THE

LIGHTNING

CONJURER

- The Christening -

Rachel Rener

Cover art by Selene Regener | Jacket design by Joey Rener

Cover by Selene Regener | www.deviantart.com/selenada

ISBN: 9781687576750

For K.E.E.

Destiny is no matter of chance. It is a matter of choice. It is not a thing to be waited for, it is a thing to be achieved.

– William Jennings Bryan

Prologue

ancing flames emanated from dozens of wax candles, casting long, ominous shadows on the ancient stone walls of the Inner Sanctum. Nine hooded figures regarded the formidable man who stood at the head of the long table, their expressions solemn. It had been exactly two months since the Day of Enlightening, the day the Pentamancer had been named in front of hundreds of witnesses, just as the Magistrate had intended. The Aggregator had played her unwitting part even better than anticipated; she not only brought the child to him, full abilities intact, but as the pitiable woman unraveled under the mounting pressure, Savannah became the ideal scapegoat.

Still, the Magistrate's meticulous plans were not without complication, as that bespectacled worm, Strauss, nearly brought the entire scheme to an abrupt end with his impudence. If not for the auspiciously resurrected breaths of the girl's mother, the Prophet would have been lost to them forever. But two months had come and gone since that fateful day, and the Pentamancer – glory to her dawning epoch – was still cooperating.

Albeit with unanticipated challenges, Barish surmised, stroking his silver beard thoughtfully. The girl never ceased to surprise even him with her own unique – and at times provocative – brand of unorthodoxy. The Magistrate turned once more to face the others, deliberately meeting every weary eye in the chamber as he did so. Now was not the time for delicacies or lenience; he could feel the misgivings, the unrest, that permeated within those sacred walls. It was time to quell it.

"She will not negotiate on this matter, as I've already stated. We will have to yield to her wishes, or risk further discordance." Barish's deep voice resonated within the thick, stone walls of the circular room, and while his tone carried the same compelling authority that it always had, a strange timbre echoed alongside his words, tingeing them with the slightest pitch of uncertainty, of disquiet.

Kaal, one of the Magistrate's more outspoken Prelates, had risen from his seat, his crimson and violet robes draping across the marble floor. The man's gray, unkempt eyebrows furrowed, carving deep wrinkles into his papery skin. As he stood, he clasped his forearms in front of him, a feigned show of deference that shrewdly provided a glimpse of the faded black numerals embedded in his dark skin; Kaal was a powerful Elementalist, even among the Inner Circle.

"Request to speak freely, *Magistrate*," his thick accent reinforced his South Asian features, and today, there was a particular roughness touching his words, an implication. A challenge.

The Magistrate's eyes narrowed imperceptibly, but he nodded, allowing Prelate Kaal the courtesy of the Inner Sanctum's floor.

"I must again raise concerns that have been privately echoed by my fellow Prelates outside the walls of this Sanctum…"

As Kaal spoke, several members of the Inner Circle shifted uncomfortably in their ornately carved, gilded chairs.

"Like everyone in this chamber, I hold the Pentamancer – glory be upon her – in the highest esteem. Nevertheless, I must declare that I – and several others," he was quick to add, searching the room for a sympathetic nod. He found none. He cleared his throat, his resolve momentarily slipping.

"Magistrate, I – that is, *we* – worry about the precedent that we are setting, sanctioning the girl's every whim, allowing her to forego the rites and formalities that have embodied this organization for millennia. I also feel a growing apprehension about the ramifications of some of these… *unique* policy changes we are allowing her to carry out without due process…" His voice trailed off as his eyes darted around the table for an ally willing to openly voice their agreement – *Keres or Jahi, perhaps…?* – instead he found only downcast eyes and firmly clasped hands as the others took refuge in their own duplicitous silence.

Cowards, he scowled as he smoothed invisible wrinkles from his scarlet sleeves. How could he have ever hoped for such a brazen display of candidness within these walls, where every calculated utterance was steeped in tacit motives? He would need to seek out alliances, obtain formal oaths, then try again. Perhaps then, he would have enough votes, perhaps then he could—

"As I have already stated, Kaal," the Magistrate said, pressing his fingertips together, "we will continue to allow the Prophet these concessions in order to secure her trust. If it requires adding months, or even years, to our greater long-term objectives, it is of minor consequence. So long as we have her allegiance – as well as the support and enthusiasm she continues to garner – that is all that matters in the interim. We *will* usher in the glorious new epoch and our visions *will* be realized, with the Prophet as our unifying instrument."

"But to what end?" Kaal demanded, leaning forward on the table. The rest of the Inner Circle carefully avoided his steely gaze. "She has made no move to formalize her affiliation with us, yet we allow her to gallivant about the globe as a false representative, unhindered!"

At that, several eyes darted to the Magistrate, whose face appeared serene despite the Prelate's heretical outburst. Taking Barish's silence for indulgence, Kaal soldiered on. "How many laws will we allow to be broken without repercussion? How many *Deficients* will we allow to witness our existence without taking the proper steps to rectify? How long are we to blindly follow this girl and her idealistic nonsense before we—"

"Enough!" the woman seated across from Kaal hissed, just as the Magistrate's eyes flashed with anger. "You repeatedly defile the holy name of our Pentamancer with your irreverent tongue and I for one will no longer stand for it!"

Kaal gaped at her in surprise.

Keres stood to address Barish, her emerald, blue, and gold robes swirling at her heels. "Magistrate, I move to depose Prelate Kaal on the grounds of overt blasphemy and insubordination!"

Barish's eyebrow twitched slightly, but he said nothing.

A quiet gasp escaped through Kaal's lips. "How dare you? Such a proposal hasn't been made in—"

"I second the motion," Jali interjected.

"Motion granted," the Magistrate murmured.

Keres suppressed a smug smile as she settled back into her chair. Kaal remained standing, the color slowly fading from his sunken cheeks.

"Y-You can't, it simply isn't—"

"All in favor of deposing, and thereby replacing, Prelate Kaal?" the Magistrate asked softly.

After a brief pause and several furtive glances, six hands rose into the air. Kaal stared at Keres and Jahi in open horror, but both refused to meet his gaze.

"The motion passes," Barish murmured.

"No, wait – please!" Kaal cried out, but it was too late. The Magistrate's hand had barely lifted before Kaal crumpled to the ground, his heart frozen mid-beat.

"We must uphold the sacred name of the Pentamancer at all costs," Barish whispered, his violet eyes flashing. Eight hooded heads nodded in agreement as their eyes darted past their fallen Prelate, his velvet robes splayed across the floor like a crimson pool of blood.

"Keres," Barish spoke again, addressing his most reverent servant.

"Yes, Magistrate?" Her silver eyes shone with anticipation.

"You may summon Kaal's sub-Prelates – King, Park, and Lawson – for their final appraisal. I expect his seat to be filled by the week's end."

Keres dipped her head obediently, hoping her wide hood would conceal the upturned corners of her mouth. "Of course, Magistrate."

Chapter 1

"We're getting closer," Eileen shouted over the din of the crowded bazaar, which only moments before had erupted into screams and chaos. "Hey, watch it!" she snapped as a man shoved past her with his wheelbarrow of assorted Indian silks, plowing his way through the furor. Several of the colorful embroidered scarves tumbled onto the dusty street, but he didn't stop to look back as the ground beneath us violently shook again.

"*Bhukamp!*" a little girl cried, clinging to the folds of her mother's sari. The girl's big, brown eyes momentarily settled on mine and she cocked her head, confused by the strange color of my irises.

"Stay close," I said, pulling Eileen towards me. Her emerald green headscarf had fallen to her shoulders during the turmoil, exposing her platinum blonde hair. Normally, that in and of itself would have caused a commotion in a packed marketplace in the middle of Mumbai, but at that particular moment, the hundreds of frantic people rushing past us clearly felt they had more pressing matters to worry about. Like the earthquake that had rattled the city without any warning – despite the Indian government's sophisticated early detection system.

"We need to get out of here before we're trampled," I muttered, more to myself than Eileen. I glanced around us for a swath of ground that hadn't been overtaken by a teeming mob, feeling the tightness growing in my chest. We were standing in an open market, the blistering sun blazing down on us with extraordinary fervor, but the throngs of people closing in on us felt like the oppressive walls of a sweltering, shrinking box, and I could feel the old familiar panic of claustrophobia creeping in.

Just breathe, I reminded myself, craning my neck to find a clear line of escape. *We're outside, there's plenty of air for everyone.* Beside me, a man of considerable height stumbled and nearly fell, roughly gripping my shoulder to steady himself. I shook him off gruffly.

"Look!" Eileen shouted, "There's an alleyway over there!"

I latched onto her sleeve, doing my best not to let either one of us be carried off by the torrent of frantic brown faces that was rushing in the opposite direction. Narrowly avoiding an elbow to the forehead, I ducked between two shop stands, dragging Eileen at my heels. We shimmied between the narrow rows of silk scarves and colorful, ceramic bowls of exotic spices until we finally made it to the empty alleyway where I breathed a sigh of relief, glad to be watching the pandemonium from afar. The ground had just shuddered again, inciting a newfound wave of terror across the crowd. An old woman was nursing a bleeding arm as she struggled to keep up with the surging current of people, but I fought against the urge to try and help her. There was no time.

Eileen sank to the ground, wiping damp strands of green and blonde hair from her eyes. I knelt beside her, pressing my fingers into the dirt.

"Together?" I asked, wheezing slightly. The air was so hot and thick, it felt like I was breathing soup.

"Together," she nodded, squeezing her eyes shut. The back of my neck tingled as we concentrated on the trembling layers of Earth below us, searching for the epicenter.

"I'm starting to think it would have been better to bring some back-up after all," Eileen groused, wiping a fresh bead of sweat from the tip of her nose. "I feel like I'm barely helping."

"You're more help than you know," I muttered, straining to settle the trembling layers of rock below us. Instigating an earthquake is relatively easy, but successfully interrupting one is quite a bit more complex. "And believe me, we're not alone. I'm sure at least a dozen other Elementalists are on standby within a fifty-foot radius of here, God forbid I scrape a knee or something. Not that they're doing anything useful at the moment, from what I can tell."

Eileen grunted, "I can't tell if you're joking or not."

I chose not to answer that for the moment. "Anyway, the target's not far," I panted, once we'd successfully brought the ground to a momentary halt. "One, maybe two blocks at most." I gently released my hold on the layers of Earth below, easing away carefully to avoid further disrupting the bedrock. I was all too aware of the tightly-crammed buildings that surrounded us – and everyone else – in that overcrowded city.

"I know we have to hurry," Eileen panted, kicking her legs out in front of her to sit splayed-out in the dirt, "but between the balmy hundred-and-five-degree heat, the intermittent stampedes, and our two-woman earthquake suppression team, I'm already exhausted."

As she adjusted her headscarf, I noticed her hands were shaking. I glanced at her complexion; her normally-pale cheeks were deeply flushed, and the sweat had evaporated from her forehead. *Heatstroke,* I worried. It was a serious enough complication all on its own, let alone when paired with the exhaustion of manipulating Elements. Disregarding the harangue I'd incurred earlier that week about altering weather patterns without permission, I guided a stream of Wind into the alley, chilling it slightly as I did.

"Oh, that feels like Heaven," Eileen sighed happily, turning her face to soak in as much of the breeze as possible.

I rummaged around my satchel. "Take this," I said, handing her my last juice box. "My father used to tell me that sugar is a good temporary fix for Elemental fatigue."

Eileen took the drink from my hands gratefully, then used the straw to stab a hole through the foil. "Do you want to split it?"

"I'm okay," I lied. "Just let me know when you feel ready to stand." I glanced at my watch. We had less than an hour before the Mumbai Containment team would arrive, at which point they would take matters into their own hands... *If they haven't already*, I fretted. The situation was worse than we'd prepared for.

Eileen nodded, squeezing a stream of hot grape juice directly into her mouth before I could even offer to cool it. Nevertheless, I envied her slightly, as I myself was imagining an ice-cold root beer float at that very moment – not just drinking it, but lounging in a wading pool full of it.

"Any chance you could make it rain?" she asked hopefully, crumpling the empty juice carton between her palms. "Or maybe decrease the temperature by sixty degrees or so?"

"I wish," I smiled. "But then we'd have bigger problems, as I've already been warned."

"Such as?"

"Oh, you know… inadvertent climatic disasters stemming from altering local weather patterns. And something about eighteen million witnesses in the city of Mumbai alone. Besides, I suspect Barish's patience with me is already thinning as it is… I haven't exactly been the ideal 'prophet'." That last part I muttered under my breath.

"All of this might be true, but a girl can dream," Eileen chuckled, rising to her feet. The alleyway rumbled.

"You ready?" I asked.

"As ready as I'll ever be."

***

A quarter hour later, after making our way through the occasional earthquake stampede, diving out of the way of motorists who appeared to take no notice of pedestrians, and having to navigate a circuitous network of alleyways, we finally found our epicenter: a screaming young boy, kicking and flailing as his frightened family members unsuccessfully tried to soothe him. They raised their heads in alarm as Eileen and I cautiously approached. We were standing in between a half-dozen dilapidated buildings – *Not a great place to be during an earthquake,* I grimaced – but there were no crowds, and not a single curious face appeared in the open windows surrounding us. I hoped that meant that they'd already evacuated to a safe, street-level location, somewhere far away. Other than the distraught boy, who looked to be around nine or ten, there was one other child, a small girl who was no older than four, and two very frantic-looking adults – their parents, I assumed.

I glanced over my shoulder. *No guards*, I sighed in relief. The Inner Circle had kept their word… so far.

"Do you speak English?" Eileen asked, kneeling beside the boy's father, who was doing his best to restrain the child. The boy's eyes widened at her sudden appearance, and he let out a long series of shrieks and cries, accompanied by ground-roiling tremors.

"We do," the man replied, tightening his grip on the boy. "And I recommend you do not stay here; it is not safe for you."

As if by cue, the ground beneath our feet lurched violently, causing me to pitch forward. Pieces of plaster rained from the buildings above. I squeezed my eyes shut, doing my best to counteract the boy's Terramantic tantrum. *He's so strong,* I realized with a start. I remembered what Savannah had told me months before about an Uzbeki Terramancer who ended up killing 15,000 people when he inadvertently triggered a fault line. The memory supplied bleak, yet ample, motivation, and I was able to still the ground – but not without considerable effort. When the Earth had quieted, the boy's mother gasped, looking from Eileen to me with angry, fearful eyes. She knew what we were.

Resting my hands on my thighs to catch my breath, I watched the little boy squirming in his father's arms. His eyes rolled around his head wildly, never once stopping on mine or anyone else's; he didn't speak, but he made a string of panicked grunts that would dissolve into coughing fits, which seemed to frighten him even more. All the while, his little sister sucked on her fingers, giving her brother a sad look. She didn't seem alarmed by anything that was happening; she'd clearly seen these tantrums before.

"Do you know what your son is?" Eileen asked softly, putting a gentle hand on the boy's arm. He immediately recoiled and began rocking back and forth, clenching his eyes shut. The ground shuddered simultaneously.

"Eileen," I whispered, taking a few steps forward to kneel beside her. "I don't think this boy wants to be touched." I gave the father, who had his arms wrapped around the child like a straightjacket, a pointed glance. His wife put an arm in front of the two of them, as if to block them from us. My eyes fell to her forearm, where a green triangle had been etched into her dark skin.

"I know what he is," she hissed. "I know what *you* are. And I know you are here to lock us away."

I shook my head firmly. "No. We're here to help you."

Her brown eyes narrowed at me. In that moment, I wished I'd inherited my mother's talent for affecting emotions, if only to soothe the poor woman. I opened my mouth to stammer some likely-ineffective response, but Eileen rested a placating hand on my arm. She smiled at the boy, who was watching her through squinted eyes.

"Would you like to see something cool?" she asked, pulling her scarf back to reveal green-streaked, platinum blonde hair. The boy gasped, cautiously opening one eye, and then the other. He promptly stopped rocking to reach forward with a tentative finger.

"Go ahead," Eileen grinned.

Ever so shyly, he leaned away from his father to stroke the bright green stripe framing her face, shrieking excitedly as his fingers touched it. He ran his hand across her cropped curtain of shiny pale hair, entranced by the feel of it.

"I'm like you, see?" Eileen said as she floated a small, nearby rock in front of the boy's face. He immediately dropped her blonde tresses and yelped in delight. Eileen smiled, lifting two more stones in the air to dance in front of the boy's face. He cried out happily, pushing away from his startled father to play with his new friend. The boy's mother gaped first at her son, then at Eileen. As her eyes fell back on me, she gingerly reached forward to lift the sleeve of my tunic.

"Pentamancer?" she gasped, her round eyes widening further.

I nodded. "Your son is very powerful. We can help him."

The woman frowned slightly, exchanging a furtive glance with her husband. As her eyes fell on her small daughter, who was gazing at the spinning rocks with a delighted expression, she sighed, her shoulders heaving with reluctance.

"My gifts are very small, almost nothing," she finally admitted. "My parents were part of the Order but I ran away from home many years ago to marry my husband. He and my daughter are not like us." Though I said nothing in response, her brows furrowed defensively. "I know the laws and I kept my gifts a secret for many years. But our son was born with these abilities, much stronger than mine. He cannot control them and I am not strong enough to intervene… Please," she whispered, clasping my hand. "Please do not punish us."

I squeezed her hands tightly in mine. "I won't let any harm come to you or your family. I promise. We only want to help you."

She said something then but I winced, not hearing her response. The headache was coming back, this time worse than before. I rubbed my temples, hoping to ward off the bright flashes that sometimes accompanied my persistent migraine. There was no sign of them – not yet, at least.

The alarm on my watch started beeping. I pried my eyes open to glance at Eileen, who nodded at me tersely. I could feel her anxiety spike. But the boy was calm now, his parents placated, the Earth still. Surely all that would count for something? I silenced my watch just as the sleek, black limousine turned into the alleyway. Eileen let the floating rocks fall to the ground as she stood, wiping the dirt from her pants. The little boy hovered at her side, unfazed by the approaching vehicle, a wide smile stretched across his face as he tugged on her sleeve. Rising to my feet, I beckoned to the boy's mother.

"Come," I said gently, reaching for her hand. She took it tentatively, standing as the car pulled up to us. Her husband rose as well, positioning his small daughter behind him. He was staring at the vehicle with obvious apprehension.

"Don't worry," I said, forcing a tight smile despite my growing uncertainty. "Everything is going to be okay."

Chapter 2

It took ages to reach the towering, mirrored building in the middle of Navi Mumbai, as throngs of people still lingered in the street, fearful that another earthquake might hit. But the little boy, Tosh, was well past his Earth-shaking outburst – an outburst, his mother had informed us, that was triggered by the loss of his most cherished toy, a stuffed monkey named Kapi. Now, one hour later, he was joyfully staring out the window of our luxury Mercedes-Maybach Pullman, his thick, dark hair blowing in a cold stream of air conditioning. The specific brand of car was not something I would have ever taken the time to learn myself, but the boy's father lit up with excitement as we stepped inside, marveling that he'd only ever seen something that magnificent in movies.

He wasn't wrong. The limousine had four creamy, quilted leather seats in the back, which faced each other like a club lounge, and they were the widest, most luxurious car seats I had ever sat in. Tosh's parents took the two seats that faced the front – his mother cradling his sister on her knees – while Eileen and I had our backs to the driver, who was separated from us by an electrical partition screen. Tosh refused to sit, instead pressing his palms and forehead against the glass to admire the passing views outside.

"Bottled water, San Pellegrino... *champagne?*" Eileen asked incredulously, rummaging through the bucket of ice wedged between our seats. "Is this stuff free?"

I nodded.

"Oh, thank God," she moaned, retrieving the bottle of champagne to press it against the back of her neck. She passed cold bottles of water to the rest of us, which I gulped down gratefully.

I glanced out the window while Eileen and Tosh's parents chatted, wondering how many clandestine escorts the Inner Circle had sent to accompany us to the Mumbai Chapter. At least four of the nearby cars that flanked us on any given side would be driven by Asterian guards – that much I knew – but it was always hard to tell who they were, since they wore plain clothes and drove inconspicuous vehicles.

Like Strauss' beat-up brown Corolla, I shivered.

Luckily, I wasn't able to dwell on that particularly unpleasant thought for very long, because the traffic in Mumbai was gut-wrenchingly awful – quite literally. The lack of traffic lights, continuous cacophony of horns, potholes the size of crockpots, and never-ending parade of nonchalant pedestrians casually sauntering in and out of lethal traffic conditions kept my mind off of other topics, such as the vile man who nearly killed my mother – and ultimately died, himself, in the attempt.

When we finally pulled into the circular drive of the Mumbai Asterian Chapter well over an hour later, I was having trouble keeping my eyes open; sleep had become a rare commodity during those last few weeks of traveling and training. So when the door to the car opened and the four Heads of the Chapter greeted us – proudly displaying their brightly-colored Asterian sashes across formal black suits – I scarcely heard what they were saying, instead slipping once more into autopilot: mechanically shaking outstretched hands, flashing a polite smile as needed, nodding my head when it seemed appropriate. Eileen, astute as always, had tacitly relieved me from my unwanted responsibilities by making introductions herself, and was doing a wonderful job in her newfound role as Public Relations Manager to the Pentamancer. *If only I'd been able to bring her along sooner,* I couldn't help but think as she chatted amiably with their Head of Medicine, a smiling Auromancer who wore a purple-embroidered turban atop his head.

However, I was immediately pulled from my somnolent reverie by the half-dozen uniformed soldiers who guarded the front entrance with a startling arsenal of assault weapons. They watched us with narrowed eyes, not bothering to feign any such niceties as a smile or a polite nod. *Is this the norm for this chapter, or is it because* I'm *here?* I wondered. Either way, I carefully avoided their steely gazes as I, along with the precession of people trailing behind me, shuffled through the metal detector outside the doors. And I couldn't help but breathe a sigh of relief after I passed them, the silver zippo lighter in my pocket going thankfully unnoticed.

Eileen took my arm as we approached the entrance, with little Tosh trailing right at our heels. From the outside, the building was like any other building in that sector: ten stories of silver reflective windows, just one of the many sleek, modern office buildings in the sweeping district of New Mumbai. But just past the sliding glass doors, in what I'd come to learn was typical Asterian fashion, was an opulent interior, replete with marble columns, a grand staircase framed by twin sandstone statues of elephants, and a forty-foot high, elegant domed ceiling that glittered from its many conjoining pieces of stained glass. In striking contrast to the Denver Chapter, which had a prosaic, monochromatic design, the inside of the Mumbai Chapter was a dazzling rainbow of brilliant magentas, deep ocean blues, lush purples and greens, fiery vermillion, and vibrant splashes of turquoise. Rainbows bounced off the glass domed ceiling like a disco ball, while iridescent mosaic tiles adorned the lower half of each arch-supporting column, and polished gold leaf wrapped every pillar and parapet.

"We need to steal their interior designer," Eileen muttered, gripping my arm tightly.

"No kidding," I whispered.

Just then, their Regional Aggregator – a kind, older man whose gentle, candid demeanor made him appear as different from Savannah as cactus from sea coral – informed me that the conference room had been prepped for the daily briefing.

"I do apologize," he added, "but the Magistrate made it clear that only the Prophet—"

"Rowan," I interjected, doing my best to avoid making eye contact with Eileen. The reverent title was embarrassing enough without having to observe her poorly-concealed smirk.

"I'm terribly sorry, Miss Rowan," the Aggregator stammered, bowing his head obsequiously. "But ah, as I was saying, only the Pentamancer will be allowed in the briefing. No other guests have been authorized, I'm afraid." He straightened to give Eileen an apologetic look.

"That's okay," she replied, before I could interject. "Maybe I could stay with Tosh and his family, then? Get the grand tour of the place and help them get settled?" I gave her an appreciative smile, then glanced over her shoulder at Tosh; he, his father, and sister were marveling at their surroundings in wonder. His mother, however, looked anxious, her eyes glued to the two guards standing on either side of the front entrance.

"That would be quite satisfactory," the Aggregator said, nodding grandly as he turned to answer Eileen. "In that case, please follow me. We'll meet, uh, Miss Rowan after she's finished with her duties."

I reached for Eileen's hand before she could walk away. "Would you stay close to Tosh's mother?" I asked softly. "I trust Barish when he says the Order will stop locking Elementalists away for non-violent infractions, but…"

Eileen nodded. "Loud and clear, Proph – I mean, *Miss Rowan*." She winked.

"Yeah, yeah," I replied, chuckling despite myself.

"Right this way, Miss Rowan," the Chief of Security said, guiding me to the grand staircase. She was a petite woman but her royal blue sash indicated that she could likely pack a nasty Hydromantic punch. "The Inner Circle is ready for you now."[1]

***

Moments later I settled into one of the four high-backed chairs surrounding the round, mahogany table in the darkened conference room. The walls had been painted a deep mauve, making the stark, windowless room seem even smaller than it was. On the wall behind the far-side of the empty table, a huge flat screen TV flickered on and ten 4k, high-definition faces gazed down at me from the round table of their own meeting room, seven hours away in Istanbul. Barish clasped his hands together tightly, a jocund smile stretched across his fleshy cheeks. He had forgone his usual tri-colored robes and opted instead for a khaki-colored blazer and a white button-up shirt. I arched an

---

[1] See *Elemental Class Appendix* on page 156 for a complete list of Inner Circle members and sigils.

eyebrow. The simple attire made him seem almost... human.

"You were magnificent today, Rowan – I could not be prouder of you!" he enthused.

"I couldn't have done it without Eileen's help," I replied, but he was already steamrolling ahead in his usual verbose style.

"I must admit, I was skeptical at first, but it has been a nice change of pace to skip the velvet robes in this terrible June heat," he chortled. "It's been unusually hot in Istanbul."

Is Barish actually attempting to make small talk? I wondered, momentarily taken aback. I realized then that the rest of the Inner Circle had opted for business-casual as well, which was... surprising, to say the least. I'd never seen them without their ceremonial hooded robes before. Talking to the Inner Circle like this – in street clothes, chatting about the weather over Skype – made the daily briefing seem more like a business meeting and less like an ancient underground gathering of the Illuminati. I raised an eyebrow, wondering whether the others had really been on-board – or whether Barish had insisted. Jahi, in particular – I noted with a hint of satisfaction – looked rather uncomfortable in his unadorned, button-up shirt. His full lips appeared even more pursed than usual.

"What was it you said last week, my dear?" Barish mused, snapping me back to the conversation. He was stroking his chin thoughtfully, a wry smile tugging at the corners of his mouth. "That the robes were – how did she put it?" He turned to one of his five female Prelates, Keres, who gave me an obliging smile as she answered.

"I believe the Prophet said our robes call to mind an image of medieval wizards, Magistrate, but she stressed that that was *not* to be inferred as a compliment." Barish laughed loudly, slapping his hand on the table. The other nine Prelates quickly joined in. *Wait,* I frowned, quickly scanning the faces on the screen. *There are only eight of them.*

"Where's Kaal?" I asked. His was one of the few names I'd managed to remember, as he, Keres, and Jahi were the most outspoken members of the Inner Circle, apart from Barish. Kaal, like Jahi, was part of the small handful of Prelates who seemed to openly dislike me, often frowning when I spoke or imperceptibly shaking his head when I'd offer a suggestion.

The chortling immediately ceased. Keres and the others glanced at Barish, whose shoulders slumped slightly.

"Prelate Kaal, who was a devoted member of the Inner Circle for more than a decade, passed away suddenly, just last night."

What? Kaal had to have been in his late fifties – at most – and the man seemed perfectly healthy two days ago.

"I would have preferred to have told you in person," Barish added, "but I didn't want to keep you out of the loop."

"Was he unwell?" I asked, confused.

"He headed a large corporation in addition to his many Asterian duties," Barish replied sadly. "I believe the stress of it all was simply too much for his heart to take. But he passed quickly, without any pain or suffering, which is all anyone could ever hope for…" He cleared his throat.

"I… I'm sorry to hear that," I answered, not sure what else to say.

"There will be a great funeral for Prelate Kaal in three days' time," Barish smiled. "Elementalists from all around the world will come to pay their blessings, and also witness the formal ordaining of his replacement… I believe it would be prudent for you to attend as well," he added. "Your presence would honor his memory and provide great comfort to us all… And it might also be a wonderful opportunity for your own official induction…?" He trailed off hopefully, tempering his last request with a question mark.

I shook my head, inviting several raised eyebrows as I did. While one doesn't turn down a request from the leader of the Asterian Order lightly, I'd been making a habit of it in recent weeks.

"I've already extended my travels by a week and a half, and I would like nothing more than to go home to see my family and friends. This evening, as we discussed."

"Of course," Barish conceded, gracious as always. "Certainly, you must be exhausted from all of your travels. I wonder, however, if we might be able to raise the subject of your official Christening, which we've put off, at your request, for two months now? As you know, we are eager to formalize our arrangement, if only for the sake of ceremony."

"I haven't forgotten," I replied, rubbing my forehead. "I just need more time… and some reassurance."

"What further reassurances may we provide?" Barish asked. I could hear the slightest trace of impatience creeping into his voice.

I raised my eyes to the screen. Inside a small square in the lower-right hand corner, I could see my own face staring back at me, pale as always, but the new appearance of my eyes still unnerved me. After my mother subjected me to the equivalent of Electromantic shock therapy to reinstate the majority of my memories and abilities, my blue eye had deepened in hue, making both of my irises a vivid purple color, like tanzanite glinting in the sun. I cleared my throat, focusing on Barish's strange violet eyes instead of my own.

"For starters, I want you to tell me exactly what will happen to Tosh and his family. No sugar-coating. Will his mother be placed in Containment for marrying a non-Elementalist? Or for inadvertently exposing her secret to her husband?"

"Certainly not," Barish chafed. "I have already assured you of this."

"And what will happen to Tosh, who may or may not always have the means to control his abilities at all times?" I pressed. "I believe this is more than a simple matter of a child acting out. I believe he may have autism, which will require additional attention and resources."

Keres cleared her throat, looking to Barish for his assent before she spoke. Younger than the rest of the Inner Circle by at least a decade – but easily fifteen years older than me – Keres was the obvious favorite of the Magistrate. With her olive skin, piercing silver eyes, and cascades of chocolate-brown hair that fell nearly to her waist, she was one of the most beautiful women I'd ever seen. The Polymancer was also one of the most frustrating, as I'd learned from our previous real-time interactions.

"If that is the case, *Prophetis*," she replied in her typical captivating, diplomatic fashion, "we will place the child in specialized training and counseling, as you've recommended for similar cases. We will also provide his family with the proper resources to handle his potential Elemental outbursts. I will have my own sub-Prelates personally ensure that this occurs."

The back of my neck pricked. Everything she said was what I wanted to hear, but somehow it never made me feel better. Barish, however, was nodding in avid agreement. I watched the two of them carefully, feeling for any sign of deceit. It's much harder to rely on Empathic Electromancy when you are separated by thousands of miles and two screens. Still, I didn't get any indication of pretense. With them, it was rare that I ever did. I leaned back in my seat, satisfied for the moment.

"And what about the Containment Centers? Have they been emptied yet?"

Keres, along with several of the other Prelates, shifted awkwardly.

"My child," Barish sighed. "You know we are willing to take these steps, but as I've already stated, we cannot do this without your full commitment to the process. If we were to suddenly release all of the current, non-violent offenders from Containment, it would cause pandemonium, hysteria, wide-spread dissemination of rumor and conspiracy." I could see Jahi nodding fervently as Barish spoke. "We need to first unite our members worldwide, give them a trusted figure on whom they can rely, a leader..."

"A mouthpiece," I interjected, ignoring the gasps my unceremonious interruption incited. "A figurehead... Yes, I know what it is that you want from me."

"You will be so much more than that," Barish insisted. "You will be a guiding light for the entire Community, which is exactly what we will need to offset such a controversial, unprecedented move! We simply cannot introduce such chaos and confusion to the Order without first instating a unifying force," he stressed, clasping his fingers together tightly. "But, if we could formally present you as the true Pentamancer, the Prophet that our Community has been waiting generations to meet, well... I believe that that would be enough to keep our Community from shattering beneath the stress of such profound change."

The tone of his voice was polite, but unwavering. *I won't be winning this one*, I conceded, clenching my hands beneath the table.

"I understand," I replied tersely. "And I will give you my answer soon. That being said, I have nothing else to report from my side. May we conclude?"

"Magistrate, if I may…?" Keres asked. Barish nodded graciously. *"Prophetis,"* she began, again addressing me in her native Greek.

"Rowan is fine," I interjected. "I'm no Prophet."

Keres turned to Barish as if for help, but he merely shook his head. "It is as the Pentamancer wishes."

"As I mentioned during our last few briefings," I added, forcing what I hoped was a polite smile, "I'd prefer it if we could skip the formalities altogether and just stick with my name."

Keres turned back to me, mirroring my stiff expression, yet somehow her face appeared lovely as ever. *"Rowan,* then." She practically cringed at the informality. "Ah, could you tell me, how strong would you say the boy's Terramantic aptitude is? Level Two? Level Three?" she asked hopefully.

"I would say it's very likely he's a Level-Three Terramancer," I answered carefully. "It took my full concentration to counteract his abilities. I think with proper training and support, he'll be extraordinary." Keres bit her lip with excitement. "…That is, if that's what *he* wants." At that, her smile wavered ever so slightly.

"Will that be all…?" I asked, rising from my seat.

"Just one thing from me," Jahi said, "if I may, Magistrate?" A Nigerian-born aristocrat, Jahi was a powerful wielder of Wind, Fire, *and* Water, making him a Polymancer as well. Along with Barish, Keres, and Mei (one of the older Prelates I'd yet to exchange a single word with), he was one of the most powerful Elementalists in the world. And for whatever reason, I just didn't like him very much. For one, he'd asked me on more than one occasion to arrange for a meeting between him and Sophia; I could only assume that desire stemmed from coveting her incredible Auro-Hydromantic abilities, so I repeatedly "forgot" to mention it to her, much to his evident disdain. He was also, from what I could tell, a self-righteous, borderline-fanatical stickler. He spoke of rules and policies the way Eileen would talk about rocks and minerals – with unbridled, eager reverence. However, I found Eileen's love of rocks to be infinitely more interesting than Jahi's obsession with bureaucracy and technicalities. I slumped back down in my seat, doing my best to remain cordial.

"Yes?"

"We received several sub-Prelate reports indicating that you used unauthorized Auromancy earlier today," he stated, rifling through a stack of papers in his usual officious manner, "and I must again remind you that, even for the Prophet, such transgressions pose a serious risk of
—"

"You'll have to forgive my impatience today," I interjected, rising to my feet. Jahi's mouth hung open in disdain. "I can understand not wanting Elementalists to juggle balls of Fire in the middle of a playground or flatten an ex-boyfriend's house with a hurricane – I think we can all agree that these seem like good, common-sense ideas. But when a friend of mine is suffering from a bout of heatstroke in 105-degree heat in the middle of Mumbai, I'm not going to sit on hold with the nearest Containment Division to obtain authorization to whip up a cool breeze for her. I'm just not going to. That being said, if I feel the urge to alter the prevailing ocean currents of the Indian Ocean in order to plunge the entire subcontinent of India into a deep-freeze with a handful of my closest Auromancer buddies, I'll be sure to check in with you first... Now, if there's nothing else, I'd like to catch my flight home."

Nine sets of astonished eyes stared back at me from the giant screen, thoroughly unaccustomed to such brazen insolence. I abruptly broke off my staring contest with Jahi and swallowed tightly, realizing a moment too late just how far I'd crossed the line that time. *Evelyn, Mom, Sarah, Ted!* A voice in my head shouted at me. *This is bigger than just you!*

"That is — if his Magistrate approves," I added quickly, bowing my head ever so slightly.

Barish hesitated a fraction of a second before letting out a good-natured laugh. "By all means, my child. Go home and get some rest. Your efforts these last several weeks have been valiant, and while the majority of the Community may not have the privilege of knowing about your heroic deeds just yet, rest assured that one day, very soon, every Elementalist in the world will know your name, Rowan Elizabeth Fulman." He leaned forward slightly. "And mark my words, they will tremble in awe of it."

I nodded slowly, carefully composing my features before speaking again. "Magistrate, Prelates, I thank you for the honor of your presence today," I murmured, reciting the customary farewell in as gracious a tone as I could muster.

"The honor is ours," Barish replied, bowing his head slightly. His remaining eight Prelates mechanically followed his lead, bowing as I quickly made my way for the door.

Apart from regrouping with Eileen and seeing Tosh and his family safely off, I had only one, singular intention at that moment: to get the hell out of there and finally go home. But the instant I stuck my head out of the door, I was greeted by the Aggregator, who immediately broke off his discussion with the Chief of Security once he saw me.

"Miss Rowan!" he exclaimed, reaching forward to hand me a crystal goblet of ice water. "I trust everything went smoothly? May I offer you some refreshment? We also have chai, coffee...?" I quickly waved away the offer.

"Everything went fine, thank you, Aggregator." Though he beamed with pride at the formality, I honestly wasn't trying to be decorous – I just couldn't remember his name for the life of me. He was the fifth Aggregator I'd met in two weeks, and just one of the dozens of Asterian officers I'd recently been introduced to.

"Before you go, might there be any way we could convince you to do a demonstration, just for our Chapter Heads?" he asked, his expression hopeful. "I understand you have not been formally introduced to the Community just yet, but we would be honored if—"

"I'm sorry, but I really have to get going," I said, doing my best to keep my voice congenial; it wasn't *his* fault I'd been away from home for weeks. But I was exhausted, my head was killing me, and, thanks to a rather impulsive moment that involved flushing my Asterian-issued cell phone down a public toilet the week before, I was about five days overdue for a thrice-postponed conversation that I couldn't bear to delay a second more than was absolutely necessary.

At my clipped tone, the Aggregator's face fell. In what appeared to be too well-timed to be a coincidence, the two other department heads had just arrived, conveniently blocking my beeline for the staircase. Sporting matching, hopeful expressions, they seemed blissfully unaware that I'd already declined the request for a demonstration. I crossed my arms, rubbing my tattoo self-consciously. The fresh black "III" that had recently been stamped beneath the five-colored star still felt sore and inflamed. *Sweets, one of these days you will need to learn how to tell people 'no',* Evelyn's voice chided in my ears.

I guess that day isn't today, I sighed, motioning for the four of them to follow me back into the meeting room. The television screen was black once again. Probably a good thing, since Barish and the others expected me to adhere to a strict agenda during my international tour of the various Chapters, and an impromptu Pentamantic demonstration was certainly not on their list of sanctioned activities.

I don't have to report everything, I thought wryly. *And anyway, what are they going to do – fire me?*

As I pulled the silver lighter from my pocket, the Aggregator – a Pyromancer, as his red sash indicated –

immediately perked up, while the rest of his associates exchanged eager glances. I flicked the lighter open and pulled the flame from the wheel in one fluid motion, adding a dash of oxygenated Wind to fuel it into a white-hot torch of Fire. The Aggregator gasped softly, just as the Security Chief shielded her eyes from the brightness. I reached into my other pocket and took out a sizeable chunk of coal (or, rather, 'carbonaceous shale', as I'd been haughtily informed), which was left over from a Terramantic conference Eileen and I had attended a few days earlier. The black rock hovered next to the flame between my palms, faintly glowing red from the inside out.

With as much force as I could muster in my dog-tired state, I clapped the fiery orb and the heated chunk of rock together, causing the coal to burn white-hot while at the same time eliciting stunned gasps from my captivated audience. The chandelier above us flickered as I borrowed some of its electrical current for good measure. Exciting molecules to such an extent takes a lot of energy, but if you can wield more than one Element, there are shortcuts, as I'd been learning. I gritted my teeth together, compelling the molecules of the molten carbon to squeeze together as though undergoing tremendous pressure. It was tricky enough, manipulating carbon atoms in such a profound way, but I also had to control the surrounding air temperature, ensuring the room didn't heat up too much from the extreme exothermic reaction I was forcing. If I'd let my concentration slip for even a moment, that conference room would have quickly transformed into an oven, and the five of us would all be in for a painful visit to the chapter's Pyromantic Burn Unit.

With a final flick of my wrist, I summoned the ice and water from the Aggregator's glass, encapsulating the rock in liquid ribbons as I focused on continually cooling and re-condensing the steam. The resulting summit of molten hot, highly pressurized carbon and frigid, cyclically-cooled Water created an explosion of hot vapor as the shocked molecules were forced from their highly-energized states into cold, crystalized stone much faster than the laws of physics ever intended in the natural world. When the thick plumes of steam drifted away, I stood there, damp from the steam and panting from the exertion, a golf ball-sized diamond resting in my open palm... Albeit a fairly yellowed diamond that was filled with tiny inclusions. I frowned slightly. *Graphite would have worked so much better...*

But the four Department Heads didn't appear to notice the shoddy quality of the diamond – they were staring at it, and me, in stunned, open-mouthed stupor... Until I pressed a finger against the spherical crystal, shattering it into tiny pieces. The Chief Medical Officer nearly shrieked, clasping her hands to her open mouth. I suppressed a chuckle as I poured the handful of rough diamonds into the hands of the Chief of Finances, a portly man in his early forties who was no taller than me. He looked from the pile of rough diamonds, then back to me, then back to the diamonds.

"I'd like you to use the money generated from these to invest in the local community," I instructed, meeting his wide eyes. "And I don't mean the Asterian Community – I mean the *entire* community, as far as you can stretch the funds. There are far too many children on the streets of Mumbai, and I'd like our Community to start giving back in meaningful ways."

"Certainly, Miss Rowan," he stammered. "I wonder though, whether this has been authorized—"

"I'm authorizing it," I answered simply. "I don't want a penny going into this Chapter or any of your pockets. Whether you establish a new charity or donate the money to an existing one that tends to children and the homeless, it doesn't matter to me. But I am personally counting on you to see that my wishes are carried out." I gave him a stern look, doing my best to appear intimidating despite the overwhelming exhaustion I felt.

He bowed his head. "It will be as you wish, Prophet," he answered, and I smiled – my first real smile of the day – knowing he meant it.

Chapter 3

I sank into my plush seat, gazing out the window at the hazy skyline below us. The sun had just set beneath the outstretched horizon, and the crowded buildings of Mumbai glinted against the last vestiges of its fading red light. We were steadily nosing upward, cresting the dark pillars of clouds that billowed below the narrow underbelly of the private jet. I rubbed my eyes tiredly, trying to ignore how small the inside of the cabin felt. Our tiny plane had departed from a private terminal, meaning that our entire five-person traveling party was able to skip past security and everything else associated with 'typical' airline travel. Such posh treatment normally left me feeling uncomfortable, but that evening, I couldn't help but feel grateful for the quick exit. I was finally heading home.

I closed my eyes as the jet soared upwards, trying to remember the blur of events from the last week. Even with most of my memories restored, my knack for recall felt... hindered. Uncomfortable, at times. For one, all of the events from the first twenty years of my life, the ones that had been eradicated and then, years later, reinstated by my mother, were difficult to piece together in the proper chronological order. I couldn't always find the right memories from the corresponding time period – it was as though they'd somehow been misfiled in my brain. Sometimes one memory would inadvertently get cross-wired with another: for example, a week earlier, I had been reminiscing about a trip to the San Francisco zoo with my parents many years ago, but without warning, the scene suddenly shifted to the terrible hail storm that shattered a window at my family's house and ripped all the lilac blossoms off the tree in our front yard – even though the hailstorm happened two years after the trip to the zoo, as my mother gently reminded me.

Accessing those old memories – which were usually shrouded in a strange incandescent light, like a roll of film that had been over-exposed – took effort. It was easy to become fatigued while trying to remember specific things. Sometimes, the simple effort of retrieving them left me with debilitating headaches – the older the memory, the more painful it was for me to access for prolonged periods of time. In a way, it felt like I was trying to flex muscles that had been atrophied for years, which, for all intents and purposes, was exactly right. Those neurons *had* been cut off for years. Even my most recent memories were sometimes hard to organize, and more and more in those recent weeks, I was left feeling tired or frustrated when I actively tried to call them to mind.

But the blur of the last week didn't have anything to do with the procedure I'd recently undergone; it was simply due to the fact that I'd been going and going for days on end, sometimes doing tours, meetings, and Containment initiatives in multiple countries within the span of the same day. I'd slept little and had forgotten which city I was in on more than one occasion. So yes, the days had been blurring together for weeks by that point, and it had been useless trying to keep track of them. But that was all going to change soon. In just nineteen hours, things would be back to normal.

Well... as 'normal' as things can be. I shifted uncomfortably in my seat, doing my best to avoid fretting over what that meant, exactly.

As soon as the 'fasten seatbelt' sign switched off, Eileen plopped down beside me, blowing stray hairs from her eyes. Her nose was peeling from the sun and there were eggplant-colored splotches beneath her eyes. Not that I could have looked any better. She'd only been able to tag along for the last few days of my intercontinental slog, after I'd insisted on having a familiar face join me at the Terramantic Conference in Johannesburg – which I didn't want to go to in the first place. Eileen was thrilled when she got the invitation, but not half as glad as I was to have a friend accompany me. It had been weeks since I'd seen the others, and days since I'd last spoken to anyone back home, since one of the sub-Prelates had let it slip that the Asterians were monitoring my calls. *Your safety is our one and only concern,* Barish had insisted later that same day, during our daily briefing. As far as I could tell, he wasn't lying. But that didn't mean I would ever use an Asterian-issued cell phone ever again.

"Someone needs to educate this organization about the massive carbon footprint that private jets leave behind," Eileen huffed, crossing her arms. "Couldn't they have just put us on a commercial airliner? I mean, I flew coach all the way to Johannesburg. All thirty-two hours of the way!" she rolled her eyes. "I certainly wouldn't have complained if we had flown back to Denver first-class in a lay-flat bed, but having a jet all to ourselves just feels excessive."

"It is exorbitant," I agreed, rubbing my temples. "I'll mention it to Barish." *Again.*

Eileen frowned. "Another headache?"

I nodded.

"Can't your mother do anything about that? Rearrange your neurons a bit, fix whatever defective circuit that might be causing the pain?"

I smiled wistfully. "I don't think it's that easy. But I haven't mentioned the headaches to her yet. She's got enough on her plate right now, settling back into a routine outside of the Containment Center, getting used to life in Colorado… Not to mention constantly worrying about me. I don't want to overburden her. Not right now. Besides, the headaches come and go. They're not always this bad."

Eileen started to say something, but I shook my head. "I know what you're going to say. If it makes it any better, I spoke to Robert about them last month and he told me that this kind of headache is a common side effect of Mnemonic Manipulation. I remember I had a bad headache after I woke up the first time around, a few years ago. But it feels different this time. Robert says it may or may not go away."

"That's terrible," Eileen said softly. "I'm really sorry, Aspen."

I shrugged. "I'm one of the lucky ones, I guess. Most people don't get nearly as many memories returned as I did. And, you know, things could have gone a lot worse…" My stomach knotted then, as my thoughts drifted to Ted's daughter, Jenny – my childhood friend who had died after undergoing the exact same procedure a few years ago... against her will.

Eileen quickly changed the subject. "Well, apart from a persistent Electromantic headache and some minor structural damage that was miraculously confined to a ten-mile diameter in Mumbai... I'd say our mission was a success!"

"Tosh did seem really happy in the arena, didn't he?" I asked, remembering how he'd actually run up and hugged us as we bid him and his family goodbye.

"He was like a kid in a candy shop," Eileen agreed, "except all the candy was pretty rocks."

Over Eileen's shoulder, I noticed that one of Jahi's personal assistants had risen from her seat to approach us. The other two sub-Prelates – both gorgeous, large-bosomed women, I couldn't help but notice – who were accompanying us home remained in their seats, reading over a document they were attempting to translate. I tried to remember this particular assistant's name as she stepped into the aisle. *Kaylie? Or is it Kylie?* Try as I might, I just couldn't keep track of everyone. But I *was* finally beginning to understand the top tiers of the Asterians' organizational system. Apart from Barish, who had the entire Inner Circle (and the rest of the Order worldwide, for that matter) at his beck and call, each of the other nine members of the Inner Circle – called *Prelates* – was granted three personal assistants, or *sub-Prelates*. While Jahi, in particular, seemed to have an affinity for young women with large breasts, the other eight Prelates appeared to have chosen their deputies using a more pragmatic set of criteria: raw power, influence – both within the Community and outside it – as well as reputation and seniority. It quickly became obvious during my travels that being selected as a delegate for the Inner Circle was a tremendous honor, one that nearly all of the Chapter Heads aspired to. Not that I could fully understand why; I hadn't met all of the sub-Prelates, but from what I could tell, they were effectively round-the-clock interns – albeit incredibly Elementalists of all ages who came from every corner of the globe. They learned closely-guarded secrets of the trade from their specific Prelate mentor, competed among themselves to earn a coveted promotion into the Inner Circle itself – on the off-chance that a seat would become available in the next decade or so – and essentially did whatever bidding was required of them by their nine superiors: scheduling meetings, translating ancient Asterian documents, dry-cleaning velvet robes, babysitting Pentamancers...

I crinkled my nose in annoyance. For the past two months, everywhere I went, I'd had an entourage of at least six sub-Prelates babysitting me... That is, until I finally lost my temper the week before, when one of them had followed me into the washroom to check on me. She shamelessly burst through the bathroom stall when I didn't immediately respond to let her know I hadn't – I don't know – drowned in the toilet or something equally absurd. That's when Barish had finally conceded to my demands, removing half of them from active stewardship duty. He even allowed me to invite a friend for my last two errands, an obvious attempt to appease me. It worked, though. Having Eileen around for that last week had been a godsend.

The woman – *Kelly?* – stepped in front of us, bowing her head graciously. "Forgive my intrusion, but we just received word of a call that will be coming in for you shortly. It was routed from D.C. I've asked them to transfer the call in about five minutes so I have time to set up the video screen, Miss, uh... R-Rowan," Kelly/Kylie added, avoiding my eyes.

I did my best to stifle a sigh. It had been a constant battle, but I'd finally managed to convince most of the Inner Circle and their secretaries to stop referring to me using various cultish euphemisms, such as the ubiquitous "Prophet" nonsense they had been slinging around, or the austere-yet-objectifying "Pentamancer" salutation. I'd about lost it when someone called me "Her Eminence" during my last training session, refusing to return to the D.C. arena until every person in that room had solemnly sworn to call me either "Rowan" or "Aspen". Since the return of my memories, I hadn't forced anyone to pick one name over the other, as both names felt equally natural by that point. But I had noticed that it was Grandma Evelyn, Robert, and my close friends who chose to stick with "Aspen," and I was perfectly content with that arrangement.

"That is, if it's convenient for you?" the woman added uncertainly, and I realized I hadn't actually replied yet.

"Oh, um, sure. That's fine," I answered. "Thank you very much, uh... Kaylie." I looked up at her hopefully, praying I hadn't gotten it wrong. But she merely bowed her head again, excusing herself to the control panel to set up the video monitor. I sighed, wondering if she'd have corrected me even if I had gotten her name wrong. I hoped so. While I didn't appreciate the sub-Prelates' constant, hovering presence, I didn't want to be openly hostile, either.

Eileen let out a low whistle. "You weren't kidding about the weird vibes," she said, raising an eyebrow. "They don't even know what to do with you – it's like they're stuck somewhere between veneration and cowering in fear. And wanting to encase you in bubble wrap," she added, snickering.

"Tell me about it," I muttered, kicking off my boots to draw my knees up to my chest. "The awkward, reverential gazes and constant pomp and ceremony are bad enough," I said, keeping my voice low, "but it's the over-protectiveness that's making me crazy. It's not just the Inner Circle and their assistants; I have this convoy of plain-clothes guards that follows me around everywhere I go – I don't know who most of them are, or where they're stationed. I just know they're there, constantly on the lookout. I've been banned from using public transit, hence the gaudy limos and private jets. I can't even make a call without being monitored!" I buried my face in my knees. "The cell phone they issued me was tapped."

Eileen's eyes widened to saucers. "Seriously?"

"When I realized that they might have heard certain, um… *sensitive* conversations, I chucked my phone down the toilet," I muttered, flushing hotly.

"What do you mean, 'sensitive' conversations? …You mean, of a romantic nature?"

I nodded miserably.

"No!" she gasped.

"I've been totally incommunicado with everyone back home for almost a week, but I refuse to let them replace my phone."

"Man, I'd have lost it if that happened to me," Eileen said, shaking her head. Her eyes darted to my three nannies at the back of the plane. "Have you ever considered throwing in the towel?" she whispered. "You know, just washing your hands of all of it? I can see it's taking its toll on you, all of this..." she swept a hand, and I knew she wasn't just referring to the constant air travel.

"I... can't," I muttered.

"Why?"

I sighed, turning my attention back to the view outside. My stomach told me that we'd finally leveled out, and it was right. We were well above cloud-level now, chasing the perpetual sunset west. I could see the wind currents as they rushed over the wing of the aircraft.

"Because..." I said softly, biting the inside of my lip. "Because I'm finally getting through to them, Eileen. About the Containment Centers... About the Electromantic mind control stuff... It's been a constant battle, but I'm finally making headway. If I give up... who will fight that battle in my place? It's only because I'm considered some sort of 'Prophet' that they're even considering what I have to say."

I didn't tell her about the other side of that double-edged sword, the fear and paranoia that fueled my resolve and kept me awake at night: if I turned my back on the Order, would my family and friends remain safe? If I no longer played along, embracing my newfound role as an 'almighty Pentamancer' from the legends, would my mother, Ted, and Aiden's sister still be allowed to walk free? What about Evelyn? Barish had promised me there would be no quid pro quo for my cooperation or lack thereof, but a nagging feeling – my own deep-seated cynicism perhaps – warned me otherwise.

Eileen was about to reply, but the large video screen in front of our seats suddenly chimed to life. I took a deep breath, steeling myself for whichever Asterian Official was waiting on the other side of that screen. An impromptu, mid-flight call couldn't have just been for a simple exchange of pleasantries.

When the video screen flickered on, however, my jaw dropped.

Chapter 4

"*Evelyn?*" I spluttered. "How in the *world* did you manage to get this number?"

My grandmother's arms were crossed. She was giving me her signature "you've-done-something-wrong-and-I'm-about-to-give-you-what-for" look. That's when Robert popped his head into the frame, giving Eileen and me a cordial wave, and adjusted the camera zoom.

"Mom!" I practically shouted as she came into view. She, Robert, and Evelyn were huddled in front of the ancient desktop computer sitting in Evelyn's living room, the early morning sunlight streaming through the pink curtains behind them.

"Hey Rosebud," my mother smiled tightly. "Everything alright over there?" I was glad to see she finally had some color in her cheeks. Her face was still thin, but I had every faith that Evelyn was already doing everything she could to address that since my mother would be living with her indefinitely.

"Yes, everything's—"

"It's been six days since we last heard from you, young lady," Evelyn interrupted, peering at me through a stink-eye.

"I know, I'm so sorry," I stammered, glancing at Eileen, who appeared far too amused to offer any form of support.

"You might have Barish and the Inner Circle wrapped around your finger, but you're not getting off the hook this time," Eileen sniggered, hiding her laughter behind an old SkyMall magazine. I dug an elbow into her ribs, which only made her snort louder.

"Uh, it's been *really* crazy," I said, turning back to the screen. "I was in Athens last week, then I met Eileen down in Johannesburg a few days ago, and *then* we had to make a last-minute trip to Mumbai to help—"

"You were in *Mumbai*? During the *earthquake* there?" Evelyn's eyes bulged.

"We were in Mumbai heroically *stopping* the earthquake there," Eileen chimed in, drawing a sharp glance from me. "Which was actually just a little b—" I nudged her again. That information wasn't exactly for public dissemination.

"Evelyn—" I started.

"*Grandma* Evelyn," my mother corrected.

"Oh, it's perfectly okay, dear," Evelyn smiled warmly at my mother. "I frankly like it. Going back to 'Rowan' and 'Grandma Evie' doesn't feel quite natural after three years of being the two Musketeers, Aspen and Evelyn."

"'Evie'?" Robert marveled. "That's a darling nickname! May I use that?"

"Oh, I'd like that very much!"

I glanced over my shoulder at the three sub-Prelates sitting a few rows behind us, who, to their credit, were doing their best to pretend as though they weren't listening.

"You really are okay though, right sweetheart?" Mom asked once I'd turned around again. She was watching me carefully. "No, um, *issues* of any kind?"

"I'm doing great," I replied quickly. "Even better now that I'm finally coming home." I gave her my best reassuring smile. "But I really do have to know… How were the three of you able to get this number? We're currently flying forty-thousand feet over the Indian Ocean."

"Forty-five, I think," Eileen remarked, casually flipping to a page advertising a laser-powered, hair-growing cap.

"Oh, it was easy," Evelyn replied, waving a hand nonchalantly. "After we didn't hear from you for nearly a week —" she gave me a pointed look, "— I got the number to the Asterian's Denver Chapter from Ori, who came over just the other day to help us fix a blown circuit. Anyway, after a few attempts, they offered to transfer me to the security division in D.C., and, after a dozen or so phone calls to their receptionist – who's a darling, I might add – I was escalated several more times through various departments until I finally made it to the Magistrate's personal secretary – Carrie, was it—?"

She spoke to Keres? I marveled.

"—who patched me right through to Mister Barish as soon as she learned you were my granddaughter. After chatting with him for a while, he graciously made a few phone calls, because I reminded him of how dreadfully we were treated in his facilities back in April – he did apologize again, by the way, quite profusely – and now here we are." Evelyn beamed.

By that point, Eileen had put down her magazine and was openly gaping at the video screen. I, on the other hand, was shaking my head in not-quite-disbelief. *Only Evelyn could sweet-talk her way all the way up to the most powerful man on Earth.*

"Your grandmother may very well be the most impressive person in this family," my mother winked, wrapping a loving arm around Evelyn's shoulders.

"I couldn't agree more," Eileen quipped. "It's been a real drag having to fly around the world with *this* bum," she added, jerking a thumb in my direction. "Terribly uninspiring, really."

"Barish was telling us the same thing," Robert was quick to chime in. "He was pontificating about the fact that Aspen has just been lazing about for the last few weeks, floundering about in paltry mediocrity…"

My eyes were suddenly pricking with tears. "I've missed you guys so much," I half-laughed, half-sobbed. "I'll come see you the moment we land, which should—"

"Don't you dare," Evelyn interjected, eliciting a startled look from Robert.

I blinked. "Er… why not?"

"I think we both know that you have one, extra important stop to make first," Evelyn replied, a mischievous grin spreading across her face. "And I for one will be *very* disappointed if you don't take care of that particular errand beforehand." Robert looked rather confused, but both Evelyn and my mom exchanged knowing smiles as my face flushed redder than the tip of Eileen's nose.

"By the way, he came back yesterday," my mother added, a little too casually. "And he asked us to let you know that he's looking forward to seeing you."

I swallowed tightly, only then fully realizing that the next nineteen hours were going to be, by far, the longest nineteen hours of my entire life.

Chapter 5

*A*fter sleeping through most of the flight, including the pit stop we made in New Jersey to refuel, I finally trudged off the plane the next day just in time to see the sun rising over the Rocky Mountains. Eileen stood at my side, the two of us wordlessly admiring the fluffy pink clouds that hovered over the craggy mountain peaks like tufts of cotton candy. I stretched my arms over my head luxuriously, feeling the compressed spaces between my vertebrae pop and expand, now that I and my spine were finally free from that confining tube. My depressurized ears immediately appreciated the absence of blaring car horns, my lungs took in mouthfuls of crisp, clean Colorado air. The signs on the tarmac were written in words I could understand without having to stop and ask a translator.

As I breathed in the fresh, non-recirculated air, I sighed in contentment. During the brief moments of the flight that I'd managed to stay awake, I calculated that in the last month alone, I'd been on twelve different planes for a total of sixty-three and a half hours. Plush private jets or not, if I never had to set foot on another aircraft for the rest of my life, it would be too soon.

Tapping my foot on the tarmac beside the jet, I waited restlessly for the other three to join us. The five of us had landed at a small, regional airport not terribly far from home, but before I could even make a phone call, we still had to get our luggage from the belly of the plane, rendezvous with the chauffeur, then—

"Miss Rowan?" A gentleman in white gloves appeared at my side.

"That's me?" My tired answer sounded more like a question.

"Good morning," he replied. "I have a message for you from the Magistrate." He handed me a sealed envelope, the crimson-red wax stamped with an elegant "B". I cast Eileen a weary glance. It appeared that the pomp and circumstance had followed me home. I tore open the envelope to find a short letter inside, penned in elegant script:

If you make your way to the lot just outside the east entrance, I think you'll be pleased with what you find there.
-B

I frowned. If the events of the last few weeks were any indication, I was fairly certain that whatever surprise was waiting for me out there would not, in fact, be pleasing. Beside me, Eileen was chuckling at her phone.

"It sounds like Sophia slept through her alarm – as well as the six additional snooze alarms she set to pick me up this morning. Mind if I catch a ride home with you?"

"Sure," I replied, glancing toward my three-woman sentry as they finally stepped off the plane. "So long as you don't mind rolling up in a limo, or a helicopter, or whatever extravagance they've arranged for our ride home."

Kaylie was chuckling as she approached us; it was the first time I'd seen her crack a smile in the twenty-plus hours we'd been traveling together. I also couldn't help but notice that her curled auburn hair and meticulously-applied eyeliner were flawless. *How did she manage that?* I wondered, self-consciously running my fingers through my own tangled tresses.

"I don't think you'll be disappointed in the transportation arrangements this time, Miss Rowan," she said, casting the white-gloved messenger a knowing look.

***

Barely ten minutes later, I stood rooted to my spot, my mouth dangling open in stuttering disbelief.

"You're not serious," I whispered. "He couldn't have... He didn't!"

"He did," a voice behind me replied.

"B-But... *How?*" I stammered, running a hand over the cool chrome finish of my grandfather's bike. The key was sitting in the ignition; a sleek jacket and expensive-looking helmet had been slung over the handlebars as well. The dead bugs I'd acquired from the road trip to California had been polished off the headlight, the chrome exhaust buffed, the gas tank filled.

"You know what," I said, holding up a hand to interrupt myself, "I don't even care at this very moment." I turned to Kaylie. "Are you telling me that you're going to let me ride this home?"

She nodded.

"Without an escort?" I asked incredulously.

"The Magistrate only asks that you wear a helmet and steer clear of semi-trucks." The man who had delivered Barish's letter gave me a small smile as he held up the cerulean-blue-and-white jacket for me to put on. It fit like a glove and had protective padding all along the spine.

I did my best to suppress a happy squeal as I flung my leg over the seat and switched on the ignition. The bike roared to life, sending a flock of birds that had perched on the fence behind us scattering into the air. I revved the engine a bit to give it some juice, causing Eileen to clamp her hands over her ears.

"Yeah, I'm going to go ahead and hitch a ride home with your special guard here," she shouted, motioning to the black Mercedes that had just pulled up to the curb. "I'm not a big fan of being smeared across the asphalt."

I nodded, barely hearing her. "I missed you, baby," I whispered to the shuddering engine. I remembered my grandfather complaining, years ago, that the bike was a "thumper" in the lower gears, but I didn't mind it a bit.

"How about Sophia and I bring you your bags this afternoon," Eileen suggested as I continued to stare at my bike lovingly. "Though I understand you probably have an, um, eventful morning planned, so if you just want us to drop them off on the porch…"

"I absolutely want to see you both," I assured her, missing the obvious inference altogether as I strapped on my new helmet. It fit perfectly. "Bring Ori if he's free!"

"You got it," she grinned.

A sheepish look must have crossed my face then as I was hit with a sudden stab of guilt about abandoning her with the Asterian Babysitter's Club.

"What am I doing? I'm so sorry, Eileen. I can't just leave you—"

"What are you still doing here?" she half-yelled, half-laughed. "Don't you have better things to sit on than an idling motorcycle? Go on! Get out of here!" Crude innuendos aside, we both knew she was right, and I was already calculating the fastest route home.

"I owe you," I said, pulling her in for a tight hug. "For everything."

"I know," she replied. "Now shut up and go."

I revved the engine again, grinning like a Pyromancer on the Fourth of July. "Thanks for everything, be well, say hi to the folks at the Denver Chapter for me!" I practically sang as I tore away from Eileen and our travel companions. She was waving cheerfully, but the other three women looked a little put-out as I sped off, tires squealing. I'm sure they were hoping for a more formal farewell, but I for one was done with ceremony. I was finally home.

Once I was clear of the parking lot and airport traffic, I yanked on the throttle, sending my stomach careening into my toes. *Barish, you old son of a gun,* I practically laughed as I sailed down the straight, hilly stretch of road that led me home. The rolling prairies on either side of the two-lane road were still green, blanketed by blossoms from last month's spring showers. And the early-morning sky was bluer than I remembered, the air fresh and crisp – and *clean*. I lifted my face mask to breathe in the sweet morning air. Flying over the crest of one of the many steep hills, I could see the empty road stretching ahead of me for miles. It was a strange and glorious sight to behold after braving the harrowing traffic of Mumbai.

I rolled back on the throttle and leaned into the wind, exultant, untethered, *free*. After weeks of being told where to go, what to do, how to act – weeks of constantly being chauffeured, accompanied, and monitored – *this* was exactly what I needed. Perhaps Barish sensed that. Perhaps this was his way of showing his gratitude, his camaraderie... Or maybe it was just his cunning way of winning me over. At that particular moment, I didn't care either way. For the first time in a very long time, everything was just like old times: just me and my grandfather's bike on the open road.

***

What should have been forty-five minutes later – but was actually closer to thirty minutes – I carefully leaned my bike against the side of my cabin, unstrapping my helmet as I surveyed the place. I half-expected the grass and weeds to be overgrown, the generator by the well to have been knocked over by winds, extensive hail damage to the roof from the storm I'd heard about last month. But the grass was freshly-mowed, the roof intact, and the generator was nowhere in sight. I frowned. I did expect – hope, rather – to see a certain black Jeep, and couldn't help but feel disappointed when I didn't. But there *was* a car in the driveway, and a familiar one, at that. I jogged up the front porch, which had been swept clean, and burst through the door, breathing in the familiar smell of home.

"Ted?" I called, dropping my helmet on the end table.

"Hey! The prodigal daughter returns!" he yelled back. I followed his voice to the kitchen, where he was standing on a wooden chair beside the table, the end of a lightbulb carefully clenched between his teeth.

"What are you—" I started, then stopped. Behind him, another person was hunched over the counter, plugging in a... a *microwave*? I gaped. The man installing the appliance straightened as I approached, turning around to face me with that same, familiar smile. My hands flew to my mouth.

"Aiden," I whispered, rooted to my spot.

"Hey, stranger," he smiled.

"Well," Ted grunted, hopping off the chair, "I think that's my cue to leave."

Eyes still locked on Aiden's, I did my best to recover gracefully. "You don't have to go—" I started to say, simultaneously kicking myself as the words tumbled out. *Now's not the time for etiquette, woman.* Fortunately, Ted just snickered at my half-hearted attempt at decorum.

"Oh, I'm already outta here, sweetheart. Your mom needs a few things. But before I go, I do have to show you this." He flipped a switch by the sink, and the garbage disposal, for the first time ever, roared to life. "And this." On the same switch plate, he flicked on the switch for the light above the kitchen table, which hadn't even housed a bulb in years. But the fresh, incandescent bulbs inside glowed to life, bathing the entire kitchen in warm, yellow light. I made a noise somewhere between a gasp and a yelp.

"You installed electricity in here?" I exclaimed, my voice rising several octaves.

"Well, since we no longer have to worry about inadvertently triggering latent Electromantic powers, and because you officially have a legal name and documents again, we figured you might appreciate not having to live like a Mennonite anymore. We also installed a phone in here—" he pointed to the far wall in the kitchen, "—as well as in your bedroom, and uh, I brought you an old laptop which you can go ahead and borrow indefinitely—" Ted's words suddenly broke off as I flung my arms around him.

"Thank you," I breathed into his good shoulder.

"Easy there, sweetheart, it was nothing," Ted wheezed. "Couldn't have done it without Mr. Lawson here," he added, giving me a quick squeeze before delicately prying my arms away. My gaze fell on Aiden again, who still hadn't moved from his spot beside the new microwave.

"I haven't been around much," he admitted, almost sheepishly, "but I did stock your pantry with popcorn in celebration of your new microwave. Your favorite meal, right? Apart from grilled cheese." He flashed me another crooked grin.

I gaped at him stupidly. I wanted to laugh, cry, say *something*, but the words weren't forming in my mouth correctly. Instead, the two of us just stared at each other dumbly across the kitchen.

Ted cleared his throat. "Alright, kids, I can see you both have a lot of awkward sexual tension to attend to – or not – but either way, I'm gonna see myself out."

At that, I could feel even more blood rising to my cheeks, if that was even physically possible by that point. Ted made his way for the door, dropping the spare key on the table as he knelt to grab his toolbox from the floor.

"By the way, your mom and grandma did a whole bunch of stuff to the place. I'm supposed to point out every little thing, but I'm sure they'll tell you all about it, in detail, over dinner..." He swung the front door open. "Which, ah, I'm supposed to invite you to tonight, though Evelyn made it abundantly clear that you are not allowed to decline." Behind me, I could hear Aiden chuckle.

I nodded at Ted stupidly. "Mandatory dinner at Evelyn's tonight, check."

He winked, then started out the door. "Oh, one last thing," he said, his voice suddenly serious. "I did a thorough check, with Aiden and Ori's help, to make sure that no cameras or surveillance equipment were installed anywhere inside or outside the cabin. And I've been crashing on your couch every night since we did that sweep, so I can personally assure you that, so far, at least, they appear to be keeping their word. Your place remains bug- and wire-free."

"Thank you, Ted," I breathed, feeling my shoulder muscles release. "That's, uh... *really* good to know." For some reason, my face grew hotter as I said that.

"Take care, kid. Try to get at least a *little* rest today," he grinned. "And I'll see you both tonight." As he turned to go, I could have sworn he gave Aiden a stealthy wink, but he was already out the door by the time I did a double-take. The moment the door clicked shut behind him,

Aiden finally crossed the linoleum threshold to approach me.

"Aspen—"

Without warning, I threw my arms around his neck, practically flinging my body against his to kiss him fiercely. Aiden teetered in surprise, though it only took him a half-second to regain composure. He wrapped his arms around me to lift me up, returning my kiss with as much enthusiasm as he'd received. More, even. The taste of his lips, the scent of his breath immediately dispelled all of the fatigue, the anxiety, the frustration, the loneliness that had been building up inside of me for weeks, filling those empty spaces instead with hunger, with desire... with *fire*.

After a long, breathtaking moment, he eventually pulled away, his lips still brushing mine. "Do you need anything, a nap—"

"The only thing I need is you," I replied, roughly pulling his mouth against mine. As close as we were, I didn't need to be an empath to feel his growing excitement. "I've been waiting months for this, Aiden. And I'm not waiting another second... If we burn this house to the ground in the process," I added, knotting my fingers in his dark curls, "so be it."

He made a noise closely akin to a growl as he bent to kiss me, fumbling with the buttons of his shirt as he did.

I took a half-step backwards to tear off my own shirt, flinging it somewhere on the kitchen counter, then reached forward to help him – though it didn't take long for me to lose patience with the buttons altogether. As I tore his shirt open, a handful of them went bouncing across the linoleum.

"I'm so sorry," I gasped as he leaned down to pull me in for another kiss, hungrily grabbing fistfuls of my hair as he did so.

"I couldn't care less," he muttered into my mouth. My hands shot up to his chest, which had somehow become more muscular since I'd last seen him without a shirt on that fateful – and fiery – night in Tulsa. My eyebrows arched in surprise as I traced my fingertips along the ripples of his sculpted chest.

"This is not the body of a professor," I muttered, almost accusatorily. Aiden laughed in earnest. "But seriously, have you been working out?" I asked as his chiseled arms encircled me to unhook my bra from behind. In one smooth movement, he removed it and tossed it to the floor, not bothering to admire the lovely blue lace I'd chosen just for the occasion.

"Yes," he replied, leaning down to kiss my neck. "Apart from everything else, that's been one of the few things that's helped pass the time while you've been away." As if to illustrate, he lifted me into the air as though I weighed nothing. I wrapped my legs around his torso and pulled his face into mine, kissing him deeply as he carried me to the couch.

"This is new," I breathed as he laid me across the cushions. I couldn't help but marvel at the plush, black upholstery as I kicked off my boots.

He gently climbed on top of me, murmuring a distracted "uh-huh," as he bent to kiss my throat, my breasts, my stomach. "You're so unbelievably beautiful," he whispered, his eyes burning into mine.

A soft moan escaped my lips as my thoughts drifted to other, more pertinent topics – such as Aiden's warm, wet lips tracing their way to the top button of my jeans. He cradled the small of my back as he unclasped it with his teeth.

"A dress would have been much better suited for the occasion," I heard him mutter against the inside of my leg, kissing every inch of my exposed skin as he peeled away the tight jeans I was wearing.

"I agree," I replied, arching my back luxuriously. It was so good to finally have a couch with intact springs. The smooth chenille fabric felt soft and comfortable against my bare back. "But you try riding a motorcycle in a dress and tell me how that goes for you."

Aiden didn't reply. He'd finally noticed – and stopped to admire – the blue lace panties I was wearing. His dark eyes met mine as he pressed his lips between my legs. I bit my lip, stifling the moan that was threatening to overtake me.

"Just so you know, Aspen…"

"Mmm… Yes?" I asked, running my fingers through his thick curls.

"I'm never letting you leave me again," he murmured, kissing my thighs as he slipped his warm fingers beneath the soft, blue lace.

"You won't have to," I whispered, tilting my head back to receive him. "I'm not going anywhere."

Chapter 6

*Q*iden stroked my hair gently as I lay on his chest, both of us working to catch our breaths. The black and purple blanket my mother and Evelyn had bought to replace my old, moth-eaten comforter had been kicked to the floor; the lavender satin sheets were tangled around our bare legs. Late-morning clouds passed lazily in-between the fresh curtains that had been hung from my bay window while streaks of sunlight splashed across the bed and our naked bodies, which were entwined around one another like vines on a trellis. We'd migrated from the couch to the living room floor to the hallway to the bathroom – where I was delighted to find fresh, blue towels in place of my ratty, beige ones – then on to the bedroom, where I made a feeble attempt to take a nap that ended up not being much of a nap.

"You know," I mused, tracing small circles on Aiden's chest with the tip of my finger, "if I had known that making love to you was going to be like *that*, I never would have agreed to leave."

"Oh?" he chuckled. "Is that all it would have taken to keep you here? The promise of phenomenal sex?"

"Mmhmm… I would have just said, 'Barish, old buddy, I'm really sorry but you'll just have to find another Pentamancer to tackle global corruption… ' and then I would have dragged you to the nearest hotel and not emerged again until it was absolutely necessary to eat."

"With the help of room-service, it may have been weeks before anyone saw us again."

"Months, even."

Aiden laughed. "Well, in that case, I would have had to find a way out of my own obligations as well," he murmured, running his fingers down my spine. The skin on my arms erupted in goosebumps. "After resigning from the university, which I obviously would have been forced to do—"

"Obviously."

He ruffled my hair playfully. "I suppose I would have just had to tell my sister 'Good luck', and to text me once she was settled – that I had other, more pressing matters to attend to in the meantime."

"Hmm… I don't believe you," I murmured, biting his ear. He tilted my chin to kiss me tenderly, entwining the fingers of his other hand into my still-damp hair. The lamp beside the bed flickered alive.

"I guess some things never change," Aiden smiled. I waved a lazy hand at the bulb to turn it off.

"It's going to take me a while to get used to having electricity here." I nuzzled against Aiden's chest, letting the intoxicating smell of him wash over me. I'd never smelled anything quite so good. "…Anyway, now that I'm here and no one's listening in on our conversations, tell me everything. You have a full week of news to catch me up on."

"Oh no," he replied. "I'm not letting you get away with that this time."

"Get away with what?" I asked, arching my eyebrows at him.

"That thing where you gloss over major developments in your life and then skip straight to 'but enough about me, how are you?'"

I stuck my tongue out at him. "That sounds nothing like me. Where would you like me to begin?"

"Well, first of all, I hardly got anything out of you even before you chucked your phone down the toilet. So, I suppose my most pressing question is, how are you doing? With everything, I mean."

"I'm fine," I replied.

Aiden rolled his eyes. "You recently underwent an agonizing procedure to reinstate your memories, then sat through some intense negotiations with the people you previously considered to be your enemies, and have since been bouncing all over the world without a moment to breathe. And all I've gathered from your brief phone calls and emails is, 'I'm fine, I'm tired, I'm making progress'. But now you're trapped in my clutches," he grinned, squeezing his arms around me as though they were restraints. "Therefore, I insist you give me something other than 'yada-yadas' and sound bites." He relaxed his arms around me and stared into my eyes, clearly watching for any sign of evasion. "So... How *are* you, Aspen?"

I rubbed my forehead. His question was straightforward enough, but the answer was... complicated. Mostly because I myself wasn't really sure how I was. There were a hundred pieces of news, a thousand thoughts and feelings from the last two months that I'd been dying to share with him, but there were so many details and pieces – pulling them together into one coherent picture felt overwhelming.

"I'm, well..." I trailed off, sighing gratefully as Aiden's fingertips pressed against my scalp, gently massaging my temples. He knew about the headaches.

"I'm... exhausted," I finally admitted. "I've been touring all these different Chapters, meeting with dozens of officials to talk about pressing issues, going to lectures and conferences, making endless small-talk and answering the same questions again and again. And, throughout all of that, I've been worrying about things back home non-stop – my mom and Evelyn, Ted's recovery, everyone's transition back to the Denver Chapter... Missing you," I added, kissing his cheek. "Not to mention, it's been two weeks since my last training session, but I swear I'm *still* sore from it."

Aiden chuckled. "Well, let me reassure you: your mom's doing well. Having her move in with Evelyn was a good idea. And Ted's great. He's been acting as the part-time interim Security Chief here in Denver, per your request, but I think he ultimately spends most of his time playing *Call of Duty* with Ori, or here, making repairs... Or at Evelyn's, where he's been almost every night..." He cleared his throat.

Hmm... I thought.

"Anyway, your training session in D.C., as brutal as it sounded, is the one part of that international tour that I actually envied. You got to work with the most powerful Elementalists on the planet – including a handful of Polymancers. And the Magistrate himself! I'd have given just about anything to see that."

"Ugh," I groaned. "Those people worked me so hard, I'd wake up in the middle of the night hearing drills being barked in my head. Once, I jumped out of bed and nearly threw a Fireball into the wall, thinking I was hearing a real command. It was honestly like Asterian Boot Camp... but with sadistic drill sergeants who simultaneously worshipped me for being 'The Prophet'."

"I still would have given anything to see it in real life," he smiled. "Thanks for sending that video you managed to record. Is the frostbite completely healed?" He kissed my fingertips gently.

I nodded, wincing at the memory. I'd learned the hard way that ice tornadoes tend to get unbelievably cold in a vacuum – and unruly. "I have another training session in a week. Now that you're off for the summer and your sister's all settled, come with me."

"I can't tell you how much I'd like that," Aiden said, continuing to kiss my fingertips. I shivered slightly. "So, what happened after the training session? Athens, right? I believe you were chatting with the Greek Chapter heads about that Pyromancer with the fiery temper." He chuckled at his own joke, but I could only grimace.

"God, he was a pain," I muttered. "Here I am, advocating for the guy so he can get anger management coaching instead of Containment, and what does he do? He stubs a toe and abruptly sends two non-Elementalists to the burn ward! Nothing I said could convince them not to wipe the memories of the burn victims. That's a battle I just can't win yet." I clenched my jaw. "And some of the Chapters I've visited aren't totally on board with my suggestions. Putting people like that through therapy is expensive. And labor-intensive. If we empty out the Containment centers, we're going to need to set up a lot of rehabilitation centers in their place."

"But all of that is still probably less expensive than Containing them for the rest of their lives," Aiden remarked.

"Yes – and they are starting to see that. It helps that this particular trouble-maker is loaded, so they're able to tack the additional therapy fees onto his monthly membership dues. But how are we going to do that for Elementalists who are too poor to pay their way out of Containment?"

Aiden nodded thoughtfully. "It's not simple, these fixes you're proposing. But we'll find a way, even if it means speaking in terms the Asterians can understand – dollars and cents," he rubbed his fingers together. "What happened after you flushed your phone down the toilet? The last email I got from you was in South Africa, right before you met up with Eileen. How was the conference?"

"The parts where I managed to stay awake were interesting. There were Terramancers from all over the world – hundreds of them – which was incredible. They had seminars on mineral excavation, quelling fault line activity, gem and mineral exhibits... I've honestly never seen Eileen so excited about anything before. I was getting into it too, until I got roped into doing a bunch of demonstrations for the officers there. Keres and the other high-level Terramancers just about lost their minds when I was able to successfully make a diamond on my second attempt."

"Bet you never expected you'd be working in the diamond industry," Aiden remarked with a sly undertone. "At least they're conflict-free. Did you enjoy entertaining an unctuous audience, at least?"

"Oh yeah," I rolled my eyes. "Until I agree to be formally christened, I'm not supposed to advertise my abilities around the Community. But all of the Asterian Officers at every Chapter know who and what I am, so there's never a shortage of questions or requests for some kind of demonstration. It makes me feel like a cheap circus performer."

"That was my next question," he said, still running his fingers through my hair, "not about the circus bit – sorry about that – but whether you'd put more thought into this whole initiation business. I have to tell you… despite the changes you're seeing, the idea scares me."

"It scares me too," I admitted. "But Barish keeps telling me that he's willing to do just about anything to formalize my membership with the Order. He's assured me at least a dozen times that he'll rewrite whatever laws I'm uncomfortable with, that they'll reform the current Containment policies to only include violent prisoners, that we can discuss abolishing, or at least limiting, Electromantic manipulation of memories. He swears he'll do all of these things… And the crazy thing is, I believe him."

Aiden chuckled. "In other words, he doesn't make your Electromantic Spidey senses tingle?"

"No," I answered. "But more than that, he's *showing* me that he's on-board. Just this week, he allowed me to break just about every established protocol when I was in Mumbai. And yeah, it got a little dicey for a minute, but the local Containment unit never intervened. They let Eileen and me handle it, our way."

"Sophia told me a little bit about that. From her and Eileen's perspective, you're a hero."

I shook my head firmly. "It's not enough. Individual interventions like that aren't enough. There are still hundreds of Elementalists stuck in Containment, families who haven't had the luxury of being reunited like ours have. And until I've been formally introduced as the Pentamancer or 'Prophet' or whatever nonsense they want to style me as, I can't do much more than air my suggestions, and they're free to ignore them. They can probably sense that I have one foot out the door, so I can understand why they aren't exactly in a tizzy to accommodate my radical ideas. The fact that they are entertaining them at all is a miracle in and of itself."

Aiden touched his lips thoughtfully. "I think I can guess your answers, but let me play Devil's Advocate for a moment. If you can tell that Barish is being honest with you, why not go through the initiation, if only so you can formally address the corruption? You're not dealing with nutty Aggregators or local Chapter Heads anymore. You're dealing with the top decision-making body, and it sounds like they're willing to do whatever you say, so long as they can call you, the world's only Pentamancer, an official member of the Asterians. So, what is there to feel torn about?"

I propped myself up on an elbow. "I just... I have so many negative feelings and associations with The Asterians. They've done terrible, unforgivable things. It's almost like..." I sighed, trying to find the words. "It's like going back to an abusive boyfriend who swears that he'll be better, that he'll never hurt you again... In your heart, you know you're probably being manipulated, but you go back anyway, in hopes that he might actually change."

Aiden stiffened. "Are you speaking from experience?"

"No, no," I replied hurriedly. "Wes would never hurt me – or anyone else, for that matter. But I volunteered at a women's shelter for a few months in college and I heard some really terrible stories there. So, I can't help but wonder... if I agree to join the Asterians, can I truly make a difference? Will they actually change? Or am I setting myself up to... to..."

"Develop a severe case of Stockholm Syndrome?" Aiden supplied.

I nodded.

"I think, particularly if you feel they're being honest with you – and, above everything, I trust your abilities to discern the truth – that you *can* make a difference. I know that's what you want, more than anything, but I think it's also my responsibility to remind you that it's not your job to save the world," Aiden said softly, reaching forward to stroke my face. "You don't have to sign anything; you don't have to *be* anything you don't want to be. You don't owe them anything, Aspen."

"But I do," I pressed. "My mother is free because they made an exception for *me*. Same with your sister, and her fiancé, and Ted, and Vivian – she should have been charged with treason for letting us escape with all of those prisoners. Evelyn's memories should have been fried, for all that she's witnessed of our world. But, for the first time in recent history, the Inner Circle is allowing their ancient laws and traditions to be broken; they're allowing me to tweak policies that would otherwise land people in Containment. People like Tosh and his mother – and the dozens of other people I've helped in the last few weeks – are getting second chances that they never would have been granted before."

"Yes, because of you, the Asterians are finally fixing a broken system," Aiden replied. "But it's not a personal favor *to* you. They owe *you* for giving their organization a much-needed jolt back into modern times. Right? Look at it this way: the Asterians were becoming archaic at best, and barbaric at worst. It would have eventually lost them loyalties, and, even more importantly for them, monthly dues. You know they make millions of dollars off of those membership fees alone. So it's not about some debt or courtesy you have to repay – *they* need *you*. But you can walk away, right now." His dark eyes burned into mine. "The Magistrate swore to you that there would be no retribution if you left. And, more importantly, you believe him. That's the part that matters most to me."

"It's not just about retribution or debt," I said softly. "It's about turning my back on people I could otherwise help. I went to school to be a doctor, to save people. Barish says he can get me in touch with the greatest surgeons in the world, Elementalists who can help make my dream of using Electromancy to cure neurological illnesses a reality."

"I can certainly see how that would be attractive," Aiden conceded.

"And, on top of everything else that's wrong *inside* the Asterian Order, I can't help but feel like there's this growing feeling within the Community that Elementalists are somehow better, more evolved than the rest of the world. It's like... even though we could easily help with things like worldwide water shortages, forest fires, hurricanes, famine, and so on, the Asterians don't seem to think that helping non-Elementalists – *Deficients*, I've actually heard them called – is worth the time and effort.

But I could fix that… I could…" my voice trailed off as the enormity of what I was saying caught up with me.

Hundreds, thousands *of years of tradition have made the Asterians who they are.*

"…I could try to fix that," I finished weakly, my voice barely a whisper.

Aiden pulled me back into his arms. "You don't have to fix every problem of the world right this minute. And you don't have to decide anything yet. There's no ticking time bomb." He kissed my lips softly. I returned his kiss, still thinking about all of the lives that had been disrupted or ruined by the Asterians, family members that were still living in isolation… or worse.

But then my stomach suddenly growled – loudly.

"Maybe we can continue this conversation over breakfast?" I asked, rubbing my hollow belly sheepishly. I couldn't remember the last full meal I had eaten. "Or lunch – whatever meal we're supposed to be eating right now?"

Aiden put a chagrined hand to his mouth. "It's official. I'm the worst boyfriend in the entire world," he groaned, scrambling to get out of bed. "What can I make you? Eggs? Coffee? Toast? I should warn you – your mother and Evelyn stocked enough food in your refrigerator and pantry to feed an army."

At least, that's what I *think* he said. I'd stopped listening the moment he stood up, abruptly forgetting all about my empty stomach as he stretched in front of the window, his lithe muscles rippling in the morning sun. As I stared at his exquisite naked body, I felt myself flush with a different kind of hunger.

"You know, all of a sudden I'm not thinking about food anymore," I said, crawling to the edge of the bed where he stood, looking sexier than any man had the right to look. I rose on my knees and pulled his warm, naked body against mine, pleased that, even after all of the morning's 'activities', he immediately stiffened with excitement.

"Once more?" I whispered, pulling him on top of me. He slid deftly between my legs, pressing his pelvis firmly against mine.

"Fine," he growled, biting my neck. "But after this, you irresistible temptress, I'm making you food."

I tried to answer him, but a soft moan of pleasure was the only sound to escape my lips.

Chapter 7

S ome indeterminate amount of time later, the smell of sizzling bacon came wafting through my open bedroom door as I basked in the silky comfort of my new satin sheets and enjoyed the quiet, blissful solitude of lying in my own bed. I hadn't realized how much I'd missed my home until I was finally home. In the last two months, I'd only been at the cabin a handful of days, and never for more than forty-eight hours. This last absence of three weeks was the longest period of time away yet. But coming home to find a new couch and working appliances, fresh linens and towels, family photos on the walls, and a sparkling clean house made my homecoming that much more poignant.

I glanced at the digital clock on the nightstand. There was still plenty of time to take that nap before Eileen and the others stopped by. It was safe to assume that they had already gotten invites to dinner as well, since Evelyn's place had apparently become the central hub for everybody to gather during my absence.

Ted never told me what time to come over for dinner, I realized, reaching into the nightstand to pull out the old brick phone Aiden had gotten for me. I switched it on. A quick text to Evelyn would do the trick – or maybe to Robert, whose response was more likely to be confined to a single message.

"How does my Pentamancer prefer her eggs?" Aiden called from the kitchen.

"That's 'Prophet' to you," I shouted back, rolling my eyes. I could hear him laugh. "Over-easy, please! Super runny yolk!"

"Two eggs with a side of salmonella, coming right up," he replied, eliciting an inelegant snort in response.

The cell phone powered on with its customary jingle, then chimed with a handful of messages that had been sent sometime over the last few weeks: an old message from Ori, who had forgotten to text my other cell phone, several frantic messages from Evelyn when I'd gone incommunicado last week, an advertisement for some new smartphone that was being released with a special feature I didn't care about, a random text message from four days ago…

My heart thudded to a heavy stop. There wasn't a name attached to the message, but I immediately recognized the number. I shot a quick glance at the bedroom door as I opened it, my pulse quickening.

Hey Rose... Or, sorry, I guess I should say, "Rowan". I apologize that it's taken me so long to get back to you. I was caught off-guard when you reached out a couple months back. That was... unexpected, to say the least. I won't lie – I seriously considered ghosting you, the way you ghosted me for years. Getting your message opened up some fresh wounds, I guess. Not to mention I'd just gone through a break up with the girl I'd been seeing for a long time. So yeah, a lot to take in all at once. But now that I've had some time to reflect, I'm glad you finally reached out. I've always felt bad about how things ended. You were going through something serious and all I could think about was myself. I'm sorry for that. I know it doesn't make up for my past behavior, but I want you to know that I spent months trying to track you down after that phone call. It would have been a lot easier if you had given me your number... or your actual name. Sorry. Better to leave the past in the past, I guess. Anyway, judging by your area code, I guess you're in Colorado now? What brought you there? What are you up to these days? To answer your questions, apart from the break up, I'm doing well. I just finished my third year of med school. You'll probably laugh, but I ended up taking the anesthesiology route, after all – shocking, I know! I bet you're well on your way to becoming a world-class neurosurgeon. Right now, I'm getting ready to head out for another month-long stint in Mali with my dad. When I told him about your message, his eyes teared up. No joke. He and my mother never stopped talking about you. It irritated my ex to no end, haha.

Anyway, I hope you're doing well. Write back when you can. I would be lying if I said I haven't thought of you often over the years.

-Wes

PS – Happy Birthday. Just so you know, I've had a drink in your honor every June 22nd for the last three years. This year, I'm just glad to know you're still out there somewhere.

Sitting there, wide-eyed in my underwear, I stared at his message for a long moment. I felt as though a brick had been lodged beneath my ribcage. "Wes," I whispered, the sound of his name feeling foreign on my lips. We hadn't spoken since our abrupt break-up that bitter February morning more than three years ago, if only because I'd been made to forget he existed – until I found his letters in my family's safe deposit box two months ago. Shortly after that, I'd texted him in a moment of recklessness and desolation, the night Aiden and I had our first and only fight. With the whirlwind of events that happened since then, I'd completely forgotten I'd even sent that message. Or, perhaps, 'willfully forced it from my mind' is a more apt description.

I leaned my head against the pillow, remembering that night clearly. I'd just found out that my actions the previous week had left Tom, the Denver Chief of Security, dead. It was the night Aiden had confessed to playing a minor role in my parents' ruin. The night I realized my mother was the cause for his sister's imprisonment. The night that forced Aiden and me to face a grim reality: that our families had been locked in an ongoing war for years, the effects of which were devastating to both sides even now. At the time of our fight, my mother hadn't seen the light of day for years, nor had Sarah. My father was dead – killed during his interrogation or shortly thereafter. And Aiden and his father may as well have been dead to each other. The night we saw Terry in D.C., not a word was spoken between the two of them – not then, not in the days of negotiation that happened afterward – though we all sat at the same round table for hours on end.

After an informal agreement was forged, and I returned to D.C. for more training, Terry and I were careful to avoid one another, never entering a room where the other was present unless we had to. I had my suspicions, and had many opportunities to find out, but I couldn't bring myself to ask Barish whether Terry had had a direct hand in my father's death. To me, foregoing that knowledge, which would only create more pain, was a sacrifice I needed to make in order to safeguard an already-tenuous situation. And to protect my new relationship with his son.

I glanced down at the message in my hands, feeling a profound wave of guilt. *How will you explain this to Aiden? Things are complicated enough right now.* And then a more distressing thought came: *You've dragged enough people into this mess, and on top of that, Wes isn't one of us – he's vulnerable – a Deficient, like Evelyn... Like Jenny.*

That did it. Try as I might, "Deficients" who had knowledge of Elementalists were still being targeted for their memories. It was a battle I didn't have the footing to win – not yet, at least. I hated the thought of ignoring him, especially after everything I'd put him through, but Wes' well-being was not a gamble I was willing to chance. Not after what happened to Ted's daughter.

I highlighted the message for deletion just as Aiden entered the room.

"Everything okay in here?" he asked, carrying a mug of steaming coffee. I quickly set the phone face-down on the bed.

"Everything's great," I lied.

"Then, madame, your breakfast awaits," he smiled, making a sweeping gesture towards the kitchen with his free hand. He winked as he took a sip from his steaming mug. Only then did I notice he still hadn't put his shirt back on. "I made us undercooked eggs, bacon, and a side of white cheddar popcorn, for the lady with disconcerting taste."

"Don't you mean 'discerning taste'?" I asked, pulling an undershirt over my head.

"I meant what I said," he grinned. "And feel free to refrain from putting on any additional articles of clothing." Laughing, I threw a pillow at his head, which he easily dodged.

Leave the past in the past, a voice in my head warned. *Where it belongs.*

***

"Hey – how's your sister doing?" I asked suddenly, after I'd downed enough coffee and food to feed a small family. "And her fiancé, Kurt – how is he?"

"She's doing well," Aiden answered, reaching forward to take my empty plate. "She and her fiancé – well, 'husband', I should say, since they eloped at the courthouse… Anyway, they stayed with me until the semester finished, as you know, then the three of us flew back east together with the goal of finding them a cheap apartment." He rose from the chair, balancing a stack of dishes as he did. "Sarah is steadily recovering. But Kurt's not adapting as well. Where she's relieved to be free – grateful even – he's angry. And feeling understandably paranoid, looking over his shoulder everywhere he goes. Beyond that, I think his ego is bruised, having to start over with no assets."

I followed him to the sink with the rest of the dishes, raising an eyebrow as I handed him an empty mug. "No assets?"

"Barish did keep his promise," Aiden clarified. I stood close beside him, washing the dishes while he dried them. "They were offered a substantial amount of money as a sort of reparation, but Kurt refused to accept it. Any of it. So, they're currently living with my mother, trying to make ends meet while finding new jobs outside of the Community."

I nearly dropped the plate I was holding. "They went back to live with your family? After... after everything that happened?"

He nodded. "That's what I was doing all last week – helping them move into my mother's townhouse in Virginia. It's been a strange transition, for everyone – people who renounce the Order are almost always shunned by their friends and families. As you know, my parents stopped speaking to me entirely when I left. It's even worse for those who become Contained. The small majority that are eventually released are typically forbidden from having any contact with other Elementalists as part of the discharge agreement – that is, until you intervened on Sarah's behalf," he added, kissing my forehead softly. I gave him a tight smile before turning to rinse the last of the soap suds off the pan I was washing. Just then, my freshly-caffeinated brain caught up with everything he had been saying.

"Wait – so you actually saw her? Your mother?"

He nodded.

"How many years has it been?"

"Almost five."

"And your father?" I breathed, remembering the gruff, weathered version of Aiden I saw in D.C. "Sarah was just willing to move back in with him, after everything that happened? After he hid her Containment from you and everyone else?" I suddenly felt a profound shift in Aiden's emotions, but I couldn't name the feeling – it was something resembling anger, mixed with grief... But there was relief as well. Sorrow. Suspicion. Worry.

I tossed the pan on the drying rack, then hoisted myself up on the counter to sit. Aiden stood in front of me, resting his hands on my thighs. His eyes didn't meet mine.

"What's wrong?" I asked softly.

"It's just the three of them at the flat – Sarah, Kurt, and my Mom. My parents, uh... they split up."

"Oh, Aiden," I whispered, feeling the combined weight of our grief. "I'm so sorry..."

He gave me a tight smile. "It's for the best... It turns out that my mother didn't know everything my father did – her security clearance wasn't as high, and she had no choice but to believe the version of events that he told her. Basically, she knew that Sarah and Kurt had been taken into Containment, but she didn't realize that they had been separated from one another, or the terrible conditions they'd been placed in. And she wasn't told the truth about their actual 'crimes'. My father led her to believe they had actively committed treason, as opposed to just speaking out against the corruption. He also apparently told my mother that he'd tried to obtain permission for the family to pay her monthly visits, but that my sister refused to see any of us."

I gasped softly.

"Sarah adamantly denies that. She says she begged to see us every day for years... and eventually had no choice but to assume her family had disowned her."

"That's terrible," I whispered. "How could he have done that to her? To your mother? And you – you didn't even know she was locked up to begin with. All this time, you were both just wondering where the other was..." I swallowed tightly, my eyes burning with angry tears. *Thinking your family is dead is bad enough... But to let Sarah believe that they were alive and well and simply wanted nothing to do with her?* I gritted my teeth, not wanting to say what was on my mind – that only a monster would do that to his child.

Aiden was quiet for a few minutes before he spoke again. "Their marriage had apparently been suffering for years. I was just too self-centered to see it back in the day. But when my mother found out the truth about Sarah, that was the last straw. She left my father and moved into her own place. She's still an Officer in Washington, but she transferred to a different division and hasn't spoken to my father since April. I don't think Sarah fully forgives her yet, but, in my mother's defense, she's doing everything she can to repair the damage that was done. I think, for the time being, it's a good situation for the three of them to rely on one another while they rebuild their lives..." his voice trailed off, his eyes somewhere far away.

"What about you?" I asked, cupping the side of his face gently. "How are things between you and your mother?"

He turned to look at something outside the kitchen window, pausing a moment before answering. "I endured a lot of guilt and vitriol from her when I left the Asterian Order – it's difficult to forget. But I'm doing my best to forgive."

"I'm just glad that you have part of your family back," I said, kissing his cheek softly.

"I'm glad you do as well," he smiled.

I glanced at the clock on the wall – the afternoon was already half over. *So much for a nap,* I thought ruefully.

"I'd better get dressed," I said. "It might be awkward if Eileen and the others show up and I'm not wearing pants."

Aiden chuckled. "Then I'd better stay out here – if I follow you in that bedroom, you might not be wearing *any* clothes when they arrive."

"Good idea," I winked, giving him a long, tender kiss before hopping off the countertop.

"Mmm," he sighed. I peeled off my tank top, casually tossing it over my shoulder as I walked out of the kitchen wearing nothing but my skimpy, blue lace panties. Behind me, I heard Aiden make an appreciative noise and I grinned, thinking myself clever.

That's when the doorbell rang. I let out a shrill yelp, practically skidding across the linoleum to make it to the hallway before the others had the chance to peer through the window – if they hadn't already. The sound of Aiden's laughter followed me into the bedroom as I slammed the door behind me, panting. Moments later, I heard the voices of Eileen, Sophia, and Ori as Aiden let the three of them inside.

"She'll be right out, she's just changing," I heard him say. His lingering grin was evident, even through the walls.

I yanked open my closet doors to find something to wear. To my surprise, several new shirts and dresses had been carefully hung inside. "Mom," I whispered, fingering the soft cotton of a pale blue sundress. As much as I had missed Aiden and the others, I had missed my mother the most. I'd spoken to her more than anyone else during my absence, partially for that reason, but also because I needed the constant reassurance that she was still here, that nothing bad had happened while I was away.

I could hear Ori and Eileen laughing in the living room, so I quickly pulled the blue dress over my head, running my fingers through my hair to smooth out the tangles. From the bed, my phone chimed, causing my heart to skip a beat. But it was Robert, not Wes, that was messaging me, letting me know that dinner was at six. Heart pounding, I sunk into the mattress, gripping the phone with two hands. Wes' message stared back at me from underneath Robert's, filling me with guilt and apprehension. And the tiniest bit of curiosity.

I hung my head as shame quickly replaced idle curiosity. Wes had been my closest confidante for years, a friend, a lover. Our relationship wasn't perfect, and my feelings for him were complex even back then, but I never expected things to end so abruptly, with zero opportunity for closure. Was it so wrong for me to want to properly end that chapter of my life?

Let it go, I thought to myself. *It's not fair to Aiden and it's* certainly *not fair to Wes. He's not part of your world anymore. And it's safer that way, even if it hurts him.*

But then, another thought came: *I don't have to tell him anything about this new life. I can just let him know that I'm okay, just one message, and be done with it.*

It immediately cheered me up, the notion of not having to leave him pondering yet again... *But it's more than that*, I was forced to concede to myself. The very idea that he *wasn't* an Elementalist, that he *was* so far-removed from all of the recent, overwhelming events, was... comforting, somehow. He wasn't linked to any of the recent drama or hardships; he was just Wes, the sweet, funny, *normal* guy whose parents used to invite me over for brunch every Sunday. The guy who made me laugh harder than anyone I'd ever met. The guy who got me through Organic Chemistry – not because he understood it any better than I did, but because he'd do these ridiculous things, like drawing a cartoon of a giant, monstrous jellyfish being shoved into a tiny briefcase to illustrate how ungainly molecules can fold into such tidy packages. It didn't help me understand the concepts at all, but it certainly kept me engrossed as we stayed awake until four in the morning studying for that horrible final.

I smiled wistfully. Wes was the guy who hid a pearl engagement ring in a bag of chips, then pretended to choke on it. It was almost four years ago and only now was I able to laugh at the idiotic memory of me frantically trying to give him the Heimlich maneuver just moments before he dropped down on one knee to propose...

Stop it, I chided myself. *That was a lifetime ago.* I glanced at the bedroom door, feeling a fresh wave of guilt. *Just let him know you got his message and be done with it.*

I opened his text, skimming it just once more, then did my best to write a friendly-yet-suitably-cagey response:

Hi Wes, thanks for your message. And thanks for everything you said. I'm really sorry too, about how things ended, and I'm especially sorry that my last message came at such a bad time. I hope you're doing okay. Congratulations on Med School – you'll be surprised to hear it, but I actually never went. I know, I know – after all that nagging, you're the one who's three years in and I'm the one who's –

I bit my lip, not knowing what to say.

I'm the one who took another path. Anyway, all is great here. I wish you the very best and –

And what? I frowned. 'Hope to be in touch soon'? 'Look forward to seeing you'? I sighed in frustration.

I hope things in Mali go well. Bring plenty of mosquito spray. Take care, Aspen.

– Rowan! I chided myself, replacing my newly-adopted name with something he would recognize. I hurriedly hit 'send', then flung the phone back on the bed.

My head was starting to hurt again. From the other room, Eileen was calling my name – well, one of them.

"Aspen!"

"Coming!" I shouted, glancing at my reflection in the mirror of my closet door. Standing there in my new blue dress, my disconcertingly-purple eyes staring back at me, I felt like I hardly recognized myself.

I sighed. *Getting my memories back was supposed to answer all of my questions... not create more.*

Chapter 8

"How am I being offensive?" Ori demanded, stuffing another bite of chicken parmesan in his mouth even though he hadn't finished the first bite yet. "I'm just making the observation that those three women who showed up in the arena today were hot. I mean, *hot* hot. Like, carwash bikini model hot. So, all I'm asking is, how do I become a sub-Prelate?"

Beside him, Eileen groaned.

"First of all, you have to be extraordinarily powerful—" I started.

"I am!" he retorted, a piece of spaghetti dangling over his lip.

I arched an eyebrow. "As in, Level-Three powerful. Preferably in two Elements or more. All five of the most powerful Polymancers in the world are either in the Inner

Circle or working directly under them, if that tells you anything."

"I'd love to work directly under those three," Ori muttered beneath his breath.

Evelyn raised a scandalous eyebrow at him. "Wipe your chin, dear, you've got sauce on it."

He grinned, daintily dabbing his beard with the pink cloth napkin she had tucked into his collar.

"Interestingly enough, the man those women work for, Jahi, has taken quite an interest in Sophia," I mentioned, trying to keep my voice casual. I'd seen the way he looked at his sub-Prelates, one of whom had already been replaced by a younger, more bosom-y model in the short amount of time I'd been involved with the Inner Circle.

"Oh?" Sophia asked, raising an eyebrow.

I nodded. "He's asked to meet you once or twice now." *In the last week alone.*

"I haven't personally seen Jahi's current harem – er, team," Ted smirked, leaning back in his chair. "But I do know he's notoriously picky about his Subs' level requirements. So, if those women are as good-looking as they are powerful, I'd be impressed. At the very least, you should take his interest as a compliment, Sophia."

Sophia wrinkled her nose. "I've heard rumors that some of the sub-Prelates earn their way into the Extended Circle through specific types of 'favors'… So, I think I'll pass."

Eileen shrugged. "I mean, it's yucky and corrupt, but those women *were* really good-looking, so you'd be in good company…" Sophia shot her an appalled look. "I jest, I jest!" Eileen added, throwing her hands up defensively.

"Is this type of conversation really dinner-appropriate?" Evelyn asked, giving that side of the table a reproachful look that was only slightly undercut by the upturned corners of her mouth.

"I'll say this much," my mother said, causing the rest of the table to immediately fall silent, "people will do anything for the chance to be in the Inner and Extended Circle. And as someone who routinely worked to suppress knowledge, I can tell you that some of the things I saw and heard were… indecorous. At best." She took a sip of wine, glancing at me over her glass. "The corruption doesn't stop at Containment and memory suppression. As is the case with many other hierarchical organizations, depravity and corporeal abuses of power occur in more intimate areas, as well."

I swallowed tightly.

"So, what you're saying is, Asterians are sleeping their way to the top of the token pole?" Ori asked.

Evelyn shot him a look. "It's 'totem', dear. How do you like your dinner? It was Aspen's favorite growing up." She gave me a quick wink and I smiled, relieved for the abrupt change of subject.

Ori took a big swig of wine before patting his flat stomach. "As always, *Evelinkeh*, dinner was incredible. Have I mentioned that I've gained at least three kilos since we met?"

"Well, thank you, sweetheart!" she beamed, adding another tong-full of spaghetti to his plate.

At the same time Eileen demanded, "Where could you have possibly gained seven pounds? In that over-inflated head of yours? Because when you turn to the side, everything except your head disappears. You're built like a lollipop!"

Aiden squeezed my fingers beneath the table, chuckling. Looking around the room, it readily occurred to me that I'd never seen so many people inside Evelyn's tiny dining room before. In fact, apart from her and I, I'd never seen anyone else sitting at her table, period. After my grandfather died and my parents disappeared, she really didn't have anyone – just me. And even then, I'd been conditioned to forget that we were family. But here we all were, the leaves in the table fully extended, every mismatched chair in the house clustered around a crowded dinner table set for nine. My mother sat to my left, and beside her, Ted. Sophia and Ori had sandwiched Eileen in the middle of them, and across from Aiden and me were Robert and Evelyn, clasping hands beneath the table like high school sweethearts. Even back in California, our dinner table never held more than the five of us – Mom, Dad, Ted, Jenny, and me.

For a brief moment my heart ached, thinking about Dad and Jenny. When my eyes momentarily caught Ted's, I could have sworn he was having the exact same thought. But, in his usual 'Ted' style, he immediately perked up when he caught my glance, flashing me a breezy smile and a wink. *Has he been back to California at all since Mom was released?* I wondered. *Or has he been couch surfing at our houses this whole time?*

"Aspen?" Ori was waving a hand in front of my face. "Did you hear me?"

"Um, no – sorry," I said, reaching for my glass of lemonade. "What did you say?"

"I asked what the deal was with your eyeballs," he repeated, suddenly wincing as though he'd been kicked. He shot a dirty look at Eileen, who looked positively angelic.

"I mean, they're stunning as ever," he quickly stammered, "like two lovely amethysts set beneath lush, dark lashes…"

Aiden cleared his throat.

"I'm just stating a fact!" Ori protested.

"Darling," Eileen whispered loudly to Sophia, "why don't you ever wax on about my lovely gem-colored eyes?"

"I think Ori's question has more to do with the change in color," Robert interjected. "Which, I confess, I've been wondering about as well. I've never stumbled across anything like that in the Asterian archives."

"Oh, well, uh…" I glanced at my mother, who was giving me a wistful smile. "Mom?"

"I'm not really sure why Rowan's eyes have changed color again," she admitted.

"Again?" Aiden asked, surprised.

"Her eyes used to be similar in color to mine – dark blue, with just a hint of gray around the iris, from her father. But when we, uh… affected her memories a few years back," she looked down at the table, still seeming uncomfortable with the subject, "one of her eyes flickered during the process, then permanently shifted to that purple hue. And now, after this most recent procedure, both of her eyes have darkened to violet. I don't know how – or why. It's not something I've heard of."

I frowned. "I didn't realize you hadn't seen this happen before."

Robert cleared his throat. "You know, Aspen has mentioned that she can consistently see colors now that she couldn't see before, which I suspect may fall in the ultraviolet spectrum based on what she's described to me – bright, shimmering lines around certain light bulbs and electric lines, a glowing remnant in the aftermath of a lightning strike. I wonder if that has anything to do with the change?"

"It's possible," my mother replied, though she sounded skeptical. "I certainly can't see those things the way she can, so I can't rightfully say. But I suspect there's more to it... I just can't say what exactly that is."

"I bet Barish can," Aiden said, brushing a strand of hair from my face. "If you felt comfortable asking him, that is."

I stared down at my plate. It was true – Barish and I both shared the same strangely-colored violet eyes. But a part of me shuddered to wonder why that was, and like other things, I couldn't bring myself to ask him.

The hush that had fallen on the table was interrupted by Evelyn abruptly pushing her chair away from the table. "Robert, dear, would you help me with something in the kitchen?" she asked sweetly.

"Oh, ah, of course, my pet," he replied, straightening his shirt as he stood up. "You know," he chuckled, giving Ori a quick wink, "I think I've gained a few pounds in the last few weeks myself." He patted his slightly protruding belly. "Unfortunately, I no longer have a hollow limb to store it all in – and it shows!"

Without missing a beat, Ori turned to Eileen and said, "Don't."

"What?"

"You're going to refer that my head is the part of my body that's hollow, right?"

"How could you think I'd say something so hurtful?" she asked, her eyes widening in bemusement. "And also, it's *in*fer, not *re*fer."

"Going back to the subject of your induction," Ted cut in, leaning forward in his chair to look at me, "has there been any further news? Or pressure from above?"

"Only about every single day," I replied. "They're inducting a new member into the Inner Circle in a couple days and Barish was really hoping I'd—"

"Wait," he interjected. "They're *what*?"

"One of the Prelates – Kaal – passed away suddenly," I answered, "and he's being replaced. Barish was hoping I'd attend the ceremony so he could kill two birds with one stone and induct me at the same time."

Ted and my mother exchanged weary glances.

"I don't understand," I frowned. "What's the big deal?"

Just then, Evelyn and Robert stepped outside the kitchen, carrying a homemade cake with candles. My face immediately flushed as Evelyn, a wide grin on her face, set the cake down in front of me. If Wes hadn't reminded me earlier that afternoon, I never would have remembered that it was my birthday.

"Happy birthday, sweetheart!" she exclaimed. "I'm just so glad we can celebrate it properly again! Now, I know you hate it when people make a big fuss over it, but don't worry – your mother and I warned everyone in advance – no singing, no presents!"

I stared at the cake, feeling a strange sensation growing in my chest. Two dozen white candles blazed alongside pink frosted roses, their tiny drops of wax settling upon the dark chocolate icing. As I stared at the candles, I was suddenly transported to a strangely-shimmering memory of my grandmother setting the same cake in front of me, but with far fewer candles. Over the tops of the candles were my father's pale, twinkling eyes, the reflection of the flames dancing across his glasses.

"Happy birthday, Rosebud," he smiled. A flash of pain seared across my vision and my hand immediately jumped to my forehead. "Rosebud?" his voice echoed.

"Rosebud?" I felt my mother clasping my shoulder. "Are you all right?" My hand fell back to my lap, where Aiden squeezed it gently.

"I-I'm fine," I replied, forcing a smile. "I just remembered something. Uh, Evelyn, this cake looks amazing."

"Family recipe. Your mother helped me," she beamed, the corners of her smile not quite meeting her eyes. "Now hurry and make a wish!"

I stared at the candles, blinking a few times to clear my father's face from my mind. Then, with a quick flick of my wrist, the candles went out.

"Cheater!" Eileen laughed.

"So, Aspen, how old are you now?" Sophia asked. I hesitated a moment, trying to remember. My mother squeezed my shoulder reassuringly.

"Twenty-four, I guess," I finally answered. "I've been lying about my age for so long, I almost forgot."

"Wait – Aiden, how old are you?" Ori asked.

"Thirty," Aiden replied dryly. "Thirty-one this August."

"So that means that when Aspen was just a little baby of twelve, you were already in college?" Ori gave a low whistle, then turned to my mother. "Mrs. Fulman, I hope that doesn't appall you or anything."

My mother laughed lightly. "Rowan's always been very precocious for her age... and Aiden's a good man." She exchanged a quick smile with him, before her eyes swiftly fell back to the cake sitting in front of us. There wasn't a coldness between her and Aiden, per se, but there was a palpable discomfort. I could certainly feel it, and I was fairly sure the others sensed it as well; the historic bad blood between our families hadn't escaped the memories of anyone at that table.

Evelyn quickly served me a piece of chocolate cake, then set a fat slice in front of Ori, sending the plate clattering against the table as she did. "Shut up and eat, dear," she smiled, pinching his cheek.

I glanced over at Aiden to make sure he didn't appear too dour, only to find him staring down at his phone, a concerned look on his face.

"Hey... Everything okay?" I asked.

"Uh – yes. Just, uh... Please excuse me for a minute," he replied, getting up from his seat. "I'll be right back." He gave me a quick kiss on the forehead before making his way for the front door.

"Did I hit a sore spot?" Ori asked with a mouthful of cake. Surprisingly, he actually looked contrite.

"The news might have been made public by now," I heard Ted whisper to my mother.

"What news?" I asked, bringing a sheepish look to his face.

"Nothing that needs to be brought up right this moment," my mom replied tersely.

"But it has something to do with Aiden?" I pressed.

My mother shot Ted a look, which was quickly replaced by an apologetic one when she turned back to me. "I think Ted might be *speculating* about Aiden's father, who's worked very closely with Prelate Kaal over the years."

I set my fork down on the table. "What do you mean?"

Ted glanced at my mother, who appeared to give him the tiniest shake of the head. He sighed. "I'm sorry, Ro. I didn't realize you weren't aware. Terry was bumped up to sub-Prelate a couple years back. He's been working under Kaal for some time."

Across the table, Eileen let out a small gasp.

"Wait, so you're saying…" my voice trailed off.

The front door had just slammed shut, and a moment later, Aiden entered the room. The second his eyes met mine, I knew. But the immediate thought that entered my mind wasn't about the man who hunted down my parents, disowned his son, and allowed his own daughter to be abandoned in Containment... It was an errant memory from five years ago, of Wes' father serving me homemade birthday pancakes – a tradition in their family – a wide smile spread across his cheeks as he ruffled my hair fondly. I blinked, trying to clear away the image, as well as the tears that came along with it.

"I'm so sorry," I whispered, and for the briefest moment, I wasn't quite sure who exactly I was apologizing to.

Chapter 9

*L*ater that night, Aiden and I sat side by side on the front porch swing outside my cabin, our somber expressions exposed only by the pale yellow light filtering through the kitchen window behind us. We'd been sitting in complete silence for nearly a quarter hour, each of us trying to absorb the news: Aiden's father was about to be initiated as the Inner Circle's newest member, making our already-complicated lives all the more difficult. For the remainder of dinner and the ride back home, I'd been doing my best to suppress my own negative feelings, knowing that Aiden was struggling just as much as I was – if not more. But my thoughts were in chaos. *How am I supposed to cooperate with a man who's caused my family so much pain and suffering? A man whose only concern appears to be executing the law, no matter the cost?* Based on everything I'd ever heard, Terry Lawson was a fanatical, cold-hearted, and Draconian man – the kind of man who felt he could justify any level of barbarism, simply because some antiquated law prescribed it. He and Jahi would probably be great friends, if they weren't already.

How is this going to affect the policies I've been working so hard to change? I wrung my hands together, idly picking at a loose hangnail. On paper, the Magistrate had the final authority regarding current Asterian laws, but any formal change in policy would have to be voted on by the Inner Circle. With a super majority of opposing votes, they could – in theory – overrule him. That hadn't happened in years, but if Terry had enough influence, he could hypothetically sway enough votes in his favor...

I winced as a sharp prick quickly snapped me back into the moment. Muttering a curse under my breath, I stared at the drop of blood forming where the hangnail on my thumb used to be, concentrating on staunching it before it could drip onto my new dress. Beside me, Aiden was staring at his own tightly-clasped hands, lost in thought. I rubbed the fresh scab on my thumb, gazing up at the dim stars that had appeared in the night sky just moments before. The sun had long set below the horizon, leaving a crimson slash of twilight peeking through the trees. To the east, dark clouds were forming over a jagged line of evergreen trees as the wind ushered them in our direction. I sighed, searching for the right words to break the silence, but it was Aiden who spoke first.

"My mother is a mess right now," he muttered, raking his curls away from his face with both hands.

"Because of your father's promotion?" I asked.

"Because of the rumors," Aiden replied.

"Rumors?"

He flicked open his lighter, rolling the flame between his fingers – an anxious habit of his, I'd come to learn. "There are rumors swirling around the D.C. division that my father and one of the Prelates have been having an affair for months... maybe longer."

I gasped softly. "An affair?"

"My parents haven't filed for divorce yet, but I imagine these rumors will give my mother fresh motivation." The fire in his hand flared from orange to blue.

"Aiden, I'm so sorry," I whispered, squeezing his free hand. Inwardly, I tried to wrap my head around the news. There were five women in the Inner Circle: Nadia, Izabel, Keres, Mei, and Valeriya. Nadia and Mei were well into their seventies and their somber demeanors gave the impression of being above such corporeal indulgences; Izabel was married to one of the other Prelates, Felipe, and Valeriya didn't seem interested in men at all. Not to mention she appeared to have a particular disdain for most things – including the English language – and I doubted Terry spoke enough Ukranian to entertain an affair.

But Keres... That, perhaps, I could swallow. With her stunning looks and disarming manner of speaking, she seemed to charm everyone around her, particularly Barish... Though I could never quite tell whether his affection toward her was fatherly – or something else. Still, Keres had such an air of elegance about her, and she certainly didn't want for attention from the opposite sex. Why stoop to having an affair?

"It's possible that those rumors are just stemming from jealousy," Aiden continued. "It sounds like my father's only been a sub-Prelate for a short time, and while there are no hard and fast rules regarding promotion into the Inner Circle, it's traditionally based on ability level, influence, and seniority..." Aiden snorted derisively. "Compared to the other two candidates, my father doesn't have strength or seniority in his favor... but it *would* appear that he has influence."

"*If* the rumors are true," I pointed out, then started. *What's that noise?*

Behind us, from inside the house, an unfamiliar sound drifted through the window.

"Is that a phone ringing?" I asked, frowning. It occurred to me then that *I* didn't even know my own phone number yet.

"It would appear so," Aiden answered. "Please, go ahead. I wouldn't mind a moment alone, anyway."

"I'll be right back," I said, kissing his forehead as I stood. "It's probably just my mom or Evelyn. I'll bring you a drink when I come back out."

By the time I'd made my way into the kitchen, the phone had stopped ringing. But a few seconds later, it started again. My hand shot out and I grabbed it on the first ring.

"Hello?"

"Hello, Rowan," came Barish's deep voice. "I'm so glad I was able to reach you this way. I didn't want to trouble you with a visit from one of my messengers at this hour."

"Barish," I breathed. "How did you get this number?"

"You know I'm always happy to explain, my dear, but I'm afraid we're short on time."

My shoulders tensed. "Is there a problem?" I asked, my thoughts immediately drifting to my family next door.

"No, no. Well, certainly not one that impacts you... directly," he clarified.

Here we go, I thought to myself.

"As I mentioned the other day, the Inner Circle had an unexpected vacancy and the seat requires an immediate replacement. This is normally a straightforward process; either the incumbent Prelate goes into voluntary Sequestration – retirement, if you will – and formally names his successor in a subsequent announcement, or, in the rare case of a sudden passing, such as Kaal's, we would look to his Register. It's a formal log we all keep that contains Community-related notes, personal records, as well as named beneficiaries and replacements in case of certain emergencies. In this case, Kaal's Register has gone missing."

I frowned. "I don't understand. What does all of that mean, and what does it have to do with me?"

"It means," Barish said, "that the legitimacy of Kaal's rightful successor is in question. One of his sub-Prelates, Terry Lawson, insists that Kaal verbally promised him succession rights in the weeks before his passing. We took his word on that and made the formal announcement to the Chapters early this morning. However, as of this afternoon, one of Kaal's other sub-Prelates , Darius King, is challenging Lawson's assertion, insisting that their departed master promised *him* his chair."

I blinked at the phone in my hand. *You've got to be kidding me.*

Barish's voice continued from the receiver. "Given the untimely disappearance of Kaal's Register, which would have easily confirmed his appointee, I'm sure you can see how this complicates matters."

"So, what exactly do you need from me?"

"There is to be a formal Challenge to determine the rightful successor; therefore a vote may be required, depending on the outcome. Because I must traditionally abstain from such designations, and because our Circle currently has an even number of members, we require a ninth vote. And I have respectfully requested that it come from you."

"Why me?" I asked, my voice reflecting the growing lump in my throat. *I only just got home...*

"Because the sanctity of the Inner Circle is in question, and, unlike any other proxy, the legitimacy – as well as the impartiality – of your vote would not be questioned." It wasn't hard to read between the lines. What the Magistrate was really saying was: *Because you are the Pentamancer... and because I am asking you to.*

I forced myself to exhale the air I had been accumulating in my lungs before speaking.

"I see..." I said carefully. "And if I refuse?"

"I think, my dear Rowan," Barish replied, his voice level, "it would be prudent for you to graciously accept this honor. Your requests have been causing somewhat of a division within the Inner Circle; I sense a growing feeling of ambivalence among its members with respect to our present one-sided arrangement."

"Yes, but—"

"However," he continued, "I have every reason to believe that your cooperation in this matter will win you much favor. If the Prelates sense from you a willingness to support the Asterian Order – and not just your own agenda – I guarantee that their newfound positive impression will benefit you… as well as your ambitious goals."

I bit my lip. I couldn't detect any hint of threat embedded in his words, only logic. But for some reason, those words made my spine tingle. I rubbed the back of my neck, glancing at Aiden through the kitchen window. He was still sitting on the porch swing, cradling his head in both hands.

"I'll come on one condition," I conceded, fairly certain that what I was about to ask for was a radical request, even for me.

"And what is that?"

"Let me bring Aiden," I said. I heard Barish take a sharp intake of breath.

"Certainly not," he snapped. "Outsiders may not encroach upon the Inner Circle's governance – it's heresy!" His sharp tone made me raise an eyebrow in surprise, but his voice quickly softened. "That is to say, my dear, it deviates from our policies in the utmost extreme. Terry Lawson's estranged son does not have a voice or a place within the Sanctum."

"As an uninitiated member of the Asterian Order, I technically shouldn't have a voice, either," I replied, doing my best to channel the smooth, mollifying tone that I had seen Keres use on him before. While I may have looked down on her particular brand of coquetry, more than anyone else, she almost always got her way when it came to Barish. The least I could do was try to mimic her skills in diplomacy. "Besides – I'm not asking that you allow him to vote or have any sort of influence in the matter. I just want him by my side – a companion. For moral support." I leaned against the counter, trying to allay the tension I felt creeping inside my ribcage.

Barish was silent for a long moment before he spoke. "Historically, I suppose it is not unheard of for family members to attend such challenges, in case of casualties…" he mused.

That caught me off-guard. *Casualties?*

"And," he continued, "the event would occur in the public arena, after all, and not inside the hallowed walls of the Inner Sanctum..." He sighed. "*İnatçı kızım...* If this is the only way to secure your involvement, so be it, my plucky Pentamancer... But know this."

I chewed on my lip, anticipating his next words before he spoke them.

"With every provision we make for you, with every special accommodation we provide on your behalf, the Inner Circle grows more and more anxious to make our... *arrangement* official."

In other words, we're officially in quid pro quo territory.

I swallowed tightly. "I understand, Magistrate."

"Very good, my child," he said, his voice brightening. "Please expect a car to arrive for you and Mr. Lawson shortly. *İyi geceler.* I'm very much looking forward to seeing you in İstanbul."

"Yeah... me too," I muttered to the dial tone. My fingertips were tingling from gripping the countertop so roughly.

What did Barish mean by 'casualties'?

I glanced back outside to check on Aiden, but the porch swing was empty. Suddenly I didn't feel so confident about my 'plucky' request to bring my boyfriend along to what sounded like an Asterian cockfight involving his father. But if there was a chance Terry could get hurt in the challenge, Aiden would want to be there to provide him support… right?

Or did I just make an already-painful situation that much worse for him?

As if on cue, the front door opened.

"Aspen? What's wrong?" Aiden asked, stepping into the kitchen, his forehead creased with worry. The contents of my stomach suddenly felt very heavy. My first instinct was to lie, for his sake. But that had gotten us into trouble in the past, and at the very least, I knew he deserved better than my pity.

He gently rested his hand on mine as he approached. "Is everything okay?"

"Not exactly," I answered, rubbing my forehead. "It's… about your father."

Aiden was silent, turning his head away from me as though he were deliberating something. A moment later, he reached into his pocket and pulled out a small, white box.

"Before we get to that," he said quietly, setting the box on the counter beside me. "I got you something for your birthday."

I looked at him, surprised. "You remembered my birthday? Even I almost forgot."

"Open it," he said, the corners of his mouth flickering into a small smile.

I took the box and gingerly pulled open the lid. Inside was a pair of deep purple earrings, the color of the sky just before sunrise. I gasped softly, fingering the precious gems.

"Tanzanite?"

He nodded. "I briefly considered getting you pearls or moonstone, because I know that's your birthstone – but when I saw these, and how perfectly they matched your eyes, I knew I had to get them for you."

My fingers went to the matching pendant around my neck, one of only two other pieces of jewelry that had ever been given to me.

"I don't know how to thank you," I whispered.

"No thanks needed," he smiled, reaching forward to caress my face with his fingertips.

The emotions interwoven in the space between us abruptly changed, as though the atmosphere of the kitchen itself had become charged with Electricity. It made the hairs on the back of my neck rise up, and for the briefest moment, I tensed, wondering if lightning was about to strike close by. But it wasn't a storm that was causing the shift. My gaze settled back to Aiden's face, peered into the dark pools of his eyes. In that moment, there was no trace of anger or sorrow there. Only love.

Love? My breath caught in my throat. The word had only been spoken between us once, when I was about to undergo that terrible procedure that could have left me dead. Two months ago, it was the strongest emotion I could recall ever feeling for another person. Now that my memories were more or less intact, it occurred to me that I hadn't spoken the word to him again. Had he been wondering this whole time if my feelings for him had changed, or somehow diminished, now that I had my past to color my current perceptions? I bit the inside of my lip anxiously. I'd only tasted love with one other man, but it had felt so different all those years ago: safe, comfortable… expected, even, after spending most of high school and college together. With Wes, saying 'I love you' had been automatic, perfunctory. But the feelings I had for Aiden were so intense, almost overwhelming. They distracted me, consumed my thoughts, left my chest with a hollow, gnawed-out void during those long weeks apart – so much so that I'd had to bottle them away in order to function properly.

Gazing into his eyes, I wanted to tell him all of this, to let him know that my newfound memories hadn't changed my prior feelings for him; if anything, they strengthened them. But the words – those three simple words – took the breath right out of my lungs. I had only loved seven people in my entire life, and I had lost each and every one of them at one point or another – three of them forever. Most of those losses, I suddenly realized, were at the hands of the man that Aiden called 'Father'.

That's when I understood the crux of the fear gripping my chest: Now that Terry was about to obtain even more power, would he take Aiden from me as well? I quickly blinked my eyes, but it did nothing to halt the stinging tears that fell from them.

"Hey, it's okay," Aiden said softly. He cradled my face, gently brushing my tears aside with his thumbs. "You don't have to say anything you don't want to," he whispered, centimeters from my lips. "I'm not going anywhere."

How did he know? I thought to myself, overwrought with emotion.

I stretched up on my bare tip-toes, sliding my hands behind his neck to kiss him deeply. He wrapped his hands around my waist, pulling me close. The warmth of his lips, the sweetness of his breath stirred something deep within me, giving me the strength that I knew we would both need for what was coming our way. After a long moment, I gently pulled away, taking a shaky breath as I did.

"I have to go to Istanbul – tonight," I said softly. "Will you come with me?"

I expected him to counter my request with a dozen questions, to consider all the reasons why he should decline, and rightfully so. But without a moment's hesitation, he simply said:

"Yes."

Chapter 10

*I*t didn't take me long to pack – no time at all, to be precise – since I never unpacked my bags from the weeks before. But Aiden needed to grab some things from his house, so I asked him to drop me off at Evelyn's on the way. When we pulled into the driveway, Ted's car was still there. I gave Aiden a quick hug, then jogged the rest of the way up the drive, stopping at Evelyn's front porch. Before I could knock on the door, however, my mother pulled it open, her eyes trailing on Aiden's headlights as they pulled away. When she looked at me again, she was crestfallen.

You're leaving again? she asked, her lips unmoving.

I nodded.

Evelyn and Robert are already asleep. Come, sit. Let's talk. She ducked inside to grab a blanket, then sat with me on the wooden bench in the front yard.

"Where are they sending you this time?" she asked out loud, draping the quilt across my shoulders before settling next to me.

"Turkey," I replied. "They need me for a vote..."

"A vote?" she asked, then quickly nodded in understanding. "I see. A vote you want nothing to do with... That accounts for the dejection I sense, but I still don't understand – what's frightening you?"

I sighed, staring down at my hands. "I've been stalling as long as I can... but this time, I don't think I'll be able to talk my way out of being initiated. And once that happens... the entire Community will know my face. There won't be a way to turn back. Back to the way things were."

Her eyes lingered on mine for a long moment, then trailed to my ears. She fingered my new earrings gently. "These are lovely," she said. "They're the exact shade as your necklace – and your lovely new eyes," she smiled tightly.

"That's what Aiden said, too." I pulled the quilt that we were sharing closer around my shoulders as a damp breeze ruffled my hair. The forest outside Evelyn's cabin was dark, the half-moon quickly becoming obscured by dark clouds. A strange quiet had settled on the woods; even the crickets were still.

"A storm is coming," my mother remarked. "Can you feel it?"

I nodded. The last remaining twinkling stars had disappeared behind dark, billowing clouds. I could feel the air around us ionizing in anticipation of the storm.

I'm so sorry for dragging you into this world, Rosebud, my mother's voice drifted in my head. *More than anything, I regret the choices your father and I made, the choices that trapped you on this path...* As she took my hand in hers, I felt her shiver. *I can't tell you how to protect yourself from it, I can't tell you how to escape it. I can only pray that your abilities will safeguard you in a way that we couldn't.*

Her gentle voice in my head fell silent; somewhere close by, thunder rumbled.

"I heard from Wes today," I said softly.

Wes? She turned to look at me. *He knows...?*

"Of course not," I answered quickly. "He knows that Electricity seems to do weird things around me. Nothing more. But I... I reached out to him again, a couple months ago. I didn't tell him anything; I only asked how he was. I guess – I just..." I sighed, idly tugging on a loose thread in Evelyn's quilt.

"You miss him," my mother said simply. "It's understandable. The two of you were very close… and you never got to say goodbye. Not properly. I'm so sorry for that."

I leaned forward, resting my elbows on my thighs. "I miss my *life* with him, Mom. I miss the way he made me feel normal, the way he made me forget about my abilities, the Asterians, the fear, the *heaviness* of it all. And Wes' family was always so warm and welcoming…" I grimaced, remembering what Aiden had once said to me: *I wish I could have courted you… taken you to my parents' house, where my father and mother would welcome you, the first girl I've ever brought home, with open arms. Sarah would regale you with embarrassing stories from my childhood. It would be awkward and uncomfortable… but that would be the worst of our worries.*

I sighed. *Yeah… In an alternate universe, perhaps.*

"Wes and his family were very nice people," my mother agreed. "Your father and I always liked them."

"They were nice," I said. "And they were so open, so… so *boring*." I leaned my head back, watching the swollen rainclouds flicker above. "The biggest scandal to rock their household was when Wes got a C-minus in Physics. I'd give just about anything for that kind of normalcy."

"I suppose extraordinary people just weren't meant for ordinary lives," my mom replied, just as a silver fork of lightning streaked across the sky. "But you were meant for amazing things, Rowan. Not settling with someone because they make you feel ordinary."

"Does that mean you approve of me dating Aiden?"

The words slipped out, and I wanted to kick myself. Of *course* she didn't approve. I'd seen the sideways glances in his direction, the way the corners of her mouth pursed ever so slightly whenever he spoke. His father was the reason she'd been locked up, torn away from me – the reason her husband was dead. Just being in the same room with Terry's son was probably difficult enough, let alone having to live with the fact that he was dating her daughter.

"I'm sorry," I muttered, embarrassed. "We don't need to talk about that."

"I think Aiden is absolutely wonderful," she replied, startling me.

"You do?"

She nodded. "Wes was a sweetheart – always making you laugh. And I know he brought some much-needed normalcy to your life. But the few times I've seen you with Aiden… Well, it doesn't take an Electromancer to see the spark between you two," she winked. "But more than that, he's brilliant and capable and confident enough that you'll never need to diminish yourself to accommodate his ego. When you're with him, Ro, I see a great power in you that I believe he helps nurture. So, no, I don't care who his family is. If you love him, so do I."

My eyes stung, and for the second time that night, I found myself blinking away tears. "I *do* love him, Mom. Which is why I'm so afraid to lose him. Part of me still wants to run, to take all of you with me."

"I know." She turned to look at me, clasping my hands in hers. "For the last two months, I've been thinking about all the different ways we could try to do just that – run away and never look back. When I think about you becoming one of them, it terrifies me…"

I wanted to comfort her, say something reassuring, but a lump had formed in my throat, blocking my words.

"But you're not weak like I was, Rowan. You see what's right and what's wrong in this world, so clearly, better than I ever could, even when I was much older than you. As much as I want to tell you to run, to adopt one last alias somewhere far away… I know it would be wrong. You've spent too much of your life hiding."

"But what if facing them head-on is worse?" I whispered. "What if all of this is a terrible mistake?"

She shook her head firmly. "You can't let yourself doubt your instincts; too much depends on them. You have to do what you were meant to do, Rowan. If anyone can fix this broken world, *you* can. I can't shield you from your destiny anymore."

"My destiny?" I repeated, wiping my eyes on my sleeves. "You're starting to sound like Barish."

My mother started to say something, but above us, a peal of thunder crashed in the sky just as the rain began to fall. I parted it in curtains around us to keep us dry; it slid down two diagonal sides of an invisible roof, collecting around our bench in little pools. A flash of lightning illuminated my mother's dark irises just before she leaned forward to kiss my forehead gently. When she pulled away, her storm-blue eyes bored fiercely into mine.

"I don't believe in many things in this world, Rowan, but more than anything, I believe in you. Don't you ever forget that."

Chapter 11

ourteen hours and half a world later, my ears were all at once accosted by a disharmonious eruption of chants as mosques from every corner of the street announced the late afternoon call to prayer. Though I was already sweating from the blistering heat of the sun, I tightened the purple shawl I'd borrowed from Evelyn around my head and craned my neck towards the source of the incantation closest to us: a set of speakers perched atop one of the six towering minarets of the colossal, blue-domed mosque to our west. Its haunting call drowned out the shrill cries of the seagulls circling above it, but did nothing to drown out the clamorous calls from its neighboring mosques, which converged upon my ears from five different directions. The rest of the people we passed on the narrow street continued on as though nothing unusual had occurred, paying my startled reaction more heed than the startling noise itself.

"The *Adhan* is beautiful, isn't it?" Aiden murmured, pulling me close as a group of passerby stared in our direction. "Though not particularly inconspicuous. Kind of like you," he chuckled, kissing the side of my head playfully. I flushed even hotter beneath my scarf.

As we followed our guide, Yusuf, through the bustling bazaar that was nestled within the cobblestone streets bordering the Blue Mosque, I gripped Aiden's hand in mine, both awed and overwhelmed by the old city of Istanbul. All around us, gregarious merchants peddled hand-spun Turkish rugs, scarves, painted dishes, and apparel in a dozen different languages, all the while twirling colorful prayer beads in their fingers, a porcelain cup of Turkish coffee or cigarette resting on their lip. I hid a smile as we passed an old man who nimbly sucked on both at the same time, since any display of friendliness – genuine or perceived – would summon an onslaught of entreaties from the merchants to come and browse, along with fervent affirmations that everything inside was "genuine, handmade, and the best in the world". Our guide, Yusuf, waved away their invitations as we passed, stopping only once to purchase the three of us delicate, steaming teacups of sweet tea, which tasted tart and crisp like hot apple cider.

When we eventually emerged from the far side of the market, everything opened up into a vibrant backdrop of even more extraordinary sights and smells. I sucked in an awed breath, my eyes jumping from the multitude of spectacular landmarks all around us: at our backs was an ancient Egyptian obelisk that rose twenty-five feet from the ground; to our right was the great Blue Mosque, its series of massive domes and six towering spires rising majestically above the square. Across the plaza was a gate with twin turrets, leading to a sprawling palace-turned-museum, and beside that—

"Our destination is just ahead, beneath the walls of the *Aya Sofya*," Yusuf said, pointing to the stunning structure in front of us. Its magnificent spires were similar in style to its neighbor, the Blue Mosque, but its tiers of gray-capped domes and desert rose-colored exterior was framed by lush trees and foliage, a sparkling fountain, and colorfully-flowering gardens.

"This building is also called the Hagia Sophia, right, Yusuf?" Aiden asked, shielding his eyes from the late afternoon sun.

"Yes, *aynen*," Yusuf replied, giving Aiden an approving smile. "In Latin, it is *Sancta Sophia*, also called

Church of the Holy Wisdom. It was built in the sixth century, first as a Greek Orthodox Christian cathedral, later adopted as an Ottoman mosque, and now it is preserved as a museum." He motioned us to follow him across the lawn, where dozens of people stood to pose for photos in front of the shimmering fountain outside.

"And of course," he said, lowering his voice, "it is the home of our Community's headquarters, which we will access through the gardens in the back. Follow me, please – we will take a path away from these crowds," he added, scowling at the busload of Japanese tourists that were headed for the front entrance.

"This place is incredible," I enthused as we walked around the walls of the colossal domed building. "I've never seen anything like it."

From up close, I could see that the main dome had to have been a hundred feet in diameter; the top of it – which was perhaps two hundred feet tall – rose well above even the tallest palm trees in the surrounding gardens. The smaller, gold-ornamented gray domes around the front and sides of it glittered in the sun; their supporting walls were the same pink hue as a desert sunset. As we walked along the winding gravel trail through the gardens, my nose was greeted by the honeyed scent of hundreds of artistically-arranged tulips and the delicate blossoms of exotic flowering trees.

"It is easy to see why İstanbul was selected for the Asterian Headquarters," Yusuf said as we approached a pair of armed guards. They stood on either side of a small, nondescript metal door embedded in the side of the sandstone brick; their eyebrows narrowed sharply until Yusuf flashed a piece of paper with the Magistrate's seal – as well as his blue Hydromancer's tattoo. They gave him a curt nod, then stepped aside for us to pass. I tried not to let my eyes linger on the semi-automatic weapons they carried.

"*Tabi ki*, İstanbul is the most beautiful city in the world," Yusuf continued, opening the heavy door for us. "But more than that, our Aya Sofya is a symbol of harmony and peace, a meeting point of two great religions. That is why this historical place is perfect," he said as we headed down a dark, winding staircase. "Because the Order transcends religion itself, uniting all followers of nearly every worldly faith. While the rest of the world continues to wage war on one another, Elementalists find solace in everlasting peace."

Since when is it 'peaceful' to turn a blind eye to the rest of the world's suffering? I mused, using the wall for support as we descended down the steep stone steps. My hands were starting to feel clammy from being in such a tight space, but in an odd way, the darkness of the stairwell helped; all I had to do was imagine it as a much wider stairwell than it actually was.

"Well, I'll say this much," Aiden said lightly. "The Asterian occupation of the Hagia Sophia has proven to be beneficial for the building. It hasn't been razed since the Community took possession of it in the eighth century."

"You are very insightful, *beyefendi*," Yusuf chuckled. "Yes, that is true. After the second Aya Sophia burned in the Nika Riots, the Order has made certain that this third and final version would never be threatened again. And to this day, it has weathered the storms of more than a thousand years of human history."

A muffled yelp was all I could contribute to the conversation as my toe caught the edge of one of the steps. I tried to catch myself in the near pitch-black darkness, but all I managed to do was scrape my sweaty hand on the way down. Luckily, Aiden's unyielding backside prevented me from tumbling the rest of the way down the seemingly never-ending staircase.

"Are you okay?" he asked, helping me to my feet.

"Yeah," I grunted, wiping my bloodied hand on my shorts. "It would have been thoughtful of them to install a light in here, though…"

Aiden pulled out his lighter to create a torch of Fire in his palm. "I hope you don't mind, Yusuf?" he asked, pouring some of the flames into my uninjured hand. I accepted them gratefully, holding my ignited fingers out in front of me to better make out my surroundings. The flames did wonders to help me stay upright, but my chest immediately tightened when I looked ahead and saw no end to the steep stone steps that spiraled down into the darkness and out of sight.

"It is no problem," Yusuf said with a wave. "Just be sure to first seek permission before conjuring in the Inner Circle's presence. That is rule number one. You must also always address them by their proper titles – Magistrate and Prelate. And it is forbidden to bring electronics of any kind past the antechamber. I do not suggest you try sneaking them in, either… *He* will sense them."

Yusuf paused, glancing over his shoulder. "I wonder what the Inner Circle requires from two young Pyromancers such as yourselves?" he asked casually. His eyes trailed to the place my tattoo should be exposed, and not for the first time that day.

"Nothing all that interesting," I muttered, casting a quick glance to make sure the sleeves of my tunic properly covered the unmistakable tattoo on my forearm.

Yusuf shrugged. "If you say so, *hanımefendi*."

After the hundreds of introductions I'd been subjected to in the last two months, I'd eventually gathered that it was considered rude to keep one's tattoo concealed in the company of other Elementalists, who often inquired about one's Elemental class even before exchanging names. Keeping my Pentamancer tattoo covered had certainly caused some recurrent awkwardness between myself and the non-officers I'd met, such as Yusuf – not just because of the inherent social gaffe, but because the majority of Asterians appeared to view the five classes of Elementalists as separate fraternities; Pyromancers immediately seemed to be drawn to other Fire-wielders, Terramancers to other Earth-movers, and so on. But by hiding my class from most of the Elementalists I'd met, I – or, rather, Barish – was effectively ensuring that I would remain an outsider. I suspected that was by design, just in case my formal initiation fell through, for whatever reason.

I crossed my arms tightly over my chest, feeling a sudden chill in the air. *Even still*, I reasoned, keeping my 'unique capabilities' a secret from the majority of the Order was one of the Magistrate's few non-negotiables that I was more than happy to adhere to. I'd take awkward glances and false assumptions about my abilities over shock and veneration any day.

Though the stairs continued downward, Yusuf abruptly stopped at an unmarked metal door embedded in the wall to our left, removing a long, gold colored skeleton key from his pocket to fit inside the formidable lock.

"They are waiting for you both through this door, which leads to the antechamber where you will be greeted and debriefed by a small security team – perhaps even one or two sub-Prelates, depending on the nature of your business. The welcome committee will instruct you further on proper decorum and etiquette. From there, if they are satisfied, they will take you to the Inner Circle. Remember what I told you about the rules, and you shouldn't encounter any problems. Now, if you'll please extinguish your flames."

Problems? I frowned slightly, flicking my wrist to snuff out the fire in my palm. The staircase was plunged into pitch-darkness once more.

But I didn't have time to ponder Yusuf's implication for long, because moments after he opened the door for us, we were greeted not by guards, but by the Magistrate himself.

Chapter 12

"*R*owan, my child!" the Magistrate boomed, clasping my hands in his. "I am so very pleased to see you again so soon." He was back in his formal robes, which, unlike the rest of the Prelates', had silken cords of thick, gold rope hanging from the hood.

"Nice to see you too, Magistrate," I replied coolly. It hadn't really fazed me that Barish and his eight Prelates had forgone their typical security procedure, opting instead to greet us personally. I was frankly half-surprised that Barish hadn't been the one to pick us up from the airport.

Yusuf, however, nearly fell to the ground when he stepped inside the doorway to find the most powerful man in the world warmly clasping my hand. He immediately jerked his head toward the stone floor in reverence, as if his eyes were not worthy of the sight they beheld.

"*Sizinle tanışmak bir şerefti, Hakim Bey,*" the poor man stammered, pressing his forehead to the tri-colored tattoo on Barish's arm. I didn't speak a syllable of Turkish, but I surmised from Yusuf's stunned reaction that this was his first time seeing the Magistrate in person.

"*O şeref bana ait,*" Barish replied, placing a formidable hand on the man's trembling shoulder. Yusuf took a step back, still muttering formalities, and continued to keep his head bowed as he backed out of the room. Without another word to either Aiden or me, Yusuf staggered backwards into the stairwell. The door slammed shut behind him, echoing against the high stone ceiling of the otherwise tiny antechamber.

"Young Mr. Lawson," the Magistrate boomed, turning his attention to Aiden. "It is a pleasure to see you again as well."

"Magistrate," Aiden replied, bowing his head slightly. I could see the corners of the Magistrate's mouth twitch, perhaps because, unlike Yusuf, Aiden didn't throw himself at the man in awestruck veneration.

Is that what I should have been doing this whole time – prostrating myself in front of him? I wondered as I glanced at the other Prelates standing behind Barish, surveying Aiden and me with their usual solemn, hooded expressions. *After I'm initiated and the courtship ends, will the informality be allowed to continue? Or are the rules of engagement about to change?*

I looked around the room, the tightness in my chest from descending down the narrow, musty stairwell only slightly dissipating in the small, confined antechamber. The ancient brick walls were bare and had only two doors; the one we came in, and another door directly across from it. Five torches hung from the walls, but I quickly realized that the flames that burned from them were not orange, but red... and purple? And *green*? I gasped softly. They each burned a separate color of the five Elements, the same five colors embedded in the tattoo on my arm.

"Ah, yes," Barish smiled, seeing my awestruck expression. "You can thank Prelate Piotr for the inspired ambience."

One of the oldest Prelates, a wizened man dressed in emerald and crimson, tilted his head in my direction. "Pyromantic Fire mixed with copper, strontium, sodium and potassium chloride each," Piotr spoke, his raspy voice resounding with surprising enthusiasm. "And a dash of sodium borate to create the perfect shade of purple." He raised a pale, wrinkled hand to the torch nearest him, fingering the violet flames lovingly.

I gaped at him in surprise. In all my daily briefings with the Prelates, I'd never heard Piotr utter a single word before... *But then again*, it occurred to me, *I've never asked him anything about Terramancy.* I felt the corners of my mouth tug upward as my thoughts drifted to Eileen and the way her eyes would light up the moment the conversation veered towards anything mineral-related.

Keres stepped forward then, her gold, sapphire, and emerald-colored robes sweeping elegantly around her strappy, sky-high heels. "Prophet, I pray your travels were comfortable," she said demurely, taking my hand in hers. "Oh, what's this?" she asked, looking at the dirty cut on the inside of my palm.

"It's nothing," I said, pulling my hand away.

"Please, may I?" she asked, holding a tentative hand over mine. Out of curiosity more than anything else, I nodded. As she swept her hand over my palm, dust and tiny bits of gravel rose from the fresh scrape; the shallow wound all at once was clean and dried.

"Th-thanks," I said, frowning slightly at my hand.

"It was my honor, *Prophetis*," she replied. Her eyes darted past me to Aiden, who was watching her closely. I hadn't told him my suspicions about Keres and his father, but looking around the room of otherwise-wizened, solemn faces, it wouldn't be hard for him to put two-and-two together. Keres' long dark hair tumbled from her hood and spilled onto her velvet robes, which hugged her narrow waist and full bosom in an impossibly-seductive way. She'd painted her plump lips the color of candied apples for the occasion, though her stunning silver eyes and long, black lashes didn't need a drop of make-up.

"And of course, we welcome back the Prophet's closest supporter," Keres breathed, releasing her grip on my hand to clasp Aiden's. As she eyed him up and down, my chest tightened. For the briefest moment, her eyes looked... hungry.

I took a step closer to Aiden, linking my arm around his. "It's Rowan," I said, doing my best to keep my voice light.

"Of course," she purred, dropping her eyes – and Aiden's hand. "As you've already reminded me. Forgive me, *Rowan*."

Jahi stepped forward to address Barish. "It's almost time, Magistrate. But before we can proceed..." As his black eyes fell on Aiden, I stiffened.

"Ah yes, of course," Barish replied. He cleared his throat. "Mr. Lawson, there is one small formality we must address before we can allow you to pass through this door."

"And what might that be?" Aiden asked warily.

Barish held up a pacifying hand. "It is nothing nefarious," he chuckled. "But it has come to my attention that you renounced your Asterian membership some years ago. We will need to renew that membership – in full – before we can allow you to enter. I'm afraid," he added, his eyes darting to mine, "that this is non-negotiable."

"But you never said anything about—" I protested.

The Magistrate raised a silencing hand. "My child, I was not aware of the specific circumstances regarding young Mr. Lawson's forfeited membership; therefore, I could not have possibly prepared you ahead of time. The renewal does not require any pomp or ceremony; it simply requires his renewed oath and signature."

"Aiden, you don't have to—" I began.

"It's okay," he said, squeezing my hand reassuringly. "I was expecting nothing less from them on this matter."

What? I drew a sharp breath. *He knew this was going to happen, but he came with me anyway?* I glanced over at him, but his eyes were glued to Barish. Outwardly, Aiden seemed calm enough, almost relaxed, but the feelings I felt emanating from him were anything but.

He was terrified.

"Excellent," Jahi smiled, producing a pen and long piece of paper from the pocket of his cloak. "Mr. Lawson, if you'll just sign and date here," he pointed to the thin black line at the bottom of the page. "I'm happy to go over the contract with you, though I believe you are already familiar with it. Prelate Mei has the Compendium for you to swear upon once we've finished."

"Wait," I blurted out, stepping between the two of them.

"Aspen—" Aiden started.

"What if I trade you – his membership for mine?"

Jahi opened his mouth to speak, but Barish interjected.

"Done!" he exclaimed. His booming voice echoed off the stone walls like a leather drum.

"Aspen, wait," Aiden hissed. But I'd already taken the pen and paper from Jahi's hand. Because what Aiden didn't realize in that moment was that my initiation was inevitable – whether they indirectly forced my hand that day or the following month or in five years, it would have to happen at some point. For their antiquated policies to change, for the Containment centers to be emptied – for the imprisonment of my mother, the deaths of my father and Jenny and countless others to mean anything – it was the only way. I pressed the pen to the paper, my hand shaking slightly… Then, without another thought or flourish, I signed my name.

Rowan Elizabeth Gulman

As I handed the paper back to Jahi, Aiden raised a knuckle to his lips, shaking his head. I could almost hear his thoughts in my head: *Oh, Aspen...*

"Excellent, my child!" Barish exclaimed. "We'll arrange for the Christening to occur at sunset tomorrow, immediately after the funeral proceedings conclude. However, let's not waste a moment before making it official with the oath ceremony..."

He motioned to Prelate Mei, a diminutive woman around Evelyn's age whose blue, purple, and green robes identified her as a Polymancer. She carried a large, gold embossed book against her chest and smiled warmly as she approached me. I could see the corners of her tri-colored tattoo peeking out from beneath her sleeve, the once-colorful ink now blurred and faded by time. As she held the weighty book aloft in one hand, her other hand reached for mine, gently setting it atop the gem-encrusted cover. Barish stood beside Mei, his lips pursed with a bourgeoning smile. The rest of the Prelates stood behind them, their eyes flashing with the multicolored Fire that burned brightly against the dark, circular walls of the chamber. For the first time that I could remember, most of the Prelates had smiles etched across their faces, even Jahi. And I couldn't help but notice that Keres' crimson, candied smile was the widest of them all. I rubbed the tattoo on my arm with my free hand, trying to ward away the goosebumps that had erupted across my flesh.

"This book contains all of our laws and commandments, as well as the name of every member of the Asterian Order, past and present," Mei said quietly, drawing herself close to me. The top of her gray bun barely came to my chin, and I had to strain to hear her soft voice above the sound of my own heart throbbing loudly against my eardrums. "To utter an oath upon its binding is to speak a promise to thousands who came before you, and thousands who will come after your body has become one with the Elements once more."

I swallowed tightly, suddenly feeling as though there wasn't quite enough air in the room.

Mei's almond eyes burned into mine. "Do you, Rowan Elizabeth Fulman, pledge yourself to the Asterian Order; its mission, its philosophy, and the Asterian Community, from this moment forward until the end of your days, for the good of all Elementalists everywhere?"

For the expanse of one heartbeat, the room fell completely silent, the wind from our combined breaths as still as death. The only movement in the chamber came from the five fluttering torches on the walls. From somewhere behind me, I could hear Aiden's sharp intake of breath.

Don't, Aspen.

"I do," I whispered hoarsely.

"Welcome to the Asterian Order, Prophet-*sama*," Mei answered, taking a step back to join the other Prelates.

"Welcome to the Asterian Order," they echoed, bowing their heads in unison.

Barish put his hand on my shoulder, squeezing it gently, and in that moment I felt as though everything was going to be okay, as though this were the missing piece that simply needed to fall into place.

"I couldn't be prouder, Rowan," he whispered softly, his amethyst eyes gleaming. I smiled, remembering the day my college admissions letter came in the mail. My father had clasped my shoulder in exactly the same way, his eyes twinkling with pride from beneath his silver-rimmed spectacles.

"The hour grows late, Magistrate," Jahi said, tucking the signed parchment back into his cloak. "The Challenge must begin before sunset."

"Too right you are, Prelate Jahi," Barish replied, his voice jovial. "Let us move to the arena."

He gave my shoulder one last squeeze, then turned on his heel toward the far door. The Prelates bowed their heads deferentially as he passed; then they, too, turned to follow him out the door. As Barish's robes disappeared through the doorway, I could feel my newfound sense of optimism wane slightly.

"You shouldn't have done that, Aspen," Aiden murmured as we fell into step a few yards behind the others. "We could have bought you more time, stalled the decision—"

"I couldn't bear to watch you sign your life away again," I whispered, idly fingering my mother's pendant around my neck.

"So, you would rather sign away yours?" he demanded.

"I signed my life away the moment I conjured that tornado," I replied darkly, my thoughts drifting to the semi-truck that nearly killed me. I wasn't sure whether the sinking feeling in my stomach was due to the grim memory, or something else.

Aiden fell silent, running an anxious hand through his curls. As much as he probably wanted to argue with me, he must have heard the truth in my words. My life was no longer mine, hadn't been mine for a long time. There was no arguing that.

Chapter 13

We followed Barish and the others through a long, stone corridor and down several more winding staircases much like the first, until we finally arrived at one of the steel-door entrances leading to the arena. The Magistrate pressed his hand against a touch-screen embedded in the damp bricks of the ancient wall – a striking contrast of modernity-meets-archaic – and the double doors swung open to what appeared to be a balcony, illuminated only by the dim light filtering in from the hallway. Eleven of us trickled inside, one by one. My eyes strained to make out the black expanse that stretched ahead of the balcony, but we were suddenly enveloped by total darkness as the doors slammed shut behind us. Aiden's hand found mine and I could feel him tense; for the briefest moment I was taken by a wave of panic, wondering if this was somehow all an elaborate trick staged by the Magistrate and his Prelates.

But then, all at once, a hundred torches suspended from the walls burst into flames, illuminating the immense chamber. Their ruby, gold, emerald, sapphire, and amethyst Fires cast wide, cascading orbs of light that didn't quite make it to the very tops of the five towering stone walls, which ascended well above our heads and up into the blackness. The eight Prelates took their seats on the second stone bench, the one closest to the door, but Barish beckoned Aiden and me to stand with him at the edge of the balcony. I drew a daunted breath as we approached the low stone balustrade that overlooked the floor of the arena, spreading out before us some three dozen feet below. Like the five other Asterian arenas I had been inside, this one was shaped like a giant pentagon. But very much *unlike* the others, this stone coliseum was ancient and utterly colossal, stretching two hundred feet between any two of its five opposing points. With rows of stone-carved stadium seating at the bottom and dramatic parapets and archways that housed additional balconies only slightly smaller than the one we stood in, it reminded me of the Roman Colosseum.

"Impressive, isn't it?" Barish asked from beside me. I could only nod. "It's been dramatized a bit for the occasion," he chuckled, gesturing toward the supernatural

torches, "but what good is a challenge without a little…
spectacle?"

"What exactly is this 'challenge' going to entail?"
Aiden asked. His hand had found mine on the edge of the
balustrade and was squeezing my fingers tightly. I wasn't
about to complain; his grip was the only thing that kept my
hand from visibly shaking.

The Magistrate raised a surprised eyebrow in
Aiden's direction. "I had assumed, given your history with
our organization and the extensive research you've done,
that you'd be familiar with such an extraordinary event.
After all, you've been granted an unprecedented privilege
in witnessing it today."

Aiden shook his head. "I'm sure you're aware of
how unusual it is for *any* of the Inner Circle's clandestine
activities to make it into the archives – or anywhere that's
accessible to the general public, for that matter. I couldn't
have learned more about this particular event if I'd
interrogated my own father."

I glanced nervously in Barish's direction. It was one
thing for me to push boundaries, since the damned
Pentamancer's sigil emblazoned on my arm had granted me
a kind of unspoken immunity within the Order. Aiden, on
the other hand, had secured no such imperviousness.

After a brief moment's pause, however, the Magistrate merely flashed his usual gregarious smile. "Then you're in for a real treat, my boy," he replied genially, clapping a hand on Aiden's shoulder.

I breathed a small sigh of relief, then jumped as something in my pocket buzzed. Barish's eyes trailed to the source: my cell phone.

"I'm so sorry," I muttered, fumbling to get it out of my pocket. "I forgot to give this to you in the antechamber."

Barish waved his hand lightly. "It is no problem, my dear. You are no plebian among this crowd!" He laughed at his own joke. "By all means, keep your device. I trust you won't record anything you see within these walls?" he asked – though, by the tone of his voice, it sounded more like a command.

"Of course not," I replied, slightly distracted by the message that had just come in.

Rose, I'm so sorry to even ask, but is there any way we can talk? I'm trying, I really am, but I just can't stop thinking about you.

Blushing furiously, I quickly switched the phone off and stuffed it into my pocket. When I looked up again, Aiden was watching me closely. Had he seen Wes' message? Or was it my startled reaction that had caught his attention? Thankfully, there wasn't time for either of us to ponder the question I saw forming on his lips, for the wide double doors on the far end of the arena floor had just burst open. With a gust of Wind, the torches in the room abruptly went out. I squinted my eyes, trying to make out the figures standing behind the elongated shadows in the illuminated doorway; just then, a sharp, resounding sound, like a blow to a drum, filled the air.

"It's time to take your seats," Barish said, motioning to the empty bench in front of the Prelates. "We're about to begin."

Several explosions sounded in the air, which was quickly becoming crisp and fragrant with the smell of ionization – like a rainstorm on a warm, summer afternoon. The hair on the back of my neck tingled. I exchanged a nervous glance with Aiden before sitting on the very edge of the cold stone bench beside Barish, praying I didn't accidently trip over his dark robes. Aiden dropped down next to me, his eyes glued to the arena floor.

Does Terry know we're here? I suddenly wondered. *If he sees his son in the audience, will he be relieved or upset?*

I didn't have the opportunity to consider that question for long. Down below us, rows of men and women in black robes began trailing into the arena, their arms outstretched above their heads. The sound of heavy, leather drums cracked through the air, pulsing with a quivering, rhythmic tribal beat. With no drums or percussionists in sight, I searched for the source of the deafening noise in bewilderment – until I saw the gold and purple tassels trailing from the hood of a young Elementalist at the back of the pack. His long, thick cords of black hair bounced in the air as he yelped and leapt with excitement, deftly weaving invisible bands of Electricity and Wind through the air like an instrument, summoning great peals of thunder that shook the entire balcony – as well as my insides.

The rest of the sub-Prelates carried glowing orbs of Elements that matched the colors of the tasseled ropes they donned from their black hoods, moving in a graceful, synchronized fashion as they glided into the coliseum alongside the rhythmic drumbeat of thunder. Wind and Fire, Water, Earth and Electricity were held aloft like torches. And most of the Extended Circle wielded more than one Element, which made the display all the more dazzling. I squinted, recognizing some of the illuminated faces. One woman with tasseled green and red cords hanging from her neck – she was one of Piotr's – swirled thick bands of lava just inches above her head; another man with purple and yellow tassels – one of Nadia's apprentices

– carried a miniature thunder cloud with flashing Lightning above his.

"Oh wow," I heard Aiden murmur as a young Pyromancer in a wheelchair rolled in, holding aloft a blaze of Fire that had been shaped into the lithe form of a running wolf. Flames danced and sizzled along the wolf's back and tail like raised hackles. My eyes widened; I'd learned from Sophia that Water could be shaped into elaborate shapes, but *Fire*, as unruly as it was?

I leaned forward to rest my hands and chin on the stone balustrade. In total, two dozen sub-Prelates had entered the room, arranging themselves before us in eight small groups of three. They danced and writhed as the "drums" thundered through the arena – even the old and feeble-looking ones. I gasped softly as I recognized Kaylie in her impossibly tight black robes, as well as the other two voluptuous Auromancers that made up Jahi's team of young women; and there beside them were Keres' three sub-Prelates: two exceptionally tall, dark-haired Hydro-Terramancer twins who were in their early thirties or so, and a tiny, middle-aged woman who barely came to their chins, yet she carried aloft a brilliant purple sphere of Electrified Water that made me gape in amazement.

"Is that woman handling *three* Elements?" Aiden whispered, pointing in Kaylie's direction.

"I don't think so…" I replied, squinting at the blue ribbons that danced and swirled above her elaborately-styled curls. "I'm only seeing Wind and Water."

"Look closer," Aiden said quietly. "She's got some wispy blue flames in there as well. She's a Polymancer."

I gaped in disbelief at the woman as she let out a wild cry, her expression one of pure elation. On the plane, Kaylie's shy, eye-averting politeness had bordered on ingratiating. I hadn't noticed her tattoo beneath her long sleeves and never thought to ask. But Aiden was right – she *was* a Polymancer. One of only a tiny handful among the world's five thousand known Elementalists. I glanced over my shoulder at Jahi, who was sitting directly behind me. He was smiling down at his apprentice widely, clearly pleased by what he saw. And yet, there was another feeling emanating from him, one that didn't match his expression… Anxiety? Fear? Beside him, Keres appeared to be radiating the same peculiar energy, but when she caught me staring, the feeling abruptly disappeared. I frowned slightly. What did the two of them have to be worried about? Their apprentices making them look bad?

I brushed the strange sensation aside, turning back around to watch the incredible display below. Having so many Elements manipulated in one place set my senses aflame, and I found myself fidgeting in my seat like a child, every nerve in my body prickling with excitement. The back of my neck grew warm from the Pyromantic Fire while at the same time the Hydromancers' Water spells sent goosebumps trickling down my spine.

The Electricity that surged down there was the most enticing, however; white-hot tines of Lightning splintered between the fingertips of the handful of Electromancers on the floor, flashing in colors I could name, like white and yellow, as well as that strange band of purple hues only I could see. I blinked my eyes, but the crackling lines of violet that danced along the edges of the electricity didn't fade. More than anything, I wanted to reach out and seize the Lightning myself. Every time the thunder cracked through the air like a whip, I felt a surge of raw energy ignite me from the inside-out, felt my toes dig into the ground as though I might leap off the balcony to join the frenzy below...

What's wrong with me? I started, glancing around the balcony self-consciously. Did the five Polymancers in the room feel as I did? After all, they were being inundated by their three different Elements from twenty different sources all at once. But I felt no such excitement from Jahi and Keres, or from Barish, who was only inches to my right. He stared straight ahead, a pleased, almost serene, expression painted on his face. As for me, I sat there

trembling in my seat, overstimulated, intoxicated –
aroused, even. I could only pray that the other Empathic
Electromancers in the box – Barish, Keres, and Izabel –
hadn't noticed.

Flushing slightly, I glanced at Aiden. Like Barish,
his eyes were still glued to the floor... but he was anything
but serene. Even through the thick, electrified air of the
arena, I could feel his anxiety steadily rising.

Get it together, I chided myself. *Aiden needs you!*
With some effort, I pried my eyes away from the
Electromancers and forced myself to survey the illuminated
faces of the Pyromancers instead, looking for Terry.

He's not here, I realized, quickly understanding the
reason for Aiden's growing unease. I'd searched every wild
face of the Fire-wielders below, but I couldn't find Terry's
angular, weathered face among any of them. As if reading
my mind – or, more likely, it was the other way around –
Aiden leaned over and whispered.

"I don't see my dad anywhere."

"Kaal's team must not be here yet," I replied,
practically sitting on my hands to keep myself from
squirming. Aiden didn't seem to notice. He was watching
the wide double doors at the center of the arena again, his
lips pressed together in a thin line.

Just then, Barish rose to his feet, gliding to the edge of the balcony. The lines of Elementalists below immediately grew still and the ionized drums of Wind stopped; even the unruly arcs of Lightning and Fire had settled into near-motionless spheres, resting placidly atop their bearer's outstretched palms. Behind the two dozen sets of eyes that gazed up at our balcony, the doors to the arena flew open once more to reveal two shadowy figures, their hooded faces half-concealed, half-illuminated by the dazzling spectacle ahead of them. As they stepped through the threshold, their dark robes churning around them like apparitions, they shook off their black hoods. Beside me, I could feel Aiden stiffen.

Chapter 14

*J*erry stepped into the arena, his eyes reflecting the fire he carried; like the other Pyromancers in the room, he held a massive ball of flames high above his head. But, unlike the others, his orb of Fire sizzled white-hot, almost icy blue. As I looked closer, I could clearly see the ribbons of Wind that surrounded the flames, fueling them with pure oxygen.

Of course, I remembered. *He's an Auromancer as well. That's why he was able to lead the team that tracked Mom down...*

Without warning, my thoughts shifted to the door swinging open in my old Organic Chemistry lecture hall, my parents' eyes wide with fright as they searched for my face among the roomful of students. *What's wrong?* I had wondered fretfully, shoving my notebook into my messenger bag as I jogged over to greet them. *Has someone died?*

Barish's booming voice jerked me back into the present.

"The vacancy within our coveted Circle has been contested!" He did not shout, yet his voice rumbled unnaturally loudly against the five walls of the arena, carried and amplified by the currents of Wind that he effortlessly controlled. "Therefore, a Challenge must be wrought! Step forth, Challengers!"

Aiden's father took a step forward, along with the towering man who stood directly to his left. He looked younger than Terry by about ten years, and though Mr. Lawson was by no means a small man, his challenger easily had half a foot and a solid fifty pounds on him – along with an obvious talent for Electromancy. His vermillion Fire crackled with splinters of ice-blue Lightning that surrounded the fiery orb. I could see Terry glance at him out of the corner of his eye, the muscles in his jaw tightening. It must have been exhausting to channel so much energy into two Elements like that, and I wondered whether it was custom or ego that compelled the two men to expend such resources before the Challenge had even begun.

"Sub-Prelates," Barish called. "It is time."

All at once, the men and women below flung their Elements into the air, setting loose a brilliant explosion of light and sound that rattled the stone walls of the coliseum. Water met with Fire, releasing towering pillars of white steam that roiled and hissed. Wind met with Lightning, resulting in peals of thunder that crashed against the enormous domed ceiling. Various Earth elements collided in the storm to create a shower of sparks and metals and diamonds that fell to the ground in glittering curtains. I gripped the edge of my seat, my eyes locked on the maelstrom of Elements above. When the air cleared and the arena had descended into darkness once more, the torches around the arena reignited – this time, their flames erupted in red, violet, and gold.

"Sub-Prelates Darius King and Terry Lawson, on my word, the Challenge will commence," the Magistrate boomed.

The rest of the sub-Prelates had formed a wide circle around the men. The two challengers removed their black robes to expose their shirtless bodies beneath, then tossed them atop a curtain of summoned Wind that carried the garments across the arena and out of sight. Aiden's father, I couldn't help but notice, had maintained a lithe and muscular body throughout his fifty-some years – a hardened man with a hardened body. The towering man beside him, however, had a chest the size of a whiskey barrel and muscles that bulged with the rippling ferocity of a grizzly bear. His naked torso glistened from the exertion of wielding both Fire and Lightning moments earlier; the sheen from his sweat highlighted every nook and cranny of his swollen muscles. Behind me, I felt a flush of excitement, but as I glanced over my shoulder, it disappeared as quickly as I'd noticed it.

"In the event that one of you forfeits, the other shall automatically be declared the winner. Should you both be standing with tied points by sunset, a vote shall be taken among the Prelates, as well as a very special proxy, our Order's newest initiate—" Barish turned around and beckoned me to stand beside him. I gave Aiden a shaky look that was meant to be a smile, then approached the edge of the balcony beside the Magistrate.

"—the Pentamancer!"

Several hushed gasps and murmurs erupted from the Extended Circle, who abruptly bowed their heads in reverence. I caught sight of Darius' bulging eyes a split second before the tremendous man fell to one knee, the gleaming skin of his bowed head catching the reflection of the torches. Aiden's father, however, merely tilted his head the tiniest fraction, glowering at me from beneath his furrowed brow.

I took a step away from the balcony, feeling my cheeks grow furiously hot – not just from the fawning reactions down below, but from the undeniable acrimony I felt emanating from this man; a man that I frankly held in equal contempt.

"Thank you very much my dear," the Magistrate whispered, resting a hand on my shoulder. He faced the men below once more, not bothering to use Wind to amplify his voice this time. "Though only one of you is fortunate enough to have your son present today, we have made arrangements with both of your families, in the event that you do not make it through the Challenge—"

What? My head whipped in Barish's direction, my ears taking in his words before my brain had the proper chance to register them.

"So, fight hard, and fight honorably, gentlemen, for your legacy may be the only thing that remains of you by tonight," he finished, glancing at me out of the corner of his eye.

With Barish's keen Empathic faculties, the jolt of shock that ran through me would have been palpable. Even without Electromancy, I imagine the horrified look on my face was more than enough to convey my feelings. I swayed slightly, feeling as though the balcony had suddenly pitched forward. A heavy feeling of dread had been forming in the pit of my stomach ever since we'd descended into that darkened staircase. But the Magistrate's words unleashed that dread from the iron cage of my stomach, sending forth writhing tendrils that tightened around my diaphragm, crept up and seized my lungs mid-breath. I struggled to fill them with air but they had been gripped too tightly.

This was no gentleman's duel that Aiden and I were about to witness. It was a fight to the death.

I felt the brush of Aiden's skin against mine. As he stared down at his father from the ledge of the balcony, his body was stiff, his expression unreadable. The expression on Terry's face, however, made it seem fairly obvious that he hadn't known either one of us would be there. Tension and hostility emanated from the narrow slits of his dark eyes, mingled with shock, eagerness, heaviness, dread... and desire. Desire to win? Desire to prove himself in front of his son? I rubbed my forehead gingerly.

"Why would he do this to himself?" Aiden whispered. "Risk his life for... for *what*? For glory? For pride?" My hand reached out to clutch his. He squeezed my fingers reassuringly, as though it were *my* father, and not his, who might die in front of our very eyes that afternoon. But I couldn't bring myself to look at him. I knew first-hand what it was like to lose a father, and because of me,

Aiden might have to witness his own father's death – and even worse, as a helpless spectator. In that moment, I hated myself for bringing him there, hated myself for my selfishness, for my unforgivable ignorance.

As I squeezed my eyes shut, I could hear my own father's voice whispering in my ear, the last words I ever heard him speak before he died: *Everything's going to be okay, Rosebud. I promise.* I sucked air through my teeth as his words were accompanied by a searing flash and a sharp stab of pain in my head.

"The Challenge will begin on my mark," the Magistrate continued. "During the fight, there is to be *no* channeling of *any* kind, by any*one*, other than the two challengers. Should this rule be broken, the penalty would be extremely severe – and I shall remain unsympathetic to anyone who attempts to provide an excuse for such a transgression. As for our challengers, there are no rules but three: "Fight for the honor of the Asterians, stay well inside the white lines at all costs…"

My father's face floated in front of mine, his grey eyes blazing as purple as an early morning thunderstorm.

"…And do your very best to survive."

Chapter 15

The heels of my hands dug into my forehead, doing their best to clear the tempest raging inside my head. By the time I eventually managed to unclench my eyes, Darius and Terry were striding away from one another, each walking to opposite points of the white pentagon that I had only just noticed in the middle of the arena. It had been painted – or perhaps, chalked – directly onto the floor, each of its five sides about twenty-five feet long. The two men stood just within their respective inside angles, eyeing one another from across the pentagon. *Stay inside the white lines at all cost*, Barish had instructed them. What would happen if they didn't? Would they be killed?

I heard a rustle behind me as Jahi rose to stand beside the Magistrate. He held his long, slender hand out past the ledge of the balcony, the sleeve of his robe pulling back to reveal his striking purple, blue, and red Polymancer tattoo; not many other Elementalists in the world had full stars embedded in their arms.

As I stared at his tattoo dumbly, the back of my neck grew warm, as though wax had been poured down my scalp. The torches flickered ominously throughout the coliseum.

"You can't let this happen," I whispered to Barish, finally finding my voice once more. "You can't let them kill each other!"

Turning to look at me, his eyebrows had gathered into a frown, but when he saw the tears threatening to spill over my cheeks, his expression softened. "Oh, no, my child – you've misunderstood!" he whispered, gripping both of my shoulders. "A death hasn't occurred in a challenge such as this in more than a century. It's a ceremony that relies upon tactic and discipline, not brutality. In fact, resorting to overt aggression is frowned upon."

Immediately, the tendrils that had wrapped themselves around my insides loosened. "You mean, all that talk about legacies and surviving the night…?"

Barish suppressed a smile. "All for pomp and spectacle, I assure you, child."

Aiden draped an arm around my shoulder as though to comfort me, but I could immediately sense his own relief as well. "Thank god," he muttered darkly.

From Barish's other side, I heard Jahi clear his throat.

"You may proceed," Barish told him.

In an instant, the red, gold, and purple flames of every torch in the room flew to Jahi's hand, coalescing together to make one crimson colored flame so deeply saturated, the color reminded me of blood. He held the scarlet torch above his head, momentarily bathing our entire balcony in red light, then hurled the flame to the center of the pentagon. There it remained suspended a few feet from the ground, halfway between the two men. At the same time, two fiery numbers appeared in the air twenty feet above the floor, but close enough to us that I could feel the immense heat rolling off of it in waves. The dancing flames read: *10 – 10.*

"Let the Challenge begin!" Barish bellowed.

The flame hovering between the challengers abruptly tore in two, each ragged half flying to opposite sides of the pentagon as the men hungrily seized the fire in their palms. I tensed, thinking they might lunge at one another immediately, but the two challengers just stood there for a moment, eyeing one another over the tops of their flames. Barish and Jahi returned to their seats and I hurriedly followed, slumping down beside Aiden.

"What's the feeling down there?" Aiden asked, leaning close to me. "Can you tell?"

"Darius seems very relaxed," I replied, watching the larger man carefully. "Save for a bit of performance anxiety, he's almost..." I rubbed my forehead, trying to eradicate the last dull vestiges of my earlier headache, while at the same time struggling to put a word to another human's feelings, on which I was discourteously eavesdropping from afar.

"...playful," I finally finished. "Your father, however, is a knot of emotions. I can't even begin to pick them apart."

Aiden sniffed. "Yeah, sounds about right."

"I wonder what they're waiting for?" I mused, half to myself.

Barish leaned towards me. "The opponents will not rush to attack, as they are unfamiliar with one another's abilities. As custom dictates, Kaal would not have mentored his apprentices in the company of one other."

"So, this is their first time sparring?" I asked.

He nodded. "As I told you, the Challenge is not meant to be a display of brute force or haste, but rather a calculating strategy of Elemental acumen and endurance. It's a showcase; something that's meant to be both elegant and methodical – because more than a battle, or even a competition, this Challenge is an audition."

"Is that why you needed Aspen here?" Aiden asked. "Because you needed help making a casting decision?"

I swallowed, glancing down at the two men below. They had begun circling one another, slowly stoking the flames they cradled as they paced inside the pentagon.

Barish chuckled. "Not quite. The Challenge is based on a point system. It rarely ever requires a vote – though it has been necessary in the past."

"How are the points tallied?" I asked. I fanned my face, wishing I could use Auromancy to cool the stifling air of the balcony. Between the fiery scoreboard hovering in the center of the stadium and the red-hot flames below, the arena was rapidly heating up.

"Each challenger begins with ten points," Barish explained, gesturing to the numbers floating in the air. "Watch the sub-Prelates surrounding the pentagon – each has a section they will personally be overseeing. Now, should any part of a challenger's body touch the white line of the pentagon, he will be deducted a point. If, at any moment, one of the challengers crosses the white line while another part of their body remains inside the pentagon, he'll be deducted three points. However, if his entire body ever fully passes the white line, he will lose the Challenge on the spot."

"Is that the only way they can lose?" Aiden asked.

Barish shifted ever so slightly. "If one formally yields to the other, he loses. If a challenger becomes too weak or injured to continue, he loses. While it has been over a century since a death has occurred in this arena, in the unlikely event that someone dies..."

"He loses," Aiden supplied dryly. "Got it."

A surge of Fire made my head whip towards the arena. Darius had begun tossing grapefruit-sized Fireballs in Terry's direction, one after another. Terry flicked his wrist at the oncoming projectiles, casting each one to the side before it could reach him. The men continued to circle each other near the center of the pentagon, an easy air about them.

Almost like they're sizing one another up, I remarked to myself.

"That's exactly what they're doing," Barish replied, startling me.

I frowned. I knew, of course, that he was a gifted Electromancer, but it never occurred to me that he might be able to read minds. According to Robert, an Empathic Electromancer who could sense and decode another person's emotions was one thing, but reading minds was an altogether different ability. And an exceedingly rare one, at that. *He's just drawing from your emotional cues and the context,* I told myself. *It's basic Electrical impulses, nothing more.*

"The tattoos on their arms, even Level-three distinctions, mean nothing in this Challenge," Barish continued, watching the men intently. "They must unearth the other's weaknesses, anticipate his errors... Much like playing chess. Do you play chess, my dear?"

"Not for some time," I replied tersely. A thick rope of Fire appeared in Terry's outstretched fist, lunging in Darius' direction like a striking cobra. Darius reached up to snatch it away, but its fiery tail whipped around and caught him in the ribs, leaving a bloody scorch mark in its wake. I winced, sensing the sting of it, but the enormous man didn't seem to notice. He tore the snake from the air and circled it over his head like a lasso. Terry set his teeth, grimacing at the spinning propeller as it drew nearer and nearer to him.

"Why not just extinguish it?" I asked Aiden as Terry's heel approached the perimeter of the pentagon.

"If Darius was a Level-one, or perhaps even a Level-two, Pyromancer, it wouldn't be much of a problem for my Dad to do that," Aiden replied. "But simply 'extinguishing' an opponent's Element, particularly if they are in the same class as you, is extremely difficult."

"It is?" I asked.

Aiden chuckled dryly. "For those of us who aren't Pentamancers, it is."

Kaylie, who had been standing directly behind Terry, flung her hand in the air, pointing her index finger to the sky. The back of Terry's heel had touched the line. The fiery numerals that floated above the arena floor changed from *10 – 10* to *10 – 9*. Terry lunged between the floor and Darius' spinning propeller of Fire, skidding to a stop at the center of the Pentagon. He swung out his arm and produced a basketball-sized torch of blue flames, which he held out at his side stiffly.

"Okay, well why not use one of their secondary Elements, like Wind?" I pressed. Terry certainly could have extinguished Darius' flames that way.

"It is bad form to rely on unshared secondary Elements so early in the Challenge," Barish replied. "That, perhaps, will come later – depending on the style and skill of these challengers. Besides," he added, a hint of smugness in his tone, "sub-Prelate Lawson is a Level-three Pyromancer, like his son, but he's not as gifted an

Auromancer as you or I. I wonder if he would be able to achieve such a risky move in the heat of battle?"

As if on cue, a surge of heat rose up from the center of the arena as Terry's ball of flames erupted into a massive hose of Fire. He held it palms-out in front of him, spraying a white-hot deluge of flames in Darius' direction. Strangely, Darius appeared to have been caught off-guard by the onslaught. As he flung himself away from the blaze, his arms flailing over his head in an attempt to maintain his balance, his right foot stepped cleanly over the line of chalk. The woman standing behind him shot three fingers into the air. *7 – 9*, the fiery numbers flashed. Darius flung the beads of sweat from his forehead onto the floor, along with an angry curse. The relaxed feelings I had sensed from him before appeared to have evaporated along with the sweat.

I glanced at the eight Prelates seated in our balcony, who were whispering to one another in hushed tones. Felipe and his wife, Izabel, looked smug, Piotr and Mei were grim-faced, Valeriya was cackling in delight, and Nadia – the oldest member of the Inner Circle – appeared completely indifferent, as though the outcome was of no concern to her. Keres, I noted, sat as still as stone, watching the floor of the arena with her hands tightly clasped in her lap. *Are she and Terry really having an affair?* I wondered uncomfortably. Did she root for his triumphs, fear for his safety – the way I would if it were Aiden who was fighting someone on that floor? Curiously, I tried to peek into her emotions. I knew it was eavesdropping – worse even. My mother always used to tell me that having the ability to empathize with others was a wonderful thing, but there were limits we had to respect.

Not that Mom's been a model citizen in that regard, I thought, feeling a twinge of guilt as I did. I knew she felt immense shame for her previous role in the Asterians' memory alteration and manipulation division. Still, in that moment, I just had to satisfy my curiosity. So, I prodded the air around Keres, feeling for the telltale Electrical currents that we all emit, scrunching my eyebrows in frustration. I felt… nothing.

I frowned. I'd noticed this before, how Keres' inviting façade had almost seemed like a mirage – beautiful and shimmering on the outside, but all at once vacant if you got too close. Effusive as the woman was, as warm and forthright as she often portrayed herself to be, I sometimes felt as though I knew nothing about her. It bothered me and frustrated me at the same time, as I had become accustomed to reading people almost effortlessly as of late.

Keres' pale eyes trailed to mine and she smiled, a warm, friendly smile that was meant to say, *Entertaining, is this not?* But the expression on her face felt foreign and strange and disconnected from the rest of her, which, at that moment, exuded about as much emotion as a cold chunk of marble. I composed my features into something I hoped would resemble a smile in return, trying to disregard the odd shiver I felt.

"Oh, shit!" Aiden gasped. I spun around in alarm; I'd never heard him curse before.

Darius had just flung a massive wall of Fire in Terry's direction, much like the inferno Aiden had sent my way while training with Sophia – the same one that sent me hurtling toward the ground and left me covered in burns.

"Oh!" I cried out as the flames engulfed Terry, pushing him to the very edge of the pentagon. The Elementalist closest to him, one of Keres' twin Terramancers, flung a finger in the air.

7 – 8.

A moment later, one of the other nearby sub-Prelates threw three fingers in the air.

7 – 5.

"Dad," Aiden whispered into his knuckle. I gripped his arm tightly, my blood running cold even as the air of the arena continued to heat up.

"Have faith," I heard Barish murmur. "It's not over yet."

A split second later, the coruscating wall of Fire parted like a curtain, revealing a charred, slightly bloodied Terry. The skin of his torso and arms were covered in angry red welts; the fabric of his pants was smoking. His chest heaved from obvious exhaustion – the exhaustion of having to control another Elementalist's Fire, of having to expend so much energy wielding his own. But more than being exhausted, he was *mad*.

Gritting his teeth, Terry lifted his singed arms over his head; then, with an angry snarl, he flung them downwards, as though he were snatching something out of the air and hurling it behind him. All at once, the Fire disappeared from Darius' hands, leaving him both defenseless and weaponless in the middle of the pentagon.

"This might be it," Aiden whispered as Terry ambled in Darius' direction, the Fireball in his hands the only remaining source of Fire in the arena.

"I don't understand," I whispered back.

"Pyromancers have the greatest difficulty when it comes to summoning their Element from 'nothing'," Aiden replied. "A breeze for Wind exists all around us, even in confinement – in breaths, in air vents. And Water can be found in trace amounts as moisture in the air – hell, it literally runs in our blood—"

"Along with Electricity," Barish supplied, his eyes glued to the white pentagon.

"...Right," Aiden continued, his eyebrows furrowing in Barish's direction. "The point is, now that Darius' Fire has been extinguished, the only other source of Fire in the room is in Dad's hands. And, from my own personal experience, I can guarantee he's not going to be parted from it without a fight."

As Aiden's father closed the distance between himself and his challenger, however, Darius abruptly lifted his foot behind him – as though he were about to kick an invisible soccer ball – then sent the sole of his boot skidding against the hard, stone floor, flinging a shower of white sparks into the air. With a skyward flourish of his hands, the sparks exploded into a surging cascade of Fire that ignited the entire pentagon.

"Flint!" I heard someone behind me chortle. "On the sole of his boot – how novel!"

The torrent of flames, rushing forward like a breaking wave on a riptide, caught Terry off-guard. He flung himself out of the way of Darius' surprise attack, letting the toe of his shoe land on the white line in the process. The red flames nearly caught the robes of one of Prelate Mei's Hydro-Terramancers, who let out a loud yelp as he threw his hand up into the air, his index finger pointed at the ceiling.

7 – 4.

"Bravo!" Barish clapped. "Good show!"

The hair on my arms rose suddenly.

"He's conjuring Wind," I whispered to Aiden as the flames around Terry began convulsing into white-hot tongues of Fire.

"Indeed, he is," Barish murmured from my other side. "His dwindling score must be making him anxious."

My hair began thrashing around my face as the air in the arena whipped into a frenzy, surrounding the column of Fire beside Terry, ushering it into a blazing funnel. It grew skywards, trembling and bulging as it transformed into a spinning tornado of hellish flames; the light from the inferno burned so brightly, I had to shield my eyes. Across the pentagon, Darius closed his eyes for a moment, as though he were concentrating. The back of my neck began to tingle.

"Lightning," I whispered. "But from where? Where's the source?"

"Like Prelates Keres and Izabel, Darius is a Corporeal Electromancer," the Magistrate remarked, "which gives him some ability to draw Electricity from the cells in his own body – as well as from others. It's a very risky move. I gather that, like us, Darius has ascertained that the mood of the Challenge has dramatically shifted."

I gasped softly, exchanging glances with Aiden. He looked pale; his dark curls clung to a thin sheen of sweat on his forehead. I suddenly realized I was sweating, too – the air in the arena felt like the inside of an oven.

"Hey," I whispered, gently laying my hand on his. "Your father's going to be okay."

"It's not him I'm worried about," Aiden replied, his free hand clenching his thigh.

Without warning, an image of Terry, incensed and unhinged, sprang into my mind. He was raising his hand above his head, yelling curses at me, as though he might strike me to the ground. I wanted to cower in the corner, to run, but I was too proud, too worried about what might happen to Sarah if I fled the house.

Sarah? I blinked my eyes feverishly, trying to banish the strange vision from my mind. *What the hell was that?*

Hearing Aiden's gasp, my gaze fell back to the arena. From behind his towering inferno, Aiden's father was staring at his challenger darkly. As if fueled by his own aggression, the blazing funnel began spinning frenetically, like a top on an uneven surface, its white flames shooting out from all sides in angry, violent lashes. He took a menacing step in Darius' direction, just as a flash of Electricity appeared in the other man's palm. But something was wrong; the moment it crackled alive, Darius doubled over, clenching his chest.

From behind me, Keres made a sound that sounded like a *tsk*.

"He drew out too much Electricity," Barish murmured grimly. "A fraction of a spark would have done. Careless."

Darius let out a frightened wheeze; his hunched shoulders heaved in distress.

He's having a heart attack! I realized in horror. "We have to help him!" I cried, leaping to my feet.

"No." Barish's voice was impassive but firm. "We may not intervene in the Challenge. It is forbidden in all cases. Sub-Prelate Darius will recover from his momentary blunder; I am sure of it."

The Electricity in Darius' hand began flickering, as though he were willing part of it back into his body. As I squinted, I could almost see the tiny electric current traveling up through his arm and back towards his heart. I felt a jolt of relief as his head finally shot up, his eyes directed at the hellfire that was coming his way. But he was still hunched over, seemingly unable to move from his self-inflicted heart attack. My eyes flew to the tornado, which was heading straight for him; couldn't Terry see the man was incapacitated?

"Come on, get up – *please*," I found myself whispering to the man. I wanted to help him, give him just the tiniest nudge to get enough Electricity back into his heart and cells. But I was surrounded by other Electromancers – Electromancers like Barish, who would have sensed even the slightest intervention from the balcony we shared.

Aiden strode over to the ledge of the balcony, gripping the stone balustrade so tightly, the knuckles on both of his hands turned white. "Don't do this, Dad," he whispered. "You don't have to do this."

As if he had heard his son's plea, Aiden's father glanced up at the balcony, locking eyes with the younger version of himself. The tornado wavered, momentarily slowing to a near stop; in that moment, I honestly thought he might have decided to grant the other man the chance to catch his breath after all.

But I was wrong.

Barely a second had passed before the searing tempest once again picked up speed, tearing across the pentagon in a scorching streak that left angry, black burns across the stone floor. An exhausted grunt escaped through Darius' gritted teeth as he heaved himself outside of the pentagon, landing on his left side with a heavy thud. He pressed his glistening forehead down to the ground in defeat just as one of Jahi's sub-Prelates, Rana, shot her fists in the air, her forearms crossing above her head to make an X.

0 – 4, the floating numerals flashed blue. Terry had won.

Despite his clear victory, the fiery cyclone didn't stop; it continued to charge at Darius even after his body was no longer within the white lines. Several shouts erupted from the surrounding Elementalists, who flung themselves away from the attack.

"Stop!" Aiden shouted. "Dad, STOP!"

But it was too late. I lurched over to the balcony just in time to see the vicious firestorm slam into the fallen man; he hadn't even lifted his head in time to see it coming. Within the span of one terrifying breath, crimson Fire engulfed Darius' body, burning away his clothes, his hair, his skin. I felt the pain that emanated from his body as clearly as I saw the flames that caused it. Without thinking, I leapt atop the edge of the balcony, using barricades of Wind to keep me from plunging off the side. A scream erupted somewhere close by, though I hardly registered the sound. Teetering on the narrow ledge of the stone, dozens of feet above the solid ground below, my arms flew out in front of me as I cast away the air that fed Terry's Fire, suffocating it into submission; in the handful of nanoseconds that seemed to unfurl as slow, agonizing minutes, the blaze abruptly blinked out, plunging the coliseum into pitch darkness.

Chapter 16

"Why didn't you stop him?" I asked quietly, watching Barish over the tendrils of steam that escaped from the hot cup of apple tea he had just poured me. He sat across the desk in his spacious, dimly-lit office, where the centuries-old stones had been shrouded by hand-spun rugs, and the backlit curio cabinets had been filled with museum-worthy tomes and relics from antiquity and beyond. Behind his desk hung a gilded frame that housed an elaborate oil painting of his own solemn face; on either side of that, equally-ornate picture frames of past Magistrates stared down at us, some photographs, some painted figures dating back to a time before photographs existed. Barish stirred a cube of sugar into his own tea – a strong leafy blend of black tea that smelled bitter even from across the large desk – and sighed. A deep, weary sigh.

For the first time that I could remember, the Magistrate looked tired.

"A moment, my child... if you wouldn't mind?" he added, holding his hand above the tea to cool it slightly. Just visible from beneath the folded velvet of his sleeve, I saw his old, faded Polymancer tattoo: a near-complete star of blue, purple and yellow, with a coveted "III" stamped underneath, just like mine. Excluding me, Barish was the only Polymancer alive to have achieved a Level-Three ranking in all three of his Elements. But beneath his personal Elemental tattoo was a newer-looking star, one that was a reverse image of mine: blackened triangles with the five Elemental colors painted on the inside of the pentagon:

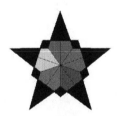

That must be the special insignia reserved for Magistrates, I thought, gazing at the unique design. I let my eyes burn into the image much longer than I needed to, letting them fixate on the peculiar kaleidoscope of colors there. Anything to keep my mind off of the horrible scene I had just witnessed.

If only I could drown out the sound of Darius' screams.

"Do you have a family, Barish?" I asked, sipping my tea with a shaking fist. The hot, sweet liquid burned my tongue.

"A daughter," he replied, taking a sip of his own cooled tea, "a handful of years older than you. She is not gifted, so I have been unable to keep in touch with her. Not many people outside this room are aware of such a fact." He regarded me then, his features softening. "I imagine it troubles you to hear, since your own father was taken from you at a young age."

I stared into my cup, where the reflection of Darius' burning body stared back at me.

"You must think me to be a very callous man," Barish continued softly, "to allow my own daughter to remain fatherless, when her father is in fact alive and well... Indeed, I *am* a callous man, Rowan. Just today, I allowed an innocent man to die in my own arena, when you and I both know I could have stopped it."

"Why didn't you?" I asked, anger slowly taking the place of shock. "Was it more pomp and spectacle? Did the murder somehow make the Challenge more interesting?"

"Do not mistake me for an unfeeling man, Rowan," Barish replied, his placid tone unchanging. "Senseless death and suffering go against my beliefs, the very core of my being. Were it up to me, Darius King would never have been allowed to die, and Terry Lawson would pay for his defamation of an otherwise honorable challenge." He grimaced as he took another sip of tea.

"'If it were up to you'?" I repeated incredulously. "You're the most powerful man on the planet. You could have stopped him at any time! Who would have questioned you?"

"No source of power is absolute; even the most powerful man on Earth is not impervious against an uprising... a mutiny," he replied softly.

"Then what the hell am I doing here?" I asked, setting my cup down forcefully. "If you don't have the power to change things, to *fix* anything, why did I just sign my life away to you?"

A brief moment of silence stretched between us, until, eventually, the meaning of Barish's words found its way into my brain. I leaned back into my chair, my shoulders slumping. *Did he just say 'mutiny'?*

Yes, there are those who secretly wish to depose me, Barish's eyes flashed ultraviolet as his voice rumbled in my ears. I gasped, my hand flying to my forehead. *And they may have one day succeeded. But now, with you by my side, no one will dare. If they do, they will only strengthen my design.*

"You *can* read minds," I whispered hoarsely.

"I can read minds, I can soothe minds, I can shape minds," Barish replied. "And so can you, with my guidance. I've sensed remarkable ability in you, Rowan; it shines through the very light of your irises."

"You're wrong," I countered. "I don't have my mother's ability. I can only sense… feelings. Intentions. Sometimes deceit. Nothing concrete… And I certainly can't talk inside of other people's heads like you can." I rubbed my ears uncomfortably.

Oh, you can read minds, my dear – and so much more, the Magistrate smiled at me, his purple eyes glinting. *With my direction, you'll not only be able to sense feelings, but you'll have the ability to hear others' thoughts, influence emotions, affect even the most deeply-held misbeliefs and misconceptions – not just individually, but among crowds of people. I assure you – the gift you possess is unmistakable.*

"What are you saying?" I asked, rubbing my temples. I could hear Barish's words clearly but their meaning made no sense to me.

He set down his tea and leaned forward in his seat. "Don't you see? *This* is the reason, Rowan. *This* is why I have been unable to succeed in the areas you rightfully judge me for. No matter how moral I know my own convictions to be, no matter the justness of the laws I wish to pass, I cannot implement such radical changes so long as the Order remains divided, both in principle and in structure. But together, with you as the guiding light – and with our combined abilities – we can unite thousands of Elementalists who have been hearing bedtime stories about the next Prophet for generations. If we work together, you and I, we can change the barbaric laws of antiquity: modify the rules of the Challenges, empty the Containment Centers, reunite lost family members—"

"I don't understand. You want me to… to what?" I asked, my voice shaking. "Manipulate people? Trick them into supporting these policies?"

Barish made a dismissive gesture. "Perhaps, if it came to it – but it won't, my child. Because you are the Prophet, the one who can unite our Community by the simple fact that you are what you are – a Pentamancer." He leaned his hands on his desk, rising from his seat. "And if they misunderstand, if anyone spreads falsehoods about what we are trying to accomplish, we can coax them, persuade them with the gentlest form of Electromancy so that they'll see things from our perspective, the *right* perspective."

"You're asking me to do what my mother did," I said, rising from my seat. "You're asking me to… to…" I cupped my forehead again, suddenly losing my train of thought.

"Your mother and her colleagues erased memories, altered perceptions… I am only suggesting that we could show your willing followers the correct path, guide them to support the policies you already know to be the right ones…" Barish's voice shifted. "Rowan, I would never ask you to do something you were not comfortable with doing. I know you hear the truth in my words. I just want you to know that, no matter what, you and I will ensure that Darius' death tonight will not have been in vain. Nor will your father's."

I gripped the back of the seat tightly; the dull thump in my head had grown to a throbbing pain. For months I had avoided asking Barish the question that burned in the back of my throat like vinegar; I'd been harboring some tiny hope that my father was still alive, that there was a deeper reason for why his file had said "presumed deceased" instead of just "dead". But Barish's words, which had no trace of a lie embedded in them, had utterly extinguished that hope.

My father really was dead.

I slumped back down into my seat, my aching forehead suddenly feeling too heavy to hold upright. Barish walked around the front of his desk and placed a gentle hand atop my head. I was about to shake him off but abruptly stopped; the debilitating Electromantic migraine that had been relentlessly plaguing me for the past two months all at once dissipated, as though the storm that had been raging inside my brain had been blown off by some divine gust.

Eyes wide, I gingerly pressed my fingers against my forehead. "H-How did you do that?"

Barish took a step back, surveying me with grim satisfaction. "I'll teach you everything I know, my child, for I believe our meeting was *kismet*. The universe knew we would need one another, and so it was that the universe brought us together."

Kismet, destiny, purpose... I thought ruefully. *What ever happened to free will?*

Barish let out a mirthless chuckle. "My dear Rowan – there's no such thing as free will when Providence itself has other plans... Now, come. There are some things I want to teach you."

***

Later that night, well after the last call to prayer had drifted through the city's darkened windows and silhouetted mosque spires, I walked along one of the many bridges that connected the various ports of Istanbul across the salty waters of the Bosphorus Strait. Despite the late hour, a dozen or so men interspersed along its two concrete railings dangled long poles into the water, trying to catch the hapless fish that would be sold as sandwiches the next day. Several of them murmured entreaties to me under their breath as I walked by, in French or Spanish or English as they tried to guess my nationality, but most avoided my eyes, focusing instead on the small, writhing fish they retrieved from the water, which glinted silver against the light of the bourgeoning moon.

Apart from the nocturnal fishermen, I was all alone. Minutes after Terry was declared the Challenge winner – and the Inner Circle's newest initiate – Aiden had excused himself back to our hotel, likely needing a moment of solitude to process what had just happened. I think we both assumed that the instant my meeting with Barish was finished, I'd return to the hotel, where Aiden would be waiting for me, to talk, to grieve, to hold me and be held. I could only imagine, after what had happened earlier that evening, that he needed me as much as I myself needed his reassurances. But as I made my way back to the hotel after a grueling, two-hour Electromantic training session with the Magistrate, I was plagued by the burning question: *Was it an inadvertent act of passion, or had Terry been planning to kill Darius all along?* The more I turned it over in my head, the farther I walked, until the hotel room I shared with Aiden was miles behind me.

Hours later, as I plodded across that darkened bridge, frightened and forlorn, a part of me longed to feel his warm, comforting embrace, but another part of me – a louder part of me – needed to be alone. *Or maybe...* a small voice whispered, *maybe you just want to get away from Terry Lawson's son.*

I stopped in the middle of the bridge and stared down into the murky water below, where dozens of pale jellyfish glowed in the moonlight like tiny, tendrilled phantoms. Colorful lights from the restaurants nestled beneath the bridge reflected off the oily surface of the water, creating a shimmering effect; the gelatinous forms floated between illuminated pockets of pink and green and blue, unseeing, unappreciative of the dazzling spotlights above.

It's not Aiden's fault his father is the man he is, I admonished myself, a knot of guilt settling in my stomach. But the fact of the matter was, I *didn't* want to see Aiden in that moment, didn't want to talk about the revolting monster who just happened to be his father, the monster who would soon be a close colleague of mine, free to make and vote upon his own policy recommendations...

Was it an inadvertent act of passion, or had Terry been planning to kill Darius all along?

As I stared into the water, idly drawing the thin layer of oil away from the lovely jellyfish below, it suddenly occurred to me that it didn't make any difference in my mind. I didn't want to ponder what happened any further, didn't want to discuss Terry's possible motives or reasons. I didn't want to talk about the Challenge, about my upcoming Christening, didn't want to talk about the Magistrate or any of the things he had just disclosed to me. I was done with talking about the Asterians for the evening – because in that moment, I was ashamed of being one.

I switched on my phone for the first time in hours and sucked in a breath as a half-dozen messages from everyone back home appeared on the screen. Evelyn was asking – yet again – how everything was going and was reminding me to bring home some Turkish delight for Robert. Ori had sent me a photo of the new Ducati sport bike with a caption that read, "Ask Barish for THIS!", and Eileen forwarded some joke I didn't understand ("Why wasn't the geologist hungry? Because she'd lost her 'apatite'!"). I grimaced at the bad pun after googling its meaning, but my grimace deepened further as I scanned the messages that came after it: Aiden asking where I was and whether I was okay; my mom and Ted both inquiring about the details of the Challenge and how I was holding up. And there was Wes' message from earlier that evening, pleading with me to talk. Just as I was about to delete it, however, a new email from Eileen popped up.

>*Hey there, Penta-Spice.*
>
>*I know you're probably busy drafting international peace treaties and/or practicing making babies with Aiden, but Sophia just informed me that there's a mineral and fossil show happening in Istanbul this week, and I'm more or less taking that to be a sign from God that I should be out there, with you, during this very tumultuous time. And also – shiny rocks. Ori has no work at the moment since you're pretty much his sole Electromancy student, and now that I'm in charge of training at the Denver Chapter, I'm free to give myself the week off. Yes, it's a blatant abuse of power. No, I don't feel bad about it. Besides, I just looked and there's currently a big price drop on tickets to Turkey since, apparently, for whatever reason, people don't seem to want to travel to the Middle East in the dead of summer. Go figure.*
>
>*Give me the green light and we'll come out there to keep you company. With all the big stuff happening, I'm*

kicking myself for not just hiding out in your luggage. (We
both know I could have, and with room to spare.) Also, I'm
not supposed to mention this, but Evelyn is bribing the
three of us with cranberry-orange scones if we go out there
and check on you. Extra points in the form of walnut
vanilla fudge if we bring back Turkish delight for Robert.
My hips say "No!" but my brain and mouth say "You had
me at 'scones'!"

 Love,

 Your favorite Terramancer

I laughed out loud as I read through Eileen's
message, then hurriedly replied:

Yes, PLEASE, come out here. Sometime in the next
24 hours if you can. I'll arrange for you guys to take the
private jet. Pack something nice to wear, if possible. Long
story short, I've taken the official Asterian oath and they'll
be christening me tomorrow. I'll tell you everything once
you get here. Just don't tell my family, okay? I've been
causing my mother and Evelyn enough stress as it is, so I'm
going to stall as long as possible before telling them—

That line of thinking gave me pause... If the Inner
Circle had sent out some sort of memo or announcement
about my Christening tomorrow night, could my mom or
Ted have seen it? *Probably not,* I reasoned to myself. In

our agreement to keep my mother out of Containment, Barish officially excommunicated her from the Order and all its associated broadcasts. And Ted, who was only working on a part-time basis at the Denver Chapter now, rarely showed up to work unless he was expressly asked to. Since neither one of them had called me in a panic, it meant they didn't know about my induction yet. I would just have to keep my fingers crossed that it would stay that way until I could eventually tell them myself, when the time was right.

Feeling mostly confident about my assessment, I finished my email to Eileen and quickly hit 'send', not caring about whether or not the Magistrate had given me advance permission to invite the three of them to my own welcome ceremony. I'd just signed my freedom over to the Asterians; the least Barish could do was let me invite my friends to the party. Bolstering my hypothetical argument was the fact that, even then, I could feel eyes watching me, and I knew I wasn't alone. There was no doubt in my mind that Barish had sent his guards along to keep an eye on me – "for my own protection." *And after tomorrow*, I grimaced, *there won't be an Elementalist in the world who won't recognize me on sight.* Barish would make sure of that.

I sighed. The moon was high above the horizon now, reminding me of the late hour – as well as Aiden, who, based on his incoming messages, was beginning to worry. I glanced down at Wes' message one last time, feeling a pang of sadness, then swiped left to delete it. A moment later, I vaguely registered the sound of muffled ringing from somewhere nearby.

No! I jumped, realizing my mistake a split-second too late; I had accidentally called him instead of deleting his message. I hit the red button on the screen immediately, but not soon enough; barely a second later, my phone began vibrating, and Wes' number flashed on the screen. Gripping the phone in my hand as though it were a live grenade, I inwardly lambasted myself for the idiotic gaffe. But after thirty panic-filled seconds, it finally stilled and the screen went dark.

I let out a long sigh of relief – until the phone began buzzing again. *He'll call back,* the voice in my head fretted. *And he'll keep calling.*

With another sigh – this one filled with resignation – I picked up the phone right as it started vibrating a third time.

"Hello?" Wes's voice sounded from the speaker. "Rose – er, Rowan? Are you there?"

I froze. His voice sounded exactly the same as I'd remembered.

"Hello?" he asked again, sounding increasingly anxious.

Just tell him it was an accident and hang up! a voice – a very rational voice, I had to admit – shouted in my head. But as I held the phone up to my ear and closed my eyes, I knew I couldn't rush him off the phone. Not after what I'd done to him; not after I'd left him with so many unanswered questions for so long. He may have broken up with me in a moment of panic, but I'd inadvertently left him wondering about me for years. He deserved – and I owed him – much more than a hasty *ta-ta*.

And so, I did the only thing I could do – I stayed on the phone and talked to him, well into the early hours of the morning.

Chapter 17

"*A*spen! I had no idea you were such a player!" Eileen mock-scolded me as she stuck a hair pin against my scalp – roughly. "You know, I don't find many men in this world attractive. Too much hair and general B.O. and the wrong kinds of pheromones, for starters… But of all the menfolk out there, Aiden comes the closest in my mind to being relatively hot. And he's smart, smells good, is well-employed… Not to mention he's clearly *suffering* from all this recent daddy drama. Men become so much better-looking when they have that whole 'brooding and vulnerable' thing going on, don't you think, Sophia?" From the other side of my head, Sophia nodded at Eileen in the large, ornate mirror leaning against the wall in front of us, where they were putting the finishing touches on my face and hair.

"You're not wrong. Not a hundred percent *right*, necessarily... but I see what you're trying to say," Sophia winked playfully. "His recent brooding nature *does* make him more attractive, I think – in a sparkling vampire sort of way. But I wonder; does having another man in the picture demote Aiden to more of a beta role, rather than the typical alpha-male heterosexual archetype?"

"Oh, come *on!*" I whined, doing my best to keep my face frozen in place, the way Sophia had instructed. "It's not like that, and besides, I already feel terrible about the whole thing – ow*!*" I winced as Eileen stuck another pin in my hair, which she had been piling atop my head in a meticulously-styled mound of loose curls and tightly-pinned coils. Between the extravagant updo and the thick layer of make-up Sophia was applying to my normally-bare face, I hardly recognized myself in the mirror. And I hadn't even put on the full-length, black gown that had been dropped off for me by one of Keres' sub-Prelates an hour earlier. I was saving that particular discomfiture for last.

"Sorry!" Eileen replied, not looking sorry at all. "So, how much did you end up telling Wes last night? Does he know you're about an hour away from being the most famous Elementalist in the world? Or that you can hot-wire a car using only your brain? Were pouty selfies exchanged?"

"Do I really need that?" I asked, warily eyeing the mascara wand that Sophia was holding just millimeters from my eye.

"Honestly?" Sophia asked. "Not really. Your lashes are absolutely gorgeous. But I'm going to apply just a tiny bit anyway," she smiled, gracefully pulling the black sludge through my eyelashes. She knelt in front of my face, her gold-speckled brown eyes peering closely into mine. I couldn't help but notice her perfect skin, as dark in tone as mine was pale, and flawlessly-applied make-up, which made me feel slightly better about being her cosmetics guinea pig for the evening. I could feel my eyes beginning to water from the mascara, but with a casual wave of her palm she cast the tears aside before they could fall and smudge the rest of my face.

"Helps to have a Hydromancer doing your eye make-up, doesn't it?" she smiled.

I chuckled in spite of myself. I was glad that the abrupt change of topic was enough to derail Eileen and her uncomfortable line of questioning, at least for the moment. But the fact was, I was terribly grateful to have her and Sophia with me in my underground powder room that evening. The last time I'd needed to get this gussied up was when I went to that fancy gala Wes' parents had hosted to raise money for orphans in Mali. Jenny had offered to do my hair and make-up for the evening, but unlike Sophia, whose hands were as steady as a tripod, Jenny had somehow managed to stab me in the eye at least three times. It didn't help that my lovely, satin-yellow gown was just the right color to perfectly highlight what appeared to be acute conjunctivitis in my left eye.

But it wasn't just about the two of them giving me "a much-needed make-over" – as Eileen had oh-so-tactfully put it – before the Christening. More than ever, I needed their company, their jokes. Eileen's biting candor. All of my friends – but especially Eileen – had the uncanny ability of making even the direst of circumstances seem so much less terrifying.

If only Evelyn could have been here, I thought sadly. She'd be fawning over that silly gown and pinching my ribs while making *tsk-tsk* sounds about how I needed to eat more, if only so my boobs would get bigger. (Why she always resorted to that particular line of reasoning was beyond me.) But an arena filled with Elementalists was no place for my grandmother, particularly when some of those Elementalists viewed 'ordinary' people like her as 'Deficients'.

... People like Terry, I scowled, which made Sophia clear her throat.

"Sorry," I muttered, quickly recomposing my face so she could brush a layer of some sort of iridescent peach powder across my cheeks.

I'd managed to weasel out of Kaal's funeral proceedings earlier that day and was glad that Barish, unprompted, had excused me from Terry's induction ceremony, which would be concluding at any moment. Ori, fresh from his ten-hour nap on a private jet, had offered to accompany Aiden there, once his original proposal to help me into my dress was shot down by the rest of us. I glanced at the intimidating black gown – form-fitting, sheer in some places, and encrusted with thousands of tiny, glittering crystals. It hung ominously on the back of the massive wooden door, which led into one of the many winding, underground corridors hidden half a mile beneath the Hagia Sophia. I shuddered. If I thought about how far beneath the ground we were for too long, it made me dizzy. If I thought about prancing around in that stunning, pretentious, tremendously-revealing dress, it also made me dizzy. But worst of all, thinking about the upcoming ceremony that was about to occur in my honor made me feel sick to my stomach.

The Christening was less than an hour away, and from the snippets I'd gathered from the sub-Prelates who had been scurrying in and out of my dressing room throughout the evening, there was never any reason to worry about inviting my friends to the ceremony, because all three of them would have received a formal invitation that very same day, regardless of my wishes. While all of the Chapter heads and officials had received invitations to attend Kaal's funeral and Terry's subsequent induction days ago, my last-minute decision to formally join the Asterians in Aiden's place gave the Inner Circle ample opportunity to take advantage of the serendipitous timing – and so they took it upon themselves to invite every single known Elementalist in the entire world. All five thousand of them, ("Actually," Jahi's sub-Prelate, Rana, had at one point corrected herself, "it's closer to six-thousand, since the invitations were sent to honorary Asterian members, as well.")

I'd naïvely assumed that the mass, last-minute summons to Istanbul would result in a poor turnout for the Christening, but I'd been informed earlier that evening that nearly five thousand Elementalists had arrived in Istanbul that very day. Not because of Kaal or Terry, but because of the special evening announcement that had been hailed by the Magistrate as "the Community's greatest revelation in centuries". Because I hadn't been very good at hiding my identity or abilities during those last few months, rumors were already flying that a Pentamancer had at long last come out of the woodwork – or isolated cabin, in my case.

Closing my eyes, I tried using the technique the Magistrate had shown me to ward off an impending headache. I wasn't able to get rid of my bourgeoning migraine entirely, the way Barish had, but my efforts did take the edge off. Better than Tylenol, at least. I chewed the inside of my lip anxiously as I thought about the rest of our impromptu Electromantic tutorial from the night before. Barish had insisted – rather urgently, I noted – that we practice mind-reading. It was an exercise I'd managed to fail at spectacularly, much to his dismay. The intrusiveness, the complexity, the intimacy of it frightened me, and after an hour or so of failed attempts to penetrate the steel barriers of Barish's mind, he gave up, instead showing me tricks to seal off my own mind from others – *Not that there are many verified mind readers apart from you or I in the world,* he clarified. *Not even Keres has the ability. But it's a good talent to possess… just in case.*

I let my mind slowly wander back to Eileen and Sophia, who were having a discussion about their own dresses, whether they were nice enough for the occasion, whether Eileen should wear her cropped hair down or try to pin it up. I gently felt for their auras; or rather, "the distinctive, unique electric fields that are emitted from the minds of all living humans," as Barish had explained to me. If you could manipulate the electrons of those auras ever so precisely, you could read a person's thoughts, tweak them, influence them, even eradicate them altogether...

Where did I put the damned curler? I heard Eileen murmur. *This one piece of hair just isn't working... Ah there...* Her words trailed off and I felt a wave of... Anxiety? Yes, definitely anxiety. *God, I hope I fit into my dress. Why did I eat so many of Evelyn's brownies last week?* I felt another twinge of emotion – guilt. *I should have told Aspen's mom about the Christening... she and Evie should be here. Ted, too... I wonder if Aspen knows they've been spending their evenings together?* Chagrin. *Don't even go there, Eileen, she's got enough on her plate...*

I gasped softly. Eileen wasn't talking out loud. She'd been *thinking* those things. I pried my eyes open and shook my head vigorously, trying to banish her thoughts from my mind.

"Whoa, hey!" Eileen exclaimed, jerking the hot iron away from my forehead. "I'm trying to give you a gorgeous updo, not third degree burns to your face!"

"I'm sorry," I replied hastily, though she couldn't have known what I was really apologizing for. Sneaking a peek into an unwitting person's mind felt wrong on so many levels; it was like eavesdropping, but even worse – a violation of trust, of power. I wanted to hang my head in shame, but that would have earned me another stern rebuke for moving. And yet...

My mother and Ted? I frowned. What was she insinuating?

"No worries," Eileen smiled, setting the curling iron back on the antique glass end table beside the mirror. "Hey – your eyes are doing that nifty thing again – Sophia, look!"

"Oh wow," Sophia murmured, leaning down to peer closer. "That *is* something. It's like they're glowing! I wonder why they do that?" She started rummaging through her make-up bag. "Maybe I can find electric purple eyeliner to highlight the color..."

I stared down at my hands as Magistrate's words drifted through my head: *I've sensed remarkable ability in you, Rowan; it shines through the very light of your irises.*

"That would look awesome," Eileen agreed. She used her pinky finger to scoop away some hair near my temples and ears, letting the dark curls frame my face just so, then she winked at me in the mirror. "So, about Wes?" I felt my cheeks grow hot for the umpteenth time that evening. "Does Aiden officially have competition, or what?"

"Of course not," I replied, a little too quickly. "I told you – I never actually meant to call him. And when I did, I just told him the watered-down truth: I was recruited to my parent's old non-profit organization, I'm working my way up the ranks to try and get to a position where I can actually head some of the philanthropic projects—"

"—And, after talking for hours, you eventually mentioned your boyfriend, who may or may not have a 'fiery' temper?" Eileen supplied.

"I didn't mention that part, no," I mumbled, blushing furiously. *Why didn't I tell him about Aiden?*

"Does he want to see you?" Sophia asked.

"Who, Wes?" I asked dumbly. She nodded. "Um, yeah, he did mention something about meeting up. I made some excuse about how I've been traveling a lot for these projects I'm working on. But then he wanted to know how my parents are doing..." I swallowed. "When I told him my dad died a few years ago and he got really quiet for a long time. They were close, the two of them... My dad used to jokingly call him the son he never wanted."

"I'm so sorry, Aspen," Eileen said, placing a hand on my shoulder. "I know you were hoping that there would be more to your father's story..."

I stared down at a stray bobby pin on the floor. Sophia set down her make-up brush and knelt beside me, resting her hand on mine. "I can't begin to imagine what you've been going through these last few months, Aspen," she said softly. "I don't think any of us can. You've been thrust into a world that you never really wanted to be a part of, into this overwhelming position that we all know you're only accepting out of a sense of duty. And even though we all love Aiden—"

"And we think you two are pretty much perfect together," Eileen chimed in.

"—I can see how Wes kind of represents a different path for you," Sophia continued. "A safe path, one where you don't have to be Rowan the Prophet or Aspen the Pentamancer... You can just be Rose, the med student, the future doctor... a 'normal' person who doesn't have the weight of the world on her shoulders. And that's got to feel tempting on some level – knowing that an easier, alternate reality could exist for you somewhere out there."

I bit my lip, taking in Sophia's words. They stung – not because they were unkind, but because they resonated a little too closely to the thoughts I'd been working so diligently to repress. *Is that what I've been doing?* I wondered. *Seeking comfort in an alternate version of my life that some part of me wishes were real?* Is that why I'd been entertaining thoughts of Wes? Because he represented a simple, mundane life – one filled with white picket fences instead of corrupted organizations and absurd magical prophecies?

A knock sounded on the door, pulling me out of my reverie. Sophia smiled at me and stood up again, busying herself with dusting the stray eyeshadow off my cheeks. A moment later, Kaylie stuck her head in the room.

"Sorry to disturb – I just wanted to see how everything was coming along?" she asked, her voice reflecting her typical soft-spoken demureness. In stark contrast, the amount of make-up she wore made mine look like a natural flush, and she wore a sleeveless dress so revealing, I wondered if she had forgotten to put on some part of it. Glancing at my own chest in the mirror, which was even more concealed than usual by Aiden's baggy, zip-up hoodie, I couldn't help but envy her gravity-defying cleavage, which was threatening to spill out of her extremely low-cut neckline like a couple of spray-tanned grapefruits. It seemed Eileen had noticed the same thing, because she turned several shades of red and immediately began hyper-focusing on the single black strand of hair on my head that had not been teased and curled into a perfect coil.

"We're almost ready," I replied, forcing myself to look away from Kaylie's eye-grabbing outfit. My gaze drifted to the tri-colored Polymancer's tattoo on her arm instead, now clearly visible. "Is uh... is the induction over?"

"Yes," she nodded. "It was a wonderful ceremony. You were greatly missed."

"So, Terry is officially a Prelate?" I pressed, ignoring the flattery.

"Yes," she said again. "*Prelate* Terry has also chosen his three sub-Prelates, all Pyromantic associates of his from the Washington Chapter."

"I see..." I replied. Suddenly a thought occurred to me.

"Kaal had three apprentices working beneath him, right? What happened to the third man? Is he still a sub-Prelate...?

"Ah," Kaylie said, her eyes darting from me to Sophia and Eileen. "When a sub-Prelate is raised to Prelate, he or she has the option of allowing the other apprentices to remain on their team, or they may request their voluntary Sequestration. In Mr. Park's case, he was sequestered from the Extended Circle when Prelate Terry opted to choose three new apprentices."

"What does that mean?"

"It more or less means early retirement from the Asterian governing body," Kaylie explained. "He'll be able to attend events and remain active in the Community as a trainer or low-level mentor, but he won't be able to speak about his experiences in the Extended Circle or use his prior role to benefit him in any capacity. He'll also lose any benefits he may have been receiving, financial or otherwise."

Benefits? I thought, raising an eyebrow. I wanted to ask what those entailed, but thought it might have been rude. "So how does Bar – er, the Magistrate – stay in power? Can he be voted out? If he is, does he also have to go into – what do you call it? Sequestration?"

Kaylie shifted uncomfortably. "I think that's more of a question for Prelate Jahi than for me... I hate to be brusque," she added, "But Prelate Jahi was wondering if he might have a word with Sophia before the evening's events commence? He wanted me to assure her that it would only take a few moments."

Sophia set down the tube of eyeliner and picked up a gold tube of rose-pink lipstick. She tried to act casual as she applied it to my lips, but I felt her fingers shake slightly. "And would Prelate Jahi take offense if I said no?" she asked.

"I'm afraid he would," Kaylie replied.

Sophia sighed. "Well, just... let me change into my gown and I'll be right there."

"You don't have to," I said quickly.

She gave me a small smile. "Better to nip whatever this is in the bud now," she whispered. "Your makeup is all done – just blot your lips before you head downstairs, in case I'm not back in time."

"Do you need help getting into your gown?" Kaylie asked – rather brazenly, in my opinion. In the mirror, I could see Eileen's eyes narrow to thin slits as her eyes fell once more on the young, scantily-clad woman standing in the doorway.

"We got it, thanks ever so much!" Eileen replied before Sophia could, her voice dripping with corn syrup. "C'mon, honey, I'll help you." She took her startled girlfriend's hand firmly in hers and led her to the divider screen at the back of the room, where they both disappeared behind the mahogany panels. A burst of angry whispers erupted from their corner, but I couldn't quite make out the words.

"I'll have Sophia come meet you when she's dressed," I told Kaylie, hoping she'd take the hint and wait outside. Instead, she stepped further into the room to approach me, a cloud of perfume following her from the doorway.

"You look absolutely stunning," she murmured, gazing at me in the mirror. "I've never seen a more beautiful woman. Even Keres doesn't compare to you, Prophet."

"Um, th-thanks," I replied, feeling a flush of embarrassment rise in my cheeks.

"I'm honored to serve beneath you, Rowan," Kaylie whispered, taking my hand in hers. Her lips pressed against the tattoo on the inside of my forearm, leaving a smudge of glitter from her lip gloss. "Should you need anything at all – truly, *anything* – I'm at your beck and call." She placed a small piece of paper with her phone number in my palm, then turned to leave the room, her tall heels clicking behind her.

"Who was *that*?" Ori asked, stepping into the room moments later. He was wearing a well-tailored black suit that was only slightly offset by the addition of a lightning bolt-clad yellow tie. "Is that one of the ladies who came to the Denver Chapter earlier this week?"

"Yeah," I replied, stuffing the piece of paper in my pocket. I was still inwardly puzzling over the odd interaction. "Where's Aiden? ... Hello...? *Ori*?"

"Sorry!" he replied, still staring down the hallway. "Uh, he said he wanted to try to speak to his father after the induction – which, by the way, was like something straight out of the Occultists' Guide for Weirdos... *Elohim Adirim*!" he exclaimed as he finally turned away from the doorway and caught sight of me. "Speaking of hot! What is it the American ladies always say to each other? You look *fearsome*, girlfriend!"

"I think it's just 'fierce'," I smiled. "But thanks."

"No wonder you have all these men on the side trying to talk to you! I told Aiden I better take a number! He didn't seem to find that as funny as I did."

I felt the blood drain from my cheeks. "What do you mean, 'men on the side'?"

"Well, I mean, maybe Aiden wasn't supposed to say anything? But he might have mentioned something about your ex-boyfriend..." Ori stammered, looking guilty. "He seemed concerned... Or, now that I think on it, maybe I misheard him?" His hardly-noticeable accent suddenly became much thicker. "You know, my English, it is terrible, he probably meant something completely different..."

"Ori, get *out* of here!" Eileen, clad only in a bra and panties, suddenly cried. She had stepped out from behind the divider to grab her dress, not knowing he was standing right beside me.

Aiden knows about Wes? I fretted, my fingers idly twirling one of the tanzanite earrings he had given me. Had he seen the message Wes had sent me before the Challenge? *He must have,* I thought, furious with myself all over again. How could I have let things go so horribly awry in such a short amount of time? Just two days ago I had pondered how and when to tell him that I loved him... Now, because of circumstances Aiden had nothing to do with and had no way of controlling, I was avoiding him, talking to my non-Elementalist ex-boyfriend when I should have been talking to him instead.

What is the matter with me?

"I'm going, I'm going!" Ori shouted, ducking as one of Eileen's green Converse sneakers sailed cleanly over his head. "See you soon, Aspen! Best of luck! I want an autograph afterwards – Ow! Okay, *sheesh*! Tiny devil woman!" The door slammed shut behind him and Eileen, now barefoot, stomped back behind the divider, clutching her and Sophia's gowns to her chest. I should have laughed at the ridiculous scene, but I couldn't muster so much as a titter.

I should have told Aspen's mom about the Christening, Eileen had been thinking, wrought with guilt. *Evie and Ted, too.* She was right, of course. Except *I* should have been the one to tell them what was happening, given them the chance to be part of the decision. And I should have told Aiden about Wes, not hidden the situation in some feeble attempt to spare his feelings. How many times had I gotten angry in the past when others claimed to know what was best for me, when they had robbed me of my say – my *choice* – in matters that affected me? And here I was, doing the same thing to the people I cared most about. In the end, I wasn't protecting them – I was protecting myself.

"You have to fix this," I muttered at myself in the mirror. "All of this, before it's too late."

If it's not too late already, a tiny voice in the back of my head fretted.

Chapter 18

As the sun dipped below the horizon of the disconnected world above, I once again found myself in the Asterian Order's colossal, pentagon-shaped arena, a thousand feet below the city of Istanbul. Only this time, I was to be the spectacle while five thousand sets of eyes stared down at me from the packed balconies above. From a dark, safely-concealed corner of the stage in the center of the arena, I half-listened to the Magistrate's speech, which extolled the endless virtues of his dearly-departed Prelate Kaal as well as the beautiful ceremony that had been held in his honor earlier that morning. He then took a quarter hour to welcome Kaal's "worthy successor," Terry, to the illustrious Inner Circle, stating what a proud and virtuous gentleman he was.

I kept waiting for Barish to acknowledge Darius' death, to pay his respects to the man who lost his life while trying to prove his worth to the Inner Circle – but he conveniently failed to mention how Kaal's seat had been won in cold blood, never once uttering Darius' name. I silently railed at him for the intentional omission as I stared at the place where Darius was killed – just there, a dozen feet away from where Barish was giving his speech. Of course, there was no sign of blood or scorch marks on the ground below the stage we shared, no clues to tip off the packed arena that anything unusual or sinister had taken place in that very spot, less than twenty-four hours earlier. The Inner Circle had effectively ensured that Darius' untimely, senseless passing would go altogether unnoticed by the Community that night.

But all of that is going to change after today, I consoled myself, recounting all of the provisions I would introduce to ensure that nothing like that would ever happen again.

As Barish spoke to the hushed crowd of Elementalists, his voice amplified by Wind, his features perfectly captured by the narrow spotlight that shone on his face from above, I did my best to blend into the shadows, knowing that it might very well be the last time I would be able to do so. My role on that stage had not yet been touched upon, though I already felt the thousands of curious, inquiring eyes straining in the darkness to make out the silhouetted figure lurking in the Magistrate's shadow. I felt as though the stage might give way at any moment, dropping me into a pit of lions like they did to gladiators in the days of ancient Rome. I forced a mouthful of air into my compressed lungs as I looked around the packed arena, almost wishing that the stage *would* give way – anything to avoid his next announcement, the real reason every able-bodied Elementalist in the world had been summoned there that night.

The ceremonial torches on the wall blazed with the five colors of the Elements, illuminating the faces of the twenty-seven sub-Prelates who stood as both strategic guards and glorified figureheads at the base of our platform. Above us, seated in the same balcony as before, the Inner Circle once more surveyed their cluster of apprentices; only this time, Terry was up there with them, and I was about to become the spectacle below. Grimacing, I pulled my eyes away from their robed silhouettes and searched for my friends among the rows of seats near the floor of the coliseum. But it was too dark to make out anyone's faces there – I may as well have been alone.

The time has come, Barish's voice rumbled in my head as he finished his speech. *Are you ready, my child?*

I'm ready, I answered, not feeling ready at all. As I left the comfort of the shadows to approach the spotlight where the Magistrate stood, I immediately regretted the tall stilettos I had agreed to wear, as my ankles quivered precariously on their narrow spikes.

"Brothers and sisters," Barish's voice boomed, filling the vast arena like thunder. "I have asked you to travel from the far edges of the earth, not just to honor the life of our beloved Prelate Kaal, or to welcome his formidable replacement, but to share with you great news – the likes of which has not been shared for more than ten generations."

The spectators in the arena shifted and murmured to one another as the air became electrified with anticipation; not everyone in that room spoke fluent English, but they all waited with bated breath for the one word many suspected might be coming.

"Were I to simply tell you this news, you would not believe me, for it is so remarkable, even I did not believe until I myself bore witness to the miracle that is this young woman," he said, beckoning me over. As I came to stand beside him, he reached down to take my wrist and hold my left arm aloft in the air, causing me to teeter unsteadily. "Behold, brothers and sisters – for the legend is no longer legend. Here, standing before you, is the most powerful Elementalist to walk the earth in centuries – a true Pentamancer in the flesh!"

The arena erupted in gasps and cries, as though I were naked, or had a scaly fishtail where my legs should be. Somewhere to my right, a woman actually screamed. Scores of people began talking all at once, some in hushed murmurs, others in frantic, excited shouts.

"A Pentamancer!"

"The Prophet lives!"

"Blessed be the Pentamancer! Blessed be our Prophet!"

The Electricity from their excitement was overwhelming, almost dizzying. I wanted to clamp my hands over my ears and squeeze my eyes shut, drop into that imaginary lion's pit and be carried away by a hungry feline – anything to get out of the spotlight and away from the vociferous crowd. As the walls echoed with their increasingly-frenzied exclamations, I felt like I was in the middle of a Terramantic earthquake all over again. *Are you out there somewhere, Tosh?* I wondered, scanning the crowd for the little boy and his family.

"Prove it!" a man's voice shouted from somewhere to my right. "Prove it, Magistrate!"

Soon, others joined in the chant: "Prove it! Prove it! Prove it!"

Barish released my hand to silence the crowd. "Do you think I would lie to you?" he bellowed.

"No!" several hundred voices cried back.

"Do you think I would trick you?" he shouted.

"No!" hundreds of shouts rang into the air; "Never!" hundreds more yelled.

Still, several dozen voices cried out, "Show us! Show us!" They stomped their feet in time with their chant, gaining more and more voices as they stayed their course, sending a rumble through the walls and a shudder down my spine.

Barish looked at me and nodded. *It's time to win them over,* his voice whispered in my head. *This is your moment – show them what you are. Show them what we're fighting for!* He motioned to the sub-Prelates surrounding the stage, who immediately made their way to the far walls of the arena.

I took a deep breath. My thrumming heart felt as though it might try to break free through my ribcage; my hands were cold and clammy with sweat. The feeling strangely reminded me of the day I first met Aiden – Professor Lawson, at the time – beneath the soon-to-be shattered bulbs of his and Robert's lecture hall. If only he were with me now. I closed my eyes, trying to find his energy among the thousands of dark silhouettes surrounding the stage. He wasn't far; that much, at least, I could feel.

As the Magistrate stepped out of the spotlight, I stepped into the center of it, momentarily blinded by the intensity of the bulb perched so high above. While my eyes slowly adjusted to the light, the rest of the arena faded to black, and then to silence as a hush settled over the crowd. I tilted my head back, shielding my eyes to focus on the electric arc quivering between the tungsten electrodes, glaring at me from inside the spotlight high above. The edges of the electrodes burned a piercing hue of violet that I couldn't name, since I was the only one who could see the invisible color. As I reached out with my mind to greet the electricity, it quivered with excitement; like me, it longed to be free. I held my hand in the air, frozen, basking in my final moments of namelessness, of anonymity, of safe, comfortable insignificance...

And then I snapped my fingers.

The sound, amplified by the complete silence of the coliseum, echoed against the walls as a single, blue spark fell from the bulb and into my outstretched palm. I let it rest there for the span of a long breath, whispering gentle encouragements to the both of us as my pulse fluttered with anticipation.

When I was relatively confident that I wasn't, in fact, going to faint, I flung the spark back into the air, fueling it with the electricity that trilled inside the spotlight above the stage, as well as the anticipation that buzzed among the rows of Elementalists. The spark seethed and contorted into a lurching, galloping streak that raced toward the invisible ceiling, so high above us, it was obscured from sight – but not for long. Like a noiseless missile, the towering bolt of Lightning erupted into a searing flash, bathing the entire stadium in a silent explosion of light so brilliantly white, the thousands of stunned faces in the enormous chamber momentary bleached into nothingness, as though all the matter in the room had been replaced by pure, blinding light.

Then the tail of the Lightning bolt slammed into the ground. It burrowed into the stone, the dirt, the thick layers of bedrock, sending dusty fountains of Earth high into the ionized air. From the pages of Eileen's notebook of Earth elements, I brought to mind the sample I needed, the potassium-rich feldspar rock that I knew would be found there below. Churning piles of molten orthoclase rose to the surface as I summoned them, while above, the huge spotlight shattered from the surge of Electricity, releasing a tiny cloud of sodium gas in to the air. As a thousand silent gasps erupted from a thousand open mouths, I drew the moisture from those breaths to the place where the lightning bolt had just struck, a colossal, purple stain that lingered in the air, suspended like a ghost in the center of the arena. There, sodium, Water, and pure potassium came together by my hand, and it was as if Lightning had suddenly turned to Fire; purple flames violently burst forth from the abyss, like an interstellar explosion vibrating through the ancient stones of the coliseum.

The arena devolved into terrified screams, the air from which I wove into thick cables of Wind that merged together above the stage. Startled cries became appreciative shouts and cheers as the flames of the violet nova quickly faded to vermillion, curling back on themselves to create smaller explosions of Fire and sparks, which crackled and glittered in the air like orange fireworks. As the air began to heat from the display, sweat dripped down my back, down the glistening foreheads of everyone in that room, including Barish, who stood in the flickering shadows of the stage behind me. I glanced at him over my shoulder; his eyes, like everyone else's, were glued to the cascades of Fire that continued to surge and swell in the center of the arena, fueled by powerful cords of Wind that knotted and tangled in the hot air above.

Facing my own conjured inferno once more, I chewed my lip, grunting with effort as I coaxed the two Elements into a churning pillar of fiery orange clouds. They twisted and expanded as I added Water, drawing from the condensation of thousands of intermingled breaths and the perspiration that dripped from the brows of five thousand mesmerized onlookers.

As the fire inside the clouds subsided, Water and Wind billowed outward to create a swelling storm, much like the squalls far out above the deep ocean, where the two Elements naturally converge in violent tempests. Lightning flickered from the belly of the storm, illuminating the room just enough for me to be able to spot my friends, directly ahead in the bottommost row of seats. Ori, Eileen, and Sophia were gaping at the churning torrent of Wind and Lightning above my head, but Aiden was watching me intently, as though his eyes were glued to my body. I was suddenly aware of the tightness of the gown I wore, the thinness of the damp material that hugged my waist, the deep plunge of the neckline that exposed more of my breasts than I'd ever revealed outside of the bedroom.

The thread of Electricity that bound the two of us – that had bound us together from the very first day we met – gave me a momentary glimpse inside his mind, where a dozen feelings churned and roiled like the black storm clouds above us. Waves of Aiden's emotions crashed into me, waves made from something I couldn't control; they knocked the air out of my chest, overwhelming me with their sheer force. Tenderness, astonishment, desire – I gritted my teeth together as the wind in the arena picked up speed – betrayal, jealousy, fear. I tried to close my eyes, to yank myself out of Aiden's head, but it was too late.

Sadness, grief, dread.

His emotions became my emotions, his mind became my mind, and as I tried to stay afloat in the turbulent sea of his thoughts, I heard the words that I was never intended to hear: *These people destroyed my family, destroyed* her *family, and now here she is, a puppet on the Magistrate's string.* The present scene of the Magistrate standing behind me in the shadows – as seen through Aiden's eyes – was quickly replaced by an image of my phone, of Wes' message flashing on the screen, begging me to talk. *Is she still the same woman I knew in Colorado, before all of this – before they started calling her Prophet?*

Tears burned like acid at the corners of my eyes. *I'm still me!* I wanted to cry out. *It's not like that! All of this – it's just a means to an end!* But I couldn't put those words in his head, or he'd have realized how I had violated him, taken advantage of our connection.

Have I lost her? I heard him wonder, and I once again saw myself in his eyes, my designer gown clinging to my body, undernourished from too little food and too little sleep; my heavy make-up, making me appear exquisite and at the same time unfamiliar; my long, unkempt tendrils of black hair, escaped from their pins and flying around my face wildly; my eyes, beautiful and strange, flashing not from any source within that arena, but from something burning inside of me, as though Lightning itself was coursing through my veins. In that very moment, I was both the woman he loved, as well as the woman he feared: powerful, yet vulnerable. Dangerous and in danger.

I shook my head violently, wresting my mind away from his. As Water burst free from the belly of the thundercloud above, rainwater splashed against my face, blurring with the tears that poured freely from my violet eyes. With a clap of thunder so loud it made my insides tremble, a flash of Lightning tore through the clouds, exploding in a purple streak that stretched from the broken spotlight to the molten hole in the floor. Like a spinning drain, the Elements swirled around the rod of Lightning and into the crevice, and as the hole swallowed up the storm I had created and the earth closed around the last wisps of Water and Fire and Wind and Lightning, a single blue spark of Electricity escaped from the sealed layers of Earth and into my outstretched hand. There it rested for a moment, faintly pulsing with the quickened thrum of my heart, before floating across the stadium, landing squarely on the railing in front of Aiden's softly-illuminated face.

"We're in this together," I whispered, my eyes glued to the deep pools of his. Currents of Wind amplified my voice so that my whisper carried to the ears of everyone else in that room – but they weren't my currents. I glanced over my shoulder at Barish once more, whose wide eyes burned with intensity, the way mine had burned just moments before. With a wave of his arm, the huge lights embedded into the ceiling burst to life, bathing the arena in warm light.

"We're in this together!" the Magistrate shouted, hijacking my words with a cunningness I knew I would never learn to mimic. His arms were outstretched at his sides as he addressed the open-mouthed crowd before us. "All Elements, unified as one and she—" he cried, whipping around to point his shaking finger directly at me, "—Rowan Elizabeth Fulman – Pentamancer, Prophet, divinely-appointed Magistrate's Apprentice – *she* is the One! The Queen to my Ministership, the shining beacon of our grand vision! Follow us, brothers and sisters, and you will find your true purpose in this formidable Community! Together, we shall guide the Asterians to a glorious new epoch *never seen before!*"

By the end of his speech, Barish's voice had transformed into a lion's roar that brought the entire stadium its feet; five thousand fists shot into the air, five thousand cheering mouths returned his fervency with raucous, uproarious approval. Louder than any peal of thunder I ever could have conjured, their stomps and cheers and screams were deafening, echoing off the rumbling walls like a battle cry. I wanted to press my hands against my ears, but they were too busy gripping the fabric of my dress at my sides. Even my friends had leapt to their feet, screaming; Ori flung his fists in the air triumphantly, chanting along with the rest of the impassioned crowd.

Despite their furor, Aiden was the only one in the balcony still seated, staring at the tiny spark he cradled in his lap.

"Long live the Pentamancer!" Auromantic soundwaves carried the lone cry over the ensuing pandemonium. "Long live the Magistrate!" Within moments, hundreds, then thousands more, joined the nameless Auromancer's amplified chorus. Soon, the entire coliseum thundered with the impassioned chant: "Long live the Pentamancer! Long live the Magistrate!"

Barish grinned at me victoriously, though I wasn't sure in that moment what exactly we had won. *'The Magistrate's Apprentice'?* I thought, attempting to speak directly into his mind, the way he had shown me.

I thought you might like that, he replied. *Or, rather, appreciate its significance.*

I don't remember that title being approved by the Inner Circle, I thought, more to myself than to him. My eyes trailed to the grand balcony, where the other members of the Inner Circle were regarding us from above. Though the rest of the arena continued to stomp and cheer in a feverish, standing frenzy, the nine of them remained pointedly in their seats. Some of them seemed somewhat entertained, like Piotr and Mei, who appeared to be chatting excitedly with one another. Even the normally stony-faced Nadia was smiling and pointing at something on the other side of the arena. Izabel, Felipe, and Valeriya all sported their usual harsh, unreadable countenances. Jahi, Keres, and Terry, however, sat stiffly in their seats, their expressions frosty; Keres had a look of distaste, as though an unpleasant smell had gripped her nostrils. Jahi ignored me altogether, and, though Keres eventually smiled and clapped at me politely when she saw me looking, Terry made no attempt to erase the glower plainly written on his face when he caught my eye.

It was evident that not everyone in the Inner Circle had appreciated Barish's last-minute script change. The question that lingered in my mind was, what were they going to do about it?

Chapter 19

Immediately following the Christening, while the rest of the arena had been instructed to remain in their seats, I was accompanied to another, slightly-smaller, underground auditorium by Barish and his personal guard – six somber-looking men and women who bore the star of the Magistrate upon their Elemental sashes. By the time we had entered through the wide front doors, the rest of the Inner Circle was already there, seated among the eleven velvet-upholstered chairs that had been lined up at the back of the massive hall. The layout reminded me of a medieval throne room: rows of gothic-looking, electric chandeliers hung from the high ceiling, filling the chamber with warm light, while dusty velvet curtains of the five Elemental colors hung from the arched, windowless walls, framing huge oil paintings of the Inner Circle's past and present members. As we made our way to the line of chairs

– the only seats in an otherwise-empty chamber – I couldn't help but admire the gold-framed portraits as we passed. As gaudy as the towering canvases were, some of the figures inside were dressed in medieval garb, making the paintings five-hundred years old – maybe more. But they had been maintained with impeccable care, as though the rich, glossy paint had only been applied sometime in the last decade.

As we approached the Prelates, the two tallest chairs in the center of their line of seats had been left vacant, and Barish motioned for me to sit beside him while his guards lined up directly behind us.

With the amount of raw power seated here, why does Barish bother with a guard at all? I wondered, regarding the Inner Circle. Even at seventy-something years old, I was fairly certain Mei alone could take down an entire room of dissidents with a simple wave of her Polymantic hand. *And we all witnessed yesterday what Terry is capable of doing in a fit of rage,* I thought to myself, suppressing a scowl. But sitting there on his gilded, velvet chair, he looked positively serene as he took in his surroundings, smiling for the first time that I could remember.

Primly seated between Terry and the Magistrate, Keres glanced at Barish for his nod of approval, then motioned for the two guards stationed at the front of the room to open the wide double doors. As the doors swung open, an excited, albeit hushed, crowd of Elementalists poured into the large room, filling every square foot of standing space in front of us. It was a strange and uncomfortable experience, sitting in that chair while a long line of awe-struck Community members from around the world proffered their supplications and well-wishes upon us. The Magistrate and the others certainly received their fair share of attention, and they seemed perfectly at-ease – delighted, even, by the toadying flattery. But while the Prelates each entertained a few dozen or so devotees – Barish receiving at least twice that – the line to greet me wrapped around the entire auditorium several times. I must have flushed a dozen shades of crimson while strangers knelt to kiss the tattoo on the inside of my forearm, murmuring exaltations and praise.

Apart from seeing a few familiar faces, such as Vivian, the Watchkeeper from the Tulsa Containment Center, and Dr. Chen, the Chief Medical Officer from the Denver Chapter (at the sight of each of them, I leapt from my seat and nearly knocked them to the ground with ecstatic hugs), I spent that interminable hour blushing and squirming, counting down the seconds until I could flee from that hot, stuffy room. But even then, the night would still be far from over; following the reception, there was to be a formal banquet with the Magistrate, Inner and Extended Circle, as well as Chapter heads and officers, while everyone else – my friends included – were to be served hors d'oeuvres and drinks down in the arena, ahead of the all-night after-party.

An hour after the last eager set of lips had pressed themselves against my tattoo, and those of us who ranked sufficiently high enough had been escorted to the lavish banquet hall for our private dinner, I stared glumly at the untouched glass of champagne bubbling in my hand. I wanted nothing more than to be down in the arena with my friends, out of those infernal high heels that tore at my feet, away from Barish and his roomful of sycophants, in front of whom he paraded me as though I were his prized horse.

And yet, despite my annoyance at his less-than-subtle practice of linking himself to me at every opportunity, I knew that it was in his – and my – best interest to make a good impression upon the people who were the caretakers and commanders of the various Asterian Communities around the world. After all, some of those Chapter officers were also well-known politicians, athletes, and celebrities – people who were powerful and influential in their own name and right. And despite the fact that more than anything, I wanted to run down to wherever Aiden was and sort everything out, I knew that there was no better time to discuss Containment Centers and outdated Asterian policies than right then and there, over a glass – or three or five, in some of the officers' cases – of champagne or scotch.

"Wait, so you are telling me that there are Containment Centers in the United States that have people locked up with lifetime sentences for losing their tempers in public *one time*? Showing a non-Elemental family member or two a neat trick?" A famous Chinese actress – also a Level-two Auromancer – stood in front of me, swirling her drink angrily. "If that is true, then I should also be in one of these prisons! … Zhang, are you hearing this?"

Her husband turned away from the fondue fountain to stand beside her. "I am, my love. It's an atrocity. I've been telling you about my suspicions regarding our own Containment Center in Beijing. I have always wondered if it was just another method to suppress our people there."

A group of officers from the Dubai chapter, who had been talking with Terry and his new sub-Prelates a few feet away, excused themselves to come join our discussion. So did a handful of other high-ranking Elementalists. Before I knew it, I'd amassed a rather large group of curious listeners, some of whom I recognized even from outside the Asterian Order. The very tall gentleman to my left, for example, I could have sworn I'd seen in a sneaker advertisement.

"So, in your opinion, every Containment Center should just be shut down?" the Security Chief from Dubai asked me, her eyes slightly narrowed. "What about repeat violent offenders? Or sociopathic criminals?"

"Violent criminals would require extra support and, yes, I agree that they would need to remain in some sort of confinement for the safety of others," I conceded. Even I couldn't argue that homicidal Electromancers should be left to freely terrorize the neighborhood. "But in a population of five-thousand Elementalists, how many true sociopaths would we realistically expect to come across in a single generation? Fifty, at most?" Several of the faces in the circle nodded thoughtfully. "It's my goal to empty all of the Containment Centers in the world," I edged, confident that I had found at least several sets of sympathetic ears. "We could reallocate the millions of dollars pouring into those centers to rehabilitate our lesser law-breakers instead – and only after they've been properly tried and proven guilty in Asterian court. Otherwise we have no business imprisoning them."

"It would seem the Magistrate's Apprentice is not only powerful, but judicious as well," Zhang whispered to his wife.

"We could even use some of the funds to help the rest of the community, particularly the non-Elemental—"

"Rowan, my child," Barish said, clapping a hand on my shoulder. "I'm glad to see you've already been introduced to Mr. and Mrs. Li, as well as our officers from Dubai and São Paolo. I wonder, however, if I might steal you away for a quick word?"

"Uh, sure," I replied, letting him lead me away from the crowd. The discussion regarding the Containment conundrum faded into the background as we made our way for one of the banquet hall's many arched doorways. There, Barish turned to face me.

"I think it's a little early to be discussing our radical agenda," he said, a smile tugging at the corner of his mouth.

"Why?" I asked, setting my untouched glass of champagne on a passing silver tray.

"Because I may have ruffled some feathers among my Prelates tonight, creating a position for you that no one's ever heard of, or sanctioned, for that matter," he smiled ruefully, his eyes darting to several members of the Inner Circle who stood, huddled with their apprentices, closely watching us from behind their bejeweled goblets of wine. "Let's give them a few days to settle down and grow accustomed to our new dynamic. Then we'll start some real trouble, hmm?" His violet eyes twinkled lightly.

"If you say so," I answered, doing my best to return his smile. I couldn't help but think about Aiden, his private thoughts that I'd intruded upon. Did he really think that I was Barish's puppet – that I'd somehow been changed by this whole experience? I caught my reflection in one of the panes of stained glass on the wall, remembering how he'd looked at me in the arena. As I smoothed away the last vestiges of static from my hair – I'd long since yanked out all the pins Eileen had stuck into my head, opting instead to use my long hair to help cover the gown's revealing neckline – a Pyromancer in a tight red dress walked by. My breath caught in my throat.

"Can I ask you something, Barish?"

"Anything, my dear."

"What happened to Savannah? To her sister?" I asked, biting my lip the moment the words slipped out. It was a question I should have asked months ago, but, like so many others, I hadn't been able to bring myself to ask it.

"Savannah and I made a special deal long ago," Barish replied, stroking his silver beard thoughtfully, "the details of which I am not at liberty to disclose at this moment. But suffice it to say – she and Emily are together."

"Oh," I replied, surprised by his answer. *The two of them made a deal? What kind of deal?* "Well… are they okay?"

"Your concern for a woman who has shown you such contempt is touching, my child. Though not surprising, given the nature of your character." He winked, then switched to unspoken communication. *Savannah has been in intensive rehabilitation for an opiate addiction; she was released two weeks ago. I saw to it that her younger sister, Emily – who was Contained despite being mentally disabled – was released at the same time. Notwithstanding Savannah's recent opiate-fueled transgressions, she has served me well over the years, and I have ensured that she and her sister are comfortable in their obligatory Sequestration…* "Does that put your mind at ease, my child?"

"Actually, it does," I admitted. "Thank you."

"Rowan, I want to thank you for the sacrifices you've made," Barish said, clasping my shoulder lightly, "for this organization, for me. It can't be easy, given what we've put you through. What we've put your family through. I know it's been… overwhelming for you. But the outcome will be well-worth the sacrifice – I promise."

"I – I'm sure it will be," I replied. There was a sudden surge of emotion behind the Magistrate's words, vanishing in the same fleeting instant that I registered it.

He smiled at me then, almost wistfully. "Now, I think I've kept you from your friends long enough, hmm? I'll have my guard accompany you downstairs to the party. The rest of us will be down shortly."

"Really?" I asked, surprised. "I can go?" With a good-natured chuckle, the Magistrate nodded.

"Oh, just one more thing," he added, brushing a stray lock of hair from my eyes. "Should you ever require anything from me and I'm not readily available, don't hesitate to turn to Piotr or Mei. I think you'll find that they'll be able to answer any questions that you may have."

I nodded, somewhat puzzled; apart from the non-sequitur nature of his comment, I'd only ever spoken to either Piotr or Mei one time, and it was during this trip. But, having at long last been relieved of the day's duties, I wasn't about to ask for clarification at that very moment.

As I turned to head downstairs, flanked on either side by the Magistrate's guard, I peeked at Barish over my shoulder, catching an affable wink in return. There was a time when I had seen the Magistrate as intimidating, formidable – someone to fear. But just then, as I regarded the lines in his face, his silver hair, nearly white from the candlelight of the chandeliers above, I couldn't help but think about how frail he looked.

I shook my head at the bizarre thought. Barish, broad-shouldered and taller than anyone else in that room aside from Jahi, was the single most powerful man in the world, as shrewd as he was robust. There was nothing 'frail' about him.

You could have worse allies, I thought to myself, giving him one last glance just before the door shut between us.

Chapter 20

I hadn't expected much when Barish mentioned that there would be a party in my honor after the Christening; after all, he and most of the Inner Circle were well past middle age, and most of them had personalities that were as antiquated as the dusty paintings that hung from the walls. So, I'd more or less envisioned the after-party that the sub-Prelates had been frantically putting together for the last twenty-four hours in the typical stiff-yet-extravagant Asterian fashion: Elemental operatic singers, caviar hors d'oeuvres, Auromantic cello quartets...

So, when I finally returned to the arena two and a half hours after I'd left it, I found myself staring, open-mouthed, at the massive underground rave that stretched out before me. Multi-colored laser beams crisscrossed through synthetic fog as bass-driven electronica throbbed in my ears; the source of the deafening music was an

Electromantic DJ perched atop one of the highest balconies, cranking his beats into the towering speakers at the highest possible volume. Down on the floor, several thousand Elementalist party-goers danced wildly, many of them tilting back shot glasses of green liquid that had been set aflame by Pyromantic bartenders. I stared in disbelief at the half-dozen go-go dancers suspended from airborne cages, who wore nothing but their Elements draped across their lithe, naked bodies as they swayed to the heavy beat. If I hadn't been one hundred percent sure that I was standing in the middle of an Asterian arena, I never would have believed where I was.

As I made my way into the cavern, still flanked on either side by the Magistrate's personal guard, the music was abruptly replaced by the DJ's voice, which ricocheted loudly through the speakers:

"Brothers and sisters, give it up for the myth, the legend, the reason we're all here tonight... our Community's very own PENTAMANCER!"

Dozens of fingers pointed in my direction as the crowd started screaming.

"She's here!"

"Oh my god – it's the Prophet herself! Rowan! Rowan, *hi!*"

"Long live the Pentamancer!"

My eyes widened in alarm, but the electrified crowd stayed put, parting even, as the six guards escorted me towards the back wall.

"Please remember the rules we discussed earlier," the DJ continued over the speakers. "No photos whatsoever, no touching the Pentamancer, and, please, no accosting our beautiful prodigy tonight! She's here to dance, just like the rest of us – and speaking of which, here's the latest single from yours truly, already blasting to the top of the charts in Bucharest!" The DJ gave me a thumb's up as he cranked the music back up again, sending the party-goers into a wild, dancing frenzy. The rumbling bass vibrated up through the heels of my shoes, shuddering against my empty stomach. One of Barish's guards, a middle-aged man in a decorous blue sash, leaned in closely so I could hear him over the blaring music.

"Prophet, the guests are all aware of the rules, which were specified in detail before your arrival. You needn't fear any harassment. We'll be watching from the balconies with the other guards in case you need anything at all… Your friends are just there," he added, pointing to a long bar top that had been erected along the nearby wall. My shoulders immediately relaxed as Ori waved me over, a wide grin plastered on his face.

"Have fun, Prophet," the guard smiled, turning to leave.

"It's Rowan," I muttered under my breath as he and the rest of the Magisterial Guard strode away. I leaned down to unstrap the torturous stilettos I'd been suffering through for hours, tossing them over to a darkened corner. My swollen, blistered feet grumbled at me from the dirty dance floor.

"Aspen! My little lightning bolt!" Ori shouted over the music, swirling one of those flaming, radioactive-colored drinks in each of his hands. "I've got to hand it to those old fossils: I've been to a rave or two in Tel Aviv, but I have *never* seen anything like this!" His lightning bolt tie had long since been cast aside, and the top buttons of his shirt were undone, exposing dark curls of chest hair smattered across his olive skin. "This puts Tuesday Night Trivia to shame! *Shame!*" He laughed, downing one of his drinks. I crinkled my nose at the fumes as he gasped and sputtered; the liquid smelled like a cross between kerosene and black licorice, even worse than the acrid stuff from Israel he'd had me try – right after I nearly electrocuted myself during our first Electromantic lesson. The memory brought a pursed smile to my lips.

"You were SO FREAKING PHENOMENAL tonight!" he added, wiping his mouth on his shirt sleeve.

"The only reason I didn't make it to your reception to ask for an autograph with the rest of your enamored fans is because I was too busy changing my pants... I'll let you interpret what you will from that," he winked.

"You idiot," I laughed, pushing him away from me.

"Aha! So the Pentamancer *does* smile!" he grinned.

"Aspen! My looove! We brought you a drink!" Eileen yelled as she returned from the bar, one arm draped across Sophia's bare shoulders, the other thrusting some sort of multi-colored concoction in my face. "The bartender called it 'Pentamancer Punch'! It's delicious!" Her short, emerald-green dress glittered in the strobe lights, while Sophia's floor-length, periwinkle gown flowed around her slender body like water.

"Thanks," I said, gratefully taking the drink from her hand. "Are you guys having fun?"

"Yes!" she replied, taking a swig from her own glass. "Also, may I just say – that thing you pulled with the orthoclase? Drawing the potassium out of it to react with Water? Blew. My. Mind." She mimicked an explosion erupting from her ears.

I grinned. "I couldn't have done any of it without your training. All of you – thank you. And thanks for being here. It means a lot to me."

"We're so proud of you, Aspen," Sophia smiled, giving me a quick hug. "You've come so far. And we know you're going to do great things from the inside."

"Yes, yes, *bevakasha*, very welcome," Ori replied. "Not that you have to thank us for taking advantage of the free liquor and beautiful bodies."

"That sentence sounds kind of creepy in English, dude," Eileen frowned at him.

"Yeah, it sounds creepy in Hebrew, too!" he grinned, drumming his fingertips together diabolically.

My eyes darted around the huge arena. Everyone who caught my eye raised a drink or an excited fist in my direction, sometimes yelling my name, sometimes letting out a loud cheer that was quickly echoed by a dozen or so of their closest neighbors.

"Aiden's over at the far end of the bar," Sophia said, reading my mind – figuratively speaking. "A couple of ladies were offering to buy him a drink, last I saw – but I think he declined," she added.

"Go *talk* to him, Aspen!" Eileen yelled, giving the small of my back a not-so-gentle push. "We've got eyes on you, along with your fifty invisible sentries stationed up in the balconies – so *go* already!"

"Okay, okay!" I griped, tilting my head back to swallow the glass of colorful punch in one gulp. "Gahhh!" I grimaced, exhaling fumes. It tasted like straight tequila with just a hint of fruit punch.

I straightened my dress around my hips resolutely as I made my way through the gyrating crowd of people, keeping my head down as much as possible. Several people yelled acclamations or invitations my way, but it was easy to pretend not to hear them over the deafening music. When I finally found Aiden at the edge of the bar, he was downing one of those green absinthe drinks. His tie and jacket were draped over the barstool behind him, his burgundy sleeves rolled to his elbows.

"Hi," I said, coming to stand beside him. My eyes fell on the empty glasses resting beside his elbow. "Can we talk?"

"Sure," he replied, setting his drained glass beside the others. "By the way, I believe congratulations are in order, now that you've officially been christened as the Magistrate's Pawn."

I took a step back. His words stung more than I expected them to. "Look, I didn't know he was going to say that—" I started.

Someone jostled me from behind just then, causing me to stumble forward. Aiden's eyes flashed.

"Oh my god, it's *you*!" a man behind me stammered as I turned around. "I'm so sorry!"

"It's fine," I replied.

"Jesus, I can't believe I'm talking to an actual Pentamancer!" He reached forward to squeeze my bare arm as he spoke. "Can I, uh, buy you a drink?"

"You can get your hand off her," Aiden growled, stepping between us. He pushed the man's hand away from me roughly.

"Hey, back off, man, I didn't mean anything by it!" the guy shot back, taking a step towards Aiden. The crisp blue tattoo on the inside of his arm branded him a Hydromancer, Level-three.

"Aiden, stop, it's fine!" I protested, but the other guy had already siphoned the water out of his own cocktail, obviously preparing to hurl it in Aiden's face. I quickly evaporated the floating blob of Water, until it was nothing but vapors that gently dispersed into the air. The man stared at me in disbelief.

"Holy shit," he muttered. "How did you do that...? I was the one controlling—"

"Is there a problem here?" A guard appeared at my side, eyeing the startled Hydromancer up and down.

"There's no problem at all," I responded, quickly pulling Aiden away from the bar.

"Do you know who that guy was that you were messing with?" I heard the guard snarl as we walked away. "That's Prelate Terry's son…"

Still grasping Aiden's sleeve, I made my way into the dense crowd of onlookers, who immediately parted for us as we passed; their heads bowed in my direction even as their bodies continued to dance. I tried not to pay attention, lest my face turn a brighter shade of red than it already was.

"What's the matter with you?" I blurted out, once we'd reached the center of the arena. I forced my eyes away from the place where Darius had died, the same place where dozens of bodies now danced and grinded against one another. "I've never even seen you drunk before, and now you're starting fights with random Hydromancers? Over what?"

Aiden avoided my eyes, watching a nearby group of people bending and heaving their bodies against the mounting beat. The strobe lights illuminated the sharp angles of his face, making him look strange and unfamiliar in the darkness.

"Over what?" I repeated, squeezing his hand gently.

"Nothing," he replied, finally meeting my stare.

"Look, if this is about Wes—"

"Do you want to dance?" he asked suddenly, gripping my hand in his.

"I – dance?" I repeated dumbly. I didn't even know he liked to dance.

"C'mon," he said, twirling my body so my back was pressed against his chest.

Out of the corner of my eye, I saw Eileen and Sophia dancing nearby, pretending not to watch us. Ori was just a few feet away from them, dancing with… *Kaylie?* My eyes widened in surprise. Not just Kaylie, but Jahi's other sub-Prelate as well, a young Egyptian woman named Rana who had glittering strands of silver tinsel woven into her long, black hair. The two of them had their bodies firmly pressed against Ori, sandwiching him in the middle. I gasped softly, unable to tear my eyes away. I'd gotten so accustomed to Ori's goofy, wise-cracking demeanor, it was strange to see him in such a provocative way – cool and confident, as though having two beautiful women draping themselves across his body was nothing new. The three of them swayed and writhed together like reeds bending in the wind.

Entranced by the scene in front of me, my hands traced their way behind Aiden's head as his right hand glided across my stomach. He pulled me tightly against him, his other hand sliding down the front of my thigh. The music pounded in my ears, filling my veins with the deep, throbbing pulse of the music. As Aiden guided my hips against the beat, I tilted my head back against his shoulder, feeling his hot breath against my neck, his soft lips pressing themselves against my skin. I surrendered my body to him as we moved together, rocking and grinding against the heavy synthesized beat.

I had no idea he could dance like this, I thought, feeling the cool beads of his sweat dripping down the back of my neck.

He spun me around roughly, moving his hand to the small of my back, pressing his pelvis into mine. His other hand knotted into my hair, damp with sweat, and tilted my face towards his, where he kissed me, roughly, hungrily. His tongue rolled over mine and I gasped into the sweetness of his mouth, the corrosive taste of absinthe on his breath surprisingly arousing. I hadn't met this side of Aiden yet – the voracious, animalistic side of him. As his fingers raked through my hair and his other hand roughly pulled me against his firm, muscular chest, heaving with his quickened breaths, I should have been afraid of the desire I knew he felt for me, the lust I saw in his eyes, but I wasn't. Burning from somewhere deep within, his Fire mingled with my own Fire, his longing found mine, and in that instant, I knew that everything he felt for me, I returned with equal ferocity.

If I could have, I'd have made love to him right there on the dance floor.

"I love you Aspen," he whispered against my lips, his words fierce with desire, unflinching in their truth.

I stared up into his face, so heartbreakingly handsome, so entrenched with the love and tenderness he felt for me, and I knew that no one else in the world mattered, had ever mattered; the spark I'd felt with Wes was nothing in comparison to the conflagration that burned between Aiden and me. It was a realization filled with profundity, with unshakable truth: I loved him. No matter the obstacles that threatened to come between us, no matter the cost, I knew I always would.

I pressed my hand against his face gently, and he cupped it with his own, kissing the inside of my palm, his eyes burning into mine. I trembled, feeling my knees threatening to give way.

"Aiden, I—"

I gasped; the liquid topaz pools of his eyes were suddenly replaced by a torrent of ultraviolet, flashing like a sun-kissed stone at the bottom of a river. A blaze as brilliant as Lightning flared across my vision, and in that instant, I no longer stood in the center of the arena, wrapped in Aiden's warm embrace, but at the front of a small, dimly-lit room, where dozens of wax candles burned from sconces embedded in the ancient stone walls.

Aiden! Where are you? I wanted to cry out, but as I struggled to utter the words, only silence came.

Chapter 21

*A*s my eyes focused on the walls, on the long, flickering shadows the candles cast across their stones, my nose took in their scent, damp and earthy with the distinctive smell of passing centuries. A large, mahogany table filled up most of the space in the musty chamber, surrounded by nine empty chairs. *I'm in the Inner Sanctum*, I realized – the special chamber where Barish and the Prelates would sit during our remote calls. Keres, Jahi, and Terry stood at the opposite end of the long table staring at me... But I wasn't me. I looked down at my arms, which were swathed in velvet, the thick fabric steeped in rich swirls of purple, blue, and yellow dye.

Pay attention, Barish's voice rumbled in my ears, and I wanted to cry out, to blink, but my own body was paralyzed, my mind trapped inside the impenetrable walls of his.

"So… 'the Magistrate's Apprentice'?" Jahi asked, leaning against the table. "And what exactly does that mean?"

"It means what it means," Barish's voice sounded through my lips. "It means she'll be training directly under me, as my student, my protégée—"

"Your poker chip," Terry muttered under his breath.

"But this was never voted on, Magistrate," Keres said, an iciness touching the edges of her words. "You cannot make such a unilateral decision without the Inner Circle's vote—"

"The role you've bestowed upon the girl also creates a new level of hierarchy that we as a legislative body have never seen, nor discussed," Jahi cut in. "One that appears to place her ministerial powers in line with your own. How will her votes be counted? Will it even be possible, at this point, for the Inner Circle to vote against the two of you, should you side against the rest of us?"

Barish said nothing.

"I wonder…" Keres mused, "If that was your intention all along, Magistrate? To diminish the authority of the Prelates? Or perhaps it was to ensure your long-standing throne would have a rightful heir, after all?"

Barish sighed, but I couldn't tell if it was audible to the others in the room or inside his own head. *Keres was once my protégée, the most talented of my Prelates... the most powerful Elementalist in the world, apart from me. Before your awakening, I'd been grooming her to be my replacement for many years, but it would seem that Providence had other plans...*

"What has been done, is done, my dear Keres," Barish replied, his voice calm. "What has yet to be determined is your next course of action. Will we find a way to move forward, or will you seek to depose me, as you've been whispering to the others behind closed doors?"

The corner of Keres' mouth twitched imperceptibly. "Magistrate, you know I would never—"

"Try as you might to block me, I can see through the barriers of your mind, Keres, so please – let's skip the denials and false declarations. The hour grows late and I am tired... Though I assume you will not be joining me in my quarters this particular evening?" he added dryly, causing Terry's eyes to flash with anger. A shudder of indignance and suspicion ran through the man's body almost palpably, which filled Barish with a sense of cruel satisfaction.

"We will raise the subject of your deposal at tomorrow's gathering," Keres replied, ignoring the glaring implication. "The Pentamancer will not be allowed in the

Sanctum during that time." Her voice sounded steady, confident, but it shook ever so slightly at the last syllable.

"I see," Barish replied, leaning back into his/our seat. "And I presume you would not be so reckless as to request a vote you were not confident you could secure?"

"We have the votes, Barish. You will be deposed by midday tomorrow."

My/Barish's eyes trained on Jahi, who squirmed ever so slightly. While Keres had grown adept at hiding her emotions from Barish, the Nigerian possessed no such ability. "Jahi," the Magistrate said, his voice surprisingly gentle. "You don't truly want to do this, do you? Even when you privately spoke to Prelate Kaal about Keres' plan, you had expressed to him your misgivings. Don't let your desire for power persuade you into doing something you don't truly support. Keres is a cunning woman – and I doubt very much that she'll keep the promises she has made to you." His gaze settled on Terry, whose hands were clasped behind his back. "She does, after all, have a habit of taking on pets to do her bidding for a short while, and then disposing of them once they've satisfied their... purpose."

"How dare you—" Terry started, but Keres interrupted him.

"The hour draws late, Barish, as you've already pointed out. There is no use continuing this tiresome game. You were a good mentor and a strong leader – for a while. But your agenda no longer conforms to ours, and we can no longer allow you to abuse your power. The Pentamancer has no allegiance to anyone in this room. Her allegiance is to her friends, to her own narrow-minded mission. I'll simply convince her, as you have, that I'll do whatever she wants – and as the new Magistrate, I will. I'll empty the Containment Centers, I'll put on a show of doing pro-bono work for the Community, even for some of the Deficients – just enough to make her malleable, to set her doubts at ease... and then, once she's safe in the palm of my hand, I'll use her for the Asterians' true mission, the one you seem to have forgotten."

"Ah, yes," Barish mused, speaking his next words for my benefit. "Securing enough money, power, and resources to freely step onto the world stage. To put the Deficients in their lesser place while removing the laws and restrictions we've placed on our own Community. To finally come out of our self-imposed hiding... Yes, I do confess, I have let that enterprise fall to the wayside in recent months."

Keres sneered, an ugly expression on her normally-lovely face. "Goodnight, Barish."

She turned on her heel, making her way for the door. Terry turned to go as well, followed closely behind by Jahi, who glanced at Barish over his shoulder uncertainly.

Do not trust the word of any Electromancer, for they can disguise their lies as truths.

"I wonder," Barish said, his voice so soft, he was sure Keres had to strain to hear it. She stopped, her hand frozen on the door handle. "Have you considered the fact that some of the Prelates may have lied to you when they pledged to vote in your favor? Prelates who have already come to me to warn me about your injudicious and reckless attempt at mutiny tomorrow?"

She turned around slowly, taking Barish in with a measured stare.

You must go to my study immediately, his voice whispered in my head – our head. *There you will find a leather-bound journal in the top drawer of my desk; it has information you will need. Take that, as well as the Compendium – the gold-embossed book in my curio cabinet. Break the lock to get inside it, then run. The guards will not stop you.*

What are you talking about? I whispered frantically, just as Keres began to speak.

"I underestimated you, Barish," she replied. "You always were stronger than me, more cunning. Everything I am, I learned from you – but that's your weakness, isn't it?" Keres held out her hand, where Electricity crackled in her palm. "You expect me to behave as you do, adhere to *your* principles, never stopping to consider the fact that others have taught me tricks, as well."

"What are you doing?" Terry hissed at her.

You must win the Community to your side, Aspen, Barish said, the sound of his own heart throbbing in our ears. *Amass at your back a great army of Elementalists, for you must burn down the Order and rebuild it from the ashes.*

"My dear Keres," Barish said softly, "I have but one weakness in this world, and I can assure you, it is not underestimating you." I could feel him drawing power from within himself, from the nearby electrical wires in the walls; he would need to draw a great deal to defend himself against Keres, but there was no doubt he was the more powerful of the two. I briefly wondered if I could somehow help, provide some additive effect—

Save your energy, my child.

"I'm sorry, Barish," Keres said, her palm still crackling. With her other hand, she drew a small pistol from the pocket of her robes. Barish's eyes trailed on it for the briefest moment before she pulled the trigger, sending a bullet directly into his heart.

"Forgive me," she whispered as weak cry escaped through the Magistrate's lips. "You're just too powerful... There was no other way."

Finding you was my destiny, Barish's words faded in my mind as his vision went blurry, then darkened to black. *Now is the time, Aspen, for you to write yours.*

***

I screamed, clawing at my chest as I emerged from the stifling blackness. I sucked in deep, gasping mouthfuls of air between the uncontrollable screams, convinced that a bullet was still lodged in my heart. My fingernails ripped at the thin fabric of my dress, tore at the skin beneath it, searching for the wound, the basin of blood that must have been pooling above my sternum.

Barish! I cried out in my head, searching for him. *BARISH!*

There was no answer. I pried my eyes open, where Aiden's horror-struck face was hovering inches above mine. He gripped my wrists, struggling to keep my hands from clawing my own skin away as he shouted something at me, but I couldn't register what he was saying.

"He's dead," I gasped, choking on my own words. "He's dead!"

"Who's dead?" Aiden demanded, clutching my face. "Aspen, what happened?"

My head spun around wildly, taking in my disjointed surroundings. The music had stopped, and though the torches still burned on the walls, the strobe lights above us had all gone dark. A layer of frosted glass fragments glittered across the arena floor, scattered by the feet of the crowd and the guards that pressed them back.

"Is she okay?"

"It's the Pentamancer! Something's wrong!"

"What happened? Is she hurt?"

"We have to get out of here," I whispered to Aiden, struggling to stand. My head seared with pain, fresh and raw as the gunshot that exploded in Barish's chest. Aiden helped me to my feet, then wrapped his arms around my trembling body, pulling me against him as though I might fall through the ground itself.

"What happened?" he whispered into my ear.

I stifled a sob deep against his shoulder. "The Magistrate is dead," was all I could whisper. As Aiden's arms gripped me against his chest even tighter, I could feel the cold spasm of fear run through his body.

Chapter 22

Hundreds of stunned faces stared at me from outside the circle of guards and sub-Prelates that separated the crowd from us; their questioning eyes bored into mine, smothering me, suffocating me. I felt as though the massive walls were closing in on all of us, that the ceiling might collapse at any moment, trapping us in that airless space. I squeezed my eyes shut, wrapping my arms around Aiden as tightly as I could, forcing my mind to believe that it was just the two of us, that everyone else had disappeared.

Barish's final instructions were for me to somehow get to his office and retrieve his things, that I would find the information I needed there – whatever that was supposed to be. But as I stood in that underground stadium, frozen by the paralyzing grip of a panic attack, all I could think about were the broken shards of glass cutting into the soles of my bare feet; the thousands of unblinking eyes, like a towering grove of aspen trees, that were glued to me; the frightened circle of guards and sub-Prelates that regarded my wild demeanor with incomprehension and unease.

Rowan, a voice whispered in my head. I stifled a gasp.

"Prophet," Kaylie said softly, cautiously approaching me as though I were some crazed, wild animal. "We've alerted our medical team. They and the Inner Circle are on their way. Is there anything…"

I'm here, Rowan. I'm in the stadium. Don't look around, it's okay. Just know that I'm here. Ted and I came as soon as we heard the news of your Christening. But I'm not supposed to be here, so it's best that you don't draw attention to that fact.

Mom! I cried out silently, fresh tears pouring down my face. *They killed Barish! He's dead – I was there, in his mind, when they did it! I don't—*

Show me, she instructed. *Show me the memory.*

Unable to explain, unable to even comprehend, I did my best to bring the scene to my mind, like a movie clip, showing her the parts that mattered, the parts I couldn't let myself forget…

"Prophet?" One of Barish's guards, the man in the blue sash, was addressing me this time. I felt Aiden's arms tighten around me as he came to stand beside me. "Prophet?" he whispered again, his voice dropping so low, only Aiden and I could hear him. I stared at the guard, seeing two figures in my head at once: Keres' contorted face overlapped his, twisted with emotion as she pulled the trigger of her gun.

Oh Rowan, my mother's voice wept in my head. *We can't let her find out that you know.*

"Prophet, my name is Stefan. The Magistrate has asked my team to escort you wherever you need to go," the guard murmured, the tone of his voice conveying a deeper meaning than his words. "Is there anywhere you feel you must go right now?"

"Escort my mother and her friend to the Magistrate's office," I whispered hurriedly. "Give them time to find whatever they need, then take them to a safe place. Don't leave their side for any reason."

I see the guard's face in your mind – I'll find him, my mother said, quickly understanding.

"Indeed, Prophet," he replied. "After that, we'll await your further instruction."

"Your mother?" Aiden asked, alarmed. "What...?"

Stall them just long enough to let us get Barish's things, Rosebud, then leave, as fast as you can, without looking suspicious. Tell them it was the alcohol, exhaustion, whatever you need to say. But you must hide your emotions so Keres and the other Electromancers don't sense anything.

I watched Stefan motion for the rest of his team to follow him, holding my breath as they made their way through the crowd to find my mother.

"Aspen?" Aiden said again. "Please, tell me – what's going on?"

I see them, sweetheart. We'll meet you in a safe place. I won't be able to speak to you this way for much longer. Everything's going to be okay... I love you.

As her voice trailed away, I took a deep breath, filling my lungs with as much air as I could. That's when my eyes finally locked on my friends, who were standing inside the circle of guards, watching me with frightened looks on their faces; Eileen's was smeared with tears, Ori's arms were crossed tightly over his chest, and Sophia was staring up at the balcony above, where the wide double doors had just swung open.

The Inner Circle had arrived.

Even as a sickening sense of dread washed over me, the sight of my friends snapped me out of my lingering shock, reminded me that there were other people to protect, people who were now vulnerable. As the crowd turned towards the wide shaft of light emitting from the grand balcony, I concentrated on my friends, felt for their familiar energies, for the special electrical signature they each emitted.

Can you hear me? I thought anxiously. I'd only ever practiced telepathy with my mother and Barish, two of the most powerful Electromancers I'd ever known. I had no idea whether I would be able to Electromantically transmit my thoughts to anyone other than Ori, and I certainly had never tried transmitting to a group of people all at once.

Aiden gasped softly. "That voice – was that *you*?" he whispered. I nodded, focusing all my concentration on reaching the others. I felt the flows of charged ions being emitted from their minds; billions of electrically conductive, biological wires that hummed with the energy of their souls. Their auras each resonated differently, uniquely, but if I could just focus my own electrical currents at just the right resonance...

Guys? I tried again. *Please – can you hear me?* Ori was the first to turn and gape at me, but Eileen and Sophia were only a moment behind him, whipping their heads in my direction with equally-startled expressions.

The Prelates approached the edge of the balcony, their cloaked silhouettes blocking out the light from the open doorway behind them. As the doors swung shut, I was able to make out Keres's illuminated face in the center of them, visibly distraught.

I don't have much time, please listen carefully, I thought, the familiar throb of a migraine creeping into my skull. *Keres just killed the Magistrate – I witnessed it with my own eyes.*

Sophia's hands flew to her mouth, just as Eileen let out a startled gasp.

"He's… dead?" Ori asked, his eyes flitting between me and the gathering above.

"Guards!" Keres shouted, "Seal the exits! Sub-Prelates – Code Epsilon!" In a flurry of movement, a dozen guards raced for the doors while two dozen sub-Prelates pushed their way through the crowd, heading for the area where my friends and I stood beneath the grand balcony.

She's been working behind the scenes with Terry and Jahi to overthrow him. They had a confrontation tonight. When Barish told her she didn't have the votes to depose him, she shot him.

Aiden gripped my arms tightly. "You saw this? How?"

Sophia narrowed her eyes. "Jahi told me he would soon be the most powerful man in the world... Now I understand why."

"The Magistrate has been murdered!" Keres cried, clutching the edge of the balcony. "Killed in cold blood by a coward!" Cries and shouts erupted from the arena floor as she held a red-glinting pistol in the air. "We found *this* beside his body – steeped in our Magistrate's own blood!"

"Aspen," Eileen whispered urgently. "The sub-Prelates – we're surrounded!"

My head whipped around, causing me to stagger from a rolling wave of nausea. She was right. Two rows of sub-Prelates encircled the five of us, facing us with their shoulders pressed together so that there was no way to escape. Faces young and old – some still strangers, but many of whom I knew by name – stared me down, trepidation and anger plain on their faces.

A cold shudder of realization suddenly gripped me by the back of my neck.

"She's going to pin Barish's murder on me," I whispered, feeling the blood draining from my face.

Chapter 23

"**S**ub-Prelates!" Keres cried, pointing a finger in my direction. "Keep the Pentamancer surrounded at all costs! Attack any offender who dares approach your barricade!"

The rest of the Elementalists in the arena took a hurried step away from our circle of captors, exchanging frightened glances and murmurs with one another as they did. The atmosphere of the room, only moments ago an exuberant, intoxicated party, was now staunched in terror and confusion.

"What are we going to do?" Eileen whimpered, grabbing my arm.

"There's no way she'd try to frame Aspen," Ori whispered, watching Keres closely. "That would be political suicide. She has to know that."

I pressed my fingers against my temples, doing my best to ward off the migraine I'd inadvertently triggered. With all the energy I'd expended that night, I'd drained myself almost completely of resources. It took everything I had to remain standing, even with Aiden supporting me; if the sub-Prelates did attack us in that moment, I wouldn't be able to put up much of a fight.

"Did you really think that you could step into *our* earthly house, take advantage of the munificence we've bestowed upon you?" Keres practically hissed, leaning over the edge of the balcony. The arena had fallen completely silent, necks craning around one another to find the recipient of her wrath. "Did you honestly think you'd get away with it – that we, the almighty Inner Circle, wouldn't find you?"

Beside me, I caught a glint of silver as Aiden pulled his lighter from his pocket.

Don't, I thought feebly, unsure whether he could even hear me. *Please… you can't get hurt. You just can't.*

"Traitor!" Keres shouted, pointing in my direction. "You are hereby charged with murder, for the assassination of our beloved Magistrate, which you indisputably committed in cold blood, and with premeditated intent!"

No! I wanted to shout, but the words that slipped through my dry lips were barely a whisper. As I looked around me, frantically searching for an exit we might be able to flee to, I realized that everyone in that room was staring – not at me, but *past* me.

"Oh my god," Aiden whispered, looking over my shoulder as a dozen guards dragged a disheveled man across the floor of the arena. The crowd parted for him, buzzing with hushed gasps and scandalized whispers.

"Terry Lawson!" Keres cried, pointing her finger at the man. My hand flew to my mouth. Terry's normally slicked-back hair was wild and unkempt, and he no longer wore his ceremonial robes; instead, his dress shirt had been torn open, the white fabric splattered with blood.

"You were witnessed, by myself and three other Prelates, sneaking away from the Inner Sanctum moments after a gunshot had sounded there. Furthermore, upon immediate inspection, the Magistrate's blood was found on your robes!" A handful of sharp gasps erupted from the crowd – from several of the sub-Prelates, even. "Since no one else was near the vicinity of the Sanctum at the time of the gunshot, there is no doubt in anyone's mind that *you* are responsible for his murder!"

Confused murmurs gave way to angry cries and shouts as the crowd took in Keres' shocking accusation. Terry, his arms forced and bound behind his back by two guards, scowled up at the balcony. His face was flushed, the beginnings of a bruise appeared as a purple shadow beneath his eye; the throbbing vein in his temple was visible even from where I was standing.

"Aspen," Eileen whispered, "you said—"

"I know what I said," I replied, attempting to swallow the bitter taste of bile filling my mouth. "And I'm sure of what I saw."

"Then that means…"

"By the power vested in me by our former Magistrate, as penned in his hand and notarized in his personal Register, I, Keres Galanis, Chief Prelate and now Regent Magistrate, sentence you, *ex*-Prelate Terry, to be Contained in isolation, until sunset tomorrow night, where you shall be subject to Electromantic Electrocution until your life energy has been drained in its entirety – just as you have drained the life from our beloved Magistrate!"

As the crowd once more erupted into rancorous shouts, Terry tried to wrestle away from his captors, spit flying from between his clenched teeth as he snarled in anger. He opened his mouth as if to yell, but Keres cut him off.

"Bind the Pyromancer with Water!" she shouted. "Let him drown if he continues to resist!" One of the Hydromantic guards splashed a container of Water in Terry's face; it spread across the lower part of his face like a surgical mask, covering his mouth and nose with liquid. He twisted his head, writhing and coughing as he tried to shake it off, but the water remained affixed to his face.

"Stop!" Aiden yelled, attempting to push through the line of sub-Prelates.

Sophia grabbed his arm before I could. "Don't," she whispered hurriedly. "Your father won't drown – it's just a gag. There's an air pocket around his nose."

"I can't just stand here and watch!" he snapped, shaking her arm off.

"We can't win," Ori hissed, pulling him back by the shoulder. "Not now. Not like this." Aiden let out a strangled cry, raking his fingers through his hair.

I have to help! The thought pierced the dense fog of shock and exhaustion scrambling my brain.

"Remove the traitor from this place, and take his conspirators with him!" Keres shouted. It was only then that I'd noticed that Terry's three new apprentices had also been Hydromantically bound and gagged, restrained in a far corner of the arena by another team of guards. As the four men were shoved from the room against the clamor of angry shouts and jeers, Terry took one last look over his shoulder to glower at Keres; but as his eyes fell on his son, they immediately softened. Aiden pressed himself against the line of sub-Prelates, frozen as a marble statue as the guards ushered his father from the arena.

Speak up! You have to say something! I screamed at myself, but even as I scoured my muddled mind for the right words, I knew it was no use. My body had been in the arena during the entire time in question; not a single eye had left me that night, particularly when I began convulsing on the floor, shattering every light in the ceiling in what probably looked like an epileptic fit. How could I begin to explain what I had witnessed, as seen through the eyes of a dead man? How could I hope that anyone in that room would ever believe such a baseless claim? I didn't even know if Barish's trick – Electromantically hijacking another person's consciousness – had ever been done before.

"Brothers and sisters," Keres said, her narrow shoulders appearing to slump with despondency, "it is with the heaviest of hearts that I must apologize for such a distressing interruption to your festivities, to the celebration we conceived to honor the most incredible Elementalist of our time…" When her pale eyes fell on me, it suddenly felt as though all the air in my lungs had been siphoned out. "The woman our dear Magistrate has been fostering and mentoring under his wing." Fuzzy halos appeared across my already-blurry vision; they spun around the colorful flames on the walls, synchronously pulsing with the throb of my racing heart.

"Rowan, my dear, treasured child... you are safe now. Though my heart is shattered with grief over the merciless, untimely loss of our cherished Magistrate, I can at least take some small comfort that you were not harmed tonight."

I stared at her dumbly as the sub-Prelates loosened their protective barrier around us – as though the threat from the room was actually gone.

"...And as I humbly, hesitantly take my oath as Magistrate tomorrow evening, once my master's killer is dead, I ask that you, Prophet, stand beside me, so that together we may lift this broken Community from its bruised and weary knees, and raise it up, the way Barish would have wanted – with you, as our shining, devoted beacon of light." Tears spilled over Keres' cheeks as she held out her hand to me, quivering and outstretched over the ledge of the grand balcony.

I floundered for a moment, my eyes darting from her to the other Prelates, several of whom looked weary, uncomfortable... even frightened. All around me, the Elementalists in that room watched me, their expressions reflecting the uncertainty I knew they felt. My friends, too, regarded me with an apprehension that settled heavily on their drooping shoulders. Perhaps my own dread and grief was clouding my perception of their feelings; but in that moment, with Barish dead and yet another life on the line – the father of the man I loved – all I could feel was the crushing weight of loss and defeat. I was no Prophet, no hero of legends, and certainly no savior to these people. I was an imposter, someone who had been born with talents she didn't deserve; talents that should have gone to someone smarter, more charismatic, more cunning.

You must burn down the Order and rebuild it from the ashes, Barish had said to me, knowing his final breath was coming. Did he really think that I would be able to lead his revolution? Or was it simply the last, desperate wish of a man who knew his own death was imminent?

I looked up at Keres then, knowing that she was shielding her true thoughts from me, immeasurably grateful that she couldn't hear mine.

"I'll stand with you," I replied, doing my best not to let my voice shake. As a wide smile spread across her face, the arena erupted into riotous applause.

"Long live the Pentamancer! Long live the Magistrate!" the cheer reemerged, significantly less spirited than it had been while Barish and I stood side-by-side in the arena, but vigorous nonetheless. I could feel my friends' eyes on me, but I kept my gaze firmly locked on the glass-strewn ground.

I hope you knew what you were doing, Barish, I thought, massaging my temples. *Because I, for one, haven't the faintest idea.*

Chapter 24

From the balcony windows of our hotel suite, Aiden and I gazed across the square as the sun rose behind the darkened silhouette of the Hagia Sophia, its colossal dome and four needle-like spires towering against the crimson morning sky. Somewhere, many hundreds of feet below its glittering fountains and flowering gardens, Aiden's father was being held prisoner in a Fire-proof cell, waiting for certain death. Behind us, Ted and my mother were sitting at the writing desk, poring over the thick, gold-embossed tome that they had 'borrowed' from Barish's curio cabinet. Eileen, Sophia, and Ori were perusing his black leather-bound journal, which was filled with pages and pages of the Magistrate's own hand-written notes and entries. Propped up on the mini fridge was Ted's laptop, where Evelyn – wrapped in a pink bathrobe – and a sleepy-looking Robert had joined us via Skype.

"Even using your security clearance, Ted, I can't find anything in the online Asterian archives regarding Magisterial succession," Robert muttered, adjusting his spectacles. By the reflection in his lenses, I could see he was scrolling through pages and pages of documents. Evelyn sat beside him, worrying at a hangnail. She had been unusually quiet for the last hour.

"I'm not surprised," Ted replied, his nose inches from the dusty pages he and my mother had been scanning for the better part of the night. "I doubt even Class-Three Officers have any insight into the inner workings of the Asterian high command. It seems like that sort of information is reserved solely for the Inner and Extended Circle members."

"I'm sure we can find that information in here," my mother said, running her finger along the bottom of a page. "The Compendium has just about everything else about the Asterians – laws, manifestos, past and current members… even its full history, dating back to Late Antiquity. If only someone had thought to put a table of contents in a two-thousand-page book," she added, stifling a yawn.

"Ori, have you guys found anything about this so-called 'Electromantic hijacking' in that notebook?" Ted asked, glancing across the room at the others. They were all sprawled across a Victorian sofa on the far wall of the hotel room, with Barish's journal splayed open on the middle cushion.

"Nothing," Ori replied, dangling his legs off the armrest. "This is like a diary of sorts – there's some really interesting stuff – even a few juicy details about his various love interests throughout the years – but we haven't found a lot regarding his specific abilities… Although, get this," he added, pointing to a page at the front of the book. "The first entry in here was dated November 25, 1928. Nineteen-*twenty-eight*!" he scoffed. "So, it can't have just belonged to Barish…"

"But the handwriting hasn't changed from the first entry to the last," Sophia pointed out. "Look – see how he flourishes the last letter of each word? That's been consistent throughout the journal."

"That's because the book *was* written in its entirety by Barish," my mom answered, her eyes still scanning her own pages. "Barish was one hundred and ten years old when he passed away last night."

Eileen made a snorting sound. "There's no way!" she scoffed. "I mean, I've never seen the man super up close, but I did see him from fifty feet away, and he didn't look a day over sixty."

"He told me himself, many years ago…" my mother replied. It took her a moment to notice the odd stares her comment had elicited, but when she did, she added, "There was once a time when Barish and I were fairly close. He was interested in my abilities, so he would take me aside sometimes during our trainings and chat about various Electromantic concepts he had read about. It certainly wasn't something Keres or the others appreciated."

Aiden and I exchanged pointed glances before I took a step away from the window. "Mom – what are you talking about?"

Still bent over the tome, my mother kept her eyes glued to its yellowed pages. "Many years ago, when you had just started preschool in the D.C. Chapter, I received a formal invitation to audition for the Extended Circle. Keres, who's a few years younger than me, had also received an invite. One of the Prelates was on his deathbed, and his chosen successor – an extremely powerful Electromancer named Victoria – was gathering a small group of us to audition to be her sub-Prelates."

"You were in the Extended Circle?" I gaped.

"Well, I was invited to be, yes. But I ultimately rejected Victoria's offer – something that earned me a fair share of criticism and ridicule from my colleagues – and Keres was chosen in my place. When Victoria passed away several years later – under suspicious circumstances, I might add – Keres became her successor."

"Yeah, even back then, we all thought it was a little odd for an otherwise-healthy, fifty-year-old woman to suddenly die of a heart attack," Ted muttered.

"Why didn't you tell me?" I asked. "With everything going on, you didn't think that that might have been a relevant piece of information?"

My mother gave me a wistful smile. "Would it have made a difference? Impacted your decision to take Aiden's place in any way?"

I stared at a piece of fuzz that was stuck to the bottom of my t-shirt, unsure how to answer. (Apart from requesting two grilled cheese sandwiches from the hotel's room service at 3:00 a.m., the first thing I'd done once the guards had escorted us back to the room was throw my wild hair up into a knot and change out of that clingy gown.)

"Right, I didn't think so," my mother chuckled. "But the point is, there was a time that I was considering Victoria's offer, and during those few weeks in particular, I got to know the Magistrate quite well. He truly is – or rather, *was* – one hundred and ten years old. His unique combination of powers – Electromancy, Hydromancy, and Auromancy – allowed him to manipulate his own body in such a way that he was able to ward off the effects of time. He told me once that it was his goal to live to be three-hundred years old – longer than any other Elementalist by a hundred years."

"That's... remarkable," Aiden said from beside me. It was the first full sentence he'd uttered in more than an hour.

"How did he do it?" Sophia asked. "Hypothetically, could you or I attempt the same, since we're both Level-three Auromancers? I know you're also a brilliant Electromancer, and I'm a fairly-skilled Hydromancer..."

"'Fairly skilled'," Eileen chuckled. "*That's* the understatement of the year."

My mother shook her head. "It was Barish's specific Polymantic abilities that allowed him to do it. Only he knows the exact science behind it, but it's my understanding that he was able to use Auromancy and Electromancy to reduce oxidation inside his body—"

"Oxidation?" Ori repeated. "Isn't that what happens to metal when it rusts?"

"It is," Robert chimed in from the tablet. "But it's also the process in our bodies that's directly responsible for aging. Humans, by nature, constantly utilize oxygen in various cellular processes, however a negative side effect of that is the introduction of oxygen free radicals to the body. Now, a free radical is a molecule that has lost an electron from one or more of its atoms—"

Evelyn put a gentle hand over his mouth. "Be quiet, dear, and let Lizzie finish."

The corners of Mom's mouth twitched. "Robert is right, of course. And that's where Electromancy would come in, as Barish would have to address all of those unstable electrons floating around his body. I can't even begin to wrap my head around the complexity of that process... And that's not taking into account the other Electromantic methods he would have to employ to ward off cognitive and neurogenic diseases, not to mention figuring out a way to sort through all of those memories he would be accumulating over the decades..."

"It looks like he jotted a lot of random memories down in this journal," Ori interjected. "Random stuff – people's names, little interactions he had throughout the day, letters to people. Maybe that's why? So he could clear out all the nonessential clutter from his mind?"

"Seems perfectly plausible to me."

"Theoretically, he could have used Hydromancy to clean his blood and remove any unwanted pathogens and toxins," Sophia mused.

"What – like Hydromantic dialysis?" Eileen asked incredulously. "When did the man have time to do all of this? Is there a Polymantic day spa somewhere out there?"

"Since Aspen's a Pentamancer, could she hypothetically live forever?" Ori mused.

From the corner of my eye, I noticed that Aiden had collapsed into the armchair beside the window, rubbing his eyes with the heels of his hands. It reminded me of how tired I was, having gone two nights in a row with almost no sleep. As my mother and the others continued to marvel over Barish's unnaturally long years and ruminate over life and mortality in general, I felt myself growing impatient.

"Look, as fascinating as all of this is, I think we're losing sight of the real problem at hand, which is the fact that we have less than twelve hours before an innocent man gets electrocuted—"

"'Innocent'?" Ted remarked, causing Aiden to jerk his head in his direction. "Remind me again how Terry Lawson is an *innocent* man?"

"Sorry?" Aiden asked, narrowing his eyes. "Haven't we already established his innocence, thanks to Aspen's own account of *Keres* being the actual murderer?"

Ted waved a dismissive hand. "Oh, sure, we know Terry didn't kill Barish, but he certainly didn't try to save him either. And what about Aspen's father, David? Or my daughter, Jenny? I'm pretty sure he had, at *best*, an indirect hand in their deaths."

"Ted…" my mother warned.

"I'm just saying, do we really have to risk our own necks for a guy who frankly has had it coming for years?"

"Ted!" my mother snapped, her voice rising. "That's enough!"

Aiden's eyes grew dark. "Those are some pretty high and mighty words, coming from a guy who's been sleeping with his best friend's wife."

Horrified, I whipped around to stare at him. At the same time, Ted slammed his fist on the desk, an angry retort ready to fly from his lips.

"Stop it – both of you!" I shouted, causing the light on the nightstand to burst. The two of them stared at one another coldly, but said nothing more.

The lock on the door clicked and opened, and Stefan, the chief of the Magisterial Guard, stuck his head in the door. "Prophet – is everything all right in here?"

"Yes," I replied tersely. "Everything is fine, Stefan, thank you." He gave me a solemn nod as he closed the door once more.

Even before the door had clicked shut behind him, a terrible silence had fallen upon the room. Ted was still clutching his hand in a fist on the desk, while Aiden stared at his own hands, which were visibly shaking. Arms crossed tightly across my chest, I chewed on the inside of my lip angrily, stopping only after I vaguely registered the taste of blood.

Evelyn was the first to speak up. "Ted hasn't been doing anything untoward with Elizabeth. He's been... helping her. With research." My eyes raised to the tablet, where she sat beside Robert, wringing a handkerchief.

"Helping her?" I asked, my eyes trailing to my mother. "What research?"

"It's not important now," Evelyn interjected. "What's important right now is this: Aiden's father, whether we're all crazy about him or not, is being charged with a murder he didn't commit. And Aspen, due to her extremely overdeveloped sense of justice—" she gave me a pointed look, "—is stuck playing 'bosom buddies' with a deranged psychopath. *These* are the primary issues at hand. Nothing else matters until Terry is exonerated, and, more importantly, this nutter-butter of a woman is put behind bars, where she belongs!"

"Hear hear!" Robert said, giving Evelyn a kiss on her pale cheek.

"Yeah... Evelyn's right," Ted said, flexing his fingers as he unclenched them.

"I'm always right," Evelyn replied crisply. "Now… what exactly do we need to do in order to make these two things happen?"

Even without looking, I could feel my friends' eyes on me.

"I have to tell everyone the truth about what I saw," I replied, my stomach sinking to my feet. "And pray they'll believe me."

"You don't have to do that, Aspen," Aiden said, rising to his feet. He walked over and gently kissed my forehead, his dark eyes burning into mine as he spoke. "Regardless of my father's innocence in this situation, Ted *is* right about one thing. You don't owe him anything."

"And speaking out against Keres will be a *very* risky move," my mother added. "She could do to you what she did to Terry – accuse you of treason."

"Did you see the way that arena reacted to Aspen last night?" Eileen spoke up. "They loved her. There were people actually *weeping* in our balcony at the end of the night. Since my mom's immobile, I sent her and my dad a video of Aspen's Christening and now *she's* dropping words like 'prophet' and 'savior' – my *mother*! The militant atheist, for those of you who haven't had the privilege of suffering through one of her sacrilegious harangues. So, no. There's no way they'd just stand and watch while Keres pulled a stunt like that. No way."

"Not to mention that Aspen will be surrounded by Electromancers when she tells everyone the truth," Ori replied. "And some of them will be Empathically-inclined, like her and Elizabeth. They'll vouch for her when they hear the truth in her words." My mother nodded in agreement.

I rubbed my forehead with my palms. "But what if they think I'm just using my abilities to manipulate everyone? Barish told me that certain Electromancers can make a lie sound like the truth – even to other Empathic Electromancers. They might accuse me of doing just that."

"Wait – wasn't Barish an Electromancer?" Ori asked, eliciting nods from around the room. "So then, isn't that a, uh, what do you call it… A paragon?"

"A paradox," Robert, Aiden, and Eileen all replied at the same time.

"Yeah, right – so, how do we know Barish, the most powerful Electromancer in the world, wasn't lying to Aspen the whole time?"

I stiffened at Ori's words. *Of course.* The calm feelings that would wash over me whenever Barish said something that was meant to be reassuring, the constant headaches – which would often flare up after spending any significant amount of time with him. That's why the migraines continued to linger long after my mother had restored my memories. *That's* why Barish was able to cure me of them so easily... because he knew exactly why I was having them.

"He *has* been lying to me this whole time," I muttered, sinking onto the edge of the gigantic, king-size canopy bed, which somehow only took up a small portion of the suite. "Telling me exactly what I've been wanting to hear in order to keep me happy and compliant. Keres accused him of doing it just last night, and she's planning to do more of the same. Because, apparently, I'm everyone's favorite puppet."

"I don't think so, Aspen," Sophia said, frowning at a page near the back of Barish's journal. "Or, at the very least, there was a lot more to your relationship with the Magistrate than that. Here, take a look at this."

Sighing, I pushed myself off the edge of the bed, then awkwardly maneuvered around the pile of mismatched luggage that had been dumped in the middle of the room. I leaned over Sophia's shoulder to read the entry she was pointing to, which was dated August 6, 2000:

Elizabeth and David Fulman have fled the Order, along with their daughter, Rowan.

I let out a small gasp.

"What is it?" my mom asked.

"It's an entry from eighteen years ago, the same day you and dad abandoned your posts. He mentioned all of us by name... And here's another entry, just below it – it's dated a week later," I said, reading the entry out loud so everyone could hear.

The Fulmans have settled into their new home in Sacramento, with the help of Ted Nichols (S&C Officer-I), father of Jenny Nichols (age 5), a non-Elementalist that was born from an unsanctioned sexual relationship with Luanne Bates (also N/E).

Ted pushed his chair away from the desk. "What the hell? He knew about that?"

"It would appear so," my mom replied. "What else does the entry say, Rosebud?"

"He has our old address from California scrawled in the margin," I marveled, running my finger over the faded ink. Aiden walked over and wrapped his arms around me from behind, gently kissing my temple as I read on.

My informants in the Washington, D.C. division tell me that a massive search is well underway, given the Fulmans' Class-III security clearances. But I also have reason to believe that some of the officers there are beginning to suspect what I already know – that their child,

Rowan, is a Pentamancer. There is an unprecedented sense of urgency among the D.C. officials that troubles me, as desperation can often lead to tragedy.

He knew, I thought, staring at the faded pages in my hands. *He knew about me the whole time.* The revelation left me feeling dizzy. Aiden tightened his embrace around my shoulders as the journal began to quiver in my hands.

"No way," Ori muttered. "So he just kept their location a secret while the rest of his officers were going nuts trying to find them?"

"Shh, let her finish!" Eileen snapped. She chewed at her thumbnail impatiently, her green eyes glued to the book I held.

I took a shaky breath, leaning against Aiden as I read the remainder of the entry aloud:

For this reason, I'm quite glad – for the moment, at least – that the Fulmans have opted to leave the Order. Had they stayed, their child's abilities, as well as the advantageousness of those abilities, would have been left to the unenlightened masses to interpret and exploit. But, under the vigilant training of her parents and godfather, each masters of their Elements in their own rights, she'll flourish, concealed from the world until I'm ready to introduce her to it. Perhaps then, in another decade or so, the Community will be ready for my vision. Until that time,

I intend to shield the child's family from the ongoing search, using my informants to proliferate false leads and misinformation. My faithful eyes and ears will be on young Rowan at all times, ensuring she remains unseen by anyone who seeks to find her.

Perhaps it is the foible of this old, sentimental heart of mine, but I cannot help but wonder if this is kismet – a divine intervention of sorts. Still, be it folly or design, I thank Providence for allowing me this one final chance to be a father.

Chapter 25

ven before I knew what I was, he knew.

Long after the others had abandoned puzzling out the significance of Barish's words, when they had turned their attentions back to scouring the pages of the Asterian Compendium for answers instead of attempting to decrypt a dead man's hypothetical motives, I continued to pore over the pages of his journal. When the sun had burned away the morning clouds, arcing across the early afternoon sky, I vaguely registered that someone had placed a grilled cheese sandwich beside me. By then, the others appeared to have set aside the ancient tome, opting instead to examine all the manners in which the night could go right or wrong – concocting plans, backup plans, and backup-backup plans. Still, I remained tucked into the wide armchair in the corner, skimming through every entry of Barish's notebook from the turn of the millennium through my early childhood. What precisely I was looking for, I couldn't say. But there was a reason he wanted me to read that journal, and with nothing and nobody else to point me in the right direction, it was the only tool I had at my disposal as the sun crept closer and closer to the western horizon.

It was evident that Barish had been watching me over the years, even grooming me, as he indirectly made sure that I had the proper knowledge and guidance to become the most powerful version of myself. By the Magistrate's ubiquitous hand, Ted just happened to receive extra rounds of training with the best coaches available, along with special Pyromantic and Terramantic tips and advice – the hidden objective being that he would then pass that knowledge down to me. Barish even had his insiders put Ted on the mailing lists that were specially-intended for other Elementalists as well; while my father's best friend probably never understood why he was receiving brochures on cutting-edge Electromantic techniques, he certainly never complained about it when he forwarded the information along to my mother, who then imparted it to me. In the end, it was all to benefit me, by way of my guardians, who otherwise would have been cut off from the Elemental masters of the Asterian Order. Barish even wrote about how he would secretly watch us from time to time, when I would train with my mother and father as a teenager; how – by way of Electromancy – he'd subtly plant ideas in their heads about coaching me, strengthening me, all without them ever knowing that the ideas were originally his.

The journal sickened me and angered me and all at once captivated me; the Magistrate had been part of my life for my entire life, without me or anyone else ever knowing that I was to be his tool, his progeny, his greatest triumph. His written words left me with more questions than anything else, but his death ensured that most of them would go unanswered. As I turned the page to find yet another entry with my name in it, I gritted my teeth, both eager and reluctant to read it.

June 22, 2008

There was a time when Pentamancers roamed the Earth – never in large numbers, and never without their share of infamy and acclaim (whether it was deserved or not). Still, throughout most of recorded history, one was born in nearly every generation. I, along with scores of Asterian scholars, have long pondered their abrupt disappearance so many years ago. Was it due to eugenics, as Elementalists became more and more inclined to choose similarly-abled Elementalists as mates? With the bourgeoning notion that strength and purity of Elemental blood was to be held above all else, why take the chance of producing a weak child when anecdotal evidence had, at times, shown that two powerful Hydromancers bred equally (or even more) powerful Hydromantic offspring?

Several scientists in the Community have pointed to this, stating that selective Elemental 'inbreeding' could perhaps be the cause for the disappearance of Pentamancers. Rowan's lineage is certainly a powerful testament to this hypothesis; her grandfather was a great Pyromancer, her late grandmother was a formidable Terramancer. Remarkably, they gave birth to an extraordinary Hydromancer – who then married a veritable master of Lightning and Wind. Truly, Elizabeth Fulman rivals even me in her abilities (if only Providence had seen it fit to keep her at my side – but I digress).

And yet, as my favorite Hydromantic poet would say, 'here's the rub': the most powerful Elementalists in the world have also been known to produce Deficients – a phenomenon I myself am all too familiar with. So, I must ask myself yet again: was it the perfect combination of genetics that brought this Pentamancer into the world, or something else? Is young Rowan an anomaly, or merely the first of more Pentamancers to come? And if she is indeed one of a kind – in a decidedly post-Pentamantic age – what is the reason for her coming? If not an aberration of nature, am I forced to concede that the religious philosophers are indeed correct? Is she one of the so-called Prophets the legends speak of? The harbinger of revolution? Of transformation? Of end times?

Regardless – be her existence destiny or chance – I believe with my very essence that she will be of great importance... Both to me, and to our world.

***

I felt Aiden's lips brush across my forehead. "Hey there," he smiled. "The others just left so they could clean up and sneak in a short rest before this evening."

"They did?" I blinked, looking around the otherwise empty room.

Aiden chuckled. "They didn't want to disturb your reading by saying goodbye, but I for one have no qualms about convincing you to take a break." He held out a hand, which I gratefully accepted. I carefully set Barish's journal on the armrest as I stood.

"What time is it?" I asked, knuckling my lower back with my free hand.

"Four-thirty," he replied.

I started. "Four thirty? That means sunset is—"

"In four hours."

I stared at him dumbly; Barish's journal hadn't told me anything about what was to come, and Terry's execution was only hours away. My hands felt hot and clammy as the familiar tendrils of trepidation and dread crept back into my chest.

"Hey, it's going to be okay," Aiden said, tilting my chin to kiss me. "Your mother is going to say that she witnessed Barish's death, through his eyes. It's not even a lie, since you showed her the memory."

"But—"

Aiden held up a hand. "And Ted found something in that other book about the actual process of deposing a seated Magistrate. In addition to nabbing Keres with a murder charge, we're going call into question the legitimacy of her claim. Even if she is telling the truth about Barish naming her as his successor – and we don't necessarily believe that – it doesn't matter. The Inner Circle, according to their own Compendium of laws, has to *vote* a new Magistrate into power. In the case that the incumbent Magistrate lives, a five-to-four vote is needed from the Prelates just to accept the Magistrate's nominee. In a case like this, where the incumbent Magistrate passes before a vote can be taken, a seven-to-two majority is required. In the case that a seven-two split can't be reached, the Extended Circle must also cast their votes."

"I don't understand," I said, sitting down on the bed. "If that's the case, why didn't anyone call Keres out? Why are they allowing her to blatantly disregard these laws if they're so plainly spelled out?"

"Barish has been in power for fifty years," Aiden said, sitting beside me. "So it's possible that it's slipped their minds. But I think the more realistic explanation is that she's bribing or blackmailing the other Prelates into compliance. Regardless of what she's doing behind closed doors, we're going to draw attention to the actual laws in front of a coliseum full of witnesses. Let's see her try to bribe her way out of that."

"I can't let my mother go up against Keres," I said, leaning against the mountain of pillows that had been stacked against the headboard, untouched since yesterday.

Aiden pulled me into an embrace, and together we lay atop the plush pillows, my bare legs intertwined in his. I traced an idle finger along the buttons of Aiden's burgundy shirt; he was still wearing his dress clothes from last night.

He stroked my hair gently, quiet for a long moment. "She's an amazing woman, your mother. I was frankly surprised that she volunteered to help him at all, after, well... everything." He cleared his throat.

I sighed. "She's doing it for us. For me. Time after time, she and my father have always put me first... Even when it's cost them everything."

A memory floated across my eyes, one of Dad shielding me, maybe seven years old, from the neighbor's rottweiler. The massive black dog had jumped the low fence between our yards and was bounding towards me with a foamy snarl. Wrapped in my father's embrace, I remembered how strangely calm I felt, how his bare skin felt warm and smelled of sunshine and chlorine. The dog's teeth would leave permanent marks in Dad's shoulder, but even as my mother rushed him to the hospital, he turned around in his seat to give me a reassuring smile.

It's okay, little Rosebud. I'll always be here to protect you.

Aiden bent down to kiss my forehead, snapping me out of my reverie. "Apart from helping us get the crowd's attention before they bring out my father, you don't have to do anything tonight, Aspen," he said, using the same reassuring tone my father had used that day in the car. "Once we get his name cleared, there's nothing to be done except go home. So please – let the Inner Circle deal with Keres. It's not your job or your burden to clean up their messes anymore." I could sense the tension in his voice, as though he were waiting for me to argue with him.

"Do you believe in destiny?" I asked, watching the growing shadows from the window slink across the floor.

"Destiny?" he repeated. "As in, our lives are written before we're even born?"

I nodded, closing my eyes as he ran his fingers through my hair.

"I think that 'destiny' is whatever we intend it to be. Some people aspire to greatness and so they become great; others are perfectly happy with comfort and mediocrity, and there's nothing wrong with that. But I do think that we face a series of choices in our lives – dozens of them, every day. It's what we do with those choices that determine who we're destined to become." I felt him cock his head to look at me. "Why do you ask?"

Eyes still closed, I breathed in the smell of his shirt – musky and sweet like a summer rainstorm.

"Growing up, my parents never read me any of the Pentamancer legends. Eileen and Robert have recently told me a few of them; Barish's journal touches on several stories as well. Every story, from ancient Greece to the Renaissance, revolves around the same cliché theme: that Pentamancers are the preordained heroes, the saviors – the 'Chosen Ones' of history."

"Well, Pentamancers have always been seen as harbingers of great things within the Community.

Historically, the greatest paradigm shifts have occurred alongside the appearance of a Pentamancer. That's why they consider you and your predecessors to be Prophets... It's probably also why Barish, and now Keres, are so keen on appearing closely aligned with you. Historically speaking, they know the masses will follow you."

I opened my eyes. "But where's the *merit* in any of that? I was born this way. And because of my abilities – which, by the way, I did nothing to earn – I've been characterized as this 'Chosen One' caricature. How does that make me qualified to lead anything? It's like saying, 'anyone who's born with six fingers or some other equally-rare condition should suddenly be granted hero status' – regardless of their character or accomplishments."

"Hmm." Aiden was quiet for a moment.

"So," I pressed, self-doubt and exhaustion fueling my prattle, "did 'destiny' pre-select me to be a Pentamancer based on my innate qualities, or am I just a freak of nature who everybody mistakenly assumes is worthy enough to follow?"

"Ahh, I understand now," Aiden chuckled, kissing my temple. "My brilliant, remarkable Pentamancer has been struck with Imposter Syndrome."

I propped myself up on an elbow to furrow my brows at him. "It's not imposter syndrome if you're actually an imposter. Which I think I may be."

"My love," he whispered softly, sending a wave of warmth throughout my body, "Whether it's self-fulfilling prophecy or truly prophetic, history has shown us, again and again, that Pentamancers have a way of shaking things up. And you, my lovely Aspen, are doing just that."

"But—"

"So many people see all the ugliness in the world and do nothing. But you are doing what you can, with the opportunities you've been granted, to fix it. Forget destiny, forget prophecy; do what you know to be right and nothing will stop you from greatness."

"And what if I fail?" I whispered.

"Then I'll be here to help you back to your feet." He tilted my chin to kiss me.

I returned his kiss, softly at first, but I was suddenly gripped with a growing urgency. Aiden's hand reached up to cradle the back of my head, pulling me deeper into the kiss. A small gasp escaped my lips as his tongue traced the tip of mine; the space between my thighs flushed with a simmering heat. With everything going on, I had to be crazy to have such a thing on my mind. But as I gazed in Aiden's eyes, I knew it wasn't just me.

"Make love to me?" I whispered softly, brushing a dark curl from his forehead.

Wordlessly, he rolled me on my back, his arm cradling my waist as though I might break at any moment. With a smooth tug, he lifted my shirt above my head, exposing my bare breasts to the shaft of late-afternoon sunlight spilling from the window. Aiden's soft, parted lips gently caressed mine while his other hand traced the length of my arm, draped across the pillow. As he intertwined his fingers with mine, clasping my hand above my head, he pressed his body against my hips. Though I was flushed with heat, my skin erupted in goosebumps as he bent to kiss my bottom lip, my ear, my throat...

"I love you, Aiden," I whispered against his ear.

"And I love you, Rowan," he replied, his lips tracing the side of my neck. "From the moment you tried to attack me with a frying pan, I've loved you." I closed my eyes and smiled, pulling him closer as his lips whispered soft kisses across my neck and breasts.

In all my life, I'd never had a man love me the way Aiden did that afternoon. If I could have captured and lived inside that beautiful moment forever, I would have. But the sun was setting, and soon enough, we both knew I'd have to face my destiny.

Chapter 26

*A*lone in my room once more, I sat in front of the illuminated vanity, raking my fingers through my long tangles of hair. Having shared a hot shower with Aiden, after which he excused himself to his own room to get ready, I was back in my usual black leggings and boots. The sleeves of my blue cotton shirt were unceremoniously hiked up to my elbows, and all the make-up had been scrubbed from my face; I didn't feel like playing dress-up anymore. As I eyed Barish's notebook – still resting on the armchair – in the reflection of the mirror, a knock sounded at the door.

"Come in," I called.

My mother poked her head in. "Mind if we join you for a moment?" she asked, carrying a laptop in her arms. Evelyn was on the screen.

"Please," I smiled. I rose to follow her to the couch, where she set the laptop down on her knees. "Hi Evelyn."

"Hi sweets," she said, her tight smile not quite reaching her eyes.

"What's wrong?" I asked, sitting down beside my mother.

"Nothing's wrong, per se," she answered, smoothing invisible wrinkles from her perfectly-ironed peach blouse. "We were just hoping to talk about a recent development…"

I swallowed. I could feel the distress lurking behind my mother's stoic demeanor. I glanced down at the laptop resting on her knees. From up close, the circles beneath Evelyn's eyes seemed much more obvious, the pallor of her cheeks whiter than I remembered.

"Has something happened to Terry?" I asked. "We still have a couple of hours, right?" I began to rise from my seat, but my mother put a hand on my arm.

"Terry's fine. The guards will escort us over there in a half hour or so. This is about something different," she said, taking a deep breath. "Rosebud, as Grandma Evie mentioned earlier, I've been doing some research with Ted. And we've recently gotten some help from your grandmother and Robert, as well."

"Okay?" I replied, though my tone made it sound more like a question.

"Back in D.C., you told me about reading your father's file – that it listed him as 'Presumed Deceased'. Do you remember that?"

For some reason, my pulse quickened. "Yes, of course. But if you're insinuating that there's something more to it, even Barish acknowledged that Dad was dead, so..." I tried to swallow the lump forming in my throat. "So... yeah," I finished lamely.

"Yes – Barish," she replied. "I'll come back to him in a moment." She took my hand in both of hers. "Rowan, ever since you told me about Dad's file, I've had a strange feeling about it. Why would they write 'presumed' dead? Wouldn't they know, definitively, whether he survived his interrogation or not? So, for several weeks now, Ted and I have been doing some digging. Though nothing we found proved to be substantive, we did learn that your father underwent Electromantic Shock Therapy, a brutal interrogation method that was supposed to have been outlawed in the middle ages. And while being subjected to something I can only describe as torture, your father attacked his interrogators – they all died as a result."

"Oh my god," I whispered. *Dad? My Dad, who didn't bother to hide his tears when he ran over a rabbit in the road?*

From the screen, Evelyn was staring down at her hands, which were tightly clasped in her lap... She knew something I didn't.

"I wasn't able to learn anything more about that day," my mom continued, "until last night. When Ted and I retrieved the books from Barish's office, a piece of paper fell out of his journal. At first, I didn't know what it was – it was just some numbers and the name of a hospital scrawled on a folded note. In the fuss of trying to get out of there unnoticed and back to your hotel safely, I didn't pay much attention to it. But when you read that entry earlier – the one that revealed that Barish had been watching and, in a way, protecting us for all those years – something in my mind clicked. They weren't numbers on that piece of paper – they were a date: February 9th, 2015. And the hospital that Barish wrote down is a Denver hospital. Robert and Evelyn confirmed that this afternoon."

By now, every hair on my body was standing up straight, and though the room wasn't remotely cold, goosebumps had washed over my entire body. I rubbed the back of my neck, trying to make them disappear.

My mother squeezed my trembling hand. "Evelyn and Robert called the hospital, asking if anyone named David Fulman had been admitted that day in February."

Evelyn's eyes finally met mine. "A man *was* brought in that night, sweets," she said softly. "A man matching your father's description. Except he had scarring all over his body when he was dropped off – Lizzie, what did they call it?"

"Lichtenberg scarring." My mother's eyes were red-rimmed. "Something one would only expect to see on a victim of a lightning strike – or in this case, Corporeal Electromancy."

"You can't be saying what I think you're saying," I whispered, my voice barely a rasp between my lips.

"The man – they've been referring to him as John Doe all this time – has been in a coma for three and a half years," Evelyn said, fresh tears falling freely from her cheeks. "When I asked the nurse who it was that dropped him off all those years ago, she told me that a woman claimed to have found him near some electrical lines, unconscious – her only guess was that he had been electrocuted."

My hands flew to my mouth. I knew Evelyn's next words well before she said them.

"The nurse said that the woman's name was Savannah Clarke."

I leapt from the couch to grab Barish's journal, flipping through the pages until I found an entry dated four days after my parents had been apprehended in Colorado.

February 13, 2015

I have failed. Utterly and irrevocably so. While traveling for the last two weeks, seeking out a suspected Polymancer in Tibet, something even I could have not foreseen occurred: Ted Nichol's non-Elementalist daughter was discovered, and in an effort to save her, he betrayed the location of the Pentamancer's family. Before I could even be made aware, the Fulmans fled their home for Colorado, taking the girl with them. In a desperate attempt to shield her daughter from what she believed would be a fate worse than death, Elizabeth has cut Rowan off from her memories – and every last trace of her abilities.

Whether her powers are dormant or eradicated, I cannot say. I do not know how to undo what has been done without inflicting further damage to her mind, as it has never been done before. And even if I could somehow rouse the child from her amnesiac state, she would surely rebuke me and the Order. She has been betrayed, orphaned by the very Community she was meant to lead.

The mother has been placed in Containment, and while I have ensured she will not perish there, I cannot intervene any further as it will draw too much suspicion. Rowan's true nature must not be discovered, not in her present state; neither may my involvement be brought to light. The child must persevere as she is, until I can determine if and how she may be roused from her lamentable condition.

There is but one feeble silver lining to this tragedy – David Fulman managed to escape his overzealous interrogators and is thought to be dead. (That he did not succumb to his injuries is a tribute to the man's perseverance.) By fortune's grace, it was my operatives who found him in a nearby alley and revived him from the gates of death; at my command, they transported him to a private hospital in Denver; its Chief of Medicine is an Elementalist and a close friend of mine. I have sent my most trusted and powerful Electromancer, Keres, to try and conserve what faculties of the mind David may have retained. It is my meager hope that his eventual recovery may be of some small consolation to the Pentamancer, should she ever awaken from the oblivion her mother so selfishly bestowed upon her. Perhaps I could use his survival to my advantage, telling her – when the time is right – that I alone am responsible for his continued existence (delicate though it may be). It is an admittedly weak strategy, but there is ample time to fortify it.

For now, I can only comb the Electromantic archives to see whether this tragedy may be reversed without damage – or if our era has lost its first – and last – Pentamancer.

Chapter 27

I didn't tell the others about my father – mostly because I didn't want to distract from the mission at hand: saving Terry. But the deeper, more painful, reason I kept it to myself was because I couldn't let myself believe that Dad might actually be alive. It was too convenient, too auspicious a conclusion to the last three nightmarish years of my life. And if I refused to acknowledge even the distant possibility that there was truth to the tale, then I didn't have to be disappointed when we received that inevitable late-night call from Evelyn, letting us know that she had gone to the hospital to check, that it was all some kind of trick, a sick ruse by Barish to keep me compliant. ...Or, even worse, that it *wasn't* a trick, but my father had long since died after that journal entry, succumbing to the brain trauma that he'd endured at the hands of some sadistic Corporeal Electromancer. I didn't let myself wonder if that might have been Strauss, the man who stalked me, lied his way into Evelyn's home, nearly killed my mother…

"You okay, sweetheart?" Ted asked, leaning close to me as we walked through the secret, underground tunnel that connected our hotel to the Asterian Headquarters beneath the square. "I heard about… uh, the developments."

"I'm fine," I replied, not meeting his eyes.

The wide, round tunnel was lit, but not well enough for my liking. Stefan, a Hydromancer, cast away the murky water that pooled on the slick stone floor, grimacing at the slimy, green muck that the sewage left behind. From one of the connecting tunnels, I heard a loud screech, followed by high-pitched chittering. Eileen clung to Ori and Sophia as though a zombie might stagger out of the darkness at any moment. But I was in no place to scoff, as I was squeezing Aiden's hand so tightly, I couldn't be sure that he was getting any blood to his fingertips at all. Still, he didn't so much as wince in complaint.

"My apologies for the state of these tunnels," Stefan said over his shoulder. "They are seldom used, and our decision to avoid the public entrance this evening was last-minute."

"How old are these tunnels?" Aiden asked. "Are they Asterian-built?"

"This one is," Stefan replied. "But the city of Istanbul has hundreds of ancient underground tunnels and cisterns, dating back to Emperor Constantine in the fourth century. The Asterian Order has repurposed many of the passageways, though no one knows the underground city the way the Magisterial Guard does."

"Speaking of the Magistrate – won't Keres be wondering why you've been escorting me around, and not her?" I asked, stepping around a pile of sludge. It made me all the more grateful that I'd opted for boots over stilettos.

Stefan chuckled. "My team serves the Magistrate. It was Barish's wish that we attend to you in whatever capacity you may need. As Keres is not yet Magistrate, we do not answer to her."

"But you would theoretically have to if she becomes Magistrate, right?"

"Her Coronation was never part of the Magistrate's plan," he replied, glancing at the messenger bag slung over Ted's shoulder.

"How interesting," Ted replied, arching an eyebrow.

A rat skittered across the slimy stones, causing Eileen – and Ori – to let out a shrill shriek.

"We've almost arrived," Stefan said, a smirk tugging at the corners of his mouth.

"Remember, kid, we don't need or want you to do anything tonight," Ted said, glancing over at my mother. Unlike the rest of us, who were on the lookout for sewage and rodents, she was looking straight ahead, eyes locked on the metal gate we were approaching at the end of the tunnel. "Just help your mom and Aiden secure the opportunity to speak, and we'll handle everything from there." He patted his messenger bag, where the Compendium was safely tucked.

"Do you think you guys will get in trouble for stealing that?" Ori asked, giving Stefan and the other guards a sideways glance. "Eileen said the gems in the cover alone are probably worth well over a million dollars... Not that we knew that when we borrowed it!" he added hastily, clearly for the guards' benefit.

Ted shrugged. "I imagine they'll have more pressing issues to deal with once we inform them that the Regent Magistrate is a murderer and a fraud."

As we reached the metal gate, gleaming and sturdy despite the centuries of dampness and sewage it had endured, Stefan and the rest of the guards stopped.

"Prophet," he said, an urgency in his low voice, "the Magistrate gave us explicit orders: no matter what, we are to protect you. We have vowed to carry out that command with our very lives. So, know this: no matter the circumstance, we stand with our departed Magistrate, and we stand with you."

I should have felt embarrassed by the formality of his words, the fervency in his voice. But as I regarded Stefan and the five guards who stood behind him – two women and three men, their pristine Elemental sashes bearing the colorful emblem of Magistrate – I was filled with a sense of security – and compunction. They had forsworn families of their own to devote their lives to the Magistrate, and now to me. I didn't deserve their devotion, but I hoped, with time, that I would earn it.

"Thank you," I whispered, squeezing Stefan's calloused hand.

With a terse nod, he unlocked the gate.

***

Minutes before sunset, I entered the grand balcony with just over half of the Inner Circle, as Keres and Jahi had not yet joined us, and Terry's vacant spot had yet to be replaced. Seated between Piotr and Mei in the first row of the balcony, I watched the bustling crowd of Elementalists below. Most of the Community stood on the floor of the arena instead of in the surrounding balconies and seats; the

Extended Circle was all that separated them from the small, pentagon-shaped stage in the center of the room, and the metal chair that was bolted to the center of it. Given Terry's Pyromantic abilities, the torches in the room had all been extinguished, replaced by ordinary electrical sconces that cast a dim glow throughout the cavernous room. From above, a lone spotlight – one of the few that had been repaired since my Electromantic outburst the previous night – centered on the chair, its brilliant white light illuminating the stage, as well as its first few rows of onlookers.

The sight of that metal chair made my stomach churn; I couldn't imagine how Aiden must have been feeling. I searched for him in the crowd down below, spotting him standing at the front, nearest the stage. He was leaning in to talk to Ted and my mother, just a few feet away from the ring of sub-Prelates who stared out at the crowd, their hands rigidly clasped behind their backs. If Mom had been worried about being spotted before, she clearly didn't fret over it now. After all, according to her plan, she would soon have every eye in the arena on her as she recounted the vision she would claim to have seen through Barish's eyes.

Next to the three of them, Ori, Eileen, and Sophia were huddled together, talking to Vivian. The four of them appeared to be deep in conversation; I wondered if they were confiding to her the details of our plan – well, *their* plan, as I hadn't contributed anything helpful to it. My role for the evening was to simply find Aiden and my mother the opportunity to speak; apart from that, I'd been reminded multiple times to shrink away and do my best to blend into the background.

No one, including myself, seemed terribly confident that I would succeed at that.

As I surveyed them from above, an older woman with dark, curly hair made her way through the crowd to approach Aiden, closely followed by a slightly taller woman in a gray hooded sweatshirt. The curly-haired woman tapped Aiden on the shoulder; he whipped around, then abruptly scooped her into a big hug. A moment later, he stepped back to gather the other woman in his free arm, pointing in my direction. As the women tilted their faces to look at me, I stifled a gasp. The woman in the hoodie was Aiden's sister. And the older woman, who shared Sarah's high cheekbones and chocolate curls, had to be his mother. She was lovely, but her shoulders were stooped with fatigue. When she caught my eye, she smiled at me – a sad smile – and Sarah gave me the tiniest of waves. Their appearance caused a lump to form in my throat. Did they know about the plan, or were they here to witness Terry's execution? I rubbed the bridge of my nose, squinting my eyes shut. *Did Aiden mention that they were coming, or was their arrival a surprise to him as well?* I'd been so absorbed in Barish's journal for the last day and a half, I couldn't be sure.

They shouldn't be here, my mother's voice fretted in my head. *Sarah's been excommunicated, just as I have. If they're recognized—*

I won't let anything happen to them, I replied tiredly. *Not to any of you.*

Rowan, if, after all of this, we confirm that your father is, in fact, still alive—

Mom, I shook my head slightly. *Please, I can't talk about Dad. Not now.*

Listen to me, she pressed, her eyes darting in my direction. *Do not do anything reckless tonight. We have to get home to him. If his condition is as bad as Barish described, it will take* both *our efforts to resuscitate him. I can't do it without you. Even if I could, if something were to happen to you before that time, he would wake up only to find that his suffering has been for nothing. So you must promise me, Rowan. Promise me, you won't put yourself in harm's way tonight.*

Her words caught me off guard. My mother, ever logical and level-headed – a devout scientist before and after her time as an Asterian Officer – truly believed my father was alive. If the story turned out to be a ruse, as I suspected, what would it do to her, to have that hope shattered? She was already so fragile, having suffered alone for so many years in Containment.

I promise, I replied, doing my best to hide the lie. There was no way I was simply going to stand back if someone threatened her – or anyone else I cared about.

Even from the balcony, I could see her eyebrows furrow.

Just then, Mei leaned over in my direction. "Prophet-*sama*," she whispered softly. "It would seem the Compendium went missing from the Magistrate's office late last night... Do you happen to know anything about that?"

Oh, shit.

I stared at Mei wordlessly, praying my startled expression hadn't given anything away. *Does she know?* I wondered, my pulse quickening. *If so, does that mean Keres knows...?*

Suddenly, I remembered something Barish had said to me shortly before he died: *Should you ever require anything from me... don't hesitate to turn to Piotr or Mei. I think you'll find that they'll be able to answer any questions that you may have.*

Had he been trying to tell me something?

"Without it, Prelate Keres will be unable to take her oath as Magistrate," Mei whispered. "Or, at the very least, it won't be a legally-binding coronation. She's extremely distressed by its sudden disappearance."

Was it my imagination, or was there a twinkle in her eye? Despite the alarm conveyed by her words, I felt no such distress from her demeanor… If anything, she seemed almost *smug*.

"We have it," I replied, surprising myself.

"Wonderful," she smiled, glancing past me at Piotr as she spoke.

"Clever girl," Piotr whispered, giving me an approving nod.

I wanted to say more, to ask them what else they might have known, but the double doors to the grand balcony swung open just then and Keres stormed in, her normally silky-smooth hair looking somewhat disheveled. Jahi followed closely behind her swirling robes, staring at his own clasped hands. I noted that Keres had already donned the Magistrate's gold cords around her neck. The silken ropes swung from her lowered hood, and as the metallic threads caught the light of the balcony, I could just make out the tiny splatters of dried blood still crusted on the edges of the tassels.

At the sight of Barish's blood, a surge of raw anger rose up inside of me, surprising me with its potency; the man had used me, had lied to me, had kept countless secrets from me – but whatever his flaws may have been, whatever complex emotions I carried for him, somewhere deep down, I cared for him, and he for me.

The realization was both startling and comforting: Barish wasn't my enemy. He never had been.

Chapter 28

*T*he Prelates mechanically rose from their seats as the Regent Magistrate entered the balcony, and I, gritting my teeth, followed suit. Only Felipe and his wife, Izabel, bowed their heads. Valeriya, despite her usual churlish style, gave Keres a polite nod – which was practically a curtsy in her book. But Piotr and Mei stood tall, unwavering, and Nadia, an Electro-Terramancer clad in time-worn gold and emerald robes, did not so much as turn to look as Keres burst through the door. White-haired and older than even Mei, Nadia was the oldest Prelate in the Inner Circle, and the only Prelate who still had not uttered a word to me. I wondered what she thought about all of this – about Barish's sudden death, about Keres attempting to seize his place, about Terry, about *me*.

Without so much as an acknowledgement to the Prelates or to me, Keres hurriedly approached the balcony, while Jahi took a seat beside Felipe at the far end of the back row. His gaze still locked on his folded hands in his lap, he seemed outwardly perturbed – but he wasn't my primary concern at the moment.

"Bring in the murderer!" Keres cried out, skipping past any preamble.

The murmurs and hushed conversations on the floor of the arena immediately ceased, as all heads in the room turned to stare in our direction. Several of the guards stationed around the perimeter of the arena left their posts to exit through the wide double doors where Terry and his apprentices had been dragged out of the arena last night. As the doors slammed shut behind them, the rest of the coliseum remained frozen in silence. My breath caught in my throat. There wasn't any time to delay.

I rose from my seat, casting Piotr and Mei a quick glance as I did. I thought I saw Mei give me the tiniest of nods, but if she did, it was so subtle I wasn't sure if it was a trick of the eye or not.

"Keres," I whispered, approaching her from the side. My eyes swept the floor of the arena, where Aiden and the others were watching the balcony intently.

Keres stiffened, then slowly turned to look at me, a smile plastered on her candied-apple lips. "That's '*Magistrate*', my dear. Magistrate Keres, if you insist."

"*Regent* Magistrate." Piotr coughed politely from behind us.

Keres' smile tightened at the corners, but otherwise didn't waver. "Of course, Prelate Piotr. I seem to have gotten a half hour ahead of myself."

The doors burst open again and a wide column of light filled the far end of the room. Twelve guards surrounded a bound and gagged Terry, who was being dragged on his knees by two of them. I gritted my teeth, doing my best to keep my face composed – and more importantly, my rising emotions under control. Though Keres was no mind-reader, she *was* an Empath.

"Regent Magistrate," I said, tilting my head demurely. "My friend, Aiden – Terry Lawson's son – would like to say a few words before the… the execution."

Keres arched an eyebrow. "Oh no, my dear, I'm afraid I cannot allow that. Terry Lawson is a killer and a traitor. To pay respects or otherwise humanize the man who brutally murdered our cherished leader would be entirely unacceptable."

Below, the crowd had parted to make way for the guards. Even from the balcony, I could see that Terry somehow looked even worse than he had the other night. His bottom lip was split open, and his right eye was swollen shut. As the guards pulled him up the stage, he appeared to be struggling to keep his head up.

"I-It's not to humanize him *or* pay any respects," I said quickly. "It's a tribute – to Barish. Aiden's going to end it by saying goodbye to his father, but that's the only acknowledgement. I—" I swallowed, putting on my very best poker face. "I heard the speech myself. It's beautiful."

Keres' eyes narrowed at me, and as they did, my heart leapt into my throat. Evelyn always teased me that I was the worst liar in the world. Despite the efforts I was making to hide my emotions, the way Barish had taught me, did Keres know I was lying?

Below, the guards were forcibly strapping Terry to the metal chair, making no efforts to be gentle despite the fact that he wasn't putting up much of a fight. The people in the crowd were murmuring softly to one another; several of them were curiously regarding our exchange on the balcony.

"Let the boy speak, Prelate—er, Regent Magistrate," Mei said softly. "What harm could it do?"

Keres regarded her with cold, silver eyes. "I will not cave to petty sentimentality on this day, *Prelate* Mei. Our leader is *dead*. Killed at the vicious hands of a newly-elected *Prelate* – the absolute worst kind of betrayal!" Her gaze fell back to the stage, back to Aiden, who appeared to be watching us with bated breath. "No, I will not have the murderer's son – who is not even a recognized member of this Community – speak on anyone's behalf. Aiden Lawson should not even be permitted to be here – nor should your mother – but that is a subject we shall deal with later," she said, flashing a glamorous smile in my direction. "Now, dear Pentamancer, please be seated. There is no reason to make every moment about you."

I took a step backwards, but didn't sit. My heart was thrumming in my throat, my thoughts racing wildly out of control.

"Sisters and brothers!" Keres cried to the audience below. "We will not spare but a moment on this criminal, for he has taken from us that which we cherished most – the life of our beloved Magistrate!"

Several angry jeers and shouts erupted from the crowd, though I couldn't help but notice the hushed whispers that rippled among and between the throngs of people, the feeling of uncertainty that emanated from below. Was it possible that not everyone bought into Keres' narrative? Were there those who doubted her but were too frightened to speak up? I took a step forward, and then another, my eyes scanning the faces below. There was Vivian, her face scrunched together in consternation as she watched Terry slump over in his chair, as well as Terry's estranged wife and daughter, who clutched one another tightly. But there were also the officers I'd met from the Mumbai and Dubai chapters, who seemed tense, and the Li's – Zhang had his hand to his frowning wife's ear, whispering something – as well as countless other officers who seemed uneasy. None of them looked happy about the execution; in fact, nearly half of the faces in that room looked disturbed – and frightened, and helpless.

"Dear ones," Keres said, leaning over the edge of the balcony, "I ask that you back away from the stage, for your own safety. For those of you who brought children, now is the time to turn them away."

Children? I thought, bewildered. *Who would bring—*

A shriek sounded in the crowd, and my eyes darted to the source. Tosh – sweet little Tosh, who had traveled with his family all the way from Mumbai – was scrambling away from his mother's arms. As he darted between her legs, she wasn't looking at him, but up at me. She looked haggard; the purple circles under her eyes almost made it look like she'd been in a fight, but the paleness of her skin told me that she was simply exhausted. And suddenly, as I searched for Tosh's father and sister, I understood – she was all alone. Despite Keres' promises, the boy's family obviously had not been allowed to remain intact, not with his father and sister being non-Elementalists. Had their memories been wiped? Or something worse?

"Since this man took from me that which I loved most," Keres called, "I thought it would be fitting for me to be the one to take his life from him. I consider it a final tribute to my late mentor."

She held her hand out over the edge of the balcony, her open palm aimed directly at Terry. I could feel the air around her fingers becoming ionized with Electricity. Down below, my mother and Aiden had their heads together, whispering furiously; Ted stood beside them, his hands clutching the messenger bag. By the light of the spotlight above, I could see the familiar glint of Aiden's silver lighter as he removed it from his pocket. As my mother stood up straight, I felt the brush of Wind rushing to her lips – she was going to amplify her voice to speak. From the perimeter of the stage, several of the Auromantically-inclined sub-Prelates and guards twitched, their eyes searching for the source of the unauthorized threat.

"Stop!" I yelled, lunging my outstretched hand at Keres. As I yanked her arm down, her head whipped in my direction, her eyes glinting as silver as Aiden's lighter. For a moment, I thought she might attack me, but within the span of a haggard breath, she clenched her hand shut, dropping her fist at her side.

"What is the meaning of this?" she demanded.

"This man is innocent!" I cried, eliciting hundreds of stunned gasps from the crowd below.

"Sit. Down. Now," Keres hissed at me from between clenched teeth.

Rowan, don't! My mother cried in my head. *She could kill you!*

"Terry Lawson didn't kill the Magistrate," I shouted, turning to face the crowd. Bands of Wind lunged at my mouth to stifle my words, but I waved them away. "...She did!" I jabbed my finger in Keres' direction. The room fell completely silent then, as though the breath had been wrenched from the lungs of every person in that room.

Keres blinked, losing her composure for only a fraction of a moment. "The poor child is ill!" she cried, loud enough for everyone to hear. "Struck by a seizure just last night! She swore to our medical staff that she was well enough to make it tonight. But the brain trauma, paired with the immeasurable grief of her mentor's death, is clearly too much for her!"

It was a good lie; scandalous whispers and incredulous murmurs permeated the arena below – and why not? Most of the people in that room had seen me convulsing on that very floor less than twenty-four hours ago, screaming as though I'd been possessed. They had every reason to doubt my word.

"You killed Barish, and I can prove it," I whispered; the rage etched between Keres' eyes momentarily dissolved into fear.

Without pausing to hear her response, I empathically reached into the crowd below, searching for the familiar resonance of my fellow Electromancers. I found my mother's mind first, and beside her – though not an Electromancer – I found the warm comfort of Aiden's. As I reached out to Ori, I vaguely registered the sound of Keres' voice shouting commands from my right, but I didn't bother to listen. There was no time. I combed the crowd, locating each and every Electromancer in that room. Though rare – only about one in twenty Elementalists are able to wield Lightning – they were easy to find, as their electrical signatures were unique among the crowd. Some had ultraviolet auras surrounding them that pulsed faintly, while others – the more powerful ones – radiated their distinctive electrical force fields far into the darkness. Invisible to the rest of the world, like crackling powerlines or the faint purple hum around a fluorescent bulb, I could sense them.

One by one, I merged the electrical web of my mind with theirs, knowing that among the thousands who had amassed in that arena, they alone would be attuned to receive my message. Shudders and gasps rippled across the room as my grid of Electricity expanded, though only the Lightning wielders would have been able to see the intricate net, the fine crackling lines that flowed from every Electromancer in the room and back to myself. Even Keres, the last to be drawn into my web, let out a ragged gasp.

I gripped the side of the balcony, holding myself steady despite the gushing river of Electricity that coursed through my veins and through my mind. I wasn't prepared for the backflow of Electricity that flooded my body, streaming from the hundreds of minds I had linked to. I felt glimpses of what they were feeling, saw flashes of what they were seeing: me, standing in the center of the balcony, my eyes glowing violet, tendrils of black hair dancing around my head on the currents of ionized air. A hundred different versions of myself – all from different angles and vantage points – floated in front of my vision, as a hundred foreign emotions filled my mind. Whatever shock, fear, confusion, and wonder they were feeling down in that crowd, I felt as well. If I had wanted to, I could have freely accessed the minds of every Electromancer in that room: touched their emotions, raked through their thoughts, their memories, their innermost secrets. But it was not my intention to breach the confines of their minds or memories. It was the opposite: to each and every one of them, I needed to transmit my own.

Gritting my teeth against the chaos and confusion of so many minds linking together with mine, I brought forth the memory of Barish's death – of my consciousness being ripped from my own body and fusing with his. Shuddering gasps and startled cries erupted from the widely-scattered Electromancers in the room, while the rest of the Elementalists could only stare at their neighbors in alarm. Beside me, Keres was clawing at her head, whimpering as she slunk to the ground.

Despite the searing pain that threatened to split my skull apart, I willed myself to project the memory – every moment of it – into each and every Electromantic mind in that room. I did my best to keep the memory from flickering or jumping ahead, forced the edges to stay crisp and clear in spite of the vertigo and light-headedness that was creeping in. As I relived the horrifying moment that Keres drew the gun from her pocket, the gasps and cries quickly devolved into blood-curdling screams. A split-second after Keres pulled the trigger, however, I released my grasp on the web of Electricity, not wanting to subject them to the pain, the indescribable horror of witnessing – of *feeling* – someone die while being held hostage inside their body.

Panting, I opened my eyes just as the violet threads of Electricity dispersed into the air, infusing the arena with the sweet fragrance of a thunderstorm. As my vision adjusted to the bright spotlight on the stage once more, my eyes settled first on Terry. From the confines of his metal chair, he was staring up at me in bewilderment, much like the vast majority of the people in that chamber. The entire coliseum simmered with fear and confusion; only a handful of the Electromancers had gathered themselves well enough to explain to their frightened neighbors what had just happened. I let go of the railing and took a wobbly step backwards; my fingers had been clutching the balcony with such force, the edges of my nails were ragged and broken.

Rowan, my mother's voice whispered. *How on earth did you do that?*

Still cowering on the floor beside the balcony, Keres let out a furious sob.

I stood doubled-over for a few moments, pressing my hands to my thighs to catch my breath. Then I cautiously lifted my head – the small movement made the entire balcony feel as though it had lurched forward – and regarded the mounting tumult of the Inner Circle. All but two of the Prelates had leapt to their feet – some to hurriedly attend to a wailing Keres, others to rush to the edge of the balcony. But Prelate Nadia rose to her feet slowly, her weathered face impassive. She didn't so much as wince as Jahi brushed past her to kneel beside Keres, or when Valeriya practically knocked her aside, yelling sharp-sounding questions to her sub-Prelates in what I presumed was Ukrainian.

"What's happened?" Mei asked, gliding past me to lean over the stone balustrade. Her almond eyes were wide as saucers she surveyed the chaos and clamor of the arena floor. Beside her, Piotr said nothing in response; he wordlessly regarded the scene below, disquiet etched into his already-lined forehead.

Izabel, an Electro-Pyromancer – and an Empathic one, at that – was the only one who hadn't moved from her seat. She was staring at me, mouth agape, while her husband, Felipe, shook her shoulders.

"¿Que pasó...? ¡Izabel!" he shouted at her. "¡Dime, Izabel!" But she said nothing; she just kept her brown eyes glued to me, unmoving, unblinking.

Treading a singular calm path down the center of the Inner Circle's upheaval, Nadia slowly made her way to the balcony, her gold and emerald robes trailing behind her on the floor. As she passed, she turned to me and held up her palm; blue veins snaked across her translucent, crêpe-like skin like delicate vines, and the gnarled bones of her fingers revealed that she was even older than I had previously guessed. She placed her hand on my shoulder and gave it a gentle squeeze, then continued to the edge of the balcony where she waved it over the crowd.

"Sub-Prelates," she whispered, though a gust of Wind from Mei carried her papery voice to every corner of the coliseum. The amplified whisper, like crisp leaves fluttering on a cool autumn gale, brought the arena to a complete and immediate stand-still.

"Release that man."

Nadia's three apprentices quickly ascended the stage, moving past the mystified guards to free Terry from his binds. He staggered to his feet with their help, leaning on the broad shoulders of two of Nadia's sturdy-looking Terramancers. As Terry made his way to the bottom of the stage, he collapsed straight into the arms of his wife, sobbing as she stroked the back of his head with shaking hands. Aiden and Sarah watched the scene unfold from a few feet away, where they both stood frozen for a long moment. But as Terry extended a quivering hand to his children, it was Aiden who took the first step. He and Sarah reached for their parents, wrapping their arms around the two of them. Tears spilled over my cheeks as Terry let go of his wife to clutch his children against his chest, kissing the top of Sarah's head fiercely. A few feet away from them, my mother and Ted hugged one another tightly, while Vivian and my friends were looking up at the balcony, wide smiles spread across their faces.

"For those of you who have not yet been made aware, the Prophet has shown some of us an extraordinary sight," Nadia whispered, her frail voice still carried by Wind. "It seems Prelate Terry has been framed for a murder which he did not commit. As witnessed through the eyes of Barish himself, I – and every Electromancer in this room – can personally attest that it was, in fact, Prelate Keres who fired the bullet straight into the heart of our Magistrate."

Keres scrambled to her feet, casting wild locks of hair from her red-rimmed, silver eyes. She regarded her onlookers below with a frantic, horrified expression, her mouth silently working to find the words she so desperately needed in that moment. But what could she say? It wasn't a simple matter of my word against hers – not when several hundred people in that room had witnessed her crime first-hand. I followed her gaze to the thousands of angry faces that stared up at our balcony, at her, unable to find a single sympathetic expression among them. Even Keres' sub-Prelates were staring at the ground, avoiding the cold stares of their peers. Whether they had been in on her plans or not, they were, in that moment, guilty by association.

"Given this new, incontestable information that the Prophet has provided us, Prelate Keres' crimes – premeditated murder, treason, mutiny, slander, false accusation, and at least a half dozen more – are grounds for Electromantic Electrocution."

For a moment, I saw a flash in Keres' eyes, heard the words she was formulating in her own feeble defense – *I did it for the good of the Community, for all of you* – but in the very last moment, her plan shifted. Before I could cry out or make any move to stop her, she fled from the room, grabbing a startled Jahi by the sleeve as she did. A split second later, Felipe took off after them, shouting for his wife to follow. My eyes darted first to Nadia, then down to Aiden, who was watching me with a wild-eyed expression, still clutching his shell-shocked family. Finally, I met my mother's steel-blue gaze; her eyebrows were furrowed in such an intimidating way, she immediately reminded me of Evelyn.

Rowan – don't you dare.

But my legs moved before my brain had even had the time to sanction it.

As the heavy door of the balcony slammed shut behind me, I heard Mei shouting to the guards. "Protect the

Community! Do not let anyone in this arena in or out without my explicit order – this includes the Extended Circle!"

Good, I thought, racing down the hallway. At least someone on that balcony is thinking.

Chapter 29

ran blindly through the dim corridor, following the distant sound of footsteps as I sprinted. Behind me, there was only silence. The pounding of my feet on the stone floor reverberated from my heels and up into my skull, worsening the shooting pain in my head while also announcing my exact location to those I pursued. Somewhere in the back of my mind, I remembered my first Auromancy lesson with Sophia, how she had taught me to use the wind to dampen my footfalls, to make them softer, more discreet. And so, quiet as a ninja, I ran atop a cushion of Wind, deep into the underbelly of the Asterian compound. I did my best not to dwell on the disconcerting fact that I had no semblance of a plan and not a single guard at my side for back-up. Oddly, the absence of guards seemed to fuel my resolve – *someone* had to figure out where Keres and the others were going and what they were planning.

"You swore I wouldn't be implicated!" I heard Jahi shout from somewhere up ahead. I slowed down my pace as the winding corridor began slanting downward.

"I had no idea he was transmitting to her at the time!" Keres shrieked. "And I had no idea that she could – she could—"

"She could *what*?" Jahi demanded. "I still don't understand what happened in there!"

Their voices once more faded to muffled whispers as they turned a sharp corner; I sped up, doing my best to follow at a safe distance. I had no idea what I was going to do once they made it to their final destination, wherever that was; I only knew I couldn't let them disappear into the city. Five minutes soon became ten minutes, and with each passing minute, the rush of adrenaline that compelled me to blindly follow Barish's killer through that dark, twisting labyrinth faded, until I was left with only creeping anxiety and a throbbing headache – as well as a shrill, unrelenting voice in the back of my head that sounded remarkably like Evelyn, pleading with me to turn around.

Still, I persisted; the corridors seemed to continue on forever, sometimes cutting suddenly to the left or right – even disappearing altogether. At one point, I followed the sound of angry whispers around a sharp corner, only to find a dead-end and abrupt silence. I stared at the empty wall for a solid minute, anxiously running my hands over the cold stones. If not for the sliver of Wind coming through a crack that ran along the corner edge of the wall, I never would have known that there was a hidden door embedded inside it. Earth moved beneath my palm, aided by a strong push of Wind, and I found myself in an even smaller passageway. It was completely unlit, save for the narrow lines of light that shone underneath and between several other, presumably-hidden, entrances along the passageway. As my hand guided the rest of me along the cool granite wall, my ears strained to make out a noise in the darkness – any noise.

After a long minute, I was rewarded once more by the muffled sounds of voices, filtering in through the other side of the wall. A narrow beam of light led me to a crack in the stones, where I knelt down to peer through it. Keres, Jahi, Felipe and Izabel were standing a few feet away, clustered at the back of the large reception hall where we had all sat in a line the night before, greeting eager Community members. While our throne-like seats remained at the head of the room, the wide double doors at the front of the chamber had been closed and bolted shut. The rows of chandeliers hanging from the arched ceiling had been dimmed; their yellow bulbs glowed faintly in the massive room, casting dull shadows upon the ancient oil renderings of long-dead Inner Circle members and their shrouds of dusty, Elemental-colored drapes.

"You should not have followed these *imbéciles*," Izabel snapped at her husband as he paced in front of the line of empty chairs. He was so close to my hiding place, I could smell his heavy cologne through the crack in the wall. "No one knew we were involved – it was nowhere in the girl's vision, not even *implicado*. But you ran – like a *fool*, Felipe! And now we have no excuse!"

"Why didn't you tell me this sooner?" he retorted, raking his hands through his gray-streaked hair. "We could have hidden in plain sight, like that dog, Valeriya! ¡*Puta!*" he spat. "I hope they gut her!"

"Shut up, both of you!" Keres hissed, causing the ground to shake ever so slightly. Directly above her, the bulbs in the chandelier flickered.

"Get a hold of yourself," Jahi warned, glancing at the doors.

Keres took a deep breath. "Look – I know of a safe passage out of here, one even the Magisterial Guard doesn't know about. If we can make it there before the others find us, we can escape."

"But if we could just go back and explain ourselves, let them know why—" Jahi started to protest.

"No!" she cut him off angrily. "After the girl's stunt, the atmosphere up in the arena shifted – significantly. If we go back there now, we won't have a chance..." Keres' expression darkened. "No, Jahi, we must escape and regroup. I've learned of a growing community of Elementalists that have not yet been recruited to the Order; my sources tell me their number, which includes at least three reported Polymancers, has grown to several hundred."

"And where exactly is this so-called community?" Felipe demanded.

"You will learn the location once we arrive," Keres replied frostily. "Gathering the wilders will be our first stop; once I've reassembled enough followers to our cause, *then* we'll make our strike."

Izabel sneered at her. "Your powers of manipulation are not as strong as you'd like to think, Keres. Why have the others not followed us? Why do we stand here alone, like criminals?"

Keres grimaced at the floor. "They are simply awaiting further instructions; I am sure of it."

"No – it is more than that. Don't you get it? Even in death, Barish continues to best you! He has not only achieved martyrdom, but he's also positioned the girl perfectly! See how she captivates them, how she surpasses you without even trying? She has undone your months of scheming in a single night!" Izabel's shrill laugh was mirthless – almost delirious. "Without her, our cause is lost!"

"Spare me your melodrama, Izabel," Keres snapped. "The girl is ineffectual – gullible and incompetent. Were she not a Pentamancer, who would follow her? Who would pay her a moment's notice? Nobody!" She straightened the gold cords hanging from her hood, glancing at the door. "I thought we could win her to our cause, and it is regrettable that we have failed in that. But it doesn't matter – I have another idea."

Izabel raised a dubious eyebrow in Keres' direction. "Oh?"

"Perhaps we can discuss this from the safety of my private yacht?" Jahi suggested, darting glances at the bolted doors. No one else appeared to pay him any heed.

Why haven't the guards arrived yet? I thought anxiously. I considered turning around to get help, but Keres' next words froze me to my spot.

"We render her powerless, permanently stripping away her abilities as her mother once tried – and failed – to do," Keres said to Izabel, her tone matter-of-fact. "She'll once more be reduced to nothing, and the entire Community will see her for the worthless nobody she is. With her out of the picture, we can finally draw attention to the real issues that threaten our Community and unite once more against our common enemies."

"And her followers?" Felipe asked. "She has friends, family within the Community."

"Anyone who continues to pose a problem will be eliminated," Keres snapped. "I already took care of her father; I'm more than happy to dispose of Elizabeth next, now that Barish is no longer around to protect his poor, disgraced pet... Now let's go," she added roughly, making her way across the room. "By now they'll be done searching our quarters, and I need to retrieve something from my study before we go..."

'Dispose of Elizabeth'... 'Took care of her father'? The words sent a deluge of adrenaline straight to my blood. There was nothing I would be able to do to stop the four of them – but I could at least stall them long enough for help to arrive. Without another second's hesitation, I slid open the wall and stepped out from my hiding place.

"¡Ay, mierda!" Felipe yelped when he saw me. He tensed as though he might run, but when no one else followed me through the wall, he seemed to relax slightly.

"Enough of this," I said, doing my best to keep my voice from betraying the terror I felt. With every ounce of composure I could muster, I squared my shoulders, looking each of them in the eye as I spoke. "Enough scheming, enough fighting, enough bloodshed. There are too few of us in the world as it is. So, let's just end this, right here."

"Are you *challenging* us?" Keres sneered, taking a menacing step in my direction.

Poor choice of words, I realized a moment too late. My heart fluttered wildly in my chest; it didn't matter that I was a Pentamancer – combined, these four would take me down easily.

"No – that's not what I—"

Keres flashed me a bitter smile. "I would gladly accept your challenge, if only to get you out of my way. Because I do agree with you about one thing – there's too few of us, and too many of *them*," she said, pointing an angry finger upwards.

"What are you talking about?" I asked, baffled.

She rolled her eyes. "Naïve little Pentamancer, so concerned about insignificant drivel, pontificating at every opportunity about utter non-issues. As if anyone gives a damn about the criminals we lock up, or the Electromantic methods we employ. The world is safer *because* of our stewardship! Meanwhile, you ignore the fact that our entire Community has been forced below ground, into the holes and burrows we've carved out – as though we were rats! We remain powerless and suppressed, willfully undermining and debasing ourselves for the sake of the countless *Deficients* who freely roam the Earth above!"

I stared at her incredulously. *"That's* what all of this is about?" I asked. "You're angry because Elementalists aren't able to reveal themselves to the rest of the world and… and what? Do whatever they want, wherever they want?"

Felipe rolled his eyes. "Typical specious argument – because we no longer wish to tolerate forced oppression, that somehow makes us anarchists?"

"You must try not to be so small-minded, *hija,*" Izabel clucked. "There is no doubt that we are superior to the rest of the planet. It is time we emerge from our self-imposed hiding and take our rightful places in the world. Let the Deficients cower below-ground while we exist freely, unencumbered by the restrictions that rule us today."

"What does that mean?" I asked, trying to grasp their words, while also buying the guards more time to find us. "Are you proposing some kind of revolt?"

Felipe shrugged. "With the number of our people who have gained security access to things like nuclear launch sites, it wouldn't be much of a battle. We press a button or two, wait underground, and after most of the Deficients are wiped out, we send our best Auromancers –

like Jahi and myself – to clear the atmosphere of toxic debris."

"*What?*" I gasped.

Izabel rolled her eyes. "For the last time, Felipe, there are subtler, more sophisticated ways of eradicating Deficients that do not revolve around the end of the natural world as we know it!"

Why haven't the others found us yet? I fretted silently. I had to keep stalling; at the very least, I needed to draw out as much information from them as possible before they fled.

"Look, I feel like you're all making a pretty big leap here, jumping from 'we don't like hiding' to 'let's commit mass genocide'," I countered, glancing at the bolted doors. "Have you considered the fact that non-Elementalists might be perfectly fine with a peaceful coexistence? What if we first broach the subject with them, and *then* discuss nuclear launches?"

Felipe snorted. "The girl truly thinks she knows everything, does she not, Izabel?" He held his fingers in front of him, enumerating bullet points as he spoke. "Have you heard of the Salem witch trials? The Spanish Inquisition? Area 51's Thirteenth Division?

"*Bastardos,*" Izabel huffed angrily.

"The time for diplomacy is long-gone, my dear," Felipe said, narrowing his eyes. "The time for revolt is upon us."

These people are insane, I thought anxiously. I glanced over at Jahi, the Inner Circle's most outspoken, law-loving bureaucrat. Surely, *he* could see the absurdity in all of this.

But when he caught my eye, he merely shrugged. "We may each disagree on the 'how', but a growing number of us agree with the 'why'. Sharks do not cower in the sand beneath free-roaming guppies; nor do lions tame themselves to provide comfort to frightened meerkats. There is a natural order to things, and I believe it's high-time we embrace it. After we succeed in that, we can finally do away with all of the regulatory policies that you yourself have denounced – such as summoning a cool breeze on a hot day," he smirked.

"Hear hear!" Felipe exclaimed.

I took a step backwards, suddenly regretting my decision to run after these people alone. The four of them were surrounding me on all sides now, closing in on me as they casually discussed the topic of mass genocide. My eyes darted around the room, looking for an escape, but the front doors were bolted and Keres was standing between me and nearest exit – the secret passageway where I had followed them in. Even if I somehow overtook her and made it back to the hidden door in the wall, I would never be able to navigate myself safely back to the others, not in that dark, twisting labyrinth – which Keres seemed to know by heart. I swallowed tightly; she was standing right in front of me now, her brows knit in a tight scowl.

"You blather about Containment centers, how it's unethical to lock Elementalists away for exposing our secrets to the Deficients," she said, her red lips curled into a tight sneer. "You bore us all with your pretentious, myopic workarounds while you continually ignore the root of the problem: if not for the Deficients, there would be no need to Contain those who desire to use their gifts in public. And why shouldn't we use them? Why should *we* be frightened of what the Deficients might to do us, weak as they are individually? They may outnumber us by a million to one, but not for long. God didn't grant us the gifts he did because he wanted us to waste away underground! No!" she practically stamped her foot on the ground. "We were born with these powers because we *are* superior beings – elegant, powerful, extraordinary – the true stewards of the Earth!"

As Keres raged about the injustice of it all, I realized something: her typical cold marble exterior had crumbled away, and, for the first time, I could feel her emotions – specifically, her rampant, seething anger. It could only mean one thing: her shield was down. I carefully reached into her mind, knowing it might be my one and only chance to find some sort of soft spot or vulnerability that would help me understand her better. Perhaps an ideological common ground where we might be able to avoid a violent confrontation, a shred of rationality I could latch onto…

But there was no kindness, no lucidity, no commonality to be found. Behind her beautiful, self-possessed exterior, she was a completely different person – one filled with resentment, with uncertainty, with fear and mistrust. She was someone who had been chosen and then rejected again and again – by her father, by her lovers, by the handful of friends she never knew how to keep; someone who feared abandonment, who feared aging, who feared intimacy.

As I lingered in her mind, I felt her utter, sickening hatred not just for me, but for my mother, whose remarkable gifts far outweighed Keres' Electromantic abilities. I saw my narrow waist and smooth skin, the undeserved power that simmered deep inside of me, the love that Barish and my family and friends all had for me. I felt a surge of longing, a sickening knot of jealousy; Terry never looked at her the way Aiden looked at me, never put a protective arm around her shoulders or a tender kiss upon her forehead. In fact, Terry never truly loved her, for she had manipulated his emotions to use him, to keep him by her side. It made her feel safe, but at the same time it made her feel twisted and desperate, that the only love she could garner was artificial. The crushing wave of despair that Keres carried with her every moment of every day – the disgust and disparagement she had for herself, because she felt she would never be good enough – was staggering.

Get out of my head, the furious, humiliated whisper came. I stumbled backwards as her shield returned in full force, and as I regarded her through my own eyes – she was once again a perfectly chiseled marble statue – I finally understood Keres for what she truly was: a candy-coated apple, lovelier on the outside than any other apple in the grove, yet rancid and poisonous beneath.

"Don't you ever do that again," she whispered, low enough so only I could hear. As she balled her hands into fists, I realized the hair on the back of my neck had been standing on end. And suddenly I knew why she had allowed me to linger in her mind for so long: while I had been busy combing through her thoughts, she had been silently communicating with the others.

"Jahi, Felipe – hold her! Izabel – with me!"

Before I could react, thick ropes of Wind attached themselves to my wrists and ankles, stretching my arms outwards and over my head. My feet skidded across the stones as I fought to hold them in place. But there was no way to fend off the dual Auromantic attacks; as I struggled to counteract their combined assault with one of my own, my head suddenly erupted in agonizing pain – worse than the worst Electromantic migraine. To my horror, I could feel Keres and Izabel skimming through my brain as though it were a filing cabinet.

How will we find the access point to her powers? I heard Izabel fret from inside my head. *What we're doing is practically unheard of, and there are billions of neuronal pathways in here!*

A searing blaze of light blinded my eyes as they raked through those pathways, ruthlessly and without concern for the damage they were wreaking. I screamed, grinding my teeth together as an acrid, metallic taste filled my mouth – whether blood or Electricity, I couldn't tell.

Elizabeth already did it to her once – find that memory, and it will tell us everything we need to know, Keres replied.

The mention of my mother inadvertently called to mind her gentle face, the immense love I felt for her, igniting the thousands of feelings and memories and experiences that my brain associated with her. Using the technique Barish had tried to teach me just days ago, I fought against my own mind, doing everything I could to prevent those pathways from lighting up. Like thousands of tiny mountain streams feeding into a larger river, I knew any thoughts of my mother would guide my intruders to more significant neurological conduits – up to, and including, the memory of her taking away my powers. But with both of them fighting against me at once, my attempts to defend myself were futile.

Here, Izabel's sharp, trilling voice tore through my head.

Suddenly, Evelyn's sheer, pink curtains billowed in front of my vision and I found myself sitting on her guestroom bed, my mother tightly clasping my hands in hers. Tears flowed from her cheeks, collecting on the starchy white lace of the bedspread.

"No!" I screamed, arching my back against the wind that bound me. "Please! Get out!"

If you fight against it, you will only increase your chances of brain damage, Keres chided me, her annoyance ringing in my ears. I tried to shake the sound away, but a thick strap of Wind slapped me across the face, holding my head firmly in place.

"I promise you, Rowan, this will only be for a short time," my mother whispered softly. "We'll come back and find you as soon as we've established a safe haven, one where they can't find you. And I'll find a way to restore everything, to reunite us again."

"What if you don't come back?" I whispered.

My father entered the room then, while Evelyn – so tiny and frail in her pale pink bathrobe – watched from the doorway, her eyes wide and frightened. Dad strode to the bed and wrapped his arms around me, pulling me against his chest tightly. As my mother unclasped the tanzanite necklace from behind her neck, I heard his voice, as clear as crystal, whispering against my ear: "Everything's going to be okay, Rosebud. I promise."

We don't have time for this nonsense, Izabel snapped. *Skip ahead.*

The scene jumped; Dad was squeezing my shoulders in reassurance while my mother gently pressed her fingers against my temples. Her blue eyes were filled with sorrow.

"This will only hurt for a few moments, sweetheart. I'm so sorry for everything... May you never forget how much we love you."

Here we are, Keres whispered. *Our Electromantic roadmap, courtesy of Elizabeth.*

"Please," I whimpered, the taste of blood and tears filling my mouth. "Please, Keres, don't do this."

I'm sorry lovely, but it's the only way, she cooed, just as a zap of Electricity tore into my head like a hacksaw. *I'll do my best not to leave you brain-dead like your friend, Jenny... Or your father, for that matter. Did your beloved mentor, the Magistrate, ever get around to telling you about him?*

I wanted to cry out, to yell at her to shut up and get the hell out of my head, but my teeth were gnashing together, forcing back the screams that clawed at my throat. Inwardly, I desperately tried to seize the electricity that crackled inside of my skull, fought as hard as I could to wrestle it away from my tormentors. Had it been Keres alone who attacked me, I could have bested her; but against two of the most powerful Electromancers in the world, I was powerless.

I knew it, and so did they.

I was supposed to stabilize your father's brain when Barish sent me to check on him, but I may have accidentally damaged it further... It was nothing personal against David – my own little way of getting back at Barish, I suppose. You'd understand if you knew the things I did, the time I invested, the sacrifices I made – only to discover that Barish never intended to have me rule at his side. It was always going to be you, wasn't it? But in just a few short moments, I'll finally be the most powerful Elementalist in the world, and you'll be nothing but a sad story in the archives.

The acrid smell of burning matter flooded my nose while the sound of my own agonized sobs filled my ears. I could feel the hot torrent of Electricity drilling into my head, boring deep into the center of my brain where my powers resided. My back arched violently against the bindings of Wind that immobilized my body and I screamed – screamed like a wounded, tortured animal. Screamed until my throat bled and the Earth shook, sending forth a deep and rumbling roar that brought the enormous paintings on the walls crashing down to the stone floor like peals of earsplitting thunder.

But then something even louder ricocheted against the stone walls, as though a stick of dynamite had detonated just a few yards away. I forced my eyes wide open. As the thick, wooden doors at the front of the hall splintered into a thousand flying pieces, I suddenly realized that I wasn't the only one in that room who was screaming.

Chapter 30

*A*n apocalyptic blast of Wind and Fire sent chunks of wood tearing across the room, bouncing fifty feet away from the gaping hole where the doors used to be. As Jahi and Felipe scrambled to form a protective barrier of Wind around themselves, Izabel, and Keres, the shackles of Wind wrapped around my wrists abruptly disappeared. I fell to the ground, smacking my knees against the stone floor on the way down. Grimacing against the pain in my head and in my kneecaps, I pushed myself up on my elbows, tensing for another attack. But as suddenly as it came, the fiery typhoon dissolved back into the air, leaving a shower of smoldering splinters and ash fluttering to the ground in its wake. The five of us had fallen deathly silent, each of us rooted to our spots. Above, the chandeliers swung wildly against the ceiling, casting chaotic shadows across the walls and the swirling veil of smoke at the front of the room.

I squinted my eyes to try and make out the hazy figures approaching through the doorway, my heart pounding sharply against my chest. My thoughts were a jumbled mess, my body a hapless tangle of malfunctioning limbs. If Valeriya or any other corrupt Asterian were to walk through that door, I'd be defenseless. But as the smoke and debris began to clear, my heart leapt into my throat. It wasn't Valeriya standing in the doorway – it was my mother, her fists held stiffly at her sides. And right beside her, his outstretched palm still burning with crimson Fire, was Aiden; his expression carved into a furious glower. Ted stood a half-step behind them, holding a fistful of Fire in one hand, a handheld radio in the other.

"We found her, Stefan," he called into the radio. "We need back-up, *stat!*"

"Rowan!" my mother cried out, seeing me crumpled on the floor.

"Mom," I croaked, struggling to push myself to my hands and knees. The crackling in my skull had stopped, along with the drilling, but my entire head still raged with pain; it was so heavy, I could hardly hold it up. Aiden and my mother both darted forward to help me, but a bolt of

Lightning exploding against the floor at their feet, halting them in their tracks.

"Stand back!" Keres shouted at them. Electricity crackled in her palm, which was now pointed at me. "If you take one step closer, I'll kill her."

I vaguely registered the sound of my own voice in my head, urging me to get up, to fight back, but my body wasn't cooperating. I felt as though I had been stuck on a corkscrew roller coaster for hours, and then catapulted directly onto my head.

"Step away from the Prophet!" a voice bellowed. I had to refrain from clamping my hands over my ears at the sound.

Stefan, holding what appeared to be a staff made out of Water, had burst through the doorway. He and the five other guards stormed into the room, forming a line alongside Aiden, Ted, and my mother. Each of the guards held a different Elemental weapon in front of them, corresponding to the color of their sash; Stefan's polearm surged with Water; the red-sashed woman to his right held aloft a massive glaive of Fire; the green-clad Terramancer beside her twirled a mace made out of a hot, glowing stone the size of a grapefruit. One of the two Auromancers brandished a nearly-invisible whip of Wind, its outline discernible only because it had accumulated its fair share of smoke and debris. She snapped it at Keres menacingly, creating a deafening *crack* in the air.

"This is your one and only warning," Stefan called again, raising his polearm skyward.

"We're no match if they use force," I heard Jahi whisper to Keres. I glanced at the four of them over my shoulder; the tiny movement made me feel as though the ground was swaying beneath my knees.

Felipe nodded in agreement. "Barish's Guard has sworn no fealty to Keres. We'll be Contained for the rest of our lives – or worse."

Keres inhaled sharply.

Izabel shot her a meaningful look. "You must do it now," she hissed. "Or else it's the chair for us all."

My head still throbbing violently, I tried to army crawl away from them and warn the others, but a tendril of Wind snatched me by the ankle and yanked me back. Above, the bulbs in the chandeliers began to flicker. Stefan and the guards charged forward just as the skin on the back of my neck erupted in tingling goosebumps. I tensed, waiting for the strike that Izabel had pressed Keres to make – but nothing happened.

Seconds passed, and then a minute. My eyes darted back to the front of the room anxiously. I had expected Stefan and the others to be initiating some sort of counterattack, but they made no move to strike. Far from it, the six guards only made it a few feet into the room before they abruptly stopped, all at once appearing unconcerned by the rogue Prelates hovering above me. Stefan's polearm of Water had dropped to his side while another guard stretched his arms over his head, letting his spear of Lightning clatter to the ground where it disappeared with a subdued flash. The rest of the guards lingered in the doorway with vacant expressions plastered on their faces.

What the hell is going on? I wondered frantically. A few feet away, my mother was rubbing her temples with both hands while Ted and Aiden were whispering to one another, leaning in like old friends. Aiden had lowered his outstretched palm, a confused expression emerging on his face.

"It's working," I heard Izabel whisper. "You must hurry!"

Keres stepped out from behind their shield of Wind. "I'm afraid there's been a terrible misunderstanding," she said, loud enough for everyone in the room to hear. "It would seem we've all fallen prey to the Pentamancer's vicious tricks."

What? I tried again to pull myself to my feet, but a rush of vertigo tipped me sideways. Instead, I shakily propped myself on an elbow as Stefan and the other guards turned their gazes on me. Several of them were narrowing their eyes with disdain; Aiden and Ted were among them.

"The girl has deceived us," Keres continued, her eyes locked on the small crowd. "With her Pentamantic abilities, she was somehow able to implant false visions into everyone's minds. I did not kill the Magistrate, and I've only recently come to realize that Prelate Terry did not either. *She* killed him," she said, pointing at me from afar as though I were a wounded snake in the grass.

I stared up at her in disbelief, my head still searing in pain, my thoughts only now beginning to grasp what she was doing.

"*That* is why I fled tonight – I knew I would never be believed if I tried to speak the truth. The Pentamancer's abilities to manipulate people – even large groups of us – are simply too great. And so," she said, her voice straining against some unseen exertion, "I did what I had to do – to protect the Community."

"What have you done with the girl?" Ted asked, stepping forward. His head was cocked at a strange angle, his ice-blue eyes filled with reproach. At first I thought his scorn was directed at Keres, but as he glared at me, his mouth twisting with obvious revulsion, my heart sank into my knotted stomach.

"I cut the Pentamancer off from her Elemental abilities, as her mother was once forced to do," Keres said wistfully. "That is why you are no longer under her spell. How sad that someone with such enviable gifts would choose to use them for such wickedness."

I suddenly felt as though I'd been kicked in the gut. *Did she take my powers?* I fretted, dread trickling down my back like melting ice. I tried to reach for Electricity, for Wind, but a wave of nausea rolled over me, pinning me to the floor. Ahead, the others were making their way farther into the room, approaching me with caution, with disdain. As I struggled to grasp even one of the Elements in the room, a shadow fell on the ground in front of me.

"You lied to me, Aspen." Aiden spoke the words softly, calmly. "You lied to all of us."

"I didn't," I whispered, holding back tears as I took in his hostile expression.

He stared at me coldly. "And for what? For attention? More power?"

"No! I've never wanted any of those things!" Tears were falling freely from my face, but he turned away from me, as though he couldn't stand the sight of me.

"My father nearly died because of you."

Ted stepped forward to squeeze Aiden's shoulder, muttering something in his ear. It sounded something like,

"*She* should have been the one in that chair." My eyes widened as Aiden nodded in agreement.

Please, Aiden, I thought, feebly trying to scramble to my feet; invisible shackles of Wind kept me anchored to the ground. *Please... Don't listen to her.*

"I recommend we take her to the medical center to ensure her powers have truly been eradicated," I heard Felipe say. "From there, she can be transported directly to the nearest Containment facility."

"Actually, I disagree," Keres replied. "The girl poses a tremendous risk to our Community, as we've all witnessed first-hand. I recommend we eliminate her now, without giving her the opportunity to harm anyone further."

I was gripped by a cold shudder of dread as I regarded the faces looking down at me from above; eyes filled with reproach, mouths filled with venom. Whatever Electromancy Keres was using on them, it was working – they wanted my blood.

But one face stood out among the crowd – a face that was lined with compassion, with love.

"We're being lied to," my mother said calmly, stepping in front of Aiden and Ted. She took a tentative step towards me, and then another; her eyes locked on Keres. "Rowan did not deceive anyone in that arena; I am sure of it."

"¡Mentiras!" Izabel scoffed, crossing her arms tightly in front of her chest. "Of course, the mother will try to defend her daughter! They are modern-day witches, the both of them!"

"You are a liar, Elizabeth," Keres said, her voice straining at the edges. "A liar and an obvious accomplice to the girl's crimes. You'd think three years in Containment would have taught you better sense."

My mother came to a stop, deliberately standing between me and Keres. "The only liar in this room is you, Keres," she said, her voice cool and crisp. "But even you are not powerful enough to deceive an entire Community. Empathic Electromancers know when we're being deceived – don't we Izabel?"

The woman scoffed but said nothing.

"Even now, Keres, I can see the exhaustion creeping in," my mother said softly. "Your shoulders are tensed, there's sweat dripping down your temple. I can feel the exertion of what you're doing, the toll it's taking on you. How long can you maintain this? Fifteen more minutes? Perhaps twenty?"

"You'll never be able to take the four of us, Elizabeth," Keres whispered, visibly shaking. "Give up now."

"I'm well aware that I can't stand up to all of you," my mother replied. Her eyes darted to me briefly, and while I couldn't hear her thoughts, I felt an outpouring of inexplicable relief.

"...Luckily, I won't have to."

She smiled, her eyes darting just past Keres' shoulder; a half-second later, a high-pitched battle cry rang out from the back of the room.

Chapter 31

"*Yi yi yi yi yi yi!*"

I only caught a split-second glimpse of Ori tearing out of the secret opening in the back wall, Eileen and Sophia charging close at his heels, before the bulbs in the chandeliers blinked out, bathing the room in complete darkness. Sweeping gusts of Wind tore across the auditorium, emitting ear-splitting whistles as they whooshed past. A deep rumbling sound filled the air as the Earth began to tremble. Directly to my left, I heard a sharp scream, followed by a heavy thud. A cold spray of mist caught the side of my face as another yelp sounded in the air to my right. Felipe was screaming something to his wife in Spanish, his voice frantic and shrill. A spark briefly ignited from that direction, then hissed and went out. Another spark, this time bigger, managed to illuminate Felipe's panic-stricken face, but a cold blast of Water knocked him to the ground. I heard a loud crack in the darkness – a sickening noise that sounded like someone's head connecting with stone.

The chandeliers surged on once more, filling the room with blinding light. As my eyes adjusted to the chaos surrounding me, my jaw fell open. Beside me, Felipe was lying motionless, face-down on the ground; a thin trickle of blood seeped from his temple to the stones. Jahi and Sophia were circling one another in the far corner as torrents of Wind and Water collided in the space between them like an ocean storm. Beside the line of velvet-upholstered chairs – which had been scattered across the floor – Ori and my mother were staring down Keres and Izabel; arcs of Lightning ricocheted between them, leaving streaks of angry black scorch marks across the stones. Eileen was crouching a few yards behind Keres and Izabel, her hands planted against the quaking ground.

"Aspen!" Aiden charged across the room as a massive crack snaked along the floor, missing me by half a foot. He jumped over the fissure and skidded to a stop beside me, where he scooped me into his arms. Cradling me tightly against his chest, he pressed his face against the top of my head.

"I'm so sorry, Aspen," he murmured against my hair. "I'm so sorry!"

Ted knelt down beside us, steadying the small radius of trembling Earth beneath our feet. "That makes two of us, kid," he said, shaking his head. "That psycho really got in our heads... I didn't even know Electromancers could do that before today." He took my face in both his hands and peered into my eyes. "Why are her pupils different sizes?"

"Concussion," Aiden answered. "I'm worried she might have sustained some serious damage."

"What the hell did that woman do to you?" Ted demanded.

"Not sure yet," I grunted, struggling to my feet.

"I've got you," Aiden said, looping his arm around my waist. With his and Ted's help, I managed to stand up, though my knees still threatened to buckle beneath me.

The sound of blood-curdling screams made my head jerk to the front of the room. In a flash of blue and red robes, Valeriya had snuck up behind Stefan and the rest of the guards, who were still recovering from Keres' mind spell; five of them abruptly crumpled to the ground, leaving Stefan alone to defend himself. He flung his polearm at Valeriya, summoning a torrent of steaming Water along with it. She deftly leapt away from his attack, countering with a deluge of ice. As Stefan's frozen polearm clattered to the floor, she grinned, pulled out a lighter from the pocket of her robes, and summoned what appeared to be a winged snake from the emerging flame. The dragon-shaped coil of Fire lunged forward, singeing away part of Stefan's beard – as well as the skin on the right side of his face. He toppled to the floor, seizing his bloodied face with both hands as Valeriya raised her arm to finish the job.

"No!" I shouted. I flung my hands in front of me, trying to veer the flames away from Stefan. But my head erupted in pain as soon as I reached for Fire. I clutched at my skull, trying to hold it together. The contents of my stomach threatened to spill all over the floor as the room lurched around me.

"Don't leave her side!" Ted shouted.

Aiden tightened his grip around my shoulders as Ted released me, throwing his hands out in front of him. I watched helplessly as he grunted with effort, straining to wrest the flames from Valeriya's control. She stiffened, spinning her head in Ted's direction. As her dark eyes locked on him, he gasped and staggered, falling to a knee. I watched in horror as the skin on his arms flushed pink and then red. Just as she had done to Stefan's fallen comrades, Valeriya was heating Ted's blood.

"Ted!" I cried, pushing myself away from Aiden's protective embrace.

Before I could make a move to help, a loud, cracking noise sounded from above. My head shot up just in time to see one of the heavy, metal chandeliers being violently ripped from the ceiling by some invisible force. I thought it might have been shaken loose by Eileen's earthquake – until it soared halfway across the room and smashed into the ground, inches from where a shrieking Valeriya had hurled herself to the stones. She flung her hands over her head, cowering in terror.

"Stop!" she screamed, just as another chandelier came careening to the ground – this one was so close to crushing her skull, one of the broken bulbs drew a spray of blood from her cheek. "I surrender!"

With Valeriya otherwise preoccupied, Ted quickly scrambled back to his feet, beads of sweat dripping down his flushed face. "Are *you* doing that?" he gasped at me, doubled over to catch his breath.

I shook my head slowly as another chandelier crashed to the floor, this time landing beside Valeriya's thrashing heels.

"There!" Aiden pointed to the green and yellow robes that had just appeared in the doorway. Nadia, her frail hands raised toward the ceiling, was cackling in delight as the arms of the fallen chandeliers bent and twisted around Valeriya like a cage. For a bewildering moment, I thought I was hallucinating.

"Please tell me you're seeing what I'm seeing?" I asked, feeling faint.

"She's an Electromagnetist," Aiden replied, his eyes wide.

"Meaning?" Ted sputtered.

Aiden shielded my head with his arm as a chunk of stone fell from the middle of the ravaged ceiling. It clattered to the ground beside us, spraying the three of us with dust and fragments of rock.

"She's combining Electromancy and Terramancy to create a magnetic field around the metals."

"Like Magneto?" I asked incredulously. Aiden drew his lips into a thin line, as though he were suppressing a laugh.

"We have to help the guards," Ted interjected, his voice grim. One of the Auromancers – the woman with the whip – had staggered up from the ground and was helping a bleeding Stefan to his feet. When she caught my eye, she hurriedly beckoned me over with her free hand.

"Prophet, we have to leave. Now," she grunted, shifting her grip on Stefan as he tottered precariously. His burns were even worse from this distance, and I could see he was losing a lot of blood from his neck. From somewhere behind me, someone screamed.

"Press your hand against Stefan's wound – here," I directed, placing her hand across the worst of the burns on his neck. "Keep pressure on it. You need to get him and the other guards to safety."

She shook her head sadly. "The others are gone, Prophet, their blood has been boiled. I am alive only because I was closest to Stefan and his Hydromantic shield."

The others are gone. Her words were like a swift blow to the diaphragm. I wrapped my arms around myself, struggling against the nausea in my stomach and the panic rising in my chest.

"Get Stefan out of here," I whispered hoarsely. She opened her mouth to argue, but I cut her off. "I'm not leaving my friends, and he'll die like the others if you don't get him help! ... Please!" I added.

She grimaced, then nodded tersely. Gusts of Wind wrapped themselves around the four bodies behind her, gently lifting them from the floor as she carried Stefan out the door.

"We'll be back with reinforcements," she shouted over her shoulder.

Before I could reply, a shrill scream cut me off.

"Ori!" Eileen shouted from across the room.

A few yards away, Izabel hurled a barrage of electrified Fire in Ori's direction; he flung himself out of the way just in time, but his head struck the ground hard on the way down, knocking him unconscious. Izabel was closing in on him, her clenched fists crackling with Fire and Lightning. Eileen pressed her hands to the ground, crying as she tried to knock the woman away from Ori's crumpled body. But Felipe – still bleeding from the wide cut on his forehead – had once again joined his wife, easily counteracting Eileen's Terramantic efforts with a sharp flick of his wrist. Eileen's emerald eyes grew as wide as saucers as the ground beneath her Converse sneakers split cleanly in two, sending her tumbling into a wide fissure. A few yards away from her, the rocks beneath Ori gave out, and his body slumped into the crumbling abyss.

"We have to help!" I cried, lunging forward despite the fact that I was seeing doubles of everything. But a loud yell from the opposite direction stopped me in my tracks. Twenty feet away, my mother was facing Keres by herself, diving across the floor as a Lightning bolt charged at her from Keres' bloody fingertips. The ground opened up to swallow my mother as well, but she skidded to a stop at the last moment, rolling out of the way. As Keres fell into step beside Izabel and Felipe, the rest of the world literally began crumbling around me as layers of rock and stone fell into the fresh void they had opened.

"I'm so sorry kid, I can only do so much," Ted grunted, thrusting his fingertips into the ground to slow the massive fracture snaking toward my mother. But Felipe and Keres were working together now, and Ted's Terramantic efforts wouldn't last against theirs, not without help. My eyes darted to the gaping precipice that separated them from us, searching for a place where I could safely jump into it and help my friends.

But my half-formed plans were upended by a blast of heat that erupted from the back corner of the room. Jahi's robes billowed around him as a column of Wind lifted him from the ground, feeding the massive, rotating sphere of Fire that he was gathering in front of him.

Sophia! I thought, frantically searching for her through the smoke and scattered debris. My eyes finally found her crawling on the ground a few yards away from Jahi, holding her stomach as she approached the edge of the precipice where Eileen and Ori had fallen.

"Sophia, watch out!" Aiden yelled, hurling his own massive ball of Fire at Jahi's to try and knock it off course.

But Jahi anticipated the attack, and as his Fireball swallowed up Aiden's, it doubled in size and intensity, a blistering white comet that ignited to blue as it hurtled across the room. The drapes on the walls erupted into flames as the Fireball whooshed past, seeking not Sophia, but *Nadia*. The old woman narrowly avoided Jahi's surprise attack, but not Valeriya's; the caged woman's arm shot through the top of the twisted chandeliers, seizing the tail-end of the blaze as it flew past. Before any of us could so much as cry out a warning, Valeriya slung the white-hot Fireball back around, propelling it with lightning speed. A terrible scream tore from Nadia's lips as the attack caught her right in the center of her back, lobbing her to the ground. Her robes ignited instantaneously, engulfing her in flames. A moment later, the screams stopped.

Spitting an angry curse, Aiden flung his hands in front of him at the same time Ted did. The fire consuming Nadia's robes abruptly extinguished, but the damage was already done; her blackened robes, still smoking, were splayed across the floor like a seeping puddle of oil. In the middle of them, her tiny, charred body clung to the ground, motionless. My hands flew to my mouth as a silent scream lodged itself in my throat. Try as I might, I couldn't pry my eyes away from the terrible scene.

Nadia... the guards... Barish... Darius... Strauss... Tom... Jenny... Dad... My fists shook with terror, with rage. *So many deaths... So many needless, senseless deaths...*

As Jahi turned his attention back to Sophia, I could feel my wits returning, my burning resolve manifesting into something stronger than strength. I flung my hand into the air, reaching for the Electricity that ran through the chandeliers above, willing it – begging it – to come to my aid. Tears of desperation, of anger and grief, streamed down my filthy face as I cried out in exertion, flexing every muscle in my body to summon Lightning to my fingertips. Suspended on my tiptoes, my fingers quivering from exertion, I grasped for power, knowing if I just reached a little farther, it would surely come. As a strained growl escaped through my clenched teeth, the lights began to flicker ever so faintly...

And then I pitched forward, landing hard on my knees, and vomited all over the ground. My stomach heaved until there was nothing left, heaved until stars exploded in front of my eyes and nothing but bile passed between my sputtering lips. Heaved until my empty gags became deep, shuddering sobs and the coppery taste of blood once more filled my mouth. Gripped with sickness and the weight of my own overwhelming failure, it took everything I had to lift my head as the sounds of pandemonium once more descended upon my ears.

For a long, agonizing moment, everything and everyone in that room seemed to move in slow motion.

Aiden raked his fingers through his hair, shouting something at Ted while gesturing in my direction. Clutching the bars of her makeshift cage with a giddy, terrifying sneer, Valeriya shifted her focus on the two of them, preparing to strike. Sophia, blood seeping through the fabric of her tattered pink dress, was lowering herself down into the crumbling fissure with one hand to get to Ori and Eileen, while Jahi readied another fiery attack just behind her. Striding alongside the gaping hole in the ground, Keres, Izabel, and Felipe were closing in on my mother, who was on her elbows, shouting something to me from the floor. Meanwhile, a flurry of movement at the front of the room signaled even more arrivals as Terry, Piotr, and Mei burst through the wide doorway with a dozen sub-Prelates in tow. I locked eyes with Kaylie, Jahi's most powerful apprentice, and in that moment, I figured it was all over – there was no way she would ever betray him.

But my cynicism was quickly allayed as Kaylie turned her attention to her master – as well as the firehose that she and Vivian were carting inside the room. A boiling eruption of Water smashed against Jahi, pinning him against the wall until the foamy cascades pouring down the stones turned pink. As steaming water flooded that corner of the room, gushing outwards along the floor like an overflowing river, a fire raged several yards away. Bits of burning drapery tumbled from the walls, landing on the pile of broken paintings below. Their heavy, gold-painted frames quickly ignited, sending plumes of black smoke and smoldering furls of canvas high into the air.

Watching the faces of all those former Prelates burn away to cinders brought Barish's final directive to my ears, as though he were standing right next to me: *You must burn down the Order and rebuild it from the ashes.*

"Was all of this destiny, or did you know it would happen this way?" I murmured to the ceiling, half-hoping, half-believing he would somehow answer.

"Rowan!" someone called.

"Barish?" I whispered, squinting past the chandeliers above. It took me a moment to realize that my mother was standing in front of me, crying, shaking my shoulders, shouting my name… But inside her tear-filled, indigo eyes, all I could see were the glowing violet irises of the Magistrate.

Your story doesn't end here, dear one.

"How do you know?" I asked, trying to blink away the blurriness that was creeping into my vision.

"Rosebud, come back to me!" my mother whispered, pressing her hands to my cheeks. A hot current of Electricity filled my body, warming me from head to toe like a gentle embrace.

Come back to me, sweetheart – please.

"What's happening to her?"

My ears recognized the speaker before my eyes found him; Aiden knelt down beside my mother, taking my hands in his. Somewhere in the back of my mind, I registered that Terry and Ted had come to stand behind the two of them, shoulder-to-shoulder as they flung barbs of Fire across the room.

"When did they become friends?" I asked, confused.

"I'm trying to undo the damage Keres has done," my mother said, pressing her fingertips to my temples. "It's not just psychic impairment; there's physical damage to the brain tissue. She's hemorrhaging."

Aiden clasped my hands tightly as a painful flash of light erupted in front of my vision, making me gasp. I could hear my own, wheezing pants escaping through my lips, labored and quick.

"Hey – hey," Aiden whispered, cupping my face. "It's going to be okay, Aspen. You hear me? We just need you to hold on. Hold on!"

Another flash of light exploded in front of me; whether it was in my head or somewhere outside of it, I couldn't tell. But suddenly, Ted and Aiden's father were gone, and I could see Keres walking towards the three of us. Her robes were tattered, her entire body covered in blood and burns.

"I'll kill you," she spat, pointing a shaking finger in my direction. "If it's the last thing I do, I swear to God I'll kill you!"

Somewhere, something was tugging at my senses. Perhaps it was my mother's healing touch, or maybe it was adrenaline; whatever it was, the fog in my head was beginning to clear. As a trickle of something cold slithered down my back and a flush of warmth erupted painfully in my chest, it occurred to me that Keres was heating my blood.

Before I could so much as cry out, Aiden leapt to his feet, summoning a plume of Fire from his lighter. The warmth of his flames quickly replaced the heat spreading through my chest, but only for a moment. Like a cobra lifting its head, a massive pillar of red-tinted Water rose from the ground, churning and rippling as it towered above Aiden. Its shimmering surface reflected the bursts of Fire and light shattering in the air all around us, mimicking the Lightning storm that my mother was setting off across my brain. Each and every bolt made my head erupt with agony, but there was a strange, comforting numbness that began to unfurl in the searing aftermath.

I've almost got it baby girl, my mother whispered in my head. *Just bear with me, thirty more seconds...*

Behind her, Aiden had drawn another flame from his lighter, poising to attack. But Keres' wave of Water smashed into him, sending his source of Fire clattering across the floor. He fell to the ground, coughing and writhing as an arm of blood-infused Water wrapped itself around his face and neck, suffocating him. Keres raised her hands above her head, both her arms radiating with Electricity. As she aimed her crackling palms at the back of my mother's head, flexing her fingers as she prepared to strike, a surge of Adrenaline tore through my veins, providing me with a much-needed moment of clarity.

I love you, Mom, I whispered. *When you make it home to Dad, please tell him how much I love him. And how sorry I am.*

My mother's startled eyes caught mine for the briefest instant before I lunged past her, charging at Keres with everything I had. I heard Keres' stunned, breathless wheeze as my head connected with her stomach, sending us both hurtling towards the ground. The arm of Water that had wrapped itself around Aiden's neck abruptly lost its shape, sloshing against the broken stones at the same instant the back of Keres' head smacked against them. She gasped and sputtered, her long hair dangling over the edge of the precipice, her wide eyes rolling around wildly in her head. Crouching on top of her, I suddenly realized that the fighting in the rest of the room had stopped; the explosions had ceased, and several bodies lay crumpled nearby on the floor – some with robes splayed around them, others without. Piotr, Mei, and a handful of others were running in our direction, their palms outstretched to subdue the woman pinned beneath me once and for all.

It's over, I thought, searching for my friends among the crowd. ... *Thank god it's over.*

That's when Keres lunged forward to snatch my face in both her hands, her jagged fingernails tearing into my skin. A white-hot nova ripped through my vision, replacing everything in that room with a flood of searing white light. Like a swarm of wasps, a terrible buzzing sound filled my ears as every muscle in my body began to twitch violently. The pain was like nothing I had ever felt before. My spine arced violently, cracking and popping as it did, but I couldn't scream – my tongue had curled itself back against the roof of my mouth; my teeth ground together uncontrollably. I could feel my heart thumping, battering against my sternum like a pommeling fist—

And then it stopped... Everything stopped.

As blinding white faded to black, the last words I heard were: *Tell Barish I send my regards.*

Chapter 32

- AIDEN -

July 12, 3:28 a.m.

I can't sleep.

Images from that night come back to haunt me every time I close my eyes. The dead guards. My father's vacant eyes. Keres, blood-splattered and screaming. But the image I can never seem to shake is my fearless, frail Aspen, her limbs crumpled on the ground unnaturally, her raven hair splashed across the stones. The angry, red scars scrawled across every inch of her skin.

A hundred different choices could have yielded a hundred different outcomes and I can't stop running through each one in my mind: If only I had been quicker, stronger... If only I had ushered her out of there when I first had the chance... If only I could have bought Elizabeth just thirty more seconds.

Robert has continually reminded me that this line of thinking is self-defeating, that nothing logical or useful ever comes from looking backward instead of forward. But it's hard to ignore the what-ifs when so many outcomes that night, so many lives, hinged on mere seconds. At his suggestion, I've turned to journaling to try and combat the compulsive thoughts. A blank page is no substitute for confiding in the woman I love, a woman who always had the most insightful and surprising things to say, a woman whose gentle voice I miss every moment of every day. But it does help to pass the time at 3 a.m. while the others sleep and the hospital gym won't be open for another hour.

It's comforting to finally hear Robert's snores from the corner. I can't imagine how difficult it must be for him and Elizabeth, feeling the pain of everyone in the room while simultaneously masking their own suffering. It makes me think about Aspen's ability to read me – and everyone else around her – so well. Up until two weeks ago, I never knew I could feel so much grief all at once – it's as though my pain is too big for the vessel that carries it. As an empath, there must have been times when Aspen wanted to crawl out of her skin from all the emotions she felt, both internally and externally. But like everything else, she took that burden in stride – not because she had to, not because anyone forced her into it, but because she felt that it was the right thing to do.

Aspen's mother just stirred awake again, and now she's quietly climbing past the cluster of armchairs in the corner. Robert and Ted are still asleep, but I can see Evelyn sitting awake, quietly watching her daughter-in-law through a slanted eye. It's the same ritual Elizabeth has done every night for the last two weeks: sitting on a stool between their two hospital beds, a hand in each of theirs, whispering silent pleas under her breath.

At least the Magistrate was honest about one thing: David *is* alive – if you can call his current existence 'living'. But in a way, it makes me even angrier at Barish. All those years Aspen spent alone, wondering where her parents were… The months she spent afterwards, believing her father was dead. Meanwhile, David was here, in Colorado, just thirty minutes from her cabin. The longer I dwell on it, the closer I come to breaking down. The last time that happened, poor Evelyn burst into tears. Since then,

I've excused myself from the room when I feel the stirrings of a panic attack. The stairwell outside of Aspen and David's hospital room has seen its fair share of meltdowns this week. But I can't handle another one. Not now.

Elizabeth is crying. I just set my laptop down to go and comfort her, but Evelyn beat me to it. I won't intrude on their moment.

The Chief of Medicine, an old friend of Barish's, told Elizabeth that David is in a "persistent vegetative state" with extremely limited brain stem function. Those brain waves, weak as they are, are the only thing keeping the hospital from labeling him as brain dead. Elizabeth has spent hours with her hands pressed to his sunken cheeks, working to find a way to rouse him, but she describes his mind as "static". I've heard Robert and other philosophical Electromancers define the concept of a 'soul' as Electricity-bound consciousness. If that's the case, it would appear that David's soul no longer resides in his body. I can only imagine how Elizabeth must be feeling, having waited so long to see her husband again, only to find his body 'alive', so to speak, while his mind remains unreachable.

Aspen, Liz and the medical staff have repeatedly assured me, is a different story. Her brainwaves are strong. Neurologically, they're off the charts, according to her doctor (a Corporeal Electromancer who flew in from Tehran last week to monitor her). Elizabeth believes that this implies extraneous, ongoing activity in Aspen's brain, but she's not offering any further speculation on what exactly that might be. What confounds me – and everyone else – is this: After doctors treated Aspen's brain hemorrhaging in Turkey, the top neurosurgeon in the world, a Level-III Electromancer, combed her brain for damage, repairing everything he could find. All of this was done under the watchful eye of Elizabeth, myself, and an army of equally-paranoid sentinels, so no one suspects foul play. The surgeon reassured us that he expects Aspen to have most, if not all, of her powers returned to her when she wakes up. At that time, he estimated that that would take anywhere from two to three days after her transfer to Denver.

But two weeks later, she's still in a coma. The doctors here seem baffled. She has two small cerebral contusions, as well as some minimal scar tissue and swelling, but for all intents and purposes, she should be awake.

So why isn't she?

The five of us begrudgingly take turns leaving, one at a time, to go home, shower, and gather extra clothes. But apart from that, no one is willing to leave Aspen's (or David's) side. Elizabeth has been reaching out to her daughter Electromantically, periodically trying to rouse her. For the first week, I stood beside Elizabeth as she worked, clutching Aspen's hand with bated breath, looking for an outward sign – a flutter of her eyelids, a twitch of her finger. But nothing happened. And nothing has happened since.

Each time Elizabeth attempts to speak to her empathically, she re-emerges with a perplexed look on her face. It's not static, she's assured us time after time. But she's unable – or perhaps, unwilling – to explain further. Yesterday, when Robert asked her if she could hear anything from inside Aspen's mind, she offered only slightly more detail: "Yes and no. It sounds absurd, I know – but as far as I can tell, it's like she's having a conversation with someone I can't see, far away, behind a locked door. I call and I call to her – but for whatever reason, she's not ready to answer."

The explanation startled me, but as Elizabeth slumped down on the couch beside Ted and Evelyn, Robert shook his head in my direction. Based on his cue, I didn't press further.

Looking at Aspen now, it's like she's in a deep sleep, illuminated by the blue glow of beeping consoles. I catch myself looking over at her twenty times an hour, half-expecting her to sit up and begin speaking to us. Every time she doesn't, my heart sinks slightly further. At this exact moment, I don't know how much farther it could slip…

Robert, if he were not presently snoring like a chainsaw, would tell me to focus on the positive. In that respect, I suppose I could say that the cuts and bruises on her face have all but disappeared. Her cheeks are hollow, but their color has returned slightly. And the scarring on her neck and arms has certainly faded. The raised white lines are delicate now, hardly noticeable unless you're looking closely. But when the sun rises through the hospital window and the rays hit her skin in just the right way, you can see them – fine dendritic webs that look like interlaced lightning bolts, running up and down the pale skin of her arms.

Eileen wheeled Ori over the other day for a visit and the first thing he said was how "badass" Aspen looks, that he's "jealous of her battle scars". Despite the fact that the poor guy's confined to a wheelchair with two shattered ankles, I was gripped with the sudden, uncharacteristic desire to slug him. But when Elizabeth laughed – her first genuine laugh in two weeks – the rest of us had to laugh, too. The two of them have been here every day since, in-between physical therapy. The lime-green cast on Eileen's arm is covered in stick figure drawings and glitter from all the time she's been spending in the children's unit. I imagine it brings her some small comfort while Sophia continues to recuperate here in the ICU. Aspen's grandmother keeps saying that it's a miracle Sophia made it out of Istanbul alive, but really, it was Sophia's own quick thinking that saved her life – along with a good amount of sheer luck. If she hadn't used Hydromancy to staunch her own internal bleeding; if she and Ted didn't share the same rare blood type for the emergency transfusion; if the surgeons had waited even five more minutes to perform the splenectomy, we'd have lost her.

Like Dad.

6:24 a.m.

It took me some time to recollect myself and continue writing. I abandoned my laptop to escape to the gym, where I've been exhausting myself until the pain becomes manageable once more. Evelyn and Elizabeth thrust plates of food in front of my face several times a day, but when I eat the food sits in my stomach like a brick. The flashbacks of my father's lifeless body are almost too much to bear. A few minutes ago, Ted came over to remind me (again) that there's nothing more either of us could have done that night; Keres wanted my father dead almost as much as she wanted Aspen dead. And Dad must have known that. When he jumped between Keres and the rest of us, I don't think he believed he had any real chance of overtaking her; I just think he was trying to buy us time. Or perhaps it was his way of apologizing – for everything. As he hugged Sarah and me in the arena earlier that night, he told us for the first time how sorry he was for abandoning her, for abandoning me. For abandoning our family.

My mother told me that before he left her to join Mei and the rest of the search party, he claimed that Keres was using her powers to lure him into the affair. He also swore that he had nothing to do with Barish's death, that he and Jahi didn't know she had a gun on her that night. About that, I believe him. But about the affair, I'm not entirely sure – he's always been drawn to power. Still, I'm thankful that his explanation brought my mother and Sarah some much-needed comfort. As for me, there are so many things I wish I could say to him, so many questions he'll never be able to answer. And I'll never be able to thank him for saving me... for saving Aspen.

But I can't write about that now. It hurts, and Elizabeth is close-by. She doesn't need to feel more pain than she already does.

Robert is awake now. He's back to scouring the Asterian archives on his laptop, reading aloud to us (with a mouthful of bagel) all the new articles that have been cropping up daily as more and more public details come to light. Along with my father, most of the Inner Circle snuffed itself out that night. Mei survived. So did Piotr. Izabel, the lone survivor of Keres' troupe, was on her way to Containment when she suffered a massive heart attack and died. Those escorting her to her cell are fairly certain that her death was self-inflicted.

Regarding the abrupt collapse of the Inner Circle, we all disagree about the Magistrate's motives – I think Barish was planting the seeds all along for the nine of them to turn against one another and wipe themselves out (Elizabeth seems to believe this as well). Robert, on the other hand, doesn't think he deserves that much credit, that no one could possess that kind of cunningness and foresight. The rest of the Asterian Community seems to think it was all Aspen's doing, and as more and more of the cloak-and-dagger corruption becomes public knowledge – some via salacious sub-Prelate tell-alls, freely published in the archives for any and all to read – the entire Community appears to be banding together in its reverence of the Pentamancer, hailing Aspen as the true hero of our times.

On that last sentiment, at least, Robert and the rest of us couldn't agree more.

Apart from that, the dissolution of the Inner Circle is the one silver lining to emerge from this tragedy: the head of the snake has been cut off, so to speak. With the governing body eradicated and their dirty secrets finally out in the open, the Asterian Order seems to be moving in the direction of transparency, while also enjoying a renewed sense of camaraderie (a common occurrence after a collective tragedy). Widespread calls for reorganization and a complete overhaul of the hierarchy has led to the installation of elections this fall. It's an unprecedented move by Asterian officials, but for the first time in a long time, they're hearing the appeals of the masses. And probably fearing for their lives, now that the international Community is galvanized behind a unified desire for change.

The elections will be overseen by a volunteer-based committee, headed by ex-Prelates Piotr and Mei. Any Elementalist over the age of twenty-five can run for leadership positions and the ensuing government will be based on a parliamentary model of international representatives. The radical new system was outlined in a manifesto that Barish strategically left behind. It appeared on his desk – rather conveniently – just hours after Keres and the others had been eliminated. The twenty-page, handwritten document detailed, in exquisite language, his perfect vision for the Order, one where a freely-elected Parliamentary government votes upon and enacts laws based on the will of the Community. He even included his own ideas for what those rules might entail, as well as an addendum – dated one day before his death – that called for the disassembly of all but one Containment unit, which will be reserved only for violent offenders. The entire manifesto was published to the public archives within days of his passing by an anonymous source – most likely Piotr or Mei.

Robert has pored over every page of it, continually marveling at its brilliance. Despite my personal feelings for the Magistrate, I have to confess that his manifesto was a stroke of genius. Barish was a true mastermind. Even with the Pentamancer (tentatively) by his side, he knew the odds would be against him and his revolutionary (pun intended) new governing system. But as his own Prelates turned on him – and each other – he contrived a far more cunning plan, which is only now becoming clear. While the archives are lambasting the departed Prelates as "conniving, unethical, self-serving autocrats who wiped themselves out in a savage, well-deserved ending" (save for my father, who's received slightly less posthumous ire), Barish's reputation has managed to escape the carnage entirely intact. He's being hailed by the Community as a martyr – a "magnanimous champion of Elementalists" and the selfless guardian of / mentor to the Pentamancer. In death, he has achieved more than he ever could in his unnaturally long life, even drawing attention to the plight of non-Elementalist children born to, and cast aside by, those in the Community.

~~If~~ *When* Aspen wakes up, she'll be thrilled to hear about all of these developments. But I imagine she'll be horrified to see the bizarre rendering of her and Barish that's been floating around the archives: the blessed Pentamancer, half-lidded with flashing purple eyes, a halo of Lightning cresting her cascades of black hair while a disturbing, Zeus-like portrayal of Barish looks down at her serenely from the golden clouds above. It's... off-putting, to say the least. One of the nurses, a huge fan of Aspen's, actually printed and laminated it. And then dear old Ori took it upon himself to staple it to the wall between Aspen and David's beds. I can almost imagine her expression when she sees it: she'll draw her eyebrows together, purse her lips slightly, and do that thing where she crinkles her nose like a rabbit. Why did I never tell her how adorable she was when she made that face?

Why did I never tell her so many other things? Like how beautiful she is when she sleeps. How she makes me laugh harder than anyone else I've ever met. How much I worry about her, every moment of every day, despite the fact that she's the most extraordinary person I've ever met?

I can only hope that she knew how I felt – that her empathy gave her more insight into my true feelings for her than my fear and inhibitions ever allowed. Every day for the last two weeks, I've been bartering with the universe: Just let her wake up. Let her be well. And I swear I'll spend every day of the rest of my life making sure she knows just how much I love her, how treasured she is. I've been carrying that tanzanite ring around in my wallet since June, convincing myself that twelve or eighteen months was an appropriate window of time. Now, all I ask is that I have the opportunity to slip it on her finger, even if she thinks I'm an impulsive clod for doing so. After all, even Maxwell Smart was the epitome of—

Hold on.

Elizabeth and Evelyn just leapt to their feet. One of Aspen's computer monitors is beeping loudly… The nurses—

Something's happening.

Chapter 33

- ASPEN -

I've been straddling the line of wakefulness and sleep for some time now, never staying long enough in either place to fully comprehend where I am. But the last vestiges of sleep seem to be disappearing, the blackness of interminable slumber fading to a burnt orange. I can feel the warmth of the rising sun on my eyelids, hear the murmur of hushed voices surrounding me. I'm beginning to understand where I am now, but I'm not ready to say goodbye to the place where I've been. Inside the barren landscape of my father's mind, I've been searching and searching, combing through the interminable static like a blizzard, all while recounting the events of the last few years of my life – events that he's been waiting all this time to hear about. In my travels, I've encountered a few sparks, tiny remnants of his departed soul. It was to those sparks that I spoke, knowing they would carry my message on to him, wherever he is now.

In my heart, I know he's heard me. He finally knows what's happened, knows that I'm safe, that Mom and I love him more than words can say. I've given him that much, but I've also failed him. All the Electricity in the world couldn't bring him back; I've come to realize that. Time is a foreign entity to those of us who linger in the dreaming world, but even I know that I've been lingering in this place for far too long. And so, I must open my eyes and return to the waking world, even if it means accepting my father's fate.

I love you, Dad. To the edge of existence and back, I love you. Give Grandpa my love. Tell Jenny that Ted and I think of her every single day.

And please tell Barish that I forgive him.

***

The voices I hear are no longer traveling through a long tunnel to reach my ears. They're just within my grasp, almost close enough to reach out and touch. The effort it takes to open my eyes is greater than anything else I've ever done, as though hundred-pound weights are hanging from my eyelashes. Part of me wants so badly to give up, to give in to the darkness and just sleep, sleep in the comfort of effortlessness, of predictability, of painlessness. But as inviting as endless sleep may be, the voices that have been calling out to me are finally winning.

I cautiously squint open one eye, and then another. The light filtering through is overwhelming; it reminds me of the last light I ever saw, that burning, searing light that brought with it immeasurable agony. But that light was erupting inside of my head, and this warm light is trickling in from the outside.

"Rowan?" someone asks. I try to move my head toward the voice, but like my eyelids, my head feels so heavy. I let my eyes move to follow the sound, which is coming from the outline of my mother's face, illuminated from behind like an angel. It takes my vision a few moments to adjust, my mouth a few more moments to find my voice, but after several wordless attempts, I hear a strange rasp sounding from between my parched lips.

"Hi, Mom," I half-croak, half-whisper. "I talked to Dad."

Tears are pouring down her face, splashing against my fingers. A warm, familiar pressure lets me know someone nearby is squeezing my hand.

"What did you tell him, baby girl?" she asks, leaning forward to brush something from my eyes.

"I told him everything," I reply, my eyelids growing heavy once more. "But, Mom…"

"Yes, Rosebud?"

"I couldn't fix him," I murmur, letting sleep take me once more, just for a little while.

"I know baby," her voice begins to fade. "I know…"

Chapter 34

*I*t's been a week since I woke up from what doctors are calling a "self-induced coma". I don't remember much from my first twenty-four hours post-coma; there was a lot of poking and prodding. A lot of fading in and out of consciousness. But I do remember a lot of happy tears and hugs and showers of kisses. And I remember Evelyn hoisting herself into my hospital bed and refusing to dislodge her arms from around my waist until the nurses begged her to get out of their way.

The following day is much clearer. When I was finally able to remain conscious for more than an hour at a time, Barish's friend, the Electromantic Chief of Medicine, Dr. Wilke, brought in the entire nursing staff – half of whom had been flown in for the sole purpose of caring for me – to give me a standing ovation. Their applause echoed throughout the private wing of the hospital, but it became uproarious when Eileen wheeled Sophia into the room. They – along with my mother, Aiden, Ori, and Ted – were the real heroes that night, having risked their lives to protect not just me, but the entire Community.

Piotr and Mei arrived the next day with a team of Elemental archivists and historians in tow. After bestowing medals of honor and armfuls of gifts from the Asterian Order to all nine of us (including Evelyn and Robert, who were each given five-dozen roses and golden plaques for their behind-the-scenes service to the Community), they asked me to recount all of the things I heard while spying on Keres and the others from behind the wall. It wasn't hard, since I'd already been recounting all of that information – and more – to my father for the last few weeks.

After I told them everything I knew, they interviewed everyone else about what happened next, filling in the gaps from Stefan – who's recovering nicely in his home town of Belgrade – and the others. I gripped Aiden's hand in mine as he recounted how his father had sacrificed himself, leaping in front of Keres' Lightning attack to buy Aiden and my mother more time to save me. When I told them how I had gleaned from Keres' mind that she was manipulating Terry into having an affair, Aiden abruptly covered his eyes with a hand. His shoulders shook with sorrow, with relief, and I understood at once just how important it was for him to hear that.

For me personally, the most significant part of the archivists' visit was when they interviewed Mom, Evelyn, and Ted, taking down the true details of that fateful day three and a half years ago, when they and my father all risked their lives to save me. Their uncensored, six-page story was published to the archives, hailing the four of them as heroes – Evelyn included. The editors even incorporated an article about Ted's daughter next to my family's story – along with a scathing call to abolish punitive Electromantic methods of any and all types. Mei pledged her full support to ensure that that issue would appear at the top of the ballots, aptly entitled "The Jenny Decree".

Three days after the stories were published, absolving my parents of all crimes, we removed my father from life support. He passed from this world peacefully, surrounded by his loved ones and the promise that we would see him again. Aiden held me in his arms as Dad took his last breath, and we wept together – both for my father, and for his. When my mother kissed Dad's cool forehead and whispered her goodbyes, the lights in the room flickered. But it wasn't her doing, and I know it wasn't mine. We think it was Dad, letting us know he had heard us.

Yesterday afternoon was the very first moment Aiden had me all to himself. The second the door closed behind the nurse, he took my face in his hands and kissed me more fiercely, more passionately than I've ever been kissed in my life. When the lights flickered that time, I'm pretty sure every Elementalist in that hospital knew it was me. A moment later, Aiden got on one knee and retrieved a tanzanite ring from his pocket, asking me to marry him. I can't remember the beautiful, heartfelt words that accompanied his proposal, mostly because I was in complete shock. As he paused to wait for my answer, my stammers were cut off by the sound of screaming in the hallway. At least ten faces were pressed against the narrow pane of glass beside the door, shouting encouragement, congratulations, disbelief, and, in Ori's case, glass-fogging, indignant expletives. I promptly burst into tears when Aiden rose to embrace me, mainly from happiness, but partly from the peals of laughter that suddenly gripped us as we hugged one another fiercely.

When our laughter finally subsided, I gave him a resounding "no" – an answer he was fully expecting. But when he asks me again in another six months or so, we both know what my answer will be.

The sparkling indigo crystal fits the third finger of my right hand perfectly, and I find myself gazing at it every chance I get. Depending on how the light catches it, the stone fluctuates from deep blue to violet – like my eyes, which have settled back to their (almost) natural color. I've yet to take the ring off, even for the countless brain scans that I've been subjected to this past week. The MRI attendants don't particularly appreciate that, but they aren't about to argue with a love-struck Pentamancer, either.

Earlier tonight, after everyone had finished eating dinner in the cafeteria, I somehow managed to talk them all into going home. Aiden only agreed so he could clean up his apartment for the first time in a month, and Evelyn and my mother had the grand idea of dragging Robert and Ted to the grocery store so they could pack my refrigerator and pantry with food ahead of my long-anticipated homecoming tomorrow. In the hour since they've left, I've been enjoying my first full sixty minutes of silence in a week. Not that I'm complaining – not even close.

I just settled against my pillows to read more of Barish's journal, but a chime from beside my hospital bed gives me pause: it's a message from Wes. A lump forms in my throat at the sight of it; I haven't spoken to him in weeks, not since that accidental late-night phone call. I should have written him this week, let him know that I'm okay, but my heart has stayed firmly in this room – where it belongs. Still, I feel a sense of guilt for not reaching out, and a pang of worry ahead of reading his message; will he be upset with me? Anxious that I've disappeared again? Hoping to catch up? I grimace as I straighten myself up to read his message.

Hey Rose (yep, I'm reverting to your California appellation), hope I'm not disturbing. Aiden let me know you're awake and fully functional again. How the hell did you manage to electrocute yourself anyway? Didn't they teach you not to stick forks in outlets in pre-school? I'm kidding, of course! But in all seriousness, I'm relieved to hear that you're doing better. Do you remember Maddie, the volunteer coordinator from my parents' foundation? I told her that you were in the hospital and she was so upset. She asked me to forward her best wishes for a full and speedy recovery. We've been keeping in close touch while I've been overseas. She'll be coming to join me in Mali with the next wave of volunteers. I'm only mentioning that because I thought you would be glad to hear. When we talked last month, you told me not to wait around for happiness to find me. That really resonated with me. Thanks for that.

Did Aiden tell you he and I spoke a couple weeks ago? I was blowing up your phone late one night and he finally answered. (In my defense, you hadn't answered my calls in days and I was worried you'd fallen into a pit.) It takes just about every ounce of humility I have to admit this, but your boyfriend might be the nicest, most courteous guy I've ever met. And that voice! Is he a radio broadcaster or something? Damn. Anyway, we talked for an hour (yes, mostly about you, so go ahead and blush). After that conversation, all I can say is, it's clear that you are immensely loved over there. Just the way you should be.

Anyway, continue to get better and take care of yourself, all right? And just know that I wish you all the best in this world, my beautiful Rose. Give my love to your mother. (And please, for everyone's sake, keep away from any and all current-producing apparatuses.)

-Wes

As I finish reading his message, I realize I'm smiling from ear to ear. Wes is going to be okay. *We're* going to be okay. And it was Aiden's compassion that helped ensure that.

Through the open door, I hear a familiar voice. Eileen is chatting with a nurse outside Sophia's room. I practically leap out of bed to go over and say hi, since I haven't seen her at all today. As I plod across the tiles in my fancy blue gown and hospital slippers, the nurse raises an eyebrow in my direction, but doesn't protest. I haven't had any dizzy spells in forty-eight hours, and I'm tentatively cleared to go home tomorrow, pending the results of my final MRI and CAT scans. So, the nurses are being thankfully lenient today. I peek my head in Sophia's room to find her sound asleep, but Eileen is back in there, thumbing through her scrapbook of Earth elements, the TV mounted on the wall set to mute. She abruptly sets her book down and rushes forward to give me a hug as I enter.

"How is she doing today?" I ask, sitting beside Eileen as she once more takes her seat beside Sophia's bed.

"She's doing so much better," she replies, squeezing Sophia's hand as she sleeps. "I was so scared for a minute that I was going to lose the two women I love most in this world – don't tell my mom I said that – but now that you're both on the mend, I feel like I can breathe again. We're busting out of here at the end of the week!"

"I'm so glad," I reply, breathing a sigh of relief. "Have you heard anything from Ori today?"

Eileen nods. "Did he tell you? He finally got his green card in the mail this morning, compliments of certain friends in high places. So even though we had to bid him a fond farewell from the hospital, it sounds like we're stuck with him here in Denver." She rolls her eyes, but I can tell she's secretly thrilled.

"Good," I smile. "So, he's decided to stay full-time at the Denver Chapter after all... Well, until campaign season officially starts, I guess."

"Uh-huh. Except he's asked me to schedule him one last week of paid time off before he starts training. He's apparently got a hot date in Little Rock, Arkansas... And you'll never guess with who."

"*Kaylie*?" I gasp.

"Hey – no fair reading my mind!" Eileen sticks her tongue out at me playfully.

"Sorry!" I wince. I'm still getting used to the new feel of my powers. "But, seriously? Kaylie?"

"Yee-up. She and Ori have been maintaining a hot and torrid Skype love affair since the night of the rave. But I'm not supposed to tell you that, just in case you finally decide to dump Aiden and fall madly in love with a temporarily-crippled windbag instead... which, for the record, I do not recommend."

I laugh, then quickly put a hand over my mouth to stifle it. "That's a highly unlikely scenario... though it has nothing to do with his current lack of mobility," I add. "What's Kaylie doing, now that she's no longer a sub-Prelate?"

"Kaylie," Eileen begins, her voice dripping with mock self-importance, "has returned home to work on her 'fictional' novel about a stunning, busty woman – cleverly named 'Katie' – who becomes entangled in an evil, magical cult."

"No kidding..." my eyes widen. "And everyone's cool with that?"

Eileen shrugs. "Hey, the Asterians are embarking on a new era of *not* being the creepy big brother, right? And they have to keep good on their word, lest we all form another crazed, blood-lusting mob, led by everyone's favorite California-grown Pentamancer..."

I arch an eyebrow in her direction, but she doesn't appear to notice.

"Anyway, Ori says that the higher-ups are fine with her going public with it, so long as she changes every name, date, detail, and invents a fake magical system that has nothing to do with the Elements. She'll be a *New York Times* bestselling fantasy author, all for ripping off real events." She crinkles her nose as she scratches at the skin beneath the bedazzled green cast on her arm.

"Sounds like Kaylie's got her work cut out for her," I remark. "What about the other sub-Prelates? Any word on them?"

"The folks who worked beneath the Deplorable Four all took lie detector tests with Empaths – hence why Kaylie's back home, since she apparently had no idea what

Jahi and the others were up to. She was also let off the hook for drowning Señor Sociopath in a torrent of boiling water, because, you know, he was a raving, mass-murdering psychopath."

"No kidding," I answer darkly. "But what about the ones who *did* know something?"

Eileen shrugs. "Only a handful seemed to know anything about the whole 'attempted murder-slash-coup' thing. They're currently going through trial proceedings – with a grand jury and everything! Give it up for due process, *amiright*?" She winks, then lowers her voice again as Sophia stirs quietly. "Some of the so-called 'innocent' ex-Subs are running for office, not unexpectedly, but I think most of them are just enjoying the fact that they aren't crypt-dwelling lackeys anymore."

I find myself nodding thoughtfully. I'm wondering how many of the sub-Prelates prescribed to their departed masters' ideals of Elemental Supremacy; whether that notion died out with Keres and the others, or if it might come back to haunt us one day, once the dust and ashes have settled...

Eileen glances at me out of the corner of her eye. "And what about you, Prophet?"

"Hmm?"

"Well, you know, the Community is calling for the parliamentary age requirement to drop to twenty-four instead of twenty-five." I must have given her a puzzled look just now, because she adds, "Hmm, I can't imagine why... Oh, that's right – maybe it's because everyone and their adopted brother wants you to run for President?"

"If it's a Parliamentary system, I think it would technically be 'Prime Minister'," I reply wryly.

"Ugh, I think Professor Boyfriend is rubbing off on you," Eileen crinkles her nose at me. "But seriously, Aspen. If you wanted to, you know you could be the next Barish... I think everyone is sort of hoping that you will be."

"Politics aren't for me," I answer, shaking my head. "And besides, I'm pretty sure no one wants another Empathic Electromancer running for office, not after what Ke—"

I swallow. The mere mention of her name makes my stomach knot.

"—What *she* did."

"They'd make an exception for you," Eileen says simply. She's straightening the IV tube that's sticking out of Sophia's wrist, so I roll up a towel to help bolster her arm while she sleeps.

"I want to go back to school," I say, settling back in my chair.

"Yeah?" Eileen prompts.

"Mmhmm..." I realize I'm idly running the tips of my fingers along the raised scars on my arm. They don't bother me – on the contrary, I kind of like them. "I only had a few more credits of undergrad to finish before I left college, and Dr. Wilke says he can fast-track me into a special Neurology program that's geared toward Electromancers. It's a six-year program funded by the Asterians, and I'd earn the equivalent of an MD by the time I finish."

"And then?"

"I'd split my time between practice and research. Their primary mission is to discover ways in which Electromantic methods can be used to eradicate neurological diseases like Multiple Sclerosis, Parkinson's, Alzheimer's, and so on. They plan to use their findings to create non-Elemental therapies that mimic the results for the rest of the world. Barish told me all about the program, before..." I trail off as a lump suddenly appears in my throat.

Eileen squeezes my hand. "I know."

"Hey there," a voice from the bed says softly. Sophia is peering at us through one eye, smiling. "Don't worry, you didn't wake me. I have to pee."

"I'll get the nurse," Eileen says, giving her a kiss on the forehead as she rises.

I reach out to take Sophia's hand in mine as Eileen slips out the door. "You know, I never got the chance to thank you, Sophia."

"For what?" she asks, sitting up in the bed.

"You saved so many lives that night, taking on Jahi alone. If you hadn't kept him at bay for as long as you did, I don't think we would have made it out of there. I can't thank you enough for that." My eyes fill with tears as the truth of my own words hits me.

Sophia squeezes my hand tightly. "I never really understood the true meaning of love until meeting a certain green-haired Terramancer... and you, Aspen. I'd do it all over again if it meant I could protect those I love. Although, I should mention, my newfound spleen-less state will make that slightly more complicated."

I burst out laughing just as Eileen and the nurse enter the room.

"I'd better leave you to your business," I smile, rising to make room for the nurse. As I stand up, I stealthily attempt to straighten the back of my hospital gown with a strategic draft of Wind. The nurses may have ridiculous framed likenesses of me sitting around their stations, but I still can't convince them to let me wear my street clothes while being treated in their hospital.

"See you both for breakfast?"

"You got it." Eileen's eyes twinkle as I turn to go.

"Can you not stare at my butt on the way out?" I grumble over my shoulder.

"Sorry, Prophet. No promises."

***

As I settle back into bed, I reach for Barish's journal, tucked beneath my pillow. I've been reading excerpts from it every night before going to sleep, usually after the others have nodded off. I've perused just about everything up through 2015, but tonight, I have the urge to skip ahead. The last page of his journal is dated June 25th – the day he died. A soft gasp escapes my lips as I read the first line; the entry is addressed to me.

My dear Rowan,

There are so many things I wish to say to you. First and foremost, I wish to apologize: for keeping your father's condition from you; for allowing the pain and suffering that you and your loved ones have endured over the years; for somehow convincing myself that the ends would always justify the means. In my life and long after, I will have accomplished more for our Community than any other man; but as I fast approach the midnight toll of my existence, I am forced to concede that, over the years, avarice and pride have clouded my vision. But not yours, dear one. You see the world with fierce goodness, while compassion alone fuels every choice of your tender existence. Hold on to that purity, protecting and nurturing it like a flame in a blizzard.

By now, I'm sure you've come to understand my grand design. If all has gone according to plan, the Inner Circle – the undying bane and blemish of the Asterian Order – has been eliminated, and my manifesto has made its way to the hands of every Elementalist in the world. I only wish I could be there with you to celebrate our victory – and, admittedly, to have a hand in the subsequent revolution. It is not death that frightens me, for moving from one plane to another is but a phase change; in truth, I am afraid to lose control of the things I treasure most dearly. But the time for old men and ancient ideals has passed; the time for young people with radical ideas and unbridled hope is upon us. I pray you'll lead that honorable charge, my child.

Don't misunderstand – I know you well enough by now to realize you won't be running to take my place. The

world needs more healers, and fewer politicians, I think
you would agree, and as my good friend Einstein once said,
"The high destiny of the individual is to serve rather than
to rule." Indeed, truer words have never been spoken.
Along that vein, I do hope you'll continue to serve the
Community – through your vision, your selflessness, and
your influence. Because like it or not, my dear Rowan, they
will all look to you now, as the Pentamancer, the Prophet.
The savior. Whether you opt to become Prime Minister or
Neurosurgeon, you must never forget that your true place is
at the forefront of the Community.

This is the curse you and every Pentamancer before
you has had to endure: from the time of your first gasping
breath, your destiny was never up to you. Not because
destiny is written in stone, but because great people are
destined to do great things. Never forget that. I shall watch
with pride as you, the daughter I never deserved, take your
worthy place among our history's heroes.

Your faithful servant,
Barish

A stray tear falls from my cheek as I read his parting words to me. "I'll make you both proud," I whisper to the ceiling. "I promise."

As I snap the book shut, the light above me flickers.

***

Epilogue

A pale October sun peers between the early morning storm clouds; gentle rain sprinkles upon the slanted roof of the small wooden house tucked safely behind rolling green foothills. Inside the cabin, a young woman sits quietly in the dim light that filters in from a small, freshly-polished window. Wrapped in a warm quilt on a cozy armchair, her bare legs tucked beneath her, she watches the fat droplets rolling down the window. As her tanzanite-blue eyes dart across the glass, the drops of water move in synchronized patterns along with them, dancing across the window, leaving delicate trails of swirling water streaming behind them. Enjoying her brief moment of amusement, the young woman blinks; the trails of water abruptly split apart and crystalize, leaving frosted, geometric patterns of ice covering the entire window, like sparkling lace.

As the sun rises above the clouds, warm rays of light gleam against the pale skin of her arm, highlighting the inimitable five-pointed sigil embedded there, as well as the delicate, raised web of scarring that encases it. The woman smiles. The scars, unique only to survivors of lightning strikes, mark her as a fighter, a survivor – a conjurer of Lightning.

The sounds of chatter and sizzling eggs drift to her ears from the crowded kitchen, filled with far too many people for the tiny space. Intermingling with the crisp scent of early autumn rain, delicious smells fill the warm cabin – cinnamon-dusted buns, homemade pancakes, turkey sausage, and fresh coffee. The young woman, named for her mother's mother, as well as the white-barked trees that surround her cabin, glances over her shoulder at the sound of laughter, smiling to herself. Framed photos line the walls and the freshly-painted mantle of the fireplace, where the joyful faces of her parents and loved ones return her sentiments.

"Rowan!" her mother calls from the kitchen. "Eggs are almost ready!"

Rowan. Rose. Aspen. Elementalist. Pentamancer. Prophet. All of these names belong to her; all of them carry different meanings. Some carry joy; some carry love; some carry weight. But they all carry a piece of who she is: daughter, friend, partner, hero – unwitting savior.

"I'll be right there!" she answers.

"Get in here and shower me with effusive adoration, woman!" Ori hollers from the doorway.

From behind him, Aspen's best friend, Eileen, groans loudly. "I told you we shouldn't have bought him that thesaurus!"

As Aspen rises from her favorite spot, she chuckles softly to herself. She'll never tire of the noise besieging her cabin or the crowd of friends and family that's almost constantly there – not because she was forced to live in silence and solitude for so long, but because she had come so close to losing those loved ones forever.

But she didn't. And today, three and a half months after the bloody night that left the Asterian Order reeling, is a day of international celebration and merriment. Twelve Elementalists from twelve separate global Chapters have just been announced as Prime Representatives, freely and lawfully elected into the first session of the Asterian Parliament. One of Aspen's closest friends, Ori, is one of those twelve. He and the other representatives will cast their votes today for the first Prime Minister of the new Asterian government. While the Community has thrown their ardent support behind the young Pentamancer, she has refused to accept any formal title, pledging instead to act as an honorary member of Parliament where she will attend all sessions, throwing her support behind the matters requiring the most attention. In light of Aspen's abstention, popular support for ex-Prelate Mei Saito indicates the vote will go to her – until the next election cycle in five years' time, when a new Parliament and a new Minister shall be voted upon.

As Aspen stretches, two familiar hands wrap themselves around her waist. A warm flush fills her cheeks, causing the lamp on the table to flicker.

"I made you some eggs – just the way you like them," Aiden whispers into her ear.

"I don't deserve you," Aspen replies, smiling as she turns to kiss him deeply.

"I don't know about that," he murmurs, returning the kiss. A moment later, he pulls away gently, brushing a wisp of hair from her indigo eyes. "Hey, I was thinking – after we see Ori off this morning, what do you think about going for a drive?'

"In your Jeep?"

"Nah – on our motorcycles," he replies, taking a step toward the front door.

"On *our*... what...?" Aspen's voice trails off as Aiden opens the door, revealing a brand-new motorcycle parked just beside hers. Her mouth hangs open slightly as she regards the polished black chrome of Aiden's vintage bike, glistening from the freshly-fallen rain.

"How did you...? *When* did you...?"

Aiden laughs softly. "I gather that's a yes?"

"I have a better idea," she grins suddenly, snatching her helmet from the end table. "How about we take an early morning sunrise ride, right now? I know just the route!"

As Aspen races out the door, her grandmother, Evelyn, ambles out of the kitchen, a smudge of chocolate chip pancake batter streaking her rosy cheek. She watches with twinkling eyes as Aspen runs over to Aiden's new motorcycle, squealing in delight as she inspects every inch of it.

"You be careful out there, young man – that route of hers is prone to freak tornados," Evelyn warns, giving him a devious wink.

Aiden laughs as he reaches for his and Aspen's leather jackets, hanging side by side in the hall closet.

"Don't worry, Evie – I promise to take care of her. Always."

∞

The end.

Elemental Class Appendix

	Elementalist Type	Sigil Colors	Symbol
Aspen/ Rowan Fulman ♦♦♦♦♦	Pentamancer (III) *	Purple, Yellow, Blue, Red, Green, Black	
Aiden Lawson ♦	Pyromancer (III)	Red	
Eileen ♦	Terramancer (II)	Green	
Ori ♦	Electromancer (II)	Yellow	
Sophia ♦♦	Auromancer (III) Hydromancer (III)	Blue, Purple	
Ted Nichols ♦♦	Pyromancer (II) Terramancer (II)	Red, Green	

Elizabeth Fulman ◆◆	Auromancer (III) Electromancer (III) *	Purple, Yellow	
David Fulman ◆	Hydromancer (III)	Blue	
Terry Lawson ◆◆	Auromancer (II) Pyromancer (III)	Purple, Red	
Robert Borstein	Electromantic Traits (<I) *	n/a	n/a
Barish (Magistrate) ◆◆◆ ◆	Polymancer Auromancer (III) Electromancer (III) * Hydromancer (III)	Blue, Green, Purple, Red, Yellow, Black Purple, Yellow, Blue	
Keres ◆◆◆ ◆	Polymancer Electromancer (III) *† Hydromancer (II) Terramancer (III)	Yellow, Blue, Green	

Jahi ♦♦♦ ♦	**Polymancer** *Auromancer (II)* *Hydromancer (II)* *Pyromancer (II)*	*Purple, Blue, Red*	
Valeriya ♦♦ ♦	*Hydromancer (III)* *Pyromancer (III)*	*Blue, Red*	III
Izabel ♦♦ ♦	*Electromancer (III) *†* *Pyromancer (II)*	*Yellow, Red*	
Felipe ♦♦ ♦	*Auromancer (II)* *Terramancer (II)*	*Purple, Green*	
Mei ♦♦♦ ♦	**Polymancer** *Auromancer (II)* *Hydromancer (II)* *Terramancer (II)*	*Purple, Blue, Green*	
Piotr ♦♦ ♦	*Pyromancer (III)* *Terramancer (III)*	*Red, Green*	III

Nadia ◆◆ ◆	*Electromancer (III) ‡* *Terramancer (III)*	*Yellow,* *Green*	
Kaal *(deceased)* ◆◆ ◆	*Auromancer (III)* *Pyromancer (III)*	*Purple,* *Red*	
Kaylie *(sub-Prelate)* ◆◆◆	**Polymancer** *Auromancer (II)* *Hydromancer (III)* *Pyromancer (I)*	*Purple,* *Blue,* *Red*	

> * *Empathic Electromancer*
> † *Corporeal Electromancer*
> ‡ *Electromagnetist*
> ◆ **Inner Circle**

A CONTEMPORARY FANTASY

THE LIGHTNING CONJURER

Series

Book I: The Awakening
Book II: The Enlightening
Book III: The Christening

Support Indie Authors   *Leave a Review!*

Follow us online for exciting news, updates, and giveaways!

 www.thelightningconjurer.com

 facebook.com/thelightningconjurer

 twitter.com/RachelRener

 instagram.com/thelightningconjurer/

Acknowledgements

This series would not exist if not for the love, patience, encouragement, and unending support of my husband, Aaron. A mere "Thank you" does not suffice, but I know a lifetime of love will!

Joey, Marco, and Rachel, you have my everlasting gratitude for your assistance and support with this series.

Selene – no one could have made Aspen (and now Aiden!) more beautiful and riveting than you. I thank you from the bottom of my heart for your vision.

To my family and friends: thank you for supporting my work, my dreams, and the imaginary world that lives inside my head.

And to those strangers who took a chance and picked up a copy of The Lightning Conjurer, I thank each and every one of you for taking that leap of faith. It has been an honor to share Aspen's story with you.

About the Author

Rachel graduated from the University of Colorado after focusing on Psychology and Neuroscience. She lived overseas in both Japan and Turkey teaching English, then returned back to Colorado after missing her friends and the gorgeous skies there. Istanbul, however, will forever hold its special place in her heart.

When she's not engrossed in writing, Rachel enjoys painting, reading, photography, traveling, and, most recently, getting clay everywhere except centered on the potter's wheel, where it belongs. She lives about thirty minutes away from Aspen's fictional cabin, along with her husband/best friend, a stellar mineral collection, an umbrella cockatoo (a.k.a. "Jungle Chicken") and her two wonderful step-children, Josh and Leah.

Made in the USA
San Bernardino, CA
17 December 2019

61822178R00283